# THE
# TIME
## OF THE
# WOLF

# THE
# TIME
# OF THE
# WOLF

## WILLIAM D. BLANKENSHIP

DONALD I. FINE BOOKS
NEW YORK

Donald I. Fine Books
Published by the Penguin Group
Penguin Putnam Inc., 375 Hudson Street, New York, New York 10014, U.S.A.
Penguin Books Ltd, 27 Wrights Lane, London W8 5TZ, England
Penguin Books Australia Ltd, Ringwood, Victoria, Australia
Penguin Books Canada Ltd, 10 Alcorn Avenue, Toronto, Ontario, Canada M4V 3B2
Penguin Books (N.Z.) Ltd, 182–190 Wairau Road, Auckland 10, New Zealand

Penguin Books Ltd, Registered Offices: Harmondsworth, Middlesex, England

First published by Donald I. Fine Books, an imprint of Penguin Putnam Inc.

First Printing, October, 1998

10 9 8 7 6 5 4 3 2 1

  REGISTERED TRADEMARK—MARCA REGISTRADA

Library of Congress Cataloging-in-Publication Data:

Blankenship, William D.
    The time of the wolf / William D. Blankenship.
        p.   cm.
    ISBN 1-55611-548-2
    I. Title.
    PS3552.L366T565   1998
    813'.54—dc21                              98-22703
                                                 CIP

Printed in the United States of America
Set in Transitional 521

PUBLISHER'S NOTE
This is a work of fiction. Names, characters, places, and incidents either are the products of the author's imagination or are used fictitiously, and any resemblance to actual persons, living or dead, events, or locales is entirely
coincidental.

This book is printed on acid-free paper.

*This book is dedicated to the three newest in the family:*

*Risako Nakamura Blankenship*

*Shuhei [a.k.a. Che] Nakamura Blankenship*

*Johan Aron Sigurjon Cristwell*

# CHAPTER 1

Kay was running late. United Airlines Flight 828 to New York was scheduled to leave at 10:05 A.M. and she had arrived at Singapore's Changi Airport at 9:30, leaving precious little time to check her luggage, pick up her boarding pass and clear immigration. Worse yet, going through passport control would probably take extra time today because of the small steel case handcuffed to her wrist. She gave the limo driver a huge tip and leaped out of the car, a hired bodyguard following with her suitcase.

Fortunately, the client was paying for a first-class ticket, so Kay did not have to stand in a long, slow-moving line to check luggage and pick up the boarding pass. The ticket clerk cast a suspicious glance at both the small case handcuffed to Kay's wrist and the hard-faced bodyguard accompanying her, but asked no questions. Kay felt certain the clerk would call the customs and immigration desk as soon as she left the counter.

With her suitcase checked through to New York and the boarding pass in hand, Kay raced from the counter towards the passport control entrance with the bodyguard still at her side, scanning the crowd with professional intensity. Their progress was not as swift as she'd hoped because of the hordes of people streaming in and out of the shops and restaurants. No airport in the world has more shops than Changi in Singapore. *Changi isn't an airport at all,* Kay fumed. *It's a shopping mall with airplanes!*

When they reached the passport control area, she bid the bodyguard a hasty good-bye, tipped him even more generously than she had the limo driver, and went through the yellow door. A customs officer approached and took her firmly by the elbow. "Miss Williams? I am Inspector Chen. Please to accompany me."

"Inspector, I'll be glad to cooperate, but my flight is scheduled to depart in about twenty minutes. I don't want to miss it."

"Then you should have arrived two hours ahead of departure, as all international travelers are advised to do. However, your flight will be held for you if it appears necessary to do so. You will accumulate enemies among the other passengers with connections to make in New York, but that will not be my problem." Inspector Chen's chilly politeness seemed to be something put on for duty, like his heavily starched khaki uniform. He was a portly Singaporean of Chinese descent, almost six feet tall, with jowls that made his jaws seem extremely wide and the hint of a smile etched into the lines around his mouth. Behind his official facade Kay detected a sense of humor, which gave her hope that this customs inspection would not be as grueling as some others she had been through.

The room she was taken to was bare except for a long table. Another customs officer of lesser rank than Inspector Chen awaited them. He was younger, slimmer, very alert, and appeared to have had his sense of humor surgically removed at birth.

Inspector Chen took up a position next to his underling, leaving Kay alone on the other side of the table in the classic adversarial position.

"This is Deputy Customs Agent Tan. Miss Williams, the clerk at the ticket counter advised me that you were accompanied to the airport by a thug who may be a bodyguard and that you had a small carry-on attached to your wrist by what looked like a handcuff. I can see with my own dim eyes that she was correct. I will have to examine the contents of that case before you can leave Singapore. I presume you are an American citizen?"

"Yes, I'm an antiques dealer from Ridgefield, Connecticut. I've been in Singapore for a little less than a week to negotiate the purchase of an antique for a client in New York."

"May I see your passport?"

Kay handed over her passport and watched Inspector Chen flip quickly to the page where her arrival in Singapore had been noted, stamped and dated.

"What kind of antique are you carrying in that case?"

"A Fabergé egg."

Inspector Chen's eyes came alight with interest. "Surely not! My goodness. Imagine that, Tan. A Fabergé egg!"

The younger official's only reaction was to rearrange his scowl.

"Tan is not interested in such things. Would you open the case, please? I am sincerely afraid I must inspect this glorious creation to make sure it does not conceal contraband of some sort."

*Of course he's looking for drugs*, Kay thought. *The Singapore government hates drugs.* The day she arrived, Kay read a story in *The Straits Times* about a pair of drug smugglers arrested here at Changi airport. The next day she read in the same newspaper that the smugglers had been tried and convicted. The third day she read of their execution.

"This will take a moment." She fished into her purse for the key to the handcuff, found it and unlocked the wrist cuff chained to the box. In addition to the handcuff, the carrying case had a digital lock that Kay had to punch the right numbers into. If the wrong numbers were entered, an incredibly loud siren would blow when the case was opened.

"Good security," Inspector Chen commented. "I sense that people have tried to steal antiques from you before."

"Yes, I have had that experience," Kay said drily. When the case was unlocked, she lifted the lid to reveal an even smaller metal box nestled in a foam lining. Within the second box was a ceramic Fabergé egg decorated with precious jewels. The egg itself was protected by folds of silk.

"Oh my goodness." Inspector Chen showed genuine elation at the sight of the egg. "That is truly beautiful. *Truly* beautiful," he emphasized. "I am a fortunate man to gaze upon such a precious object."

Inspector Chen studied the egg in rapture while Deputy Agent Tan fidgeted. After a time, Tan reached impatiently for the egg, only to have Chen slap his hand away. "Do not touch it!" In a more gentle voice, he said to Kay, "Do you think Fabergé did all of the work on this piece himself?"

"Probably not." Kay let herself be drawn into a conversation about Peter Carl Fabergé with the comforting knowledge that her flight was being held for her. "At his zenith in 1915 Fabergé had about 600 people working for him in Moscow, Odessa, Kiev, Saint Petersburg, Paris and London. They produced all sorts of beautiful artwork out of ceramics and jewels—Easter eggs like this one, chalices, *bonbonnières*, bowls and baskets, you name it. His Easter eggs were his most popular creations and the ones that bring the highest prices today. I'm sure you know that Fabergé was the jeweler to the Imperial Court of Russia. Unfortunately for the world of art, the Russian revolution in 1918 put him out of business."

"A pity." Chen reluctantly looked up from the jeweled egg and returned to his official manner. "I must examine your bill of sale, export license and the certificate of authenticity for this antique."

Kay had the papers ready. She watched while both of the customs officials examined them closely. Deputy Agent Tan was clearly disappointed to find them in good order, signed, in fact, by one of Singapore's highest government officials. Inspector Chen and Deputy Agent Tan understood instantly that Kay had paid the government official a "gratuity" for his signature and that a percentage of that payment would filter down to them in due course, because that's the way business is done in Singapore.

Inspector Chen smiled broadly, and even Deputy Agent Tan managed to relax his scowl. "Your papers are correct in every respect." In sotto voce he added, "My superiors informed me that you would be coming through Changi today. I was told to see that you cleared customs as rapidly as possible. You may lock up that beautiful object and I will escort you to the gate."

Kay carefully closed the lid of the Fabergé egg box, relocked the steel outer box, set the alarm and retrieved her passport, which Deputy Agent Tan stamped to approve her departure. Inspector Chen then guided Kay through the airport with an air of authority that caused people to step quickly out of his path.

At the gate, Inspector Chen smiled so widely that his jowls jiggled. "I am delighted to have met you, Miss Williams. And I am equally happy to have had this opportunity to gaze upon a genuine Fabergé egg. I hope you have adequate security awaiting you in New York. The crime rate there is monstrous compared with Singapore's. An object worth more than a million U.S. dollars would be a tempting target."

"An armed guard will meet me at Kennedy Airport and take me to my client's office. I appreciate your help and your courtesy, Inspector."

Inspector Chen shook Kay's hand and sent her onto her plane with a formal bow and another brilliant smile.

As soon as Kay reached her seat at the front of the first-class section, the plane door was closed and the Boeing airliner began taxiing towards its takeoff runway. The steward offered a glass of champagne, which Kay welcomed. Although she felt more comfortable now that she was almost airborne, Kay knew she wouldn't be completely at ease until she actually delivered this particular antique to Andrew Whiteman, her client and the chairman of New York's Security Mutual Bank.

Buying the Fabergé egg had taken three grueling days of negotiations. The seller was a Russian who called himself Nicolai Leontin, a slick, handsome man who dressed in Armani suits, spoke English with only a subtle accent and looked at her throughout the negotiations with eyes as cold and lifeless as a corpse. Kay doubted that Leontin was his real name, even though she had asked to see his passport. She suspected Leontin of being a member of the Russian mafia because those people seemed to have all the money in Russia these days. They even controlled many of Russia's banks. Kay speculated that this Fabergé egg might have been stolen from the vault of the Russian National Museum. A lot of beautiful merchandise was coming on the market these days as government officials in countries like Russia, China and Mexico looted their national treasures under the guise of opening up their markets to free trade. It seemed logical that if this Fabergé egg were not stolen it would have been auctioned off at Sotheby's or Christie's for an even higher price. Kay hated to think of nations losing important pieces of their heritage in that way. But there was no way to prove it had been stolen from the Russian National Museum vault . . . or any other vault . . . so all she could do was haggle over price on behalf of her client.

After another glass of champagne, Kay felt a bit more sanguine about this assignment and about life in general. She had agreed to a flat fee of one hundred thousand dollars plus expenses for negotiating the purchase of the Fabergé egg and bringing it safely back to New York. Not a bad fee for one week's work. Although the one-million-three-hundred-thousand-dollar purchase price was a bit on the high side, she knew that Andrew Whiteman wouldn't complain even though this was not one of Fabergé's Imperial creations. The egg was genuine—she'd conducted tests and done the research to guarantee its provenance—and in good condition. For years Whiteman had desperately wanted a Fabergé egg to put into a jeweled Fabergé ceramic gold- and diamond-studded basket that he already owned, and now his dream had come true.

The passenger in the next seat leaned toward her. "Good morning, my name's John Steadman. Mind if I ask what's in that box chained to your wrist?"

Kay swiftly assessed her seatmate: Senior executive, probably in the computer or electronics business if he was traveling from Singapore . . . early fifties . . . still fit and rather good-looking . . . Brooks Brothers attire . . . wedding ring . . . ruddy cheeks indicating he drinks too much, probably from the pressure of business . . . *Asian Wall Street Journal* in his hand for light reading . . . the corner of a heavier black presentation book sticking out of his briefcase.

With a quick smile, she fed him a convincing lie. "I'm Kay Williams. Nice to meet you. No, I don't mind your asking. I'm carrying confidential corporate documents on computer disks. My company's afraid of industrial espionage, can't blame them these days. Kind of a drag being handcuffed to a steel box for seven thousand miles, but they pay me well for this sort of thing."

"What company?" the exec inquired.

She doubted he was a banker, so she gave him a vague answer. "A consortium of companies . . . financial services mostly."

"I'm in the semiconductor business." Steadman smiled. "Well, it's nice to be traveling with you, Kay. That case is going be awkward for you to handle over a long plane ride. Let me know if I can be of any help."

"Thank you," Kay said with a flashy smile, thinking that if John Steadman tried to put even one hand on the case she'd cheerfully break his wrist.

They were in the air now. The seatbelt sign had been turned off and the steward was taking orders for drinks. Kay didn't sense any danger from her fellow passenger, but she preferred to err on the side of caution. As Inspector Chen had surmised, people had tried to steal antiques from her before. From time to time she'd had some narrow escapes. Two years ago she had been forced to flee a hotel in Dublin just a few steps ahead of a lunatic neo-Nazi who was out to take Adolf Hitler's personal P-38 pistol away from her. Another time in Washington, D.C., a professional jewel thief had tried to steal at gunpoint an antique diamond tiara purchased for a client from the estate of J. Paul Getty; she drove him off with a combination of "Mace to the face" and a well-aimed kick to his most sensitive organs. Her worst experience by far had been in Tokyo, where a Yakuza gangster stole from her a samurai sword once owned by Emperor Meiji and used it to sever the heads of several people before she and the police could combine to recover it. That little adventure had almost cost her her life.

By comparison, John Steadman looked harmless enough.

After a second glass of champagne, Kay kicked off her shoes and curled up in the spacious first-class seat for a nap. She kept the steel box handcuffed to her wrist and set against the bulkhead well out of anyone else's reach.

She drifted into sleep. When Steadman was certain Kay was napping, he gave her as close an appraisal as she had given him. He had no particular interest in the box chained to her wrist. Instead he was wondering if this beautiful young woman might care to meet him some evening in New York for dinner and an evening of what he liked to call "Executive R and R—Recklessness and Revelry."

From her expensive clothes and the decisive way she spoke, Steadman guessed Kay Williams was at least at the director level in her company, that her income went well into six figures and that she possessed an independent streak that might have caused her to be either unmarried or divorced. No wedding ring, at least. He made no move to hide or remove his own wedding ring because he believed in being up front with women he was attracted to about the fact that he was married. And he was certainly attracted to Kay Williams.

As Kay shifted slightly against the cushions of her seat, Steadman admired the sensous way she moved even while asleep. Her legs were perfect, the calves athletic without being bulky, waist trim, breasts exactly proportioned to her body, neck as graceful as the late Audrey Hepburn's, face dominated by large eyes and sculpted cheekbones and chin, lustrous shoulder-length brown hair with reddish highlights. She gave the impression of a woman as soft as silk until you looked at her more carefully. Then you might notice a layer of steel underneath the silk. Very much the modern businesswoman, Steadman thought, and accustomed to playing hardball with men. You couldn't pitch some tired line past her; you'd have to make your approach to her pretty much head-on. Which was exactly what he planned to do before this flight sat down on the runway at Kennedy.

Half an hour later Steadman was still pondering his approach to his traveling companion when the steward came up the aisle and gently shook Kay's shoulder. "Miss Williams . . . I'm sorry to disturb you. There's a phone call for you."

"Phone?" Kay stretched. "Way up here?"

"Yes. Not just an ordinary phone call, either. I believe the caller is using a comsat and paying a lot of money to reach you. That's why I decided to wake you. I hope that's all right."

"Yes . . . sure." Kay uncoiled, forgetting for just a moment the steel case attached to her wrist, wincing when a corner of the case hit her thigh. "Ouch. Okay, can I take the call back near the galley? I need to stretch."

"Of course."

John Steadman politely stood up to help Kay move more easily from her window seat into the aisle. "No rest for the wicked," he said, hoping she caught a hint of his interest in her.

"Afraid not," she answered, and followed the steward back to the first-class galley area. She took the phone and plopped herself down in one of the small, hard seats used by the cabin crew for takeoffs and landings. "Hello?"

"Miss Williams?" A female voice. "This is Mr. William Watkins's secretary. Please hold for Mr. Watkins. He's on another line, but he's eager to speak with you. I'll patch him right through."

Kay was no longer surprised by the call. William "Billy Boy" Watkins was extravagant, and could afford to be. He ran his own oil company (Watkins Oil Exploration and Development) and was an occasional client with a large collection of antique guns and knives. He bought only quality pieces, paid top dollar, demanded top service in return. Although she appreciated his business, dealing with Billy Boy Watkins was usually time-consuming and tiring. Dealing with him from an airliner 35,000 feet over the ocean wouldn't be easy.

A booming voice barked at her, accompanied by static. "Kay honey! We finally gotcha. Goddam, I've been trying to connect with you since this mornin'. It's nightime here in N'Orleans, ya know."

"Hello, Billy Boy. I'm on an airplane on my way to New York. I can't hear you too well, there's some comsat static. Can't I call you when I land in New York?"

"Where are ya now?"

"I don't know exactly. Somewhere over the Strait of Malacca, I suppose."

"Shit, I got some oil rigs pumpin' in that neighborhood. Naw, that's Indonesia. Anyways, look here, I need your help real bad. Can't wait till you get to New York twelve hours from now to tell you about this. I'm real excited, honey."

"Excited about what?"

"The auction!"

"What auction?"

"There's gonna be a private auction for a very special knife in Austin, Texas, next week. I want you to do some of that good research you done for me before, make sure I ain't gonna get ripped off. Then, assumin' this piece is forty carat, jump on a plane and head on down to Texas to bid for me. I want it worse than anythin' I ever went after. Sky's the limit."

"For a knife? How special can one knife be, Billy Boy?"

"Honey, we're talkin' about Jim Bowie's knife. I mean the *original* Bowie knife. Old Bowie, he called it. The one lost all these years since Jim Bowie got his rascally self killed at the Alamo."

Kay shook her head. Was she dreaming? "The original Bowie knife? Lost at the Alamo? Billy Boy, I think someone's trying to float a fake here. I don't know much about the Alamo or the Bowie knife, but anything lost for a hundred and fifty years or more is probably still lost. I've seen too many crooks trying to peddle stuff like this. They come up with an old knife or an old piece of jewelry case or whatever . . . a piece that's legitimately old . . . and then try to tell you it was owned by Madame Pompadour or Grover Cleveland or Marilyn Monroe or whatever scam story fits the piece they're trying to sell. This time it's *the original Bowie knife.*"

"I know there's crooks around, honey. Billy Boy Watkins wasn't born stupid, I just happen to talk that way. Besides which, I've had to be a crook myself from time to time when the goddam IRS or high interest rates me into it. I know plenty about scams. More'n you do. But there's a chance this knife might be the real thing. If it is Jim Bowie's old hog cutter, I damn well want it!"

Kay could see that Billy Boy Watkins wasn't going to let her off the hook. He hadn't built a four-billion-dollar-a-year oil company with his own name on the letterhead by letting people say no to him. "Okay, here's what I'll agree to. When I get back to New York, I'll do some research on Jim Bowie and his famous knife. Then I'll call around and find out whether any of my colleagues have heard about this piece coming on the market and the alleged auction and if so, whether they think it's legitimate. I'll charge you a thousand dollars a day as a consulting fee. If it looks like this knife may have some provenance, no matter how dubious, I'll go down to Texas and do some additional investigation. Still at a thousand dollars a day for consulting. Then I'll give you my best advice on whether you should bid for the knife or not. If I think it's genuine, I'll represent you. If I think it's a fake but you still want to bid on it, you'll have to get someone else to represent you on auction day. My fee for representing you at an auction will be settled when and if we get to that point. Agreed?"

"Deal," Billy Boy said. "Damn, that was easier than I thought it would be. You must be tired."

"Yes, I am tired. I hate airports. I hate flying. And I hate being awakened from a nap while I am flying, which is just what you did to me."

His laughter was, as always, long and hard. "Ain't you the touchy one. But that's what I like about you, honey. You're tough. You'd cut off a man's balls and sell 'em right back to him. Of course, the needle and thread to sew 'em back on would cost extra."

"I'm not sure that's a compliment."

"Well, it was meant to be."

Nevertheless, Kay felt stung. She considered herself a pretty good businesswoman with a decent reputation for professionalism and for delivering what the client wanted at the right price. Billy Boy Watkins had painted a harsher picture of her, whether he meant to or not. "Why do you want Jim Bowie's knife so badly?"

"Look, I got almost a thousand knives in my collection. Most of them are beauties. Best collection in the world, I'd say. I got knives once owned by sultans and kings and famous criminals and all sorts of interesting folk. But this is the ultimate knife. The most famous knife there is. Above that, Jim Bowie started out life just like I did, workin' in the Louisiana bayous without a pot to shit in or a second pair of pants to wear to church on Sundays. Don't matter he died over there in that Texas brawl, he was a Louisiana-brought-up boy who went out and made a name for hisself, wouldn't let anybody stop him. Liked a fight, too, Jim Bowie did. Went so far as to kill a few folk with that knife of his. My kind of man, honey. That's why if that knife is genuine, I gotta have it."

Kay found herself beginning to be infected by Billy Boy's enthusiasm despite her instinct that this was just another well-worn con game. "If it really is Jim Bowie's knife, I'll do everything possible to get it for you."

"I know you will. That's why I want you on the case. Phone me when you get to New York and we'll talk about this auction some more. Gotta take a call right now from fuckin' Kuwait. See ya." The connection was abruptly broken.

Kay gave the phone back to the steward and thanked him for waking her. Yes, she told him, it was an important call. She carried the steel case with the Fabergé egg back to her seat and sat straight up with the case in her lap, not sleepy at all now, trying to remember her history, to recall exactly what happened at the Alamo, what year it happened, how many people died there to buy time for Sam Houston and the army he was forming farther north to defend the beginnings of the Texas Republic.

"Important call?" John Steadman asked from the next seat.

"Possibly. I'm not sure yet."

"I had a thought, Kay. May I call you Kay? My thought is that you might like to have dinner with me some evening this week. The Four Seasons, if you'd like. Or any other restaurant you care to name. Afterwards . . ." Steadman leaned close to her and let his hand rest on Kay's leg, just lightly enough so that he could deny that he was making a pass if it came to that. "Afterwards, you might be interested in a club down in the Village where they have some very amusing acts. Some people call it a sex club, but I prefer to . . ."

A hot jolt of pain shot up Steadman's arm from his hand. It was so excruciating he couldn't speak, couldn't cry out, couldn't move, could only shrink into his seat. He managed to turn his head. Look down. See that Kay had hold of his left hand with only two fingers, which were pressing on the nerve where his thumb and forefinger came together.

"Don't ever put your hand on my leg again, Mr. Steadman. And for the rest of this flight, don't even bother to speak to me. The gentleman I just talked with on the phone claimed I was capable of cutting off a man's balls and selling them back to him. At the time I thought that was a rather unfair comment. Maybe he was right. If you bother me again, you'll find out. Meanwhile, I'd be content to simply turn your hand into jelly. Are you still in pain, Mr. Steadman?"

He nodded dumbly, eyes fixed on hers, afraid to move or say or do anything to offend her more. He thought he might faint from the pain.

"My dad taught me how to deal with naughty boys when I was just a teenager. This is a very sensitive nerve I've got hold of and I could make the pain even worse if I chose to. Remember that."

She released Steadman's hand and watched him deflate like a balloon until he looked like a small boy occupying a grown man's seat.

Steadman spat out the word "Bitch . . ." in a choked voice, captured his wounded hand and began to gingerly massage the injured spot between his fingers. He looked hastily around the first-class cabin to make sure none of the other passengers had witnessed his humiliation. Then he turned back to Kay with blazing eyes. "I only wanted . . ."

". . . what you can't have." Kay lowered her seatback and closed her eyes, but this time she didn't try to nap. Instead she tried to recall every single fact she knew about the legendary James Bowie and his famous knife.

# CHAPTER 2

A gust of raw Montana wind swept across the highway, giving a good hard shake to Bud Wolf's old Ford pickup. He responded by coming down harder on the gas pedal and pushing his speed up by another five miles an hour until he was going almost eighty. Wolf liked raw winds. He also liked razor-sharp knives, country music, beer in long-necked bottles, the call of a coyote, the feel and smell of new leather boots, and the sweet sound of the last rasp of breath from a dying man. Bud Wolf was, by his own description, the civilized world's worst nightmare, a man who knows right from wrong but just don't give a damn.

Ten miles outside Missoula, he began to look for the dirt road leading to Jimmy Walters's house. It had been a few years since he'd been up here in Montana. In the old days, when he made most of his money from hijacking trucks, he and Jimmy Walters had done a lot of work together. Wolf handled the rough stuff and Jimmy did most of the driving. They'd hijacked just about every kind of merchandise you could think of, from auto parts to refrigerated trucks packed with sides of beef. They worked the interstates from Phoenix all the way east to Baltimore and fenced the merchandise at fifteen cents on the dollar through the organized crime families in Chicago and New York. Looking back, they'd been suckers. Fifteen cents on the dollar was chump change. Jimmy still did that kind of work, while Wolf had moved on to better things.

He spotted Jimmy's mailbox, decorated with a colorful drawing of a big old rattlesnake with its fangs showing, and made a sharp turn onto the dirt road at sixty miles an hour. About five hundred yards farther on he slowed his pickup to forty and began looking for Jimmy's house. He recalled that there were four other houses on the road before Jimmy's. The neighbors were the reason Wolf moderated his speed. He didn't want some dumb shitkicker taking note of a fast-moving pickup and maybe getting the license number. Not that the license number on this truck would do the police much good. The plates were fake, he'd made them himself in his own machine shop. He could manufacture a set of license plates for any state in the union, and for Mexico and Canada, too, make them so authentic the cops couldn't tell them from the real thing without a close examination. One of Wolf's sidelines was peddling counterfeit license plates. Not a whole lot of money in that—fifty, sixty thousand a year—but it helped put meat on the table. He knew a dope runner who'd pay three thousand for the fake California plates on this pickup, so he wanted to keep them clean if he could.

Jimmy's house appeared on the left, a low-slung ramshackle place with some trash in the front yard and a big eighteen-wheeler parked under a nearby tree. There was a Chevy pickup parked there, too. On the other side of the house sat an Oldsmobile station wagon that probably belonged to Jimmy's wife, Sharon. Wolf would have preferred having Sharon off shopping somewhere, because she was a fine little lady with a sweet ass, but there it was—she was just plain unlucky.

Not a lick of work had been done on the outside of the house since the last time Wolf had been here. The front porch still sagged, a piece of cardboard still covered the attic window, and a lot more paint had peeled off the exterior. Montana's winters were hard. You had to paint the exterior every couple of years or your house would fall apart. "Man's got no sense of pride, that's his problem," Wolf said aloud. His own house was well-tended, and he liked to see other people keep up their property, too.

He stopped the pickup on a patch of grass instead of parking on the dirt driveway so as not to leave a set of tire tracks for the cops. There was always a chance that Jimmy had seen him come up the driveway and reached for that old .38 Smith & Wesson of his, so Wolf jumped out of the truck, jogged up to the porch and knocked loudly on the door.

Right away Jimmy came to the door. He looked awfully surprised to see Wolf, which meant Jimmy had no idea that anyone was on to him.

"Wolfie! What the hell are you doing here?" He grinned and shook Wolf's hand. "Come on in."

"Good to see ya again, Jimmy." Wolf carefully wiped his feet on the mat before stepping into the house. He had been raised to wipe his feet before entering, to say "ma'am" to any woman more than ten years older than himself, to hang up his clothes at night instead of dropping them on the floor, to eat everything on his plate and to tithe ten percent of his income to the Baptist church. He still did all those things, except for the tithing. Wolf figured he had better use for that ten percent than God did.

"I'm just passin' through, Jimmy. Thought I'd stop and say hello to you and Sharon."

"She'll be mighty pleased to see you. Damn, you look good, Wolfie. Prosperous as all hell."

"Thank ya. I'm doin' all right." Wolf looked around. It was obvious that Sharon kept up the inside of the house because the carpet and furniture were clean and there were even bright-colored flowers in bowls. "Looks like you're doin' okay, too."

Jimmy led Wolf towards the kitchen, which was where they always used to sit when they were cooking up a plan to steal something from somebody. Jimmy Walters was a smallish man with bowed legs that came from bad nutrition when he was young. Consequently, he walked with a sailor's rolling gait. Jimmy was about forty now, Wolf guessed. His sandy-colored hair was a little thinner, his waist a little wider, otherwise he hadn't changed much. Jimmy's face was red and rough, but his voice had a thin, reedy quality that took some getting used to.

Jimmy took a pair of longnecks from the refrigerator and handed one to Wolf. "Still drink longnecks, I'm sure."

"Always." Wolf used a bottle opener that dangled from a string tied to the kitchen cabinet to pop the caps on both their beers. He lifted his bottle and said "Long life," as a toast, and also as a private joke.

"Long life," Jimmy repeated in blissful ignorance, and they both drank.

They sat down at the kitchen table and started in on some small talk about people they both knew. Since Wolf got around more than Jimmy did, he had the better stories. "Remember Willie Gell? He hijacked a truck last year somewhere over in Kansas. He'd been told the truck was carrying tractor parts. Well, he had bad information. This particular truck was carryin' chickens, for Chrissake. He figured what the hell, he could sell a truckload of chickens in Kansas City, no problem. And he probably could have sold them. But those damned chickens were so *noisy* he couldn't stand it. Imagine drivin' a truck with maybe a thousand chickens all goin' *cluck . . . cluck . . . cluck* together, on and on and on without stoppin'. *Never* stoppin'! The sound damned near drove Willie Gell crazy! Finally Willie pulled over and left the truck on the side of the road, just abandoned it. Had to hitchhike all the way back home to Tennessee. Never made a dime on the trip."

"Willie Gell," Jimmy laughed, shaking his head. "There's a name from the past. What are you up to these days, Wolfie?"

"Little of this . . . little of that."

Sharon Walters came into the house from the backyard, where she'd been hanging shirts and underwear on the clothesline, and gave him a big hug. "Wolfie, it's grand to see you."

Wolf returned the hug. "You too, Sharon. By God, you haven't aged a day. Got your own Fountain of Youth up here in Montana, I reckon." And she did look good to him. Pert little thing. Neat figure. Reddish hair cut real short. Always in a tight T-shirt and jeans, every time he saw her. Even in those kinds of clothes, Sharon could look like a million bucks. "Still got your freckles, too."

"I pasted them on," she teased. "Just for you. What are you doing this far north? I heard you were working mostly down in Texas and New Mexico and Arizona these days."

Wolf noted the concern in her eyes. "Just passin' through, honey."

"Good . . . that's good." Sharon went around and stood behind her husband with her hands on his shoulders in a proprietary way. "Because I won't let Jimmy hijack trucks anymore, you know. Or do any other kind of stealing, for that matter. You guys had a lot of fun out on the road, I know that. Made some good money, too. That was okay when we were young and wild, had all the time in the world, but we can't hack it anymore. Too much pressure on both of us."

"This is just a social call," Wolf assured her, spreading his hands. "Thought you might give me a dinner, watch some TV with you, just like the old days. I've gotta be on the road by nine o'clock, but I'd sure like to catch up on all the family news."

"Sure." Sharon's relief was apparent. "You came on the right day, I have a nice-looking pot roast for dinner. You still like those little red potatoes cooked with the skins on? Got them, too."

"Perfect."

"How's Emma? And the kids?"

"They're fine. All fine. Except Emma got herself a new PC and plays roulette and backgammon and some damned game called Shanghai half the day. Hardly has time to talk to me, it seems."

"The kids are how old now?" Jimmy asked.

Wolf beamed. "Bud Junior is fourteen and the girls are six and eight."

Jimmy and Sharon looked wistful. They had never been able to have children. Wolf thought that the way things were working out, it was just as well they didn't.

"Well, I've got to put some clothes on the washline or Jimmy won't have a clean shirt tomorrow. I'll get dinner going soon."

"Don't hurry yourself on my account," Wolf insisted. "I can eat anytime, you know that."

After Sharon had gone back outside, Wolf sucked silently on his beer in order to let Jimmy stew for a while. The guy couldn't keep his mouth shut, which was the reason Wolf was paying him this visit. Sooner or later he'd start yakking about his problems.

"Sharon didn't mean any offense." Jimmy shifted uncomfortably on the kitchen chair. "She's a little worried about me is all. She'll get over it."

"Why's she worried?"

"I got myself jammed up a few weeks ago and now she's scared I'll have to serve some time. I won't, if things work out all right. But that's why the only driving I'm doing these days is strictly legit. Mainly I'm taking cattle to market for the ranches around here. Smelly work, but it's safe."

"What kind of jam are you in? Maybe I can help."

"I don't think so."

"Try me."

Jimmy transferred his weight from one buttock to another, scratched his chin, let out an aggravated sigh. "I got picked up by federal narcs while I was hauling a truckload of marijuana from Miami to Chicago. Miami's where the stuff came into the country, y'see. On a cargo boat from Jamaica."

"Feds? That is bad. Those guys don't let go."

"I know." Jimmy dipped his head in gloomy introspection. "Now they've got me on the spot. I can cooperate or serve mucho years at Danbury or Atlanta."

"You're doin' a deal with the feds?" Wolf asked the question offhand-edly.

"What choice do I have?" Jimmy jumped up and went to the refriger-ator. He took out a couple more beers, popped the caps and came back to the table. "It's that or go to prison for ten to fifteen. That's the choice the feds gave me. I hate it. I'm no rat, Wolfie. You know me. But this is my whole life we're talking about. I'm thirty-nine now, I'd be in my early fifties when I got out. It'd be all over for me."

"There's parole . . ."

"No! No way! The feds tell me they'd block any parole, I'd have to serve the whole ticket. I can't take that, Wolfie. You understand, don'tcha?" He looked at Wolf plaintively, practically begging his forgiveness.

Wolf didn't understand. He was a true believer in the old maxim *If you can't do the time, don't do the crime.* Of course, his outlook was different from most people's. For starters, he had absolutely no interest in dying in bed with his grandchildren gathered around and the air filled with prayers. That was okay for insurance salesmen and shoe clerks, not for Bud Wolf. He expected a violent death somewhere along the way. Not soon, he hoped. Maybe in fifteen or twenty years when his reflexes slowed or the odds turned against him. Wolf's greatest wish was that when his time came he could at least take his killer with him.

"This is dangerous, Jimmy. The people you hauled that shit for must know the feds are gonna pressure you to cut a deal."

"I told them not to worry, I'd hang tough. I think they bought it."

Wolf shook his head. "I'm afraid they didn't buy it, Jimmy. That's why I'm here."

A sick grin crossed Jimmy's face, a plea for his old pal Wolfie to take back what he'd just said. He saw only the implacable look of a man with a dirty job to do, and he knew exactly why Bud Wolf had come to his door today. Not for dinner. Not to hash over the old days. Not to watch some football on TV. "Wolfie . . ."

"Sorry, pardner. You buried yourself."

Jimmy's chair fell over backwards as he leaped up and dashed for the kitchen cupboard.

Predictable. That was what Wolf was thinking as he drew an eleven-inch Malay throwing knife from inside his sleeve. Jimmy Walters had kept an old .38 S&W on the top shelf of that cupboard for as long as Wolf could remember. Sitting next to it would be a box of ammo.

When Jimmy reached the cupboard and threw open the door, he had to stand still while he grabbed for the pistol. Wolf had been waiting for that moment. He threw the knife with a smooth, well-practiced motion. It was a heavy knife, needed to be heavy to pierce a man's flesh and drive on through to do real damage.

Jimmy gasped and both of his arms dropped to his sides. The point of the knife had entered his back dead center and severed his spinal cord, exactly as Wolf had planned. Jimmy slumped sideways, hit the kitchen sink, knocked dishes to the floor, bounced off the sink and fell to the linoleum with a comical thump. At least it sounded comical to Wolf, who had never brought a man down with such a definitive thud.

"Gaa . . . nooo . . . Wolfie . . . *please.*" Jimmy lay immobile, unable to move any part of his body below the point where the knife had chopped through the spinal cord. The blade hadn't damaged any other vital organs and so his mind was clear and filled with dread.

Wolf stood and looked out the window over the kitchen sink. Sharon was still hanging out the wash, she hadn't heard anything to make her nervous. "I said I was sorry. That's the best I can do. You can't deal with the feds and expect to live, Jimmy. Not in these times, when life is so cheap and all."

"Not Sharon, too. Wolfie? Not! Sharon!"

Wouldn't hurt to send Jimmy on his way feeling good about Sharon, so Wolf said, "I'll leave Sharon alone. You can count on that, pardner."

There was a pitiful look of gratitude on Jimmy's face as Wolf pulled the knife from his back and used it to cut his friend's throat from ear-to-ear. The shock of his own death contorted Jimmy's features before his head lolled to the side and he was still. Wolf moved back quickly so as not to let the spreading puddle of blood get onto his shoes or clothes. He wiped the throwing knife clean on a dish towel and slipped it into the leather scabbard under his sleeve. He also wiped his fingerprints off the bottle from which he'd been drinking.

Wolf's orders were to pull Jimmy Walters's tongue through the slit in his neck and leaving it hanging out there after he had done the job. The Jamaicans had wanted that done as their way of telling the world what would happen to people who tried to rat them out. Wolf couldn't bring himself to do that, not to an old friend like Jimmy. *Fuck the Jamaicans,* he thought. *What are they gonna do, sue me?*

He went out into the backyard with a smile on his face and helped

Sharon string out a bedsheet on the clothesline. "My mom never would use an electric dryer," Wolf said to her. "She always claimed that clothes smelled better and stayed clean longer if they got dried by the great outdoors."

"Your mom was right." Sharon grinned at him, her freckles a deeper and more girlish brown in the late afternoon sun. "Where's Jimmy?"

"Finishing his beer."

When two people are married for a long time, they develop strong instincts about each other. Sharon's instincts suddenly shook her from head to toe and turned her stomach into a block of ice. She stepped back as if from a stranger. "What have you done to him, Wolfie? Where's my Jimmy?"

"He's dead, Sharon. I'm sorry I had to be the one to do it, he shouldn't have turned rat."

"Wolfie!" She stared over the top of the bedsheet at him.

Those were almost her last words. Wolf once again slid the knife out of its hidden scabbard. This time he drove the knife through the bedsheet into Sharon's breast.

"Oh no!" She grabbed the clothesline with both hands, desperate to stay on her feet. For a moment she thought she might succeed. Then Sharon realized she was actually just hanging from the point of Wolfie's knife. When Wolf withdrew the knife, it nicked an inch or so of tissue out of her heart and all the strength went out of her. She collapsed on the ground and died within seconds. The bedsheet was dragged along, covering her like a shroud.

"You should have gone shopping today," Wolf said, not out of remorse but just because he had liked Sharon quite a lot and he hadn't been paid to kill her, too. Then he remembered that Jimmy and Sharon were the godparents of his son. *Bad luck for Bud Junior,* he thought. *No one to turn to if something happens to me.*

An hour later Wolf crossed the state line from Montana into Idaho. He stopped his pickup at the first gas station and used the pay phone to make a call to L.A. He hadn't wanted to make any calls from Montana. The cops there weren't too diligent, but they might think to check the call records of pay phones in the Missoula area and on their side of the state line.

The phone rang five times, as usual. Then there was a click. A pause.

Another click. Another pause. On and on like that for a long time. The call was being transferred automatically from phone to phone by a computer. He doubted that the Contractor, as his contact was called, lived in L.A. The computer was passing his call all over the country, probably twenty phones or more involved, and then scrambling the phone records in order to make the call impossible to trace.

Wolf approved of strong security. He had no idea who the Contractor was and wasn't curious. The Contractor gave him his assignments and sent advance payments for expenses and final payments when jobs were done to Wolf's various accounts in the U.S. and the Bahamas. That was all Wolf cared about, the payments.

"Hello . . . this is the sales department." The Contractor's voice was crisp and without a discernible accent. He always referred to himself as the sales department when he answered the phone, just in case anyone was listening in.

"This is Mr. Spring," Wolf said. His code name changed every quarter. He'd been Mr. Winter, Mr. Summer and Mr. Fall. All the seasons.

"Yes, Mr. Spring. How was your sales trip?"

"Made two big sales," Wolf answered.

"Two?"

"There was another prospect, so I closed that deal, too."

"No problems?"

"None."

"You'll only collect a commission for one, you know."

"Sure. But two accounts had to be cleared."

"I understand. Hold for a minute while my computer scans the line."

"I've got a fistful of quarters and I'm holding. Take your time."

Wolf stood at the pay phone watching the Idaho sky darken into night while the Contractor's computer retraced every link and tested the line for what he called *subverts* to make absolutely sure nobody was listening in on them. Occasionally Wolf heard a spatter of static. Otherwise, there was silence. Whenever the automated voice asked for more money, he fed quarters into the phone.

Finally the Contractor said, "All right, we're clear to talk in the open. Are you ready for another job or do you need to take a breather?"

"Depends on the job."

"This is straightforward. You'll be a bodyguard for a man carrying a great deal of money."

"Is the money clean or dirty?"

"I don't know. Does it make a difference?"

"Not really. How long will the job take?"

"Four or five days. The client is a Russian. His name is Leon Donin. He'll be arriving in Dallas on an American Airlines flight next week. I'll have the date and flight number for you soon. He'll have the money with him."

"The customs people might not let him into the country with a lot of money."

"Donin has a diplomatic passport. Customs won't be able to search his luggage. You'll accompany him to Austin and make sure nobody takes his money. He's going to use the money to bid on an antique. There's nothing illegal about this transaction. He needs a bodyguard only because he's never been to Texas and he's heard it's dangerous."

Wolf laughed. "Texas *is* dangerous. You know why? Because that's where I live."

The Contractor never reacted to jokes. "You'll stay with him until he leaves the country."

"You know how much money he's carryin'?"

"At least a couple of million dollars."

Wolf whistled. "How about I do my thing with Mr. Donin and we split the money?"

"Absolutely not." The Contractor's voice was like ice. "I've spent twenty years building this business. My reputation is gilt-edged. If I double-crossed a client I'd be dead within a week. So would you. Don't ever mention such a thing to me again."

"Okay, don't get your bowels in an uproar. I was just funnin' you."

"My idea of fun is a long game of chess."

"You're a wild one, all right. I don't suppose you know what kind of antique this Mr. Donin is tryin' to buy."

"Yes, I do. It seems that Jim Bowie's original knife, the one lost at the Alamo when Bowie was killed, has surfaced and is on the market."

"Jesus H. Christ!" Wolf was stunned. "Is that possible?"

"Mr. Donin seems to think it is. The Bowie knife will be sold at a private auction next week in Austin. Only six bidders have been invited, I'm told. Mr Donin is one of them."

That was electrifying news to Wolf, though he made a point of not revealing his excitement. "What's the fee for the job?"

"Five thousand a day."

*Out of which you'll take one-third,* Wolf thought. And found himself resenting the size of the Contractor's cut even though he'd made a pile of money working for the man. "Sounds good. You'll contact me in the usual way with the details?"

"I will. Time to break off." The Contractor never talked on the phone for more than five minutes, no matter how safe his computer told him the conversation was. "I'll tell our Jamaican customer that his job has been done."

"And done right," Wolf added, hanging up the phone before the Contractor could. *That'll piss him off,* he thought with a smile.

The smile faded as he considered the upcoming auction. One thought dominated his mind—he wanted Jim Bowie's knife more than he'd ever wanted anything in his life.

# CHAPTER 3

It felt good to be back in her own antiques store again, waiting on normal customers and exchanging chitchat about fairly ordinary items like Queen Anne chairs and Revere silver. Kay had gotten into the antiques business because she loved comfortable old things and the histories behind them. The idea of flying around the world to find exotic antiques for millionaires had never occurred to her. She'd done so a couple of times for special customers and suddenly found herself in demand for that kind of work, spending half of her life on airplanes headed for places like Tokyo, Berlin, Singapore, Buenos Aires, and Zurich.

But her store, a renovated farmhouse on Route 35 on the woodsy outskirts of Ridgefield, Connecticut, was her first love. The place had been half falling down when she bought it. She had done a lot of the reconstruction herself because she was just getting started then and needed to conserve capital. She had put up the new siding, installed the window frames, helped the roofer nail down the shingles, sanded the floors, rebuilt the stairway to the second floor. The only part of the rebuilding she didn't take part in was the electrical work. Kay knew as little about electricity as Ben Franklin did on that stormy night when he sailed his kite.

"How do the books look?" Mrs. Hanratty asked.

"We had a good month," Kay said. "So good I'm starting to worry you don't even need me around here."

"Oh, hush." Mrs. Hanratty gave Kay's shoulder a playful slap. "You're the heart and soul of this place and you know it."

"No, I don't, but thanks for saying so."

When it became impossible for Kay to handle the store all by herself because of her travel schedule, she had taken on Mrs. Hanratty to manage day-to-day operations. Mrs. Hanratty was a woman in her early seventies, white-haired but overflowing with energy, who had owned an antiques store in Chester, Connecticut, for many years with her husband. When he died very suddenly, Mrs. Hanratty sold the shop. Later she regretted her hasty decision and decided to go back to antiquing for someone who would appreciate her talents. Which Kay did.

"The fee for acquiring the Fabergé egg will help us buy some new stock," Kay said. "I've been thinking, Mrs. Hanratty, that you might like to go on a buying trip up through Maine and New Hampshire."

"I'd love to." Mrs. Hanratty's eyes sparkled. "Mr. Hanratty and I always took our buying trips in the spring. That's when people clean out their attics and basements and hold estate sales. Mr. Hanratty used to say that the best antique bargains in the world can be found at New England estate sales and flea markets."

The downside to hiring Mrs. Hanratty was that she felt obliged to pass on a constant stream of wisdom from her deceased husband. Kay knew more about Mr. Hanratty's philosophies than she did about Gandhi's or Emerson's.

"Why don't you plan on driving up through New England for a couple of weeks in April," Kay suggested.

"Lovely. I'll take the van. Oh my, this will be fun." The little chime above the front door rang and Mrs. Hanratty swiveled her head. "Aha! Mrs. Oliphant is back. She was in here last week to look at the Herter breakfront. I'll bet she's here today to buy!"

"What price have we set on that piece?" Kay asked.

"Twenty-two thousand. Shall I let her have it for twenty percent off if she pays cash?"

"Absolutely. It's not in good condition and it's been on the floor for almost a year. Move it if you can."

Mrs. Hanratty moved off at such a fast clip that Kay had to smile. A deer would have a better chance of escaping a lion than Mrs. Oliphant had of getting out of here without buying that breakfront.

While Mrs. Hanratty was cornering her customer, Kay dipped into the

THE TIME OF THE WOLF

books and other research she had collected on Jim Bowie and his knife. Bowie was certainly an intriguing character. Land speculator. Smuggler. Killer. Gambler. Rancher. In his last days a colonel in the Army of the Republic of Texas and commander of the civilian volunteers at the Alamo. And finally, killed at the age of forty-two by Santa Anna's Army of Mexico, along with the other 182 Alamo defenders, who included such disparate characters as Davy Crockett and William Barret Travis.

The gallant defense of the Alamo was one of the great pages in the nation's history. An event of mythic proportions, especially in Texas. The defenders of the Alamo bought enough time for Sam Houston to raise an army that would soon afterwards defeat Santa Anna at the Battle of San Jacinto. Jim Bowie's knife disappeared in the fires, explosions and other carnage of the Alamo. Conceivably, one of the Mexican soldiers might have recognized Bowie's corpse and taken the original Bowie knife as loot. But that was back in 1836. Surely the knife would have surfaced many decades ago.

Kay's personal phone line rang and she picked it up, watching with amusement as Mrs. Hanratty slowly but surely coaxed her customer into bringing out her checkbook. "Kay Williams Antiques."

"Hi, baby."

A wave of disgust, mixed strangely with sweet nostalgia, passed through Kay. She gripped the phone tightly while getting a firm grip on herself.

"Hello, Phil," she said coldly.

"Great to hear your voice again, Kay. It's been too long."

"I wouldn't say that."

Phil's hearty laugh was meant to indicate he understood her hard feelings. "Wish you'd never heard of me, right?"

"No, I just wish I'd never been married to you."

"Aw . . . come on now . . . wasn't that bad. We had some great times and you know it."

"What do you want, Phil?"

"Nothing! Just checking in, see how you're doing. I heard from Phyllis Minx that you're traveling a lot these days. She said you looked a little tired, a little lonely. Just got back from a hard trip to Singapore or someplace like that."

"I'm feeling fine and people tell me I've never looked better."

"Glad to hear it. Business going well?"

She hesitated on that one. If she bragged about how well she was doing, a big temptation, Phil would almost certainly ask for another loan. That was the only reason he ever called. "Business isn't bad. We're overstocked, but at least I'm not in a field where the merchandise goes bad."

"Lucky for you," Phil said with a certain ruefulness. "I'm in the restaurant business these days. Food can go bad real fast, especially down here."

"Down where?" Kay bit her tongue. *Never ask questions of Phil,* she reminded herself. *That's how he draws you in.*

"I'm in Jamaica. Little place called Runaway Bay, about halfway between Kingston and Montego Bay. Cute little town. Lots of tourists. Good beach. High green mountains. You'd love it. I found a partner down here and we started a little Mexican restaurant. Why Mexican? Well, people were dying for some variety. Almost every restaurant down here specializes in jerk chicken or jerk pork or jerk beef, as they call it. Good stuff, despite the off-putting name. Very spicy barbecue. But we've built ourselves a pretty good following, half locals and half tourists, by offering something different."

"Sounds wonderful." Kay didn't care what kind of restaurant Phil had. She just wanted to get him off the phone quickly.

"Yeah, it is. Look . . . the real reason I called was to invite you down for a long weekend."

The idea of two people who had divorced in a blaze of acrimony sharing a cozy weekend in Jamaica struck Kay as bizarre. "Why in the world would you want to do that? Don't you remember what I said the last time we talked? I said, *Phil, don't ever call me again*—especially *to ask for a loan.* I believe I went on to say, *The only thing I want from you . . . you two-timing chiseling asshole . . . is complete and total silence.* What part of that didn't you understand?"

Phil's laugh was hollow but game. "I know . . . I know . . . I had that coming. Now that things are going better for me, I wanted to do something to make up for my past . . . um . . . let's call them mistakes."

"Sleeping with fifteen-year-old high school girls while you were married to me wasn't merely a mistake, Phil. It was a felony."

"I was a shit. I admit that. We got married too young, Kay. I've settled down a lot, believe it or not. Learned a few lessons, thanks to you and some good friends who stuck by me. I thought a long weekend in Jamaica would be a chance for us to say good-bye to each other with a little more civility. Cancel out some of the hard feelings. You know what I mean?

And you'd see the restaurant, understand how far I've come. Isn't that worth a weekend? I'll send you a first-class ticket on Air Jamaica and put you up at a nice little inn down the beach from my restaurant. The whole weekend won't cost you a cent. How about it?"

"What's your restaurant called?"

"*Seis Amigos.* Six Friends. Like it?"

"It's nice." Kay could not believe she was giving Phil's invitation even a second's worth of serious consideration. But she was. Phil's voice always had an effect on her. He still had that sexy voice. Broad shoulders. Easy smile. A crooked little-boy grin that used to melt her heart. Charming as a TV evangelist when he wanted to be. She shook herself. *No way! Like the song says, I was born in the dark but it wasn't yesterday.* "Sorry." Crisply now. "I'm going down to Austin, Texas, in a few days for a private auction. Don't know when I'll be back. I appreciate the invitation, but it isn't a good idea for us to see each other again."

"Maybe later in the month?"

"I don't think so." To her own surprise she added, "But we'll see."

"Whatever you say." He laughed. "Hey, this is the first time in years we've ended a conversation without yelling at each other. That's progress, isn't it?"

"I suppose."

"Talk to you later, babe. Have a good time down in Texas."

"Good-bye, Phil."

As soon as she put down the phone, there were tears in her eyes. She quickly went upstairs to the small apartment above the shop and made herself a cup of jasmine tea. Phil had gotten to her again, despite everything she knew about him. *Do I still love the bastard?* she wondered. *No. Not love. But once in a while I crave him,* she admitted to herself. *Being with Phil is like craving a giant chocolate milkshake. You buy it and at first it's very sweet and satisfying. Then it becomes gradually less appetizing. And when it's too late you realize you've had more than you wanted, you're practically sick and the whole experience has been very bad for you.*

She sipped her tea until she felt calm enough to go back down to the shop.

Mrs. Hanratty was there with triumph in her eyes. "I sold the breakfront." She waved a check. "I'll have it delivered on Friday."

"Why not tomorrow?" Kay suggested, trying to act like the boss.

"Oh no, not until Mrs. Oliphant's check clears the bank. She's a sweet woman, but I always like to see the check clear before shipping the merchandise."

"You're a jewel, Mrs. Hanratty."

"I couldn't help noticing that you were upset by that phone call."

Kay knew from experience that Mrs. Hanratty would worry and cluck over her unless she explained what the call was about. At times Kay liked having a mother hen around, and this was one of those times. "That was my charming ex-husband on the phone."

"Phil?" Mrs. Hanratty's eyebrows rose. "What did he want? Another loan? Don't give him a penny, dear. You'll never get it back, you know that from past experience."

"For once Phil didn't want a loan. He's in Jamaica. Owns a restaurant down there, he says. He invited me down to Jamaica for a long weekend. To 'cancel out some of the hard feelings.' "

"I wouldn't trust the man." Mrs. Hanratty folded her arms across her chest. "Not for a minute."

Kay was about to remind Mrs. Hanratty that she'd never met Phil, then decided she didn't want to sound as if she were defending him. She had shared some of Phil's extramarital escapades with Mrs. Hanratty and spoken of her weakness in lending money to Phil after their divorce. She did feel guilty about doing so much better financially than Phil since their divorce. That was irrational, she knew. "I don't trust him. But I do hope his restaurant is doing good business."

"Yes," Mrs. Hanratty agreed. "Then he won't have to come to you for money anymore."

Kay let the subject drop there and began to discuss what changes they might make in the display window.

Phil Williams put down the phone and looked out at the perfect blue Caribbean without feeling a trace of pleasure in its perfection. "She won't come down for the weekend. I almost had her, I could tell by her voice, she never could hide her feelings from me, but at the last minute she changed her mind."

"Shit!" The expletive was muttered by a large, bearded black man who sat in the deck chair next to Phil. His name was Chauncy Alexander. He was Phil's partner in *Seis Amigos* as well as in other ventures less legal. They were sitting in deck chairs on a patio behind the restaurant, looking out to sea while they talked. "Little bitch." Chauncy had the kind of deep, sweet, powerful voice made for singing gospel. Problem was, he had no interest in gospel. "What we do now, mon?"

"She might come later this month. She said so."

"Could be too late," Chauncy reminded his partner. They were deeply in debt, and not just in the restaurant venture. Last month they had financed a load of marijuana headed from Jamaica to a landing strip in South Florida. The light plane carrying the load had been tracked by the DEA's radar. When the plane set down, the pilot was arrested and the plane and marijuana confiscated. They owed money on that deal to members of New York City's Jamaica gang who had paid 25 percent of the marijuana's value up front. "The brothers up north, they hire someone down here slit our throats, we don't pay."

"I know!" Phil's depression was sapping his ability to think. Kay had plenty of money, enough to solve all his problems. He'd learned from one of their old friends, Phyllis Minx, that Kay had just received a one-hundred-thousand-dollar fee for tracking down a Fabergé egg for a client. And her antiques store in Connecticut was thriving. But would she share any of her new wealth with the man she'd married and loved? Maybe still loved? Hell, no! Tightfisted bitch.

"So what we do?" Chauncy was more frightened than he wanted Phil to know. The men they owed money to had given them a month to pay their debt. Their restaurant had no real equity, and business was bad because the food was bad. At first the novelty of Mexican food in Jamaica had brought in a steady stream of diners. Now they were down to about thirty customers a day, not enough even to meet their expenses. They couldn't raise a dime from the restaurant. That left only Phil's rich ex-wife.

The plan had been to get Kay down here to Jamaica and pry one hundred and fifty thousand dollars out of her, one way or another. Phil would make love to her first, then hit her up for a nice loan. If that didn't work, they'd hold her by force here in Runaway Bay until she came up with enough cash to save their asses. That would have been halfway safe. She had no friends in Jamaica, wouldn't know where to turn. Unfortunately, the bitch had refused to walk into their trap. "Speak to me, mon."

After a time Phil said, "Kay told me she's going to Austin, Texas, for a private auction. I don't know much about her business. But I do know the bidders often bring hundreds of thousands of dollars in cash or cashier's checks to those private auctions."

Chauncy perked up. "You serious?"

"You bet I am." Phil was nodding aggressively. "I've thought before of following Kay to one of those auctions, zeroing in on whoever's carrying the heaviest load of cash, and making a big score."

"How you find out who's carrying a lot of cash?"

"From Kay. Believe me, she hasn't gotten old Phil out of her system. I could tell that over the phone. If I flew to Austin and turned on the charm, she'd be in my bed straight off. Guaranteed. Then I'd just casually ask about the auction, what was being sold, and find out who was carrying the biggest roll. Yeah, I think a trip to Texas might solve our cash flow problems."

Chauncy didn't like the idea of Phil leaving Jamaica without him. "You don't even think of going up there alone. Get any idea like that out your head."

"We'll both go, of course. You stay in the background until I have the information we need. Then you hit the money man." Phil grinned. "It might even work out that Kay will be carrying a lot of money. That would make the whole deal much simpler."

"We maybe have to kill someone." Chauncy wanted to see how Phil would react.

"I don't do that kind of work," Phil said quickly.

"So I be elected?"

Phil ran a hand through his thick blond hair. In profile, his face was hard and strong and quite handsome. But when he looked someone in the eye, someone like Chauncy who could read a face with the best of them, Phil's softness was apparent. "I don't do that kind of work," he repeated.

"Might even have to kill your ex-wife."

"We can avoid that." Phil shifted uncomfortably in his deck chair. Chauncy had killed two people—two that Phil had heard of—back when Chauncy lived in New York and worked for the Jamaican drug gang out of Queens. Chauncy had left New York and returned to Jamaica two years ago to avoid a murder investigation. Chauncy was the kind of man Phil needed, but that didn't mean he wanted his ex-wife killed. "Kay and I were very close at one time. That sort of thing counts with me."

*Sure it do*, Chauncy thought. "This deal all we have anyway. We got just about enough cash left, get us to Texas, so this better work. Oh mon, I don't want to leave Texas broke, running for my life."

"Neither do I." Phil's upper lip went all sweaty at the thought.

A brown-skinned girl came out of the back door of *Seis Amigos*, slid into Phil's lap, put her head on his shoulder. She wore her hair in long cornrows and had legs so slim you wondered how they supported her. "What you boys plotting out here?"

Phil kissed her cheek absently. "Talking trash, that's all."

"You gonna take Germaine out to dinner tonight?" The girl nuzzled herself deeper into the crook of his arm.

"Why don't we have dinner right here at *Seis Amigos*? Won't cost us anything."

Germaine made a face. "Food no good here."

"She be right," Chauncy said. "This cook worse than the last. We should close down the place right now. Cut our losses. Cost more to keep it open than it's bringing in."

Chauncy was right. Phil knew he was right. But Phil hated to close the place. When it finally stood empty and abandoned, it would become still another official failure. He'd had too many such failures. "Let me think about it."

He moved Germaine off his lap and went inside the restaurant through the back door. The new cook was asleep on the kitchen floor, curled up in a corner with a bottle of Appleton's cheapest rum. Phil went into the dining room. The waitress, a sixteen-year-old girl who worked for pennies, was slouched at a corner table watching the solitary luncheon customer finish his tacos and refried beans.

The walls were decorated with sombreros and bright prints of typical Mexican tourist scenes—the pyramids . . . a matador standing toe-to-hoof with a great beast of a bull, his cape twirling bravely . . . a bright Acapulco beach . . . a young couple riding horses with *serapes* draped over their shoulders . . . an open-air market. On the tables were candles in the green, white and red colors of Mexico. The tablecloths were of the same color.

"Tacky . . . tacky . . . tacky . . ." Phil muttered. Chauncy was right. Close the place and move on to something better. Fly to Texas. Find Kay. Score big. He went outside and told Chauncy, "You're right. We'll close it today."

Chauncy was relieved Phil saw it his way. They weren't meant for the restaurant business anyway. Neither of them could cook, neither wanted to wait on tables. The idea had been basically good. Some new restaurants along the beach were succeeding by serving Italian or French food instead of traditional Jamaican fare, proving the point. But neither of them was willing to put in the hours and hard work it took to make a restaurant successful. "You close up the place this afternoon, I make the plane reservations. We fly economy, first time in years I do that."

"Where you two going?" Philip was Germaine's current meal ticket. He'd bought her some nice things, given her money when she needed it, taken her to Mo' Bay for weekends and made love to her whenever she asked for it. Besides all that, Philip was very good-looking. Germaine didn't want to lose him just yet.

"None of your business," Chauncy said in his beautiful voice.

"You'll be coming back, won't you?"

"Of course," Phil lied. He slipped his hand into her blouse. Her breasts were small but tender and well-formed. "Let's go upstairs, play hide the bone."

Germaine giggled. "Hide the bone. That too funny."

Phil put his arm around Germaine and led her up the steps to the two rooms above the restaurant where he and Chauncy lived. A few minutes later Chauncy, who continued to stare out to sea while he noodled around this Texas business, could hear their groans and moans and the gentle *slap-slap-slap* of two bellies moving against each other. *Mon like his ass,* Chauncy thought. *That about all he good for, too. Which is okay, so long he can still please his ex-wife.*

There was a terror inside Chauncy that he was struggling not to show. Phil, his mind on nothing but pussy, had no idea how cruel the Jamaican gangs operating out of New York were. Even the Chinese and Colombians feared them. Italians, forget it. See a Jamaican coming, run the other way.

Chauncy was thinking about himself lying in a back alley at Montego Bay, tongue sticking out through a long slit in his throat. That's what the Jamaican enforcers liked to do, turn a tongue into a bloody necktie. "Got to get my hands on some *big* money," he said aloud, his beautiful voice carrying out to sea.

*Phil gets the information, points me at the money.*

*Then I do my thing.*

# CHAPTER 4

Every time the phone rang that afternoon, Kay jumped. She was afraid Phil might call again to invite her down to Jamaica. Worse yet, she might accept. Phil still had a hold on her. He was her weakness, she'd known that from the first day they met. It was an addiction. *This time . . . This time . . .* she thought, *I've got to take a firm stand. No more conversations with Phil. No more cash loans for Phil. No more cozy feelings for Phil.*

And yet she couldn't resist feeling some sort of misplaced sympathy for him. When they first met, Phil had been a moderately successful Wall Street commodities broker and she'd been just a clerk in an antiques store. He was handsome, witty, considerate, poised. She'd fallen for him completely. It took a year or two of marriage before she could admit to herself that Phil was all image, no substance. In fact, Phil had more cracks than the San Andreas Fault. After a long time, she admitted to herself that Phil was a bum. At first she thought his greatest weakness was very young girls. Then she found that money was an equally strong temptress to Phil. In the second year of their marriage, Phil was fired from his job and the newspapers began running stories about the young commodities trader who had lost ninety million dollars of his company's money trying to recoup his personal trading losses. Phil avoided going to prison, but was permanently barred from working in any area of the securities industry. That didn't seem to bother him. By then Kay was making more money and Phil was content to live off her income and chase girls while she worked.

Kay had forced herself to divorce Phil and told herself (she knew it was self-deception) that she was completely through with him. *Finito.* End of story. A lie and a half. Whenever he called, her juices started flowing. True, she was doing better these days at standing up to Phil. She was like the alcoholic who still liked a drink on holidays, not totally cured but definitely on the road to recovery. *Why isn't there a twelve-step program to help women deal with guys like Phil,* she wondered.

The phone rang and she flinched. "Mrs. Hanratty, would you get that, please?"

"Of course, dear." Mrs. Hanratty could read Kay well enough to know when she was going through a *Phil phase.* She answered the phone, turned to Kay. "It's Mr. Watkins calling from New Orleans."

Kay took the phone with a smile. "Hello, Billy Boy."

"Hiya, Kay. Got any good news for me? Are we goin' after that Bowie knife?"

"I've done a lot of research. On Saturday I went through the Yale University rare book collection here in Connecticut. They had some books from the 1800s that were very helpful. Maps, too. And I've been on the phone to the University of Texas library. Between those two sources, this is what I've found out about the original Bowie knife.

"It was made in 1827 to Jim Bowie's specs by James Black, a smith in Washington, Arkansas, who also had a reputation as a maker of fine cutlery. Bowie designed the knife and Black carried out the work. It appears that Bowie gave Black a wooden model he'd carved. The blade was eleven inches long and an inch and a half wide. The heel was three-eighths of an inch wide, very thick in those days. It was weighted to be a throwing knife as well as an all-around knife. The point is at the exact center of the width of the blade in order to give it accuracy when thrown. The blade curves to the point convexly from the edge and concavely from the back. Black signed his name in very small letters at the base of the cross-guard, so that would be one way of identifying the original Bowie knife."

Billy Boy Watkins laughed in childlike delight.

"Bowie acquired the knife after that famous fight on the sandbar. Killed a state senator. Bowie didn't go to prison because the senator started the fight. Bowie was already well known, but that incident made him a sort of mythic character. After the knife became famous, all sorts of people began coming to James Black for a knife exactly like Jim Bowie's. Other knifemakers around the country, and even in Sheffield, England, started making custom Bowie knives. Fortunately, we don't have to be concerned about any knives except the ones made by James Black in the 1820s and 1830s because he signed his work."

"How many copies of the original Bowie knife did Black make?"

"Nobody knows. James Black probably made hundreds of Bowie knives. Many museums and private collectors have them."

"Well, that's a damned shame." Billy Boy's disappointment was a palpable thing, even over a long distance line.

"Don't give up yet." Kay was warming to her subject. "Bowie's original knife had one feature that distinguished it from other copies that Black made. The original had a cross-guard made of brass instead of steel. All of the other Bowie knives that James Black made had steel cross-guards, as far as anyone knows. Jim Bowie wanted brass because it's a softer metal than steel. He thought that would help him counter the thrust of someone using a knife against him. Apparently Bowie was a born knife fighter. You couldn't fault his thinking, because he used that knife between 1827 and 1836 to kill several people and save his own life in the bargain."

"Whoa! So we will be able to tell if the knife that's up for auction is the original Bowie knife!"

"Maybe." Kay hated to dampen Billy Boy's enthusiasm because she was keyed up herself. Even so, Billy Boy had to know that this could still be a scam. "Or it could be that a con man has done some good research and produced a very believable copy of the original."

"Isn't there some way to check on that? Carbon dating?"

"A clever con man would use old steel to manufacture a fake."

"I don't believe this knife is a fake."

"That's because you want to believe it's the original Bowie knife."

"I guess I do." Billy Boy sighed deeply. "What do we do now?"

"I want to go down to Austin. Represent you at the auction. And bid on that Bowie knife if I'm convinced it's the original."

"You do? Shit, I thought you were tryin' to tell me it's a fake. Let me down easy."

"Not at all. I was only reminding you that we've got to be very careful here. How badly do you want this knife, assuming I can be convinced it's the real thing?"

"You're askin' how much I'm willin' to bid?"

"That's right."

"I'd pay up to three million dollars for that knife."

"That's why you shouldn't do the bidding. Three million would be way too high."

"I know . . . I know . . . I'd get carried away and empty my goddam bank account. I don't dare go near Austin, I know that. I'm a real smart businessman in most things, but I tend to let my emotions go wild at an auction."

"I understand that."

"What do you want from me? A suitcase full of cash?"

"Absolutely not," Kay said. "Give me two hundred cashier's checks made out to cash, each one for ten thousand dollars. I'll bid in ten-thousand-dollar increments. If the provenance of the knife is at all shaky, I wouldn't bid more than one hundred thousand dollars anyway. But if this looks like it is the original Old Bowie, the bidding could go over a million. Maybe more. Everything depends on the provenance and condition of the knife."

"Sounds right to me. I'll have my accountant get the checks to you by courier. Where do you want 'em delivered, Connecticut or Austin?"

"Send the courier to the Omni Hotel in Austin. That's where I'll be staying. Have the courier deposit the package in the hotel safe in my name. The auction will be held, I'm told, a block away at the Driskill Hotel."

"Who's runnin' the auction?"

"A man named Stewart Ruddington. He's a top-flight auctioneer with a solid reputation. I've spoken to him. Only six people have been invited to bid, including you. Stewart says I'll be well satisfied with the knife's provenance. His endorsement is important. Stewart doesn't run an auction unless he believes the merchandise is good."

"Did he say who owns the knife now? Where it came from?"

"No, he wouldn't say. Stewart did tell me the owner is a wealthy Mexican citizen whose family has owned the Bowie knife since 1836. All of the recent economic problems in Mexico have hit the family hard. They need a ton of cash quickly. That's the reason they're selling."

"I don't trust Mexicans," Billy Boy Watkins said.

"It's good to be suspicious when it comes to an auction. Especially a private auction. I suspect the owner of the knife doesn't want the Mexican government to know what he's up to. That's why he's auctioning it

THE TIME OF THE WOLF

off privately instead of through Christie's or some other public auction house. He doesn't intend to pay any taxes on this windfall to either the U.S. or Mexican tax authorities."

"Can't blame him for that. I hate the goddam tax man myself." Billy Boy could be heard scratching the two-day stubble of beard that seemed always to cover his chin. "What about your fee?"

"If I decide the knife is worth bidding on, I'll take one hundred thousand dollars if my bid is successful or twenty-five thousand if I fail to acquire the knife for you. If I decide on auction day that the knife isn't worth bidding on, I'll bill you one thousand dollars a day for my time. Whatever happens, you pay the expenses for my trip to Austin."

"Fair enough."

With some clients, Kay asked for a written contract. She didn't bother doing that with Billy Boy Watkins. Though he was known as something of scoundrel in the oil business, Kay had found his word to be absolutely good.

"Kay honey, you stay in real close touch. And watch yourself in Texas. They got ripoff artists down there who can steal the fillins outta your teeth while your mouth's closed."

"I'll be careful."

"Carry a gun."

"I don't think it will come to that."

"You ever been to Texas?"

"No, I haven't."

"Carry a gun," Billy Boy repeated. "Go to one of them gun shows, they have them every week down there. No five-day waitin' period. Just plunk down your cash and walk away with any kinda gun you want, from a pistol to a Mac-10."

"If I feel the need for a machine gun, I'll do that," Kay said.

"You're humorin' me. After you've been in Texas a couple of days you'll be lookin' for a gun, I guarantee it."

"It's nice of you to be concerned about me."

"I'm concerned about you *and* my two million dollars in cashier's checks."

"I'll take good care of those checks. They'll be in the Omni Hotel safe except during the auction."

"Well, have a good trip. And honey, I really want that knife."

"I know you do. But it's my job to see that it's genuine and to keep you from overspending."

Billy Boy snorted. "I overpay by habit. For Jim Bowie's original knife, I'd overpay by a hell of a lot."

"That's what the seller is depending on."

"Bothers me that he's a Mexican."

"Don't go redneck on me."

"I am a goddam redneck," Billy Boy declared. "It's an essential part of my charm."

Kay laughed. "I'll talk to you from Texas."

"Take heed to what Mark Twain said. 'If I had a choice between hell and Texas, I'd rent out Texas and live in hell.' Some of us rednecks do know how to read."

"You're a constant surprise to me, Billy Boy."

"That's what all the gals say. Talk to you later."

Billy Boy Watkins rang off, leaving Kay to ponder how much weight to give to his warnings about Texas.

"Go for it!" Wolf yelled. "Hit that bitch with your spurs!" He gave his own horse a couple of vicious kicks that made the animal lunge forward, overtaking and then passing Bud Junior's horse.

They were in a helluva race now and Wolf was feeling reckless. The fence ahead was damned high, but he wanted to show Bud Junior that his old man was still top dog around here. He sucked air into his lungs and leaned forward, his butt about ten inches above the saddle.

Sunrise, Wolf's horse, cleared the fence, though one of its hoofs clipped the top slat. Sunrise landed awkwardly as a result, lost its footing for a few seconds, then recovered and charged ahead. Bud Junior's mare had taken the fence with more grace and he was already fifteen yards ahead of Wolf.

"Goddamn it!"

Bud Wolf had no intention of losing a race to a fourteen-year-old kid. He spurred his mount's flanks so hard that he drew blood. Sunrise responded well. Practically flew the last hundred yards. Wolf leaned forward, snapping the reins and muttering threats into Sunrise's ear. Wolf's tone told Sunrise all he needed to know—win the race or feel the lash of Wolf's belt later on. Wouldn't be the first time.

Sunrise crossed the finish line—the dirt driveway leading to Wolf's house—a good ten yards ahead of Bud Junior and his mare.

They slowed their mounts to a trot and Wolf turned to his son with a victorious grin. "Beat you! But that was a nice ride, Junior. You took that fence like a goddam steeplechase rider."

"Horse did all the work," Bud Junior replied, giving his mare a few appreciative pats along the neck.

"Don't spoil her," Wolf snapped. "If you show her too much affection, she won't give you her best ride next time. Same thing goes for women, you might as well know that right now. Bitches are all the same, whether they've got four legs or two."

Bud Junior didn't say anything, just nodded in a sullen way. Wolf was a little concerned about his son. *Boy's too soft,* he thought. *Rides well. Shoots okay. But he won't step up to the tough things in life. Doesn't even like to wring a chicken's neck, and how are you gonna have chicken for dinner if you can't do a simple chore like that?*

They slowed their horses to a walk and circled around the house to the stable and corral out back. Wolf had twenty acres of decent land in the Texas Panhandle, nice and flat with a stream running through it and a few stands of cedars here and there. Nearest town ten miles away, a little too close to suit him, he didn't like towns and neighbors all that much. He spent about half his time at the ranch and half on the road, just the right mix as far as he was concerned.

"Sunrise is bleeding," Bud Junior said.

"Had to spur him." Wolf glared at his son. "Don't get that hangdog look with me, boy. Sunrise is lazy, needs the spur now and then. It's nothin', just a few scratches."

They came to the stable and Wolf stepped down from his horse. He glanced at Sunrise's flanks and saw that he was right. Just a few scratches. He threw the reins at Bud Junior. "You're so concerned, you can wipe down Sunrise and dress those scratches, too. Teach you not to frown anywhere in my general direction."

He turned his back on Bud Junior and walked toward the house feeling hungry as a lion. Nothing like a good ride to get a man's appetite up.

"Emma!" he yelled, entering the house. "I'm hungry! Get some lunch on the table and make it quick, I got lots to do this afternoon."

"Okay, Bud," his wife called from the kitchen. "I have a nice beef stew on the stove already."

Wolf grunted and went into the living room. The girls, Mary and Charlene, were playing jacks on the floor. When their father came into the living room and plopped down in his easy chair, they scooped up their jacks and tried to scuttle away.

"Whoa there! Come sit on your papa's lap." He patted his knees and smiled. Mary, who was six, looked at her older sister for guidance. Charlene was eight and used Mary as a sort of slave. Charlene was nice enough to Mary, but she always wanted Mary to remember she was older and the natural leader of the two of them. Charlene nodded, giving Mary leave to climb up into their father's lap. Neither of the girls were greatly enthused by his attention, but Wolf hardly noticed. As always, he was delighted with his girls.

"Who's winnin' the jacks game?"

Mary rolled her eyes. "Charlene *always* wins."

Wolf laughed. "I'm gonna get you girls some new games, you must be tired of jacks. What do you want? Board games? Maybe some video games? That's what kids seem to like these days."

"We're happy with the jacks," Charlene said.

"Sure, but you must want somethin' else. A couple of dolls maybe? Barbie dolls? They still sell those?"

They were silent. In the silence, they slid down off his lap.

"What's the matter? Hey, I'm talkin' to you two."

Damned kids always froze up when he was around. His hand flicked out and caught both of them across the face with one slap. He hadn't meant to hit them, just a reaction to their sullenness was all.

They started to cry. Charlene stepped back awkwardly. Her heel caught on the carpet and she fell down on her bottom, which caused her to cry more loudly. Mary's voice rose, too.

"Shut up, dammit!" One little slap. They were girls, weren't they? Girls grow up to be women. Women have to learn to take a slap now and then, just the natural order, that's all.

Emma rushed into the room. "What's wrong? What have you done?"

"Nothin'! Damned kids just like to howl. Take 'em away. And make 'em shut up!"

She took the kids. Wolf moved restlessly around his living room, gazing at the oil painting of an Indian charge against the U.S. Cavalry that hung above the fireplace, taking down his favorite beer mug from the mantel and putting it back again.

He couldn't get the Bowie knife out of his mind. It wasn't fair that some rich old bastard could buy something as important, as beautiful, as the original . . . the *original* . . . Bowie knife! He'd be willing to bet that whoever bought it would never have killed a man with a knife, the way old Jim Bowie had done lots of times. *The way I've done lots of times. I'm a knife fighter, just like Bowie. I deserve that knife.*

After a time he wandered into the kitchen and found Emma sitting at the table, head down, eyes awash in tears. "Come on, I didn't do a god-damn thing to Charlene and Mary. They're just whiners, that's all."

Emma shook her head. "That's not why I'm crying. I just had a call from Wilma Fries up in Wyoming. She told me that Jimmy and Sharon Walters were found dead the other day in their house."

"What?" Wolf feigned shock. Actually, he was shocked. He didn't expect Emma to hear about Jimmy and Sharon so soon. Wilma Fries, a friend from the old days when he was still driving a truck, was a loud-mouthed bitch. "How'd it happen? A fire? Jimmy always had too much trash around his house, I warned him about fires."

Emma shook her head violently. She had been an attractive girl when she was in her twenties. Today, in her late thirties, Emma still had a good body and legs, and her hair was still blond with only a few random streaks of gray, but her face had become lined and haggard. Especially haggard right now. "Somebody murdered them."

"Jesus," Wolf said. "Are you sure about that?"

Emma sobbed.

"Well, you know Jimmy. He hauled a lot of illegal loads, hung out with some hard cases. Guess the chances he took finally caught up with him." Wolf's curiosity got the best of him. "Did Wilma say anything about what the police know, who they think did it?"

Emma looked up and for a moment, a split second, her eyes were on fire. Then they damped down and she said in a tight voice, "No, they don't. All they know is that Jimmy and Sharon were both stabbed to death. Some-one saw a blue pickup in the neighborhood. That's all anyone knows." Emma started to look out the kitchen window at the parking strip behind the house where Wolf's blue pickup was parked, then thought better of it. Her husband had been gone on one of his "business trips" when Jimmy and Sharon were murdered. And she knew that Bud considered himself an expert with a knife. But she didn't dare say anything. Didn't dare.

"I'll get your stew," was all she said, going to the stove.

Wolf sat down and unfolded the paper napkin at his place. "Too bad. I liked old Jimmy. Sharon, too. You know I did."

"I know," Emma said dully. She put a bowl of stew in front of him, thinking that she couldn't just let it pass, she had to say something. "Where were you last week, Bud?"

Wolf's hand caught Emma across the face with a slap that made her stagger. He'd hit her so often that he could do it without thinking. "That's a stupid question, Emma." Bud Junior had come in through the back door at the moment of the slap. His face twisted and he poised himself to attack his father, but backed off at the black look on Wolf's face.

The tension was heavy and Wolf tried to disperse it with some humor. "Hey, Junior, you know what three hundred battered women have in common? They just won't listen." He laughed, but no one joined in, so he shrugged and went at his stew with a big soup spoon.

"Come on, sit down, you two. I'm sorry, Emma. You pissed me off is all. Junior, this stew is really good. Sit down and have some." When Bud Junior didn't respond, Wolf looked up at his son with an expression that filled the boy and his mother with a sickening dread that something still worse could happen any second.

"I said sit down!" Wolf roared.

Emma and Bud Junior hastily filled bowls of stew and sat down to lunch. During the meal Wolf explained that he was leaving that evening for Dallas and other places on business and that he'd be gone for a week, maybe more. Neither Emma nor Bud Junior showed the great relief they felt at that news. They just kept their eyes down and ate their stew.

At the end of the meal Wolf wiped his mouth, threw down the napkin and beamed around the table. "That was a treat, Emma. Your mom's a hell of a cook isn't she? Well, I got some work to do out in my machine shop." He pushed back from the table and left the house.

When Bud Junior was sure his father was out in the barn, he said, "I can't take this anymore, Mama. Can't take what he does to you. He hits you . . . he hits the girls . . . he treats me like a piece of shit."

"Hush up," Emma hissed.

"On days like this I want to kill him," he said passionately.

Emma was almost in a state of panic. "Please, Junior, don't even *think* such things. You know what would happen? *He'd kill you.* You think your father hasn't killed people? He has. You wouldn't stand a chance."

"I could . . ."

"Do you think I haven't considered killing him myself? A hundred times? A thousand? Bud is tough. He's a survivor. I could tell you stories about fights he's been in, other people who have tried to do him harm. He always wins. Always." She reached out wildly and gripped her son's hand. "The best thing you can do is get out of here. Don't wait until you're fifteen, sixteen. I've got a little money put away. Take it and go. Go tomorrow morning, Junior. While your father's away on business."

Bud Junior shook his head. "I won't leave you and the girls here."

Emma slumped. "Bud's away from home a lot of the time these days, that's something."

"I hope he doesn't come back this time. Whatever lousy thing he's up to, I hope someone kills him."

A harsh laugh gave Emma's face some unexpected animation. "Plenty have tried. He's still around."

# CHAPTER 5

Kay checked into the Omni Hotel in Austin on Saturday afternoon. Before going up to her room, she made sure Billy Boy Watkins's courier had deposited the package of cashier's checks in the hotel safe. The manager took great pains to confirm Kay's identity before giving her the key. Once in the room, she decided to lie down for a quick nap. When she awoke, it was dark outside and the bedside digital clock read 9:18 P.M. Kay was now wide awake and quite hungry besides, so she threw on a pair of jeans, a shirt and sneakers and left the hotel for a walk. The desk clerk suggested she walk two blocks over to Sixth Street.

The number of bars and restaurants on Sixth Street was truly astonishing. Both sides of the street were lined with clubs featuring live entertainment. She'd expected country and western joints in Texas, but as she drifted along the avenue it was pleasant to hear a lot of jazz, rock, blues and bluegrass along the street, too.

She stopped in a place called Maggie Mae's for a hamburger and beer and to listen to a country and western trio sing numbers like *You Took My Heart and Stomped That Sucker Flat.* Kay also bought a T-shirt there because the motto of the place, emblazoned on the back of the shirt, was BEER—IT ISN'T JUST FOR BREAKFAST ANYMORE.

While she was enjoying her hamburger and beer, a huge bearded black man slid onto the stool next to hers.

"Myers's rum with coke, add a slice of lime," the black man told the bartender.

His order caught Kay's attention because his voice was as deep and beautiful as an opera singer's and he had an engaging West Indian accent.

He turned and smiled at her. "How's the food?"

"Good hamburger," Kay said. "I wouldn't know about the rest of the menu."

"They say chicken-fried steak is always a safe bet in Texas."

"I imagine so."

When his rum and coke arrived, the man ordered a hamburger well done and said to Kay, "I follow your lead."

"Good choice."

The big black man smiled down on her. "You don't have a Texas accent."

"Neither do you," Kay commented.

"No, I be from Jamaica."

"Jamaica?" Kay thought immediately of Phil. "That's a coincidence. My ex-husband has a restaurant down there."

"Really?" The black man's eyebrows rose. "What town?"

"A place called Runaway Bay."

"I been through there many times. About halfway between Kingston and Mo' Bay." He put his hand out. "Chauncy Alexander."

"Kay Williams."

They shook hands.

"What the name of your ex's restaurant? I may know it."

"It's called *Seis Amigos.*"

"Hmm . . ." Chauncy scratched his chin. "Funny name for Jamaican restaurant."

"It's actually a Mexican restaurant, I've been told."

He snapped his fingers. "Oh, new place on the beach. I never been there, but I drive past on my way Kingston. From all the cars parked out front, I think *Seis Amigos* a big success."

For Phil's sake, Kay was glad to hear that. "I suppose a lot of people have told you that you sound like a West Indies James Earl Jones."

He laughed. "I prefer people say James Earl Jones sound like me."

"I take your point."

"You got to be on good terms with your ex, you know about his restaurant."

Kay shrugged. "Sometimes yes, sometimes no."

"I believe in friendly divorce," Chauncy said. "Had two myself."

"Then you're an expert."

"Only barristers make that claim."

"Barristers. I like English words and phrases. The word *attorney* is so dull. What business are you in, Chauncy?"

Chauncy's hamburger was served and he delayed answering the question while arranging space in front of him for the plate. He also delayed answering because he hadn't anticipated the question. "Import–export," he finally said. "You?" He cut his hamburger in half and took a bite.

"I buy and sell antiques. I'm in town on business. You've been to Austin before?"

"Never." He held up his burger. "Pretty good, thanks for the suggestion. How long you stay here?"

"I should be out of here by Wednesday."

"Quick trip. You stay downtown?"

"Yes, at the Omni."

"This soul too," Chauncy said.

Kay had finished dinner. She put a ten-dollar bill on the check and slid off her stool. "Maybe I'll see you again."

"I hope so," Chauncy said. "If not, good luck to you."

"You, too."

When Kay left, Chauncy continued to slowly eat the hamburger, which had a delightful Tex-Mex sauce similar to the hot sauces of his own country, and ordered a second rum and coke.

A few minutes later Phil Williams slid onto the stool where Kay had been sitting and ordered a beer for himself.

"You ought try one of these." Chauncy held up the remaining quarter of his burger. "Much better anything we ever serve at *Seis Amigos*."

Phil shifted around impatiently. "So what did Kay have to tell you?"

"She be out of here by Wednesday. That mean the auction take place on Tuesday, not much time do our work."

"Four days." Phil drank off some of his beer. "Time enough. Did she say anything about me?"

"When she heard I be from Jamaica, she ask about *Seis Amigos*. I tell her I know the place, big success." He laughed, mostly to himself. "Mon, your ex-wife now the one and only person on earth think *Seis Amigos* makes money."

"That was smart." Phil tapped the bar. "When I suddenly show up tomorrow, she won't think I'm here to tap her for a loan."

"You be able do your big reconciliation scene, not get your face slapped." Chauncy finished the burger and downed his rum and coke in one swallow. "At least not right away."

"Did she say anything specific about me?"

"I ask if she be on good terms with you. She say *sometimes yes, sometimes no*."

"Sometimes yes," Phil repeated. He grinned in a way that many people would have described as vicious. "That's not too bad. I can work with that."

"That woman better than you deserve, mon." Chauncy swung around to face Phil. "She be beautiful, interesting, sexy too."

Phil smirked. "They're all *beautiful and interesting*. That's what makes it impossible to settle for just one."

"You a pig, mon," Chauncy said mildly. "That's why we get along so well. I watch her check into hotel, right? Manager take a long time verifying ID before giving her safe deposit key. Client sent money down ahead of her, you think?"

"Probably. We need to make sure it's cash or something else negotiable. I'll find out, don't worry about that." There was a girl at the end of the bar drinking a tequila shooter and munching on nachos. She was blond, early twenties, almost as tall as Phil, a cowboy hat tilted way back on her head, wearing hand-tooled boots and jeans so tight she had to sit with her legs splayed out from the stool. Phil called the bartender over and put some money on the bar. "Give that girl another tequila shooter, will you?"

"Sure thing."

When the drink was served, Phil lifted his own glass and gave her his patented smile. She smiled back and glanced at the empty stool next to her.

"I'll check with you in the morning," Phil said.

"Don't bring the blonde to the Omni," Chauncy warned. "Your ex might see you with her, ruin our game."

"Relax. Nothing's going to ruin our game." Phil was wondering how the blonde had gotten into those jeans and how tough it was going to be to get them off her. "Kay's a slam-dunk." He left Chauncy and wandered down the bar to sit at the blonde's side. "Howdy, y'all from around here?"

# CHAPTER 6

Wolf opened the trunk of his car and took out a pair of Ohio license plates. "This is just what you want, Ace. Ohio plates with the same numbers as the plates on a gray 1997 Ford Taurus registered to a Thomas Holtzman in Wickliffe, Ohio. He's an insurance salesman. Straight as a preacher. All you have to do is boost a gray '97 Taurus and put these plates on it. Let's say a cop gets suspicious of you, calls in your plate numbers from his patrol car. The answer comes back from dispatch that the car's legit, not stolen. The cop peels off, leaves you alone."

"Even got the tags on it." Ace Perry turned the plates over in his hands. "You made these, huh?"

"In my own workshop. Printed the tags, too. Weathered them so they look like they've been on the plates for a while."

"I have to say they look like the real fucking thing."

Wolf threw back a blanket in the trunk to reveal four other sets of plates. "I've got plates here for Florida, Colorado, Texas, California. You don't want the Ohio plates, you can have any other of these other sets."

"No, Ohio plates are fine. Nice dull state. Ford Taurus is a nice dull car, too. Cops'll get suspicious of Florida and California plates a lot faster than they will Ohio plates."

Ace Perry was a drug dealer. He moved around the country incessantly, transported coke and marijuana in his car and changed cars frequently. He didn't look like a drug dealer. Ace was middle-aged, had a little paunch, wore a gray business suit, white shirt, plain tie and eyeglasses with wire rims. His aim was to avoid fitting the police profile of a drug dealer. He liked to drive cars with low profiles, Fords and Chevys whenever possible. Dodges and midpriced Toyotas were good, too.

The technology of manufacturing license plates continued to intrigue Ace. This was the first time he'd dealt with Bud Wolf and he wanted to understand more about what he was buying. "How do you do it, use one of those stamping machines?"

"That's right. I make my own dies and I spray on the colors by hand. The colors come from the same paint brands the state governments use for legitimate plates. That's the toughest part of the whole deal, getting the colors absolutely right. Every other detail is authentic, too, right down to the metal or plastic compound each state uses to make its plates."

"And you want how much for these plates?"

"Three thousand."

"What if I want the Colorado plates, too? Do I get a discount for buying two sets?"

"Nope, they're three grand per set. Flat price."

"What kind of car do the Colorado plates match?"

"White Toyota Camry." Wolf grinned. "There's millions of them around. You can boost one with no trouble."

Ace Perry considered six thousand dollars for two sets of clean license plates a bargain. All he had to do was steal the right cars for them. "You got it." He took a paper bag from his car, counted out sixty one-hundred dollar bills from a great wad of cash in the paper bag and passed them to Wolf. "There you go, six thousand dollars. This your regular business?"

Wolf shook his head. "Just a sideline. I've got other things goin', too, but I like workin' with my hands. Gives me a sense of accomplishment, know what I mean?"

The idea of working with his hands did not appeal to Ace Perry. "I guess," he said.

Wolf threw the blanket back over the remaining plates, closed the trunk and glanced around. They were at the back of a huge Wal-Mart parking lot near Dallas. The nearest shoppers coming and going from the store were a hundred yards away. If anybody was watching, they were seeing nothing out of the ordinary. Two guys shooting the shit, that was all.

"I might call you again in a couple of months," Ace said.

"I'll be around. You can place an advance order if you want. Just tell me what state you'd like the plates to be from, what kind of car, the year, all that. My PC is tapped into the interstate motor vehicle data base, so I can guarantee the plate numbers will match some solid citizens'. I do special orders for my customers all the time."

"Nice doing business with you." Ace Perry wasn't the kind who shook hands. He just stowed the plates in his own trunk, got back into the non-descript car he was using for the day and drove off.

Wolf looked at his watch and saw he'd have to hump it to get where he was going on time.

He got into the car he was using and drove out of the Wal-Mart lot at a sedate speed despite the fact that he was pushed for time. He tried to drive at a moderate speed whenever the car he was using was stolen. The car he drove today was a white Cadillac stolen early that morning in Fort Worth. The plates were ones he'd made himself. The numbers on the fake plates he'd put on the Cadillac matched those of a car driven by a gynecologist in Waco. The car and the plates were good for at least a month, which was longer than Wolf would need them.

He drove to the Dallas/Fort Worth airport and parked at the interna-tional terminal. American Flight 32 from London had just arrived and the passengers were still going through immigration and customs. Wolf figured that Leon Donin, traveling under a Russian diplomatic passport, would breeze right through customs.

Wolf was holding up a piece of paper on which he'd written *Leon Donin* in large block letters when a tall, lean man with the face of a hun-gry hawk emerged from customs. He was dressed in a suit that cost at least two thousand dollars and held a Gucci carry-on suitbag in one hand and a square leather case in the other. He caught sight of Wolf's sign and came forward scowling.

"Put away that ridiculous sign," Donin snapped. His voice held only the faintest trace of a foreign accent. "Do you think I want all of Texas to know I have arrived?"

"Sorry." Wolf crumpled up the paper and tossed it into a trash can. "My name's Bud Wolf."

"The Contractor told me your name. Let us not waste time, I need to be in Austin as soon as possible."

Wolf wanted to bust this arrogant Russky in the mouth. Instead he said, "My car's right outside," and reached for the heavy carrying case in Donin's right hand.

"Take your hand off that case. Carry the suitbag for me."

"Whatever you say, Ivan."

"Ivan? You know my name is Leon Donin."

Wolf led Donin towards the parking lot. "Ivan is what Americans used to call all you Russian guys, back before we whipped your ass in the Cold War."

Donin smiled for the first time. It wasn't a pleasant smile because it didn't involve any warmth, but it did make him look a bit less like a hungry hawk. "I thought all Texans were supposed to be friendly and hospitable."

"And I thought all Russians wore cheap suits, smelled of stale vodka and had fat, ugly wives. I guess we were both wrong."

"Not entirely. I do sometimes smell of vodka and my wife Irina is what you Americans would call plump."

"So I guess you don't starve the bitch to save a few bucks. I'm a little surprised at that. You look like the kind of cheap bastard who only spends money on himself."

Donin gave Wolf a slantwise stare. Then he actually laughed. "The Contractor said I would like you. Now I see why."

"Just don't kiss me on both cheeks, I couldn't take it."

"That's what the French do. Russians clap each other on the back."

"Don't do that, either. I might get pissed and break your fuckin' arm."

"Better and better," Donin said, still smiling.

When they reached the parking lot, Wolf opened the trunk and they put the carry-on bag and the heavier case in it.

"The Contractor said you'd want a small but powerful handgun." He made sure there was no one around before giving Donin a Walther PPK and two loaded clips. "Will this do?"

"Yes," Donin said, hardly looking at the piece.

When they got into the car, Donin said, "What brand of automobile is this?"

"A Cadillac."

"I prefer high-quality German automobiles. The Mercedes or the BMW. The Contractor should have told you that."

"Wouldn't matter. I only drive Detroit iron. It's a matter of patriotism, somethin' you Russian assholes wouldn't understand."

Donin loaded one of the clips into the Walther and moved the slide back to put a round in the chamber. From the way he handled the pistol and the ease with which he slid it under his belt at the small of his back, Wolf could tell that Donin was accustomed to carrying a weapon.

As they turned onto Interstate 35 South, Donin said, "I trust you are well-armed yourself. Your function, after all, is to assure my safety as well as chauffeur me around."

"I'm carryin' a Colt Python and six knives."

Donin was amused. "Six knives? In your spare time do you have a circus act?" He looked Wolf over. "Where do you carry all your knives?"

Although it was a little hard to show Donin his weapons while he was driving, Wolf gladly went through his inventory. "I carry an eight-inch knife inside the sleeve of my shirt. The left sleeve. This belt buckle?" He pulled the clasp and a short, razor-sharp blade revealed itself. "This is for close-in work, slip someone three inches of steel in the gut or heart. Does the job just as well as a ten-inch blade. I'm carryin' a heavier knife inside my left boot. The Colt Python's inside my right boot, by the way." He reached into his shirt pocket. "You see this?" He showed Donin a short, slim black knife. "Plastic. Sharp as hell, very lightweight, latest technology. I once carried ten of these suckers through an airport security system, didn't set off any alarms. I've got a switchblade in my pants pocket and a Malay dagger strapped to the calf of my right leg. I'm loaded for bear, Ivan. You can feel real safe when I'm around."

"In my opinion, a knife is an archaic weapon."

"That so? Then why are you here to buy Jim Bowie's knife, if it's so damned *archaic*?"

"I don't consider that particular knife a weapon. It's a valuable antique."

"Well, I'd advise you not to look down on knives. In the hand of a man who knows how to use it, a knife is just as efficient as a gun."

"When was the last time you actually killed a person with a knife?" Donin asked, coming just short of a sneer.

"Last week I killed two people with the same knife that's strapped to my leg right now. Ask the Contractor, he sent me out on the job."

The incipient sneer lost its edge. After a time Donin said, "I have three million U.S. dollars in hundred-dollar bills in the leather carrying case. When we are not in this automobile, I want you to stay three or four feet behind me at all times. I can take care of anyone who threatens me from the front. Your job is to watch my back. I did not come all the way to Texas to be robbed."

"Nobody'll get to you while I'm around."

Donin gave Wolf a deeply appraising look. "Yes, the Contractor said you could protect both me and my money and now I believe him. What do your friends call you? Assuming you have some friends."

"They call me Wolfie."

"Then I shall call you Wolfie. If it pleases your childlike mentality, you may continue to call me Ivan." He slid down in his seat and closed his eyes. "The plane trip was tiring. I intend to sleep. Wake me when we arrive at the Driskill Hotel in Austin. There is a meeting this afternoon of all those who intend to bid on the Bowie knife. I want to be mentally alert."

"Sure, stay alert," Wolf said. "We need more lerts."

"What does that mean?"

"Just a joke."

"I do not care for jokes."

"And I don't like German cars. So what? Get some sleep."

# CHAPTER 7

The Driskill is the dowager queen of Austin hotels, a sprawling old structure fronting on Brazos Street that is still elegant, well-appointed and fashionable. Since the Omni is just down the street from the Driskill, Kay was easily on time for the preview meeting Stewart Ruddington had arranged.

She stepped off the elevator on the floor where the Driskill's meeting rooms were located and found herself facing two stolid, serious men in business suits. Their conservative garb couldn't conceal the physical builds that come only from a great deal of weightlifting. Kay gathered they were plainclothes guards hired by Stewart Ruddington to protect the merchandise and the large sums of money that would be in the room when the auction went forward. "I'm here for the preview meeting," she told them. "Mr. Ruddington expects me."

"Your name?"

"Kay Williams."

"May we see your identification?"

She showed them her Connecticut driver's license and two credit cards, which seemed to satisfy them.

"You're on the list. You can go right in."

Kay was ushered into the meeting room, where a small group was sitting at an oak conference table chatting and drinking coffee.

Stewart Ruddington jumped up and came towards her with a beaming smile and outstretched hand. "Kay! So good to see you again!" Instead of shaking her hand, he kissed it. Ruddington cultivated an Old World look and attitude. His suits were expensive but deliberately cut in out-of-date styles. He wore a monocle and parted his sparse graying hair in the middle. Once Kay had even seen him wear spats over his shoes. Ruddington went to those extreme lengths because it enhanced his image as an auctioneer of antiques. Or so he believed.

"Hello, Stewart. I'm delighted to be here."

"Now that you've arrived," Ruddington said in a whisper that those behind him strained to hear, "I know we're going to have a great auction. Please come and join us. I believe you know some of the other bidders."

Kay went down the table with Stewart. "This is Roy Scanner, who's here to bid on behalf of Wallace Wright. You probably know that Mr. Wright is a former Secretary of the Treasury and a collector of Americana. Roy . . . Kay is bidding on behalf of Billy Boy Watkins, the Louisiana oil man."

"I'm very pleased to meet you, Mr. Scanner." Kay shook Scanner's hand and almost winced. Roy Scanner was of the firm grip clan. He was big, especially through the shoulders, with a face so plain it approached being handsome. Large craggy eyebrows, prominent chin and a nose that looked as if it had been broken more than once.

"I'm mighty glad to meet you," Scanner declared in a quiet Midwestern voice.

Kay moved down the table to the next bidder. "Melanie! I didn't know you were going to be here. This is wonderful!"

Melanie Wadsworth didn't get up, so Kay leaned down while they planted insincere kisses on each other's cheeks.

"Kay, darling. What a *delightful* surprise. Dear Stewart neglected to tell me you'd be here." She shot an unpleasant glance in Ruddington's direction, a glance that promised the auctioneer some sort of payback for his treachery.

Melanie Wadsworth, whose popular antiques store graced one of the steep hills leading up to the Fairmont Hotel in San Francisco, was the one person in the business Kay truly despised. They seemed to be natural enemies, like the panther and lioness. Melanie had all the physical sleekness of a panther and much the same disposition.

"But dear, you look so *peaked*," Melanie exclaimed. "So . . . I don't know . . . *unhealthily* thin. You don't have that awful HIV thing, do you?"

She turned to the others at the table in mock despair. "The last time I saw Kay she looked *vibrant*. And now she's just gone totally to *pot*, as my dear mother used to say. Isn't that a shame?"

"My goodness, Melanie. I didn't know you actually had a mother," Kay said. "I thought you came straight out of the viper's nest full-grown."

"Ha ha." Ruddington laughed nervously. "They do so love to tease each other. Kay, you know Arthur Ward, I believe."

Arthur came to his feet and gave Kay a much more genuine kiss on the cheek. "If this is called going to pot, the world needs more of it. You look ravishing, Kay. How would you like to become my fifth wife?"

"No, thank you, Arthur. I'd much rather have you for a friend." Kay had purchased a few special antiques for Arthur Ward and liked him enormously. Arthur was ridiculously wealthy. He lived on inherited money with never a thought of doing anything except collecting antiques, drinking a great deal of wine and champagne and marrying beautiful women of whom he quickly tired. Over the years Arthur had built an enormous and varied collection of art and antiques that he kept in a heavily fortified room on his Long Island estate. Seldom did he show his treasures to anyone, preferring to enjoy his collection in isolation. Ordinarily Kay didn't care for such people, but Arthur's charm came from a great well of thoughtfulness that he showed to everyone—rich or poor—who crossed his path.

"A friend who's ready to bid against me?" Arthur said in all good nature.

"That's the game, Arthur."

"So it is." Arthur sat down as Ruddington led Kay to the other side of the table.

A Japanese man in the customary dark blue suit and quiet tie arose and bowed. Kay had done enough business in Japan to know that she should put the palms of her hands on her thighs and offer a return bow deeper than the one she had received.

"Mr. Kazuo Goto," Ruddington said.

"Very pleased." Goto had a small mustache and wore round glasses that made him look distressingly like the late Emperor Hirohito. "I followed your exploits in the *Yomiuri Shimbun* when you were last in Japan. Your quest to find the Meiji sword was very exciting. I was delighted when you emerged from that travail alive and in possession of the sword."

Kay didn't reply; she had already consigned that whole awful mess to the darkest back corner of her mind.

"Goto-san is president of Eastern Empire Insurance," Ruddington said to Kay. "He has an extraordinary collection of swords and knives from many cultures."

Kay bowed again, just to show additional respect. "I've heard of you and your collection. It's an honor to finally meet you."

Goto turned to his companion, another Japanese. "This is Dr. Watanabe, my physician. I have not been well recently. Mr. Ruddington has been kind enough to allow Dr. Watanabe to stay close to my side."

Dr. Watanabe bowed to Kay but said nothing. Looking closer, Kay could see that Kazuo Goto's complexion was not healthy and that his right hand showed evidence of palsy.

"Help yourself to a chair," Ruddington said. "And some coffee and croissants, if you like. We have one more bidder to come and then I'll get on with the business that brought us here."

Kay sat down next to Roy Scanner and let him pour her a cup of coffee. "Where are you from, Mr. Scanner?"

"Washington. I suppose I should say Maryland because I live in Chevy Chase, though I never seem to get home except for a few hours' sleep. And then I travel quite a bit, too."

"You aren't an antiques dealer?"

"Don't know much about antiques, I'm afraid. I'm only here because Wallace Wright couldn't attend. He's an old friend. Asked me to take a look at this knife, assess it, let him know if I think I should bid on it for him."

"Quite a responsibility." There was something strange about Scanner's story. How could Roy Scanner and Wallace Wright be *old friends?* Wright was in his late sixties and Scanner was thirty-five at most. "If the knife is legitimate, you could find yourself bidding in the hundreds of thousands of dollars. If you aren't an antiques dealer, what business are you in?"

"Please call me Roy."

"Okay."

"How long have you been in this business?"

Kay had the definite feeling that Roy Scanner didn't want to talk about himself at all. "About ten years."

Melanie rattled her coffee cup to attract Roy's attention. "Don't believe that for a minute, Roy. Kay has been selling antiques for *decades.* She's much older than she looks."

Kay smiled brightly at Melanie. "I think, Roy, that Melanie should be forgiven that sharp little tongue of hers. When a woman enters her *fifties* and experiences a *change of life,* shall we say, the unpleasant hormonal effects sometimes make her sound like a *bitch."*

*"Fifties!"* Melanie fluffed her auburn hair and sucked in her twenty-four-inch waist to make herself slimmer and younger-looking than her forty-plus years. "I'm thirty-eight and you damned well know it!"

"Melanie, you were thirty-eight when Ho Chi Minh City was still called Saigon."

Roy Scanner felt embarrassed to be caught in the middle of a catfight, but everyone except Kazuo Goto—clearly mystified by the conversation—seemed to be enjoying it.

"So this is what an antiques auction is like," Scanner murmured. "Not what I expected."

"Don't take them seriously," Arthur advised. "They're just sharpening their claws. In reality Melanie and Kay are great chums."

"Not on the hottest day in hell," Melanie purred.

"Actually, we're sisters under the skin," Kay said. "It just happens that my skin is much younger than hers."

"You snippy little . . ."

The testy exchange was interrupted when the security guard showed two more men into the room.

"Ah . . ." Stewart Ruddington went to greet the new arrivals. "You must be Mr. Donin." He shook hands with the better dressed of the two. The man who followed Leon Donin into the room didn't have the look of an antiques collector. His face was weathered and hard, though not nearly as hard as his eyes. He was tall, wore a brown corduroy jacket over a blue denim shirt, his pants a pair of clean but well-worn jeans, his boots highly polished.

"Yes, I am Donin. This is Mr. Wolf, my security advisor. I am in possession of a large sum of cash and require that he stay close to me at all times."

"As you've seen," Ruddington said, "we have our own security people on the doors."

"I require Mr. Wolf's presence." Donin's attitude brooked no argument. "Please introduce me to the other bidders. I wish to assess my competition."

Ruddington flapped his hands in surrender to Donin's demands. "As you will. Ladies and gentlemen, I'm delighted to present Leon Donin of the Koska Museum in Moscow. The Koska is a state-owned gallery associated with the Ministry of Foreign Affairs. Thus, Mr. Donin is both an antiquarian and a diplomat. Sir, let me present you to Kazuo Goto."

Kay sat in silent shock. She knew this man who called himself Leon Donin as Nicolai Leontin. A little over a week ago, in Singapore, Nicolai Leontin had sold to Kay the Fabergé egg she was buying for her client, Andrew Whiteman of New York's Security Mutual Bank. What the hell was Leontin . . . or Donin, as he was calling himself today . . . doing in Texas?

Donin presented himself as supremely confident to the point of arrogance. Though he was polite in a distant way during the introductions, his bearing made it clear that Leon Donin considered himself a breed above those he was meeting.

". . . and this is Kay Williams, who will bid on behalf of the prominent oil executive Billy Boy Watkins."

For an interesting moment Donin's facade slipped. He recovered quickly. "Miss Williams, this is a great pleasure." As he spoke, Donin made a quick movement that no one except Kay could properly see because his back was to the others. The index finger of his right hand crossed his throat. The movement could have meant almost anything. From Kay's perspective it was a warning to keep her mouth shut—or else. Then that same hand was extended. As they formally shook hands, Donin did his best to crush her fingers. *Another warning?* Kay wondered. *Or am I just going paranoid?*

Roy Scanner happened to be sitting where he could see enough of the exchange to interpret it exactly as Kay had. Donin's across-the-throat slash and the way he deliberately mauled Kay's fingers angered Scanner.

"And this is Roy Scanner . . ." Ruddington blithely continued, citing Roy's friendship with the former Secretary of the Treasury for whom he was bidding.

"Hiya." Scanner grabbed Donin's hand. As a boy and young man he had worked just about every hard job there was on his family's Illinois farm. How many times had he swung an ax to split a piece of firewood for the ancient wood stove that sat in the center of their living room? God only knew. What Roy Scanner did know was that nobody had a stronger grip than himself.

Donin's face went quite pale as Roy's enormous hand, still hard and callused from all those years of farm labor, closed over Donin's smaller hand with the force of a vise. Roy continued to squeeze until beads of sweat appeared on Donin's forehead and the sound of bones rearranging themselves became vaguely audible. When his hand was freed, Donin squelched a groan and lowered it gingerly to his side.

Scanner felt the prick of a sharp object in his back, right behind a kidney, and realized that Bud Wolf had sidled up behind him. Donin gave the briefest possible negative shake of his head.

Wolf, looking bored, drifted away and took a seat against the wall while Donin went to a chair at the most remote end of the table.

When Scanner sat down, Kay leaned over and whispered, "I saw what you did . . . thanks a lot."

"What's that Russian's problem?" Scanner whispered back.

Kay decided she needed advice on how to deal with Donin. Although Roy Scanner still seemed out of place at an antiques auction, she felt drawn to him. Plain faces aren't always honest faces, she knew. But where else could she turn? Stewart Ruddington probably didn't care whether the Russian's real name was Leon Donin or Nicolai Leontin or Joseph Stalin, for that matter. Neither would Ruddington care whether Donin had criminal ties in Moscow. Ruddington's job as auctioneer was to get the best possible price for the knife, that was all. "I'll tell you later," she whispered to Scanner.

"Now that the introductions are over and we're all good friends," Ruddington was saying, "let's get to the business at hand. We're here because the weapon known as 'Old Bowie,' Jim Bowie's original knife, the famous knife lost at the Alamo in 1836, has surfaced and been put on the market. I know that each of you is skeptical about its provenance. I think your skepticism will be put to rest before the end of the afternoon."

Ruddington removed the monocle from his eye and began twirling it by its ribbon. Kay recognized this as one of the auctioneer's standard ploys. The twirling monocle had the same effect as a gold watch in the hands of a hypnotist—it helped to focus all eyes on the speaker. "Assuming you accept the knife's authenticity, the auction will be held at four P.M. on Tuesday in this same comfortable room. Because you will each be carrying some sort of monetary instrument, additional security guards will be on duty outside the door and inside this room. Only four forms of payment will be accepted—cash in U.S. dollars . . . cashier's checks . . . gold coins . . . or bearer bonds. A banker will be on hand to verify that the payment is made in an instrument that is as authentic as the Bowie knife itself. I'm sorry to have to make that statement, but you all must have heard what happened at the Degas auction last year."

Kay knew only that someone had bought a Degas painting last year at another private auction in London and paid on the spot in bearer bonds that later turned out to be counterfeit.

"I know we will have no such problems with this group. However, proper precautions must be taken." Ruddington had begun to pace back and forth on the rich gold carpeting, the monocle still twirling in his hand. "Now to ownership and provenance. The present owner of the Bowie knife is Antonio de Baraga, an esteemed businessman and landowner from Mexico." Ruddington began passing out a one-page sheet of paper. "This is his biography. As you can see, Señor de Baraga has held important government posts and run his family business very successfully for many years. He is not a con man or *poseur* of any sort. You naturally wonder why this knife is not being offered through one of the major auction houses. Quite simply . . . and because I know you will understand me perfectly and respect this confidence . . . the Mexican government's tax structure has become confiscatory. Señor de Baraga wishes the results of this private auction to remain private. This is to your benefit as well as his because this antique would bring a much higher price in an open auction."

Each of the bidders quickly read the bio. They were interested in de Baraga, but more interested in the knife itself.

"I'll now introduce you to Señor de Baraga, who has been waiting in the next room."

Ruddington ushered de Baraga into the conference room with his usual fluttering of hands and show of pomp. The Mexican businessman came in carrying a walnut case about eighteen inches long. He was in his fifties with thinning black hair combed straight back, bright brown eyes and a round, pleasant face. He smiled nervously around the room, straightened his tie and let Ruddington guide him to the chair at the head of the table.

The first thing de Baraga did was put the case down directly in front of him and place both hands on it, as if fearing that someone might forcibly take it away from him. He was dressed in a conservative gray suit of Italian design and looked every inch a successful businessman. Kay thought she detected a hint of desperation and concluded that Señor de Baraga was very much in need of a big infusion of cash. Good news for the bidders.

"Good afternoon," de Baraga said. "Thank you for coming. Let me say this is a rather painful experience for me and my family. This article has been in my family for so many generations that it has become a part of our heritage. We are . . . the de Baragas . . . a proud family." His chin jutted out. "Very proud. At one time, in the early eighteen hundreds, the de Baragas owned seven thousand acres of land in central Mexico [pronouncing it *Me-hi-co*]. We grew grapes, wheat, cotton, many crops. We owned hundreds of horses and bred fighting bulls. Gradually, over the years, the revolutions depleted our land. Revolutionary leaders such as Zapata and his ilk carved out pieces of our property, *de Baraga land*, and gave it away to our peasants."

Kay found herself not enjoying the dismissive way de Baraga spoke of "our peasants" as if they were slaves. She thought that perhaps the de Baragas were too proud of themselves and probably were getting what they deserved.

"Our estate is now reduced to about three hundred acres. The family business, a group of mercantile stores of the type that you call department stores, is now under competitive pressure from foreign retailers. The NAFTA treaty has been a disaster for us. American companies have moved into Mexico in greater numbers. JC Penney . . . Wal-Mart . . . even Toys 'Я' Us." His voice dripped venom as he spoke those hated names. "As our circumstances have changed, we find we must lose still another piece of our heritage." His fingers were now drumming on the walnut case in an agitated way. He calmed himself and tried to restore his smile.

"Forgive me, I only wanted you to understand why we must part with Jim Bowie's famous knife. I'll show you the knife, then explain how it came into the possession of my family. When you hear my story, I know you'll be convinced this is James Bowie's personal weapon. His own invention."

As de Baraga opened the walnut case, everyone leaned forward. He lifted the knife out with both hands and thrust it forward as if delivering a new baby to its mother. "The Bowie knife," he said.

The first glance caused some disappointment to everyone in the room. It looked like what it was—an old knife. The blade didn't gleam. The grip was dirty. The leather scabbard from which de Baraga took the knife was scratched and bent in two places.

"You may take a closer look." He passed it first to Arthur Ward, who accepted both the knife and scabbard eagerly.

Arthur's innate courtesy prevailed. "We can all look at it together. Come on, gather 'round."

Soon a circle of people had gathered at Arthur's end of the table. Magnifying glasses and tape measures came out of purses and pockets. No one grabbed for the knife, but everyone wanted to touch it. The first impression had quickly fallen away. Each bidder felt a certain power exuding from this knife. The sensation wasn't new to any of them. Each had experienced the special aura that often emanates from a truly unique and authentic antique. Such objects were like the Mona Lisa. You couldn't assess them with purely objective criteria, you had to experience their emotional effect.

"It is signed by James Black," Melanie said. "That's a good beginning."

Arthur had quickly measured the knife. "Dimensions are correct."

"Brass cross-guard," Kay pointed out.

Kazuo Goto drew in his breath with a hiss, a peculiarly Japanese way of expressing emotion. "That weapon has killed many strong men. Can't you feel it?"

Only Donin and Scanner said nothing. Donin was not an expert on the Bowie knife; his approach was to rely on the assessment of experts. And Scanner seemed curiously detached from the group. He stood back and from time to time glanced Donin's way.

"Look here," Arthur said. "The initials J. B. are carved into the scabbard."

"Means nothing," Melanie snapped. "The scabbard isn't the knife."

"I know that," Arthur retorted.

Gradually the members of the group returned to their seats. The knife was passed down the table and discussion began.

Arthur looked searchingly at de Baraga. "What kind of objective evidence do you have that this was Jim Bowie's original knife?"

Ruddington jumped up, waving a sheaf of photos and papers. "I have some material to share. Copies for each of you." He laid each item on the table. "Close-up color photographs of the knife from several angles. Metallurgy report on the age of the steel and other components that generally bears out the premise that this knife was made in the first part of the nineteenth century. A report on James Black's smithing techniques. Eyewitness descriptions of the knife written in letters and magazines of the day. Other supporting evidence."

He scattered six copies of the photos and documents across the table with his usual flourish.

"This is just supporting material. Señor de Baraga will present his most compelling evidence in just a few minutes. First you may want to study these photos and documents."

Each bidder immediately turned to the metallurgy report, having gathered most of the other information independently before coming to Austin.

As the bidders studied the document, de Baraga leaned back in his chair and tried to relax. He knew a barrage of questions was coming and knew what he was going to say. Even so, this was taking more out of him than he'd expected. His pulse was racing, he felt flushed and uneasy in his stomach. The sooner this was over, the better.

Wolf saw the knife lying there in the middle of the table and just had to hold it in his hand. While everyone read the metallurgy report, he left his chair against the wall and went to the table. He caught the eye of Ruddington, the auctioneer, to indicate that he wanted to pick up the knife, too. Ruddington nodded curtly. Wolf picked up the knife and examined it from front to back.

It had been pitiful to watch these rich people and the suckup agents holding the knife. The loud bitch, Melanie, picked it up with her pinkies as if it was a piece of dog shit.

Whoa! Feel that! A jolt of energy ran up Wolf's arm. He didn't know what the hell that was or where it came from. An electrical shock without the pain. Jesus. He wondered if he'd had a kind of vision, even though he didn't really believe in such things, thought they were the ranting of preachers and hysterical women in menopause. Could Jim Bowie have stepped inside his skin just for a second? Was that possible? He got hold of himself, hoped no one noticed how shook up he felt. *Jesus. This knife is the real goddam thing. Jim Bowie's own throat cutter. Perfect balance. Beautiful design.* He barely touched the edge and opened a small cut on his finger. *And still sharp as hell after all these years.* He looked around. *These people have no idea what they're tryin' to buy, they only know it's famous.*

Wolf returned the knife to its walnut case and went back to his seat, thinking, *Nobody's gonna get that knife but me.*

Ruddington cleared his throat and gave his monocle a few extra twirls to get everyone's attention. "Now I'd like Señor de Baraga to give you the historical information that will confirm the origin of the weapon you've just examined."

"Yes, I'm prepared to do that." Antonio de Baraga returned to his chair at the head of the table, stared for a long interval and with a rather poignant longing at the knife that was beyond his reach, now and probably forever, and began his story. "In the spring of 1836 . . ."

# CHAPTER 8

"They bring everyone together in a conference room," Chauncy was saying. "Two large gentlemen on the door, I see they carry guns. May be more armed guards inside the room, I dunno. I just walk past, don't want to attract attention. Mon, you want one of these?" They were walking south across the Congress Avenue bridge, the Colorado River flowing swiftly below them. Chauncy had bought two tacos at a sidewalk stand, they weren't any better than the ones from *Seis Amigos*.

"No, thanks." Phil had seen enough Mexican food to last the rest of his life. "This isn't the actual auction today, is it?"

Chauncy threw one of the tacos off the bridge. "No, auction take place on Tuesday. Today what they call a preview meeting, bidders look at the merchandise and question the seller. Make sure the merchandise the real thing. I got that from the convention manager, she book all the meeting rooms. Tell her I be in town to meet with my salespeople. Welfare Life, I make up the name. I ask what days next week that room available. Free every day but Tuesday when Stewart Ruddington has it on reserve, he the auctioneer."

"Sunday afternoon. Monday. Tuesday. Not much time." Phil stopped and peered over the bridge.

Chauncy couldn't figure out what he was doing. "What you looking for?"

"Bats."

"I don't understand."

"I read the newspaper this morning, they said the bats were back."

"Back from where?"

"Mexico, someplace like that." Phil had never seen Chauncy read a newspaper or watch the news on TV. He needed to be better informed if he expected to be a success in life. "During the warm weather months a colony of bats lives under this bridge. About a million of them. They come flying out together at dusk, go looking for insects. Lots of people come down to watch."

Chauncy wished Phil would pay as much attention to their little project as he did to the morning newspaper. "Real tourist attraction. We could use them in Runaway Bay, except in Jamaica they turn out to be vampires."

"The auditorium should be a few blocks in that direction." Phil had seen an ad in the paper for a gun show at a downtown auditorium. He wanted Chauncy to be armed. He didn't intend to carry a gun himself, but Chauncy would need one.

A few blocks later they came to an auditorium shaped like an enormous Quonset hut. The parking lot was almost full and about half the vehicles were pickup trucks. "This must be the pickup capital of the world," Phil said.

"We have no trouble buying gun in this town." People were streaming in and out of the auditorium, and many of those leaving were carrying guns they'd bought inside. Rifles. Shotguns. Chauncy was sure that others, the ones with brown paper bags or small leather cases, had bought handguns.

"I showed the ad for the gun show to the bell captain at the hotel," Phil said. "He told me there's no waiting period if you buy a handgun from someone who says it's part of his *private collection*."

"Neat." Chauncy laughed loudly in his deep, rich voice. "So most sellers here aren't gun dealers, they just selling weapons from private collections. That be the scam, anyway."

"That's it."

They each paid four dollars to get into the auditorium. There was a grid of tables arranged like city streets, people flowing down the aisles in both directions. They fell into the flow and for fifteen minutes did nothing but walk and look.

"We have about a thousand dollars left between us." Phil was rubbing his fingers against the bills in his pocket. "What kind of gun do you need?"

"Mon, don't you know anything? I need short-barreled .38-caliber revolver. Something easy to conceal. Not one of your brand names, not Smith and Wesson. A cheap gun because I throw it away soon as this be over. Probably into that river, give the bats something to look at while they hang upside down."

Chauncy was aware that he attracted attention. Big black man in a white suit. Beard. Booming voice. He got a few stares, one nasty look he could pinpoint. He saw that at a few tables they weren't selling guns, there were pamphlets on the tables instead. He saw one pamphlet with the words *White Man's National Guard* across the top. Others were pushing brochures about how the U.S. government was the real enemy of the people. At several booths you could sign up for gun safety classes, learn how to kill people without hurting yourself.

"I love this place," Chauncy said.

Phil didn't feel the same way. "Makes me nervous being around all these guns. Let's buy one and get out of here."

"Fine, they sell what I need right over there." Chauncy led his partner to a table about ten feet long covered with revolvers of all calibers. Each pistol was attached to the table by a metal cord about three feet long, the cord running through the trigger guard. You could hold a pistol, sight it, look it over, but not steal it.

"Help you?" The gun dealer was a heavyset man wearing a cowboy hat, boots, silver-studded belt. His paunch hung down so far you could hardly see the silver belt buckle.

"Your sign say *Private Collection*." Chauncy picked up a .38 and looked at the price tag. "No waiting period?"

"You got it, chief. Where you from, anyway? I don't recognize the accent."

"Jamaica, land of rum and sunsets and beautiful black women. You ought come see us some time."

The gun dealer squinted in disapproval. Chauncy doubted he'd ever vacation in Jamaica. He picked up a .38-caliber Taurus with a one-inch barrel, a pretty good copy of the classic S&W, glanced at the price tag. A hundred and sixty dollars. Fair price for a used handgun in decent condition. "I take this one. You offer guarantees on your pieces?"

"Are you kidding?" The dealer unlocked the cord. "Best I can do for you is to put this piece in a clean paper bag."

"You be a gentleman," Chauncy said, putting a little extra James Earl Jones into the statement. "Phil, give this mon a hundred and sixty dollars. Make that hundred and eighty, I take a box of that ammo, too."

Phil counted out the money carefully. He now had less than three hundred dollars to his name. Nothing else. No stocks. No bonds. No real estate. No credit rating. No credit cards. His driver's license had expired. And a drug gang in New York had his name on its hit list. This deal had to be a success, he didn't care how many people Chauncy had to kill.

They left the auditorium looking at their watches.

"The preview meeting not last much longer," Chauncy said. "You got to connect with your ex before dinner."

"I know that." Phil was apprehensive about how Kay would react to his presence. "Don't worry about it. At first she'll be surprised and probably sore that I'm here. But Kay's not the kind who can stay mad for long. Especially at me."

"Strange weakness," Chauncy observed.

Phil was agitated about something else, too. "We don't know what kind of antique is being auctioned off. Doesn't that bother you?"

"No." Chauncy knew his priorities. "We not be after antiques. We want money. You find us that money, Phil. That be your job."

"Christ, this is getting dangerous, isn't it?"

Chauncy could see that Phil's nerves were already slipping, he needed to be bucked up. "We close to some big money, I feel that in my bones. Now you go find right person for me to point this gun at."

# CHAPTER 9

"In the spring of 1836," Antonio de Baraga began, "our family lost a beloved member at the Battle of San Jacinto, where Sam Houston and his Army of the Republic of Texas defeated General Santa Anna. Lieutenant Raul de Baraga, only twenty-two years old at the time, was the young man who died. Seven weeks before the Battle of San Jacinto, Raul had also fought in the battle of the Alamo, where he acquitted himself well and brought honor to our family."

Each bidder in the Driskill Hotel's conference room leaned forward. Although de Baraga was speaking quietly, his words had an intensity that made the beginnings of his story compelling. Kay and the others began making notes on the memo pads at their places.

Only Bud Wolf was left unmoved. One dead Mexican, who the fuck cared?

"In the early 1830s Santa Anna nullified Mexico's constitution, made himself president for life and gave himself dictatorial powers. An old story in our country, I'm afraid. He then proceeded to raise a large army for two purposes. First, to enforce the legitimacy of his regime. Second, to force the Anglo settlers out of Texas, which as you know was a part of Mexico at that time. Years earlier the Mexican government had encouraged people to emigrate to the territory of Texas. The settlers came principally from the U.S., but also from Germany, England, France, other countries. The idea was to draw economic wealth into the territory, make it a self-sustaining part of Mexico. That idea proved disastrous. Eventually the thousands of Anglos who settled in Texas came to think of themselves as independent of Mexico. They called themselves Texicans instead of Mexicans and began agitating to form their own Republic of Texas."

Kay discerned that de Baraga, as a member of Mexico's aristocracy, disapproved of that historical turn of events.

"Santa Anna decided to take his army north into Texas and put down the incipient revolt. Santa Anna's methods were cruel. In places where the seed of revolt was found, entire towns were wiped out." He shrugged. "Is the world less cruel today? Look at recent wars. Vietnam. Bosnia. All military leaders are cruel, Santa Anna was no different."

He took a deep breath. "In raising his army, General Santa Anna conscripted members of his officer corps from prominent families. The de Baraga family was asked . . . told, I should say . . . to send a family member for military training. Raul de Baraga was the youngest of two sons, therefore he was selected by the patriarch of the time—Don Pedro de Baraga—to join Santa Anna's army. You must understand that in our culture the eldest son inherits everything. He is protected. Raul accepted without question that as the youngest son he would have to go into the military. Though Raul had planned to study medicine, he reported for military duty, received three months of officer's training, was commissioned as a lieutenant in the army of Mexico and soon found himself in command of a platoon of foot soldiers.

"Raul marched his infantry platoon north as part of a division commanded by General Martin Perfecto de Cos, who was General Santa Anna's brother-in-law. They fought one battle and several skirmishes on their way north into Texas. Finally, on March 2, 1836, General de Cos's troops joined the advance force led by General Santa Anna himself at the small town of San Antonio de Bexar. A battle was in progress. It seems that a small band of soldiers from the newly formed Republic of Texas army and a number of volunteers had occupied an old mission called the Alamo and were putting up a fight. The soldiers in the Alamo were under the command of Colonel William Barret Travis. The civilian volunteers were commanded by James Bowie.

"By the time General de Cos and his troops arrived, the Alamo had already been under siege for ten days. General Santa Anna was annoyed at having to pause for so long at San Antonio de Bexar to deal with this small pocket of resistance. He knew that somewhere farther north, Sam Houston was training a larger force that would ultimately be more dangerous to him. However, if he didn't destroy the Alamo defenders very decisively, he might appear to be a toothless tiger.

"Another thing that greatly bothered General Santa Anna was the local popularity of one of the Alamo defenders—James Bowie. For many reasons, Bowie was hugely popular among the region's Mexican population. He had lived in Texas for several years, owned a large tract of land and spoke Spanish like a native. Bowie had also married into a good Mexican family to a lovely girl who bore him a son and daughter. Unfortunately, Bowie's wife and two children all died in a cholera epidemic that swept the area a year or more before the battle of the Alamo. Bowie's loss brought him great sympathy even though it drove him to become a notable drunk, often unable to stand on his feet after a night in the cantinas. His generosity and loyalty to friends was legendary, as was his ability to kill with either knife or gun. It is estimated that Jim Bowie killed between ten and fifteen people with the knife you have just examined, the knife he referred to affectionately as Old Bowie.

"The knife was always on his person, he was never seen without it. Next to Sam Houston, Bowie was the most celebrated figure in Texas. Like today's politicians, Santa Anna hated to share the spotlight. He wanted Jim Bowie dead.

"There had been several probes and small-scale assaults on the Alamo, each a failure. The long rifles carried by Davy Crockett and his Tennessee volunteers, and by many Texicans as well, were very effective. None of our troops had weapons that could fire so far, and the Tennesseeans and Texicans were more skilled marksmen as well.

"Finally, on March 6, thirteen days after the siege had begun, General Santa Anna organized a full-scale assault to wipe out the tiny fortress. Raul de Baraga led his platoon into battle and that was when he came into possession of James Bowie's famous knife."

At that point Stewart Ruddington came to his feet and held up several frames that displayed yellowed paper covered with lines of handwritten text. "This letter was written on March 10, 1836, by Raul de Baraga to his father. You can see the date at the top of the page. The text is in Spanish, of course. You'll receive copies of the English translation in just a few minutes, as well as copies of the original letter in Spanish. Last month I gave this letter to Professor Denton Portsman at the University of Cali-

fornia at Berkeley and asked him to study it. You may know Dr. Portsman's reputation as a leading historian on Mexico's colonization of California and Texas and as a collector of antique maps and documents from
that era. If not, there's also a bio of Dr. Portsman along with his official
authentication of this letter and his translation into English. We provided a tiny section of the letter to Cal's chemical lab for analysis. Paper
and ink are easier to date than steel or wood, and so the lab was able to
authenticate that this paper and ink are circa 1820 to 1850. Lab reports
are included in the package, of course."

Ruddington paused, well pleased with his presentation.

Kay thought he had a right to be pleased. Despite the out-of-date cut
of his clothes and hair, Stewart always used the latest technology to
authenticate his pieces. The provenance of the knife was beginning to
look promising. She allowed none of her thoughts to show on her face,
and neither did the other bidders. Any display of appreciation or emotion
might provide a clue as to how one might bid.

"I'll now ask Señor de Baraga to read the English translation of the letter Raul de Baraga sent to Don Pedro. Incidentally, Don Pedro—Raul's
father—was Señor de Baraga's great-great-grandfather." Ruddington sat
down and looked to de Baraga, who put on a pair of glasses and began to
read:

March 10, 1836

Dear Father
    Thanks to the mercy of our divine Lord, I am alive and in good spir-
its. Our present camp is located just to the west of San Antonio de
Bexar. We will be on the move soon, in what direction I do not know.
Our scouts are out at all compass points looking for signs of Sam Houston's army. With luck, we will find and defeat him and his army within
a few weeks. That event will end the rebellion and, I hope, send me
home soon afterward. This Texas is truly a terrible place, I do not understand why we want or need it. There is not much here except cactus and
rattlesnakes. I fear sleeping on the ground near the snakes more than I
fear doing battle with Houston and his troops.
    This package contains a well-worn knife that belonged to the famous
James Bowie. I thought you would be interested in having it. Do you
remember the day we saw Señor Bowie in a cantina during our trip to
Nuevo Laredo? I was only seventeen at the time you pointed him out to

me. A big, impressive-looking man carrying a big, impressive-looking knife. I can tell you he is no longer impressive. He is dead, along with more than 180 others who had the temerity to challenge General Santa Anna.

You may have heard already of the victory we won here in San Antonio de Bexar. The rebels had control of an old mission near the town. Their strategy (do you hear how military I have become!) was to hold General Santa Anna at bay as long as possible in order to give Houston time to build his army. They were brave men, I admit. They laid down their lives for their cause, but their strategy was foolish. Houston's army is said to be made up of civilian volunteers—ranchers, trappers, and merchants. They cannot hope to beat a disciplined and well-provisioned army such as ours.

I will tell you of the battle for the Alamo and how I happened to come upon James Bowie's corpse and his knife.

After thirteen days of siege, General Santa Anna organized a full-out attack. The Texicans were very deadly with their rifle fire during the day, so the general decided to attack at exactly four-thirty A.M. on the morning of March 6 when it would still be dark for more than an hour. Our unit, under General de Cos, was to be in the vanguard of the assault. I will tell you that I was very frightened. The night before the attack, I prayed as I have never prayed in my life. You may have heard my prayers all the way down there. Certainly Our Lord did hear my prayers because I survived even though half of my platoon were destined to perish.

At four A.M. on the morning of March 6, General Santa Anna ordered buglers to begin playing *The Deguello* to let those in the Alamo know that they would be shown no quarter. The music also helped to improve the spirits of our own troops, whose morale had declined during the siege because of the high number of casualties they experienced.

At four-thirty A.M. we attacked. My platoon advanced on the front gates along with other of General de Cos's troops. More infantry units charged the other walls and palisades.

Although it was dark, the blasts from the cannon illuminated the battlefield like moonlight. My men were brave, but our first assault was turned back. Many of the Texican riflemen on the walls had "long rifles" with steel barrels almost four feet long. Their fire was deadly accurate. So was the fire of several small cannons. I lost six men to one cannon blast. I was knocked down myself, not from cannon shot but by the spinning body of one of our soldiers. My platoon and the other platoons in my sector fell back momentarily under the withering fire, but surged forward again as the Alamo defenders began to reload their weapons.

I stood up rather shakily and looked around for my sword, which I had been waving above my head to signal my men to advance behind me. I couldn't find the sword then and I have not seen it since. I took a musket from the body of a fallen trooper and staggered forward yelling for my men to follow. They did follow, those still alive, even though my words must have been incoherent. We reached the wall. Ladders were thrown up against the wall. I detached the bayonet from the musket I was carrying and began to climb. Others scrambled up the ladder after me. I almost reached the top of the wall when an Anglo, a huge fellow with yellow hair and burning eyes, leaned out and pushed the ladder backwards. As he did that, one of my men shot him from below. His face disappeared in a bloody explosion. I fell backwards for what seemed a long time. My greatest fear was that I'd be impaled on the upraised bayonets of our own soldiers. Instead I landed on hard earth with such force that I lost consciousness.

I don't know how long I lay there. When I regained my senses and crawled to my feet, I found myself surrounded by corpses and by wounded men who lay moaning and bleeding. The fighting had moved inside the walls of the Alamo. Men were still climbing ladders, but without any resistance from the wall. The rebels had fallen back to form new lines of defense within the mission. I was still dizzy, but my head cleared as I forced my way into the line of men at the ladders and began climbing.

I will never forget the scene I witnessed from the top of that wall. The defenders were in their final minutes of life by that time. They stood in little squares of four or five men, back to back, fighting our men with rifle butts and knives because there were no intervals in which they could reload their weapons. The fresh troops who had just come over the walls fired down into the clusters of rebels with no danger to themselves.

The last of the defenders retreated into the chapel and closed the big wooden door. Our artillerymen seized a cannon and turned it on the door. With one blast the door went down. Splinters and rock from that blast wounded and killed some of our own men, but others pushed through the doors with wild screams and went after those inside with bayonets and rifle shot.

I climbed down gingerly to the ground and tried to locate the remnants of my platoon. They had scattered throughout the Alamo. Some went into the "long barracks," as it was called, to kill those few still alive in a series of low storerooms. No prisoners were taken. Anglos who were wounded but still alive were bayoneted. The sound of gunfire dimin-

ished, as our duty was now more easily done with steel swords and bayonets.

I heard one shot nearby, followed by frenzied screams, and rushed up
a flight of steps into a room that stank of gunpowder and death. That
is where I found James Bowie. I recognized him from the time you
pointed him out to me at the cantina in Nuevo Laredo, even though his
face was quite emaciated. He was lying on a cot. Later I learned that
Bowie had fallen so ill that he could not take part in the Alamo's final
battle. However, that did not stop him from taking a few of our troops
with him. Two empty, smoking pistols lay near his body. Two of our soldiers had been shot by Bowie as they entered his sickroom and a third
died from a deadly thrust from his big knife. On entering the room I
also saw several of our soldiers bayoneting Bowie over and over again.
Senseless. Bowie was already dead. However, I understood their anger.
Even in his final minute of life, and as ill as he was, James Bowie had
remained a dangerous man.

I sent the men outside and stood over Bowie's corpse. This may
sound strange, but I was almost afraid James Bowie might rise from the
dead. Such was his reputation here. I pulled the knife from the body of
the soldier he had killed and slipped it inside my tunic, where it would
be held fast by the pressure of my belt. I did not want anyone to know
I had the knife for fear of being accused of looting. That was naive of
me. I went outside to see all manner of looting taking place, even some
of our soldiers prying gold teeth out of the mouths of Anglo corpses.

The sun had risen and light came over the walls in bright slants. At
six-thirty General Santa Anna rode into the Alamo on his great white
mount, smiling and nodding in approval of the carnage he'd created.
The looting was temporarily brought to a halt. The general demanded
to see the body of William Barret Travis. The body was dragged out and
when General Santa Anna saw the huge bullet hole through Travis's
head he said, "Good . . . good." He also wanted to see the body of Davy
Crockett, but no one could readily identify the correct corpse. He
angrily demanded that James Bowie's body be produced. I was able to
tell my captain where Bowie had died. His body was retrieved and
thrown down in front of General Santa Anna, who relaxed and said,
"Well done."

My captain asked what should be done with the bodies of the Alamo
defenders.

"Burn them," was General Santa Anna's answer.

I was ordered to round up the survivors of my platoon and put them
to work piling up the defenders' bodies in the center of the courtyard.

While I was doing that, a few women and a child found in one of the rooms were escorted from the fort. They were appalled that we were going to burn the bodies. I could have told them that the bodies of our own troops would not fare much better, being put into a common grave. At least our men had the benefit of being prayed over by a priest.

I was very fortunate that day. I did my duty. I survived. And I did not personally have to take a human life.

It seemed somehow important that James Bowie's well-known knife should not disappear into that funeral pyre. So here it is.

Will you be seeing anyone from the Valdez family? If so, please find a way to let them know my feelings for Carmen are as strong as ever.

And tell Jaime he was right, army food is terrible. I hope to be back in our own wonderful kitchen, where the aromas are always superb, within six months. As always, Father, you and Mother have my love and respect. My thoughts and prayers are with you. And please pray for me to survive this war with my honor intact.

Raul

Antonio de Baraga took off his glasses, folded them carefully and slipped them into an inside coat pocket. "The letter I just read to you was the last that Don Pedro ever heard from his son. Raul, as I said before, was killed a few weeks after the Alamo at the battle of San Jacinto. He undoubtedly was put into a common grave on the battlefield such as the one he mentioned. You might even say he prophesied his own end. The letter from Raul was more important to Don Pedro than James Bowie's knife because it contained the last thoughts Raul was able to share with his family. That's why the letter and the Bowie knife were passed down together over the years." De Baraga's eyes were misted over and his lips had gone white and trembly.

A few moments of respectful silence were allowed to pass before the inevitable questions began.

Arthur Ward leaned forward. "You must be aware, Mr. de Baraga, of the knife on display at the Alamo that many people say was Jim Bowie's original, the one he called 'Old Bowie.' "

"May I field that one?" Ruddington jumped up, flourishing still another sheaf of papers. "This is a photo of the Bowie knife currently on display at the Alamo. After the battle of the Alamo, Rezin Bowie, Jim Bowie's elder brother, claimed that *he* had invented the Bowie knife, not his brother Jim. Rezin, a successful businessman in his own right, had come to resent the prominence of his younger brother. The knife on display at the Alamo doesn't have Jim Bowie's name or initials on it. It's engraved 'R. P. Bowie / H. W. Fowler USD,' the initials of Rezin Bowie and the name of the friend to whom Rezin presented that knife just a couple of years after the Alamo battle. The maker of the knife now on display at the Alamo also inscribed his name on the blade: 'Searles—Baton Rouge.' Jim Bowie's knife was made by James Black in his forge at Washington, Arkansas."

The next question came from Melanie Wadsworth. "Is there evidence other than the letter you just read that Raul de Baraga really existed? Birth certificate? Baptismal record? Anything?"

Again de Baraga deferred to his auctioneer, who promptly produced a church record of Raul's birth and a large, somewhat dog-eared certificate in Spanish. It was stamped with all sorts of official-looking seals and bore two colorful, though faded, ribbons. "These are Raul's birth record and his commission as a lieutenant in the army of Mexico," Ruddington explained. "Here are photocopies of the documents plus English translations."

The set of documents, lab reports and photos Ruddington had provided was now about six inches high in front of each bidder.

The probing continued for another twenty minutes.

Kay asked only one question: "Has this Bowie knife ever been out of the hands of the de Baraga family?"

"No . . . never," de Baraga answered forcefully.

"Please excuse me," Kazuo Goto said. "Has this knife ever been put up for sale before? At either a public or private auction? Or been offered to a dealer or private collector?"

"No . . . never," de Baraga repeated. "Over the years it has been shown to a few family friends. Those are the only people outside the family who ever knew of the knife's existence, and their interest was minimal."

Donin asked, "Who else have you told about this auction?"

"Only members of my immediate family," de Baraga responded. "As Mr. Ruddington explained earlier, I don't want the tax authorities to become interested in this transaction."

Roy Scanner remained silent throughout the entire question-and-answer session.

The final question came from Arthur Ward. "It seems to me that Raul de Baraga's letter is key to the knife's provenance. I understand why you wouldn't want to part with the letter, it's part of your family history. But I wouldn't think of bidding unless the original letter was part of the sale. Does anyone else feel that way?"

"You're absolutely right," Kay said. "No letter, no auction. That's my position, too."

Everyone at the table nodded in agreement.

Antonio de Baraga looked extremely unhappy with that demand. Ruddington leaned over and whispered in de Baraga's ear. They exchanged more whispers. Finally Ruddington said, "Señor de Baraga has graciously agreed to your condition." He stood. "At this point we will leave you alone." He put the knife in the walnut case and snapped it closed. "You'll need the next couple of days to examine the documents and photos we've provided. Again, the auction will be held in this room at four p.m. on Tuesday. Feel free to call me with any questions. I'm staying here at the Driskill." Ruddington shoved his remaining copies of the photos and supporting documents into a large briefcase.

"Señor de Baraga is at the DoubleTree Inn, but asks that you don't disturb him. All questions should be referred to me. If there are questions I can't immediately answer, I'll consult with Señor de Baraga and get back to you." He smiled around the room. "I feel confident I'll see all of you at the auction on Tuesday. By the way, no bid lower than one million dollars will be entertained."

Stewart Ruddington left with Antonio de Baraga, who seemed to have diminished in size. De Baraga's shoulders were slumped and his head bowed. The impending sale of the Bowie knife and Raul's letter was obviously painful, despite the large amount of money he stood to gain.

"Did you hear that parting shot?" Arthur raised his voice to match Ruddington's pitch. "*No bid lower than one million dollars will be entertained.* I'll bet Stewart rehearsed his farewell line for hours."

"That's not all that was rehearsed." Melanie patted and tucked at the expensive creation that was her hair. "Did anyone actually believe de Baraga's tears and oh-so-trembling lips when he finished reading the letter? And the whispers back and forth about whether the letter would be part of the sale? And the whipped dog look when de Baraga left us? *Please* spare me the amateur theatrics."

"I thought de Baraga was sincere," Roy Scanner said.

Everyone looked at Scanner as if he'd just arrived from some other planet where the IQ was remarkably low.

"We've all seen Stewart's act before." Kay felt sorry for Scanner, who was way out of his element. "He swamps you with historical material, photos, lab reports. Sometimes too much information can make you overlook the one important so-called fact you should have questioned."

"At one private auction I attended, Stewart actually brought in a microscope." Arthur chuckled over the memory. "Asked the bidders to examine some hairs that were supposed to be from Franklin Delano Roosevelt's head. Claimed they were found in the set of rare books he was flogging, thereby proving they came from FDR's private library. Actually, the books were owned by Harry Hopkins."

Roy was embarrassed by his ignorance. "You mean that isn't Jim Bowie's knife?"

"No one said that," Kay answered patiently. "Though Stewart Ruddington is a reliable auctioneer, you can't take everything he says at face value. Stewart represents the seller, after all. You have to carefully weigh the relevance of historical documents and lab reports. They can be helpful, but at times they can also be misleading."

"The knife has power." Kazuo Goto seemed to be talking to himself, not really paying attention to the conversation.

A voice came from the back of the room. "The Jap is right. That knife is the real goods."

Everyone turned to Bud Wolf, who sat with one leg crossed over the other. The bidders could see an inch or so of gun butt sticking out of the top of one boot.

"So good to have your *expert* and *illuminating* opinion, Mr. Wolf," Melanie sniffed.

"I know knives." Wolf wasn't at all fazed by some of the looks he was getting, the tight mouths and wrinkled brows that said he was an outsider, nothing but a bodyguard who should keep his mouth shut. "Like the Jap said, that knife has power. I felt it myself, the power."

Leon Donin didn't seem to mind that his bodyguard had inserted himself into the conversation. Or that Wolf's reference to Kazuo Goto as "the Jap" was insulting. If anything, Donin was amused. "Thank you, Wolfie." He looked around the table. "I've come to believe that Mr. Wolf has good instincts in these matters. I will take his comments into consideration and I urge you to do the same."

# CHAPTER 10

"I was impressed with de Baraga's presentation, especially the letter from the young man who fought at the Alamo and was later killed at San Jacinto."

"Just remember you were meant to be impressed." Kay sipped at a gin and tonic. She was sitting in the lobby bar of the Austin Omni with Roy Scanner, unsure whether he had spontaneously invited her to join him for a drink or whether she had manipulated him into doing so. She was attracted to him. Not for his looks, although she liked his plain, craggy, Lincolnesque face, but more for the shrewd mind she sensed behind the face. "You don't know zip about antiques or antiques auctions, do you? Not that you should, most people don't."

"That became pretty clear, I guess." Scanner shrugged. "I've been trying to calculate how big a fool I made of myself today because it goes against my grain to look foolish. By my own count, I've made a complete ass out of myself only twenty-two times over my thirty-six years."

"That's not bad at all." Kay thought back over her own string of embarrassing mistakes. "I'd guess I've looked a perfect fool at least three hundred times in my life. Probably more."

"What was the worst?"

Kay thought back. "Besides my ill-fated marriage? Well, shortly after going to work in an antiques store a man brought in a silver cigar case that he wanted to sell. Said it had belonged to J. P. Morgan, the nineteenth-century robber baron. Morgan's initials were engraved on the case. The owner of the store was out that day with the flu. I got all excited and bought the case for the shop for three hundred dollars. The next day the owner came in and pointed out to me that in small letters on the bottom of the case were the words *Made in Taiwan.*"

"Ouch," Scanner said.

"Double ouch. The owner took the three hundred dollars out of that month's salary, leaving me very little to live on. What about you? Tell me something really embarrassing about yourself. This is fun."

Scanner didn't have to think about it for very long. "Okay, somewhere around ten years ago I asked a girl to go to the Bahamas with me on vacation. Harriet was her name. Beautiful girl. I didn't know her very well, but I really wanted her. Thought I couldn't live without her. Dreamed about her every night. Sent her love letters. Jesus, I was so young and stupid. Fortunately, she told me *before* we went to the Bahamas that she was a male transvestite named Harry instead of a girl named Harriet."

They both had a long laugh over that, though Scanner's was a bit less frothy than Kay's.

After they'd gotten the laughter out of their systems Kay said, "I wouldn't worry too much about looking foolish at the auction. Wealthy buyers sometimes designate personal friends who may not know much about auctions to sit in for them, especially if they're very busy people as Wallace Wright must be."

"Wallace has been pretty much retired since stepping down as Secretary of the Treasury. The reason he couldn't be here in person is that his health isn't up to par right now."

"I see." Kay had seen a photo of Wallace Wright just last week in the *New York Times* playing in a celebrity tennis tournament. She wondered why Roy Scanner, a man with so much apparent honesty in his face, was lying to her. She conceded that separating the honest men from the dishonest ones was not one of her great strengths. "By the way, thanks again for giving Leon Donin that crushing handshake. I almost stood up and cheered when you made his face go pale. You must have some grip."

"Spent my youth on a farm. Not much to do there except work with your hands." Scanner was drinking a Lone Star beer, which he put aside for the moment. "It was pretty obvious that you and Donin had met before today. It was also obvious that he was trying to intimidate you into not revealing something you know about him. What's the story behind that?"

Kay considered her response. "Ordinarily I'd tell you. But I don't believe you've been entirely open with me, Mr. Scanner."

"Please call me Roy. Why do you say I haven't been open with you?"

"Your story about *sitting in* for Wallace Wright doesn't ring true. He's not in bad health, he got his picture in the *Times* last week by winning three straight sets in a celebrity tennis tournament against the twenty-five-year-old star of some idiotic sitcom. On top of that you're too young to be an 'old friend' of a man in his late sixties or early seventies. And Wallace Wright isn't even a serious collector of antiques. If he were, I'd have heard about it before today. You're not in this auction to buy an antique. You're here because Leon Donin is here. You look at that Russian as if the Cold War was still going strong. Why? I don't understand what's happening here."

Scanner grinned ruefully. "You're very insightful."

"A major auction like this one is a cat-and-dog fight," Kay explained. "We all study the opposing bidders to gauge how high the bidding might go. We probe to find out who the most serious bidders are. You don't appear to me to be a serious bidder. So 'fess up, why are you here?"

He had decided to level with Kay, maybe even get some help from her, when Arthur Ward appeared at their table. "May I join you?"

"Of course," Kay said, though she was disappointed to have her conversation with Scanner interrupted.

Arthur sat down and ordered a martini, very dry, and asked the waitress for a bowl of peanuts as well. "I use peanuts to keep my thirst alive so I can drink more," he explained to Scanner. "Is this your first auction, Mr. Scanner?"

"Yes, it is."

"And you're bidding for Wallace Wright? I didn't know our distinguished former Secretary of the Treasury was a collector."

"As a rule, Wallace isn't especially interested in antiques. But he went to college at Rice, absorbed a lot of Texas history back then, and so he's interested in the Bowie knife."

"Seriously interested? Or just interested?"

Scanner laughed. "Kay told me I could expect to be probed by the opposition on how high Wallace is prepared to bid."

"Naughty, naughty," Arthur said to Kay. "You shouldn't give away our little secrets to the outside world." He turned back to Scanner. "We're a very inbred group, I'm afraid. Suspicious of first-time bidders because we can't anticipate how they'll bid. But don't think you're unwelcome. I'm always happy to see someone new take an interest in antiques, especially a man as wealthy as Wallace Wright. Expanding the pool of well-to-do buyers helps keep up the prices, you see."

"Yes, I understand."

Arthur's martini and peanuts were served. "Just bring me another martini when you have the chance," he told the waitress. When she left, he downed his first drink very smoothly and put down the glass with a satisfied sigh. "They know how to mix a superb martini in Texas. What a delightful surprise."

Kay and Arthur chatted about the world of antiques for a few minutes, bringing Scanner into the conversation whenever they could. Scanner decided he liked Arthur Ward. He judged him to be a patrician in the style of Wallace Wright, who was also genuinely gracious to everyone he met. Wallace Wright was Scanner's mentor. In the first year of Wright's term as Secretary of the Treasury, he went over the personnel files and plucked Scanner from the ranks of field Treasury agents to be his administrative assistant. As Kay had guessed, the age difference had weighed against a real friendship developing between himself and Wright. But Wright had appreciated Scanner's abilities and given his career in the Treasury Department a boost. Scanner was a lousy politician, never good at insinuating himself into situations where he might please his superiors. However, Scanner knew he was a damned good field agent and Wright made sure others in the department realized that, too. When Wallace Wright left the administration, he saw to it that Scanner was promoted to a high-level field position in the Secret Service division of the Treasury Department.

"Oh my . . ." Arthur abruptly put down his second martini. "Melanie's been out trolling again, and look at the big fish she caught."

Melanie Wadsworth came parading through the lobby on the arm of an extremely tall and muscular young man wearing a Stetson hat, a blue denim shirt with the sleeves rolled up to display an impressive set of biceps, a pair of jeans so tight that nothing about his sexual organs was left to the imagination and jet-black Tony Lama boots glossed to a high shine.

"Christ, it's the original Midnight Cowboy," Scanner said.

Kay used her lipstick to hastily write the number nine on a napkin. She held up the napkin and waved it at Melanie as she passed by their table.

"You've bagged a nine there!" Kay called. "A definite nine! Congratulations!"

Melanie produced the kind of victorious smile that Caesar's generals wore as they paraded through the streets of Rome after conquering a new territory. Melanie and her companion stepped into the elevator and were whooshed upward to the seventh floor.

"Melanie's good," Kay conceded. "Our meeting ended only half an hour ago and she's already headed for the sack with a genuine Texas stud. And she managed to make sure we knew it."

"Maybe this romp with the Midnight Cowboy will improve her mood," Scanner said. "I'd never met her before today, but I thought she was incredibly bitchy. She can't always be like that, can she?"

Arthur was quick to disagree. "Sex doesn't soften Melanie's demeanor. If anything, she becomes even more poisonous after sex, much like the black widow spider."

"Why, Arthur, you sound like a man who's been personally bitten by a black widow named Melanie."

Arthur's nod was sheepish. "Smitten, then bitten." He popped half a handful of peanuts into his mouth. "Bitchiness can be a highly sexual quality in a woman. Yes, I *know* Melanie in the Biblical sense. But that was before you came on the scene, Kay. Since then I've been completely faithful to you."

"I believe you, Arthur." Kay returned the lipstick to her purse. "I also believe in the tooth fairy, alien abductions and that Congress is more interested in progress than in politics."

"You're too young to be so cynical," Arthur complained. "Mr. Scanner, I appeal to you. A man is entitled to one wretched romantic mistake, isn't he? I can see you're already as attracted to Kay as I am. Stand up for me."

Scanner squirmed at his transparency. "You can't fault him for one slip."

"What about all of his ex-wives?" Kay asked.

"All right . . . five slips all together." Scanner had seen the pulse in Kay's beautiful neck take a jump when Arthur declared he was attracted to her. Her scrutiny was becoming uncomfortable. "Give the man a break," he said, just to be saying something.

"Yes, give the man a break." Arthur's words were now vaguely slurred. "And give him another martini as well. What about you two? Another

Lone Star for Mr. Scanner? For Roy? I always switch to first names with my third martini. Another gin and tonic for you, Kay?"

They both nodded and turned their eyes away from each other. There was a somewhat embarrassed silence while Arthur called the waitress over and ordered another round and another bowl of peanuts.

From the window of Chauncy Alexander's room, he and Phil Williams could look down on the lobby bar in the atrium. Kay, Arthur and Scanner were sitting with their backs to them, so neither Chauncy nor Phil were particularly worried about being seen together, especially from nine floors away.

"Time to make your move," Chauncy said. "You don't want those two suits move in on your ex."

"Them? One's too old for Kay and the other's too ugly."

"Don't underestimate plain-faced men," Chauncy warned.

"I don't underestimate anyone. I just know what women want, especially Kay." Phil preened himself, pleased with the perfect fit of his best Ralph Lauren slacks, the elegantly casual silk shirt he'd chosen for this occasion and the subdued richness of his Bally loafers worn without socks. The clothes were the last remnants of more prosperous days and gave him confidence he'd soon be back in the money. "She's just waiting for me to show up again, whether she knows it or not."

"Then show up." Chauncy gave his partner a nudge. "Right now."

"Don't be so nervous. It's a lock."

Phil left Chauncy's room and strode confidently down the circular hallway toward the glass elevator, whistling the opening bars of a show tune.

Chauncy recognized Phil's bravado for what it was. Phil felt entitled to any woman he wanted, but he also was afraid that someday—maybe today—his smarmy charm would cease to work. If Phil's ex struck out, Chauncy had a backup plan in mind. He didn't want to use the plan because it would cost money he didn't have. Still, he needed a backup plan. *Phil too weak to depend on,* Chauncy thought.

". . . what looked to me like a highboy from the Goddard-Townsend school," Ward was saying. "Late seventeen-hundreds was my estimate. Queen Anne. Undoubtedly manufactured in Newport. There it was, sitting in the corner of this elderly woman's attic. Covered with dust and mouse droppings. Streaked with dirt. Scratched here and there, but not as badly as you might expect. Mrs. Rickets, the lady who owned it, had no idea what it was. She only knew it had been her mother's highboy and for that reason she'd held on to it for the past forty or so years. My God, I could have paid her a hundred dollars and she would have been satisfied."

"What did you do?" The antiques business was gradually becoming interesting to Scanner.

"I offered Mrs. Rickets thirty-two thousand dollars and she literally fainted, or had some kind of seizure. I had to call her physician and repeat the offer with him in attendance. I learned later that she was about to put her house on the market to pay off twenty thousand dollars in medical bills her husband ran up before he died. That's why she was selling off things from her attic, to raise a little extra money and get the house in shape for a sale."

"How much did the highboy turn out to be worth?" Kay asked.

"Once I cleaned it up, I ordered two independent appraisals. One came in at eighty-two thousand and the other at ninety-one thousand. It's still in my collection. By next year I believe it'll be worth a hundred and fifty thousand." Arthur smiled at Scanner. "What do you think, Roy? Did I cheat that old lady or not? This is the kind of situation collectors run into all the time. It's an interesting point of ethics."

Scanner realized he was again out of his depth. "Did you tell her what kind of antique it was? What period? That sort of thing? So she'd know what she was selling?"

Arthur grinned. "Very good. Yes, I did tell her it was a Queen Anne highboy, perhaps as early as the 1700s, and might be worth more than I was offering. I told her on the other hand I was taking a chance myself. The chest might have wormholes or other defects I couldn't spot up in that dim and dusty attic. It might turn out to be a very fine copy instead of a Goddard-Townsend original. All of which was true. She gambled and I gambled. We both won. My win was bigger, but I believe I treated her fairly."

"So do I." Scanner became aware that Kay's mouth had fallen open, that she was staring over his shoulder with a look of shock. "What's wrong?" He looked behind himself at a highly tanned man who had approached their table. The guy looked to Scanner like a one-time beach boy settled comfortably into his late thirties. Or maybe an actor who specialized in bit parts. Or a male model who could look equally good in a magazine layout or striding down a runway. Big and handsome. Wide shoulders. Narrow waist. Strong chin. The whole package. Scanner disliked him on sight.

"Hello, Kay."

Kay's hands jerked in a fluttery movement that upset her gin and tonic and knocked over Scanner's beer as well.

"Oh . . . I'm sorry . . . please . . . let me . . ." She grabbed a napkin and began cleaning up the mess with unwarranted intensity.

"Let me help." Scanner used his own napkin to soak up some of the beer while Arthur signaled the waitress that they were in need of a bar towel. The cleanup took a couple of minutes, during which Kay kept her eyes focused tightly on the table. Even when the table was clean and dry and no longer in need of attention, she declined to lift her eyes.

"I'm sorry I startled you, babe."

Eventually Kay lifted her eyes. "What are you doing here?"

The stranger dragged over a chair from another table. "You told me you'd be in Austin this week, so I flew up to say hello. Maybe take you to dinner. That's all, no big deal."

When Kay said nothing, the stranger offered his hand to Arthur. "I'm Phil Williams. No, I'm not her brother. Kay and I were married once."

"I'm Arthur Ward and I've heard of you." He shook Phil's hand as if it belonged to an escaped war criminal.

Scanner gave Phil a perfunctory nod, no handshake, instinctively supporting Kay's simmering anger. "Roy Scanner. Mr. Ward and I are here for the auction."

"Good luck to both of you." Phil sounded like the fair-minded referee of a heavyweight title fight. "You're even more surprised than I thought you'd be, Kay. Really, I didn't mean to pop up like some scary monster in a science fiction movie, sending everyone flying back in their chairs."

"Nobody's scared of you." Scanner wondered where this asshole got off thinking he could frighten anyone.

Phil raised his hands palms outward to show he wasn't here for a fight. "No argument. I should have phoned first, or sent a note to your room. Along with a bouquet of peonies, of course. You're still the only woman in the world whose favorite flower is the peony." He directed his words at Kay as if Scanner and Arthur had ceased to exist. "I did call a florist's shop. Do you know how hard it is to find peonies in Texas? Not exactly the state flower. And the bluebonnets are already out of season, I was told. So I have nothing to present to you except myself. Which I know isn't enough. Not nearly what you deserve."

"For God's sake, Phil." Kay sat back with an agitated sigh. "What are you really here for? Money?" She shook her head with solid determination. "Not this time. Not ever again."

Phil smiled first at Scanner and then at Arthur. "She knows me pretty well, but for once she's wrong. I don't want a thing from her."

Arthur and Scanner knew when to depart from a family argument. Together they rose from their chairs.

"I'll get the check." Arthur dismissed any objections. "I insist. I'm always the one who drinks the most." He scribbled his name and room number on the chit. "Kay, please call if you need me for anything. Anything at all."

"Ditto," Scanner said.

"Ditto." Phil mocking him. "Very eloquent. I can assure you Kay is in no danger from me. Never has been."

"I'll be fine," Kay said.

Phil saw Kay look more directly at Scanner than at the other one. *There's something between these two,* he thought. *I'm in time, they're just getting it going.* Still, he'd always figured Kay would be on his permanent hook. There for the taking, whenever he felt like it. Phil wondered who Scanner was, he didn't resemble any antiques dealer he'd ever met. *Jesus, the guy's got a face like an old boot. What's happened to Kay's taste?*

"I'll call you later," Scanner promised.

"Good . . . thanks." She waited until Arthur and Scanner were out of earshot before turning on her ex. "What's the story, Phil? The *real* story. You didn't spend a lot of money you probably don't have to fly all the way to Texas for *dinner.*"

"Come on, Kay." With an injured look. "I've been trying to tell you things are different for me. I'm financially healthy again, got a nice little business going down there in Jamaica, but I've been feeling lousy about the way I treated you. The other women, that damned mess with futures I oversold. I was a prime asshole, I know that. What bothers me the most were the other women. Believe it or not, I'm practically celibate these days. No more running around. I mean, they've got AIDS down in my island paradise, too. You've got to be careful these days."

He leaned forward, counting on Hermès cologne and his most appealing little-boy smile to carry him through. "I wanted to see you just once more. I don't know, maybe I'm an idiot to try to make you think of me without wanting to gag. Tell me to get lost and I'll be outta here like a shot. But why don't we have dinner together first? I mean, I came all this way. What can you lose anyhow?"

"My sanity."

"If you were sane, you wouldn't have married me in the first place." He shook his head as if he'd only recently come to understand how badly he'd treated her. "I was such a shit." *Groveling is good,* he thought. *Every woman likes to see a man grovel.* "You should have thrown me in a wood chipper, like that woman up in Connecticut did to her husband. An arm here, a leg there. Fertilizer—that's what I deserved to become."

"A wood chipper would have been too good for you." Kay reached for her drink, remembered she'd knocked it over and withdrew her hand. "I did consider slipping a slow-acting acid into your food."

"Waitress." Phil signaled to the girl at the bar. "Please bring a fresh drink to replace the one that was spilled. Gin and tonic, right? You still drink those? I'll have a draft beer, something local. Surprise me."

Kay felt humiliated to think he still knew her so well. Worse yet was the quickness with which the waitress moved for Phil, the supplicating look she gave him when she served the drinks, the gushing gratitude when he rewarded her with one of his hundred-watt smiles. *Déjà vu* all over again, as Yogi said.

"All right, we'll have dinner together—dinner . . . period—only because I'm curious to find out what kind of scam this is." She hated herself for saying yes, for feeling an unwelcome rush of goodwill for a man she knew damned well didn't deserve it. Roy Scanner had been about to invite her to dinner. She'd wanted to have dinner with him. He'd also seemed ready to tell her something very juicy about the mysterious Leon Donin—alias Nicolai Leontin. *So why did I say yes to Phil? Because I'm feeling all hot and moist between my legs? Don't be a dummy, of course that's why you said yes. Phil always makes you feel hot and moist down there, that's why you married the bastard. That's his talent. That's what he does for a living. Try to remember that.*

"What?" Phil leaned forward. "You were muttering something."

"I never *mutter.* It's not *ladylike.*" Kay took a drink and was grateful to find more gin than tonic in the glass. "All right, I guess you'd better tell me about your restaurant in Jamaica. I wouldn't even believe it existed if

I hadn't met a man last night from Jamaica who said he'd seen it." She bit the tip of her tongue. *Now he knows I've been talking about him,* she thought. *Which means I've also been thinking about him. Nice work, Kay.*

"Well, as I said, it's just a small place . . . in a nice beach town . . . Runaway Bay . . . where the waves . . ."

"I want Kay Williams out of this auction," Leon Donin was saying to Bud Wolf. They were watching Kay and Phil from inside the door of an art gallery at the far end of the lobby.

"How far should I go? You want her hurt . . . killed . . . or just scared?"

"Scared will be sufficient."

Wolf was glad for the assignment. Watching over Donin and his suitcase full of cash was about as exciting as a foreign movie. "Mind if I ask why you want her scared? Might help me figure out how to deal with her."

"Two reasons. First, I met Miss Williams recently in Singapore. I was selling an antique then instead of buying one. I was also using my real name. I never expected to meet her again, at least not this soon. There are reasons why I do not want my real name connected with this transaction.

"Second, she and Goto are going to be serious bidders. Miss Williams is bidding for an extremely wealthy oil man and Goto has millions of his own dollars to spend. You saw his reaction, he's in awe of that knife. He plans to bid high. However, I do not want you to interfere with Mr. Goto. His health is precarious, the tension of the auction will be too much for him. He may not even be able to attend the auction. If he does, I expect him to become too ill to function."

It didn't surprise Wolf to hear that the Russian's real name wasn't Donin. "Okay, I'll get on it." He looked at the suitcase sitting by Donin's feet. "You gonna lug that around day and night?"

"The trip from Russia to Texas was very tiring. I will go up to my room now and have dinner, then I will sleep. You will come upstairs with me to make sure the room is clear, then you can go about your business. Tomorrow is Monday, the banks will be open. I will put the suitcase in a vault in that bank across the street. What time do banks open in the U.S.?"

"Ten a.m."

"Come to my room at ten and take me across the street to the bank. After that you will be free to work on the problem of Kay Williams."

"Why wait? I'll start workin' on her tonight."

"Very good." Donin smiled thinly. "I will be interested to learn how you handle her. If I were not preoccupied with my own business, I would enjoy helping you to bedevil her."

"I'll bet you would."

The sales agent for the gallery, a tiny man with his hair artfully combed to disguise a bald spot, appeared and put a hand on Wolf's arm. "You've been standing here so long. Why don't you both come into the gallery? I'll give you a nice cup of tea and tell you about the artists we're featuring this month."

Wolf glowered at him. "Unless you're lookin' for a broken wrist, you'd best take your goddamn hand off my arm."

The sales agent drew back his hand as if it had touched a live wire. "Well I *apologize* for offering you some *sustenance*. It *won't* happen *again*, I assure you." He pivoted and walked away.

Donin gave a rattling smoker's laugh. "I may take you back to Russia with me, you would be right at home in Moscow."

"No fuckin' way."

# CHAPTER 11

**B**ud Wolf was fond of saying, "Your average hotel room is about as safe as the inside of a crack house on a Saturday night. Anybody with the right tools can break into one. I don't care whether the door has a key lock or an electronic lock. The day I can't get into any hotel room in under twenty seconds, I'll retire and buy myself the biggest fuckin' rockin' chair I can find." As a matter of professional habit, he always carried in his traveling kit a set of lock picks and a slim electronic jammer that slid into electronically activated locks to shut down the magnetic codes.

It took him only six seconds to get into Kay Williams's room. She was still down in the lobby bar having a drink with the broad-shouldered Goldilocks who acted like God's gift to the vagina. Wolf hoped she'd stay put for just another ten minutes.

Once inside, Wolf put on a pair of surgeon's latex gloves and looked quickly through Kay's suitcase, the closet and the bureau drawers in case she had left anything of real value lying around, like cash or certified checks to pay for the Bowie knife if she outbid everyone at the auction. No such luck, the bitch was too smart for that.

Wolf did find some jewelry in the pocket of her suitcase. Nothing flashy or expensive. Modest stuff. One brooch looked old, the kind of thing a girl might have inherited from her mother. He stuffed all the jewelry into his pockets because he knew that most people—especially women—hated to lose things that held sentimental value.

He took all the clothes out of the closet and tossed them on the bed. Their tumbled look dissatisfied him. This bitch couldn't be scared that easily. He took a knife out of his boot, picked up her nightgown and slashed it into pieces with three vertical cuts. He did the same to a suit. To a couple of dresses. To a pair of jeans. To her bras. To every piece of clothing except her panties. With each pair of panties, he cut out the crotch.

The final touch was to lay out each vandalized garment on the bed, turning his work into a sort of celebration of violence. Laid out like that, it became clear someone hated Kay Williams—maybe enough to return and use the knife on her body instead of just on her clothes.

Still Wolf was unsatisfied. The picture lacked something essential. He couldn't put his finger on it, he only knew he wanted the bitch not just scared but terrified right down to the soles of her pretty feet.

A crooked smile crossed his face. With a light step, Wolf went into the bathroom and rummaged through Kay's cosmetics bag until he found a jar of hand cream, just the thing for what he had in mind.

Wolf went to the bed, took the latex glove off his right hand, unzipped his pants and pulled out his cock. Standing over Kay's slashed clothing, he smeared some of the cold cream on the palm of his right hand, let the jar fall to the floor from his gloved left hand, and began to masturbate. Soon he was breathing hard, rocking in place, his body as hot as a manifold after two hundred miles. "Oh yeah . . . there she comes . . . old faithful . . . goddamn . . . goddamn . . . goddamn . . . goddamn . . ." It didn't take long after that. He groaned like a bison when he ejaculated and whipped his cock around so that the cum sprayed all over the clothing on the bed.

"Whoa! Go baby!" Then it was over. He exhaled deeply. Stood for a moment with his eyes closed. Then began to stuff his cock into his pants.

"Time to put the monster back in its cage. Hey, look at the mess. She's gonna faint dead away. Wish I could be here to see it."

At the door, Wolf surveyed his work and was fully satisfied. This was exactly the kind of shock Donin wanted to hand the snooty little bitch. The sort of vandalism that usually made women say they felt "violated," whatever the hell that meant.

He left the room and took the elevator to his own floor. The window of his room looked down on the lobby bar, where Kay Williams was still in conversation with Goldilocks. *They make a good-looking couple. Probably making plans to go up to her room for a quick bang before dinner.*

*Almost hate to spoil it for them.* He grinned down at the couple. "To think I get paid for doin' shit like this. What a great life!"

*It's a good thing,* Kay was thinking, *that Phil can't resist the sound of his own voice.* His long, rhapsodic description of his restaurant in Jamaica gave her a chance to put a clamp on her emotions and think with her head instead of . . . well . . . let's just say to think more clearly.

As Phil reached ever greater heights of eloquence in describing *Seis Amigos,* Kay began to sniff the unmistakable aroma of bullshit. Alas, she knew that aroma all too well. Did Phil say his chef was a graduate of the Culinary Institute in New York? She pictured a tipsy Jamaican with his hair in dreadlocks throwing beans in a dirty pot. Did Phil report that he'd brought an interior designer down to Jamaica from Miami to decorate his establishment? Kay envisioned walls plastered with cheap posters of bull-fighters and palm-treed beaches. Every one of Phil's elaborate details was a lie, every embellishment a rather sad wish. That was truly the story of Phil Williams's life.

Kay straightened her back and finished her drink.

"Phil, I'm afraid I can't have dinner with you tonight after all."

"What? How do you mean?"

"I've just recalled a previous engagement."

"I don't believe that."

She shrugged. "Okay, the fact is I've just invented a previous engagement."

"Jesus Christ, I flew all the way out here from *fucking Jamaica* to take you to dinner. Doesn't that mean anything?"

"I guess not."

Phil's face reddened under his carefully developed tan. "That's a piss-poor attitude. I thought you had more class."

"You were wrong." Kay rose and Phil jumped to his feet, unsure of just how to handle her defection.

"I don't get it. Why are you changing your mind? What's wrong?"

"Same thing that's been wrong with us for years."

As Kay headed for the elevator, Phil hastily signed the check and trotted after her. "At least let me walk you to your room."

"Fine. But you're not coming inside." Kay was a little ashamed of enjoying Phil's disappointment so much. *Not ladylike,* she thought. *Not ladylike at all.*

The elevator whisked them to Kay's floor while Phil tried out his reliable old pout and flexed his admirable muscles in a way that he considered subtle.

"What about breakfast?"

"No, Phil. Let's just go our own directions. I like it that way. Until the last week or so, you liked it that way, too."

"No, I never did. I've wanted to make things up to you, I told you that already." His voice was rising. "One lousy breakfast? What's that gonna cost you?"

"More than I'm willing to pay." She used her card key to open the door and slipped quickly inside, determined to get the door closed again before Phil could continue his appeals. Instead the card key fell from Kay's hand and she gave a gasp, a strangled cry, at what she saw.

"What's the matter?" Phil pushed into her room. "Holy fuck."

The door was on a spring. It closed behind them with a heavy click. For a moment neither of them moved. After a time Kay went past Phil, her eyes whipping left to right, then back the other way. Her clothes had been shredded, systematically slashed. The crotches of her undies had been cut out in what could only be a sexual threat. Kay felt herself beginning to gag.

"Somebody doesn't like you very much." There was just a touch of satisfaction there, which he quickly squelched. "I'd better call Security."

"Did you do this? Some kind of get even deal?"

"No!" Phil was genuinely insulted. "You know me better, this isn't my style." He wondered if Chauncy had been in here. You never knew what that Jamaican might do. "Does this look like my kind of thing?"

"No, I guess not." Kay's eyes roamed the bed, where various articles of clothing had been laid out after their mutilation. Here and there they looked wet. She reached out in curiosity, then drew her hand back. "Oh, my God!"

Phil had picked up the phone on the bedside table. He saw what Kay had reacted to and scowled in disgust. "Oh Jesus . . . that's terrible." He hit the operator button. "Operator? Room four-hundred-nineteen. There's been a break-in here. Send your security man up right now. Hurry!"

Kay went into the bathroom, gagging audibly but willing herself not to throw up. She splashed water on her face and stuffed the end of a towel into her mouth until the urge to vomit gradually receded. Her stomach continued to churn, though, and she was shaking besides. *Who could have done this? Did it have anything to do with the auction? Did somebody want the Bowie knife badly enough to try to scare me out of the auction?* Those and other questions tumbled through Kay's mind.

After a time the shaking subsided, she became aware of voices in the bedroom. She straightened herself, gave a fleeting glance at her pale face in the mirror and left the bathroom to find Phil talking with a gaunt man in a gray sportcoat and green slacks and an open-collared shirt, a gut that looked hard even though it was potbellied, small searching eyes, a mouth that was surprisingly kind.

"Miss Williams." Voice with a gravelly Texas burr. "I'm Ed Halley, security manager for the hotel. I'm very sorry about what's happened. This kind of incident is unusual for us, I assure you. For starters, we'll move you to another room right away. And first thing in the mornin' I'll have a man take you to Dillard's so you can replace your things—at the hotel's expense, of course. I'll understand if you want to move to another hotel. This must be very disturbin' to you."

*Another hotel.* Phil thinking, *Good idea. Separate Kay from her friends, especially that ugly asshole Roy Scanner.* "You're damned right we'll move to another hotel—Miss Williams and myself. I'm in Room 622." Phil brought his card key out of his pocket and tossed it to Halley with a contemptuous flip. "Have someone pack up my things right away."

Halley caught the card awkwardly. He gave Phil a long stare before returning his attention to Kay. "Miss Williams, besides the vandalism, has anything been stolen?"

Kay hadn't even thought of that. She opened her valise and made a quick check of the few possessions she'd brought along on the trip. "Oh, dear. Yes. A couple of pieces of jewelry. Nothing expensive, I don't wear a lot of jewelry. But a signet ring that came down to me from my mother is gone, and a gold pin, and an old brooch and necklace that are quite beautiful even though they aren't worth a lot of money."

"I'll need a description of the items for the police report," Halley said.

"If the jewelry isn't expensive, you should just reimburse Miss Williams right here and now." Phil had pumped himself up, but the mention of the police was somewhat deflating. The last thing he wanted was cops. "This should be handled quietly."

Halley gave Phil a searching examination. "You don't want the police involved?"

"I don't want Miss Williams bothered with a lot of questions is all."

"Phil, shut up," Kay said mildly. "Mr. Halley, I don't feel the need to move to another hotel. Just find me a different room." She had another thought. "Also, there's a Roy Scanner staying here. He's part of a group that's come to Austin for an auction I'm involved in. Could you call his room for me and ask him to join us?"

That really annoyed Phil. "What the hell do you want with Scanner?"

Halley took a small but pointed pleasure in ignoring Phil's objection as he picked up the phone and asked the operator to connect him with Roy Scanner.

"This vandalism has something to do with the auction. Roy may be able to help me figure out what's going on."

"I doubt that." Phil felt the advantage he'd briefly held slipping away. Goddamn Scanner. Goddamn Kay, too. She'd changed, and not for the better. It wasn't long ago that Kay would come in her undies if he just looked at her. All of a sudden she was acting like one of those femi-Nazis that Rush Limbaugh talked about. "Let's get out of this room, Kay. Go down to the bar while Inspector Clouseau here gets you moved to another room."

Halley just smiled. He could see that the hunk wasn't making his case. He'd gotten ahold of Roy Scanner, who said he'd be right up. Halley also called the desk and asked very softly for the name of the guest in Room 622. The name was Phil Williams. Same last name as the victim. Imagine that.

He put down the phone and said, "Miss Williams, I'd like to just leave all this mess as it is for the police to examine. They might get a fingerprint or two that'll tell us who was in your room. Unlikely, but worth a shot. We'll move your suitcase, handbag, other things that haven't been vandalized. Mr. Williams? Do you still want to move to another hotel?"

Phil was startled that this hotel cop already knew his name, then remembered that he'd told him his room number. "I guess not." He took his card key back from Halley. "I still don't want Miss Williams bothered by the police with a lot of stupid questions."

"I'm a thirty-year veteran of the Austin Police Department. Retired last year. I'll see that the investigation is discreet. Primarily for your sake, Miss Williams. But also because part of my job is to protect the reputation of the hotel. I hope you understand that."

"Of course."

"I'm not saying the investigation won't be thorough. I want to catch the sicko who did this as much as you want to see him caught. But I gotta tell you that professional thieves are easier to catch than sickos."

"So I've heard."

Two bellhops arrived. Kay indicated the things that needed to be moved to the other room and was given a card key for a room on another floor. Phil wrote down the room number and fired a couple of unnecessary questions at Halley, who ignored him. "Can I talk to you alone for a moment?" he asked Kay.

"Certainly."

Halley took a light hold on Kay's arm and moved her into the hallway. When Phil attempted to follow, Halley put up his hand in a warning to stay put.

"You and this gentleman share the same last name," Halley pointed out. "Is he your husband?"

"Ex-husband."

"Are you on good terms?"

"Not especially."

"Could he have done this?"

Kay shook her head. "I don't think so."

"Not enough motive?"

"Not enough guts."

Halley grinned. "You want him out of here?"

"That would be lovely."

Roy Scanner came striding down the hall. He'd changed from a suit into a pair of slacks, gray sweater without a shirt underneath, and a pair of scuffed old Docksiders. "What's wrong?" He looked at Halley and made an immediate judgment. "Police?"

"Ed Halley. Hotel security."

"You look like a cop."

"Austin PD. Retired."

"Was Kay's room burglarized?"

"That and something else besides."

"Excuse us for a moment, Kay." Scanner took Halley a few yards down the corridor, brought out his wallet from a back pocket, showed Halley an ID of some sort.

Halley responded by saying, "Have a look if you want."

Roy went into Kay's room. Phil Williams's presence surprised him, but he only nodded to him in a distracted way while he looked at the mess someone had made. He thought it significant that her things had been slashed so carefully. This didn't look to him like the work of a deranged mind.

"You aren't needed here," Phil said.

Scanner finally looked at him. "I was told that Kay asked for me."

"You aren't needed," Phil repeated. "Kay is my responsibility."

"You're divorced."

"I'm back in her life. That's all you have to know." Phil worked up a threatening scowl that drew only a vague smile from Scanner.

Some other hotel guests came down the hall, prompting Halley to bring Kay back into the room and close the door until the corridor was clear again.

"What do you think?" Halley asked.

Kay noted that Halley and Roy had formed an instinctive partnership of some sort.

Scanner said, "The cuts are all straight and even, no evidence of somebody going into a frenzy. Nothing torn to pieces with hands, that kind of thing. All the clothing laid out neatly." He walked around to the opposite side of the bed. "Even the semen's been sprayed around in a sort of deliberate pattern. A man's got to have pretty good control of his emotions to do that. No, this guy isn't your garden-variety loony tune. He was trying in a cold-blooded way to frighten Kay."

"That's the way I read it, too." Halley had been nodding along with Scanner's comments. "Pure intimidation."

Phil felt he had to regain control of Kay right now or these two would gradually separate her from him. "To make Kay stand here while you two talk about *semen stains* is just contemptible. Come on, Kay. I'll take you to your new room." He reached out for her but found Halley clamping a strong hand on his wrist. "Let go of me!"

"Sir, I'll just walk you to the elevator."

"I'm not leaving without . . ." But he was already at the door. Then out the door. Then being walked slowly but firmly towards the elevators. Phil tried to pull away from Halley, but the older man was a lot stronger than he looked. "I'll report you to your . . ."

"The hotel appreciates your patronage." Halley keeping his voice friendly. "Yes sir, we really do. A guest of your stature deserves an escort to the elevator." His soft Texas accent suddenly acquired a harsh edge. "I mean, hell, we wouldn't want anythin' to happen to you. That's why you're gettin' my personal protection." The elevator door opened and Phil was pushed inside. "Have a *very* nice night, Mr. Williams. By the way, y'all better not bother your ex again or I'll come lookin' for you without my usual smile. Y'hear me?"

# CHAPTER 12

"H it me again." Phil pushed his glass forward.

The bartender raised his eyebrows. "Are you driving tonight, sir?"

"No, I'm staying in this shitpile of a hotel. So why don't you just shut up and pour me another drink."

"Yessir, another scotch rocks coming up."

Phil realized he was taking out his frustrations on the guy. Fuck him, that's what bartenders were for. Any asshole could pour a jigger of scotch over a handful of ice cubes. A bartender—a *real* bartender—was paid to make people feel they were still in charge of their own goddamn lives. Still had an ace in the hole. Still had some good luck. Still knew which buttons to push. Phil took a gulp of scotch large enough to make him shudder. *Me? I don't have a fucking ace left in my hand, or even a joker up my sleeve. All I've got is a bartender who wants to cut me off.*

His morose view wasn't improved by the nagging thought that sooner or later Chauncy Alexander would come around. Old Chauncy would want to know what he'd learned from Kay. Phil would have to tell him he'd learned nothing. Nada. Zippo. He'd have to admit to Chauncy that Kay was a lost cause. He couldn't get to her anymore. Somewhere along the way she'd grown up. The thing Phil hated most in the world is a girl who suddenly grows up. For some reason the ones who grew up always looked at him like he was some kind of bug. *I'm not a goddamn bug,* Phil thought. *I'm a man! They should treat me like a man!*

"Gimme a light here."

The bartender struck a match and lit Phil's cigarette. He then escaped the smoke Phil blew into his face by moving down to the other end of the bar. Phil let a chuckle roll around in his mouth. *Are you driving tonight, sir?* Teach the bastard some manners.

"Excuse me, aren't you Phil Williams?"

He swiveled on his stool, poised for flight. Most people who asked that question were jerks he owed money to. "Maybe . . . maybe not." He studied the woman sitting two stools down from him.

"Don't remember me, do you?"

The woman was in her late forties. Expensively dressed, though too extravagantly made up for Phil's taste. At one time she'd probably been a knockout. Now she was holding her looks together with lots of makeup and silicone and a big pile of hair. "Oh, sure! Yeah! Melanie Wadsworth! Hey, good to see you!" Phil moved to the next stool. "What are you doing in Texas? Wait a minute, you must be in town for the same auction that my ex is here for."

"Correct."

"Okay, then, can I buy you a drink?"

Melanie patted at the outlying fringes of her enormous hairdo. "A nightcap would be fine. I was going to have a brandy before bed."

Phil rapped his knuckles on the bar. "Bartender. A brandy for the lady, and bring me a cup of black coffee." He felt his luck changing. Best to have a clear head. "So, Melanie, antique business still going strong? You've got the *numero uno* establishment in San Francisco, if I recall."

Melanie preened herself. "Yes, that's true. I've been fortunate the past few years."

"And smart, I'm sure." Phil believed you couldn't throw too many compliments at any woman.

"One likes to think one is smart. Let's face it, there's a lot of luck to any business."

"You're absolutely right."

Melanie looked him over with her shrewd eyes. "The last time we met, it was in New York about five years ago, you were in the stocks and bonds business and still married to dear Kay."

THE TIME OF THE WOLF

"Well, I'm no longer peddling stocks or married to dear Kay. I've got an idea you already knew that."

"Yes. I knew you were divorced and I did hear you left Wall Street rather, oh, suddenly."

"Got myself jammed up with the SEC." What the hell, she obviously knew the story. "I was making too much money too fast and they didn't appreciate that." He gave a water-over-the-dam shrug. "Doesn't matter. I switched to the restaurant business." He tugged out his wallet and gave her one of the last of his business cards. "I own a chain of fifteen restaurants called *Seis Amigos*—Six Friends. Just opened the latest one in Jamaica."

"Jamaica!" Melanie read the business card with surprise and a deeper interest in him. "How exciting."

"Great little island. Wish I could spend more time there. These days I'm on a busy schedule. My goal is to open a new *Seis Amigos* every month for the next three years. That's why I'm in Austin, to choose a site for a *Seis Amigos* here. This is a great restaurant town, you know."

"I thought you might be in Austin to see Kay." Her sly smile invited him to talk about her.

"Just coincidence that we're both in Texas at the same time. I did have a drink with Kay earlier tonight. She wanted to have dinner with me, but I had to tell her there just isn't anything between us anymore. Wasn't pleasant. She cried, if you want the truth." He lowered his voice and leaned closer to Melanie. "I'm completely on my own here. What about you?"

"Oh, I had a date earlier in the evening. But yes, I'm on my own, too." Melanie moved her shoulders around. "Just a lonely little girl in a strange city. And believe me, any city in Texas is strange."

"Yes, I've noticed a certain crudeness among the citizenry." Melanie's drink was delivered, along with the coffee. Phil made a point of putting a napkin under the glass, arranging the drink just so in front of her, pulling over a bowl of peanuts from farther down the bar, in general providing all the small attentions a woman like Melanie Wadsworth would expect. "Fact is, there's an awful lot of crude people right here in this bar. Maybe you'd prefer to have this drink in your room. Or in mine?"

Melanie was clearly tempted. After a time she said, "I've already had a very active day. And night, if you know what I mean."

"I understand. What about tomorrow?"

"I'm driving to San Antonio in the morning to look at the Alamo and visit the museum there. Business trip. Kay may have told you the auction has to do with an artifact from the Alamo."

"Are you driving to San Antonio on your own?"

"Yes."

"Would you like some company on the trip? I'd be glad to do the driving."

Melanie smiled brightly. "That would be wonderful. We could have a nice chat on the way down. Frankly, I've been wondering why dear Kay looks so grungy and washed out. I'd love to get the scoop on that. And could Kay have told you anything about her bidding plans when you were having that drink with her?"

"Perhaps."

"Then we'll have lots to talk about." Melanie finished her brandy and stood up. "Eight a.m. at the concierge desk?"

"See you then." Phil took a chance and leaned forward to kiss Melanie's cheek. There was no objection. Quite the contrary—they parted with warm glows on both sides.

Phil sat alone for another ten minutes sipping his black coffee and considering ways to pay back Kay for treating him so shabbily. Never let a bitch off the hook—that was one of his cardinal rules. They can wiggle and squirm. But one way or another, you've got to keep them on that old hook. Otherwise you're nothing. He was so deep in thought that he scarcely noticed the large form next to him until Chauncy leaned past him and picked up a book of matches from the bar.

"Meet me out front, we take a walk," Chauncy whispered.

With an aggravated sigh, Phil signed the check—no tip for *this* bartender—and strolled outside. Chauncy was easy to find. A huge bearded black man in a white suit could hardly be missed even when he stood in the shadows.

They strolled toward Congress Avenue and the lighted dome of the capitol building.

"Well, mon, how did you do?"

Phil had a story ready. "I got off to a good start. Kay was surprised as hell to see me, and a little sarcastic to boot. But she warmed up a lot faster than I expected, sent away the guys she was having drinks with, finally agreed to go out to dinner with me. More than dinner, actually. She asked me to come up to her room first. I think she was kind of surprised to find she still had the hots for me, that she actually wanted a nice fuck before dinner."

"Oh, really." Chauncy couldn't believe Phil was trying to sell him this sorry shit. "She say she want to fuck you? Come right out and ask for it?"

"Not in so many words. But hey, I was married to the woman for three years. No, wait a minute. Four years, now that I think about it. I know when Kay wants a fuck. Why else would she invite me up? Well, didn't matter. When we got up there, it turned out her room had been vandalized."

"What?" Chauncy was accustomed to Phil's bullshit, but this was over the top. "Don't wag your tongue so many lies. Tell me what really went on."

"You don't believe me, check it out with the hotel security guy. Name's Ed Halley, some kind of local cracker. Retired cop, none too bright." He told Chauncy what the intruder had done, described the way Kay's clothes had been systematically shredded and the cum stains all over the place. "Well, Kay went ballistic. Broke down completely. You know women, she was totally wiped out. Halley had to move her to another room. He even ordered up a policewoman to spend the night with her, she was so scared. Any chance I had of getting close to Kay this evening went right out the window." He gave Chauncy a sideways glance. "You aren't the one who trashed Kay's room, are you?"

"No." Chauncy wondered where Phil had got that idea. "Sound more like another bidder wants scare your ex-wife out of the auction."

"You think so?" Phil hadn't even considered that possibility. "That wouldn't do us any good."

"No, it wouldn't." Chauncy thinking, *We need information, only a couple of days to get it. If Phil can't deliver, learn anything from his ex, what good he be? I might better cut him loose. Or just cut him period. Wouldn't put any money in my pocket, but it surely make my day.* "You fucked up, my friend. Woman's clothes all cut to ribbons, space violated, she want someone to lean on. Man to comfort her. Perfect opportunity get close to her. You blow it."

Chauncy's narrowed eyes made Phil nervous. He quickly said, "You fucked up, too."

"What you mean?" Cut the man into as many pieces as his ex-wife's underwear.

"You looked over the bidders going into the auction?"

"So what?"

"You should have told me that Kay wasn't the only woman on the inside of this deal."

Chauncy remembered a flashy woman, flashy to cover up the fact she was way past her prime, going into the auction room. "Yeah, there be one other woman. What about her?"

"Her name's Melanie Wadsworth, an antiques dealer from San Francisco, I met her a couple of times when I was married to Kay. Some dinner at the St. Regis in New York. Another time in the bar at the Algonquin."

"Okay," Chauncy said slowly. "What you gonna tell me now? She invite you up to her room, too? But some maniac cut up her panties, empty out her shampoo, break the TV?"

"We met in the bar just before you came in. I'm having breakfast with Melanie tomorrow. Then I'm driving her down to the Alamo in San Antonio. We'll drive back tomorrow. Have dinner together. Have sex after that. Don't act like I'm lying to you. This one's in the bag, Melanie's a vicious little cat and as far as she's concerned I'm Mister Catnip. She also wants to know how high Kay's willing to bid. Fine. I'll make up a figure, feed her some bullshit about Kay's bidding strategy, the kind of stuff I remember from when we were married. By tomorrow night I'll know everything about this auction."

"Sound like a live one," Chauncy admitted.

"One problem, I'm short of cash." Phil looked right into Chauncy's eyes. "That's your department, bro. Get me enough walking-around money so that I can impress Melanie tomorrow. She'll expect an expensive lunch and a present, I can read her like a book."

Chauncy didn't like to have this pretty boy leaning on him. Had to respect him for it, though. *Mon's right, you need money to impress a woman. That what they call universal truth.* "I find us some money, slip it under your door later tonight."

"Where will you get it?" Phil was immediately worried that Chauncy might do something nasty that would bring down both of them.

"Don't worry, mon. Plenty of cash walking around these streets. Stealing a million dollars be dangerous work. Stealing a few hundred just plain fun."

# CHAPTER 13

"More wine?" Scanner held up a bottle of Clos Pegase merlot and waggled it invitingly.

Kay held out her glass. "Just a smidgee."

"How much is a smidgee?"

"Half a smidge."

Scanner smiled. "Got it." He poured about two inches of merlot into her glass and added a like amount to his own, which emptied the bottle. A toast seemed in order. "To Ed Halley. A cop. A Texan. And a complete gentleman."

"Hear! Hear!" Kay joined in the toast.

They were in Kay's new room, sitting back contentedly over the remnants of a fine meal Ed Halley had provided courtesy of the hotel. Texas-sized steaks with Stubbs famous barbecue sauce on the side. Huge baked potatoes smothered in sour cream and chives. Corn on the cob. Hot rolls. For dessert, strawberry cheesecake.

"Great meal." Scanner suppressed a burp. "I could like Texas."

"Me, too." Kay left the table with her wineglass in hand and curled up on the couch across the room. "Come on, move over here." She indicated the easy chair near the couch.

Scanner kicked off his shoes as he moved to the chair and sat down. After a good stretch and another pleasing sip of wine, he said, "Your ex is a very good-looking guy."

"Phil's handsome, smooth, intelligent, and has dozens of ways to make a woman happy." She shrugged. "Unfortunately, Phil is also a spoiled little boy who never grew up, and he'll sleep with any female between the ages of twelve and fifty."

"Twelve?" Scanner thought she must be exaggerating.

Kay looked at him seriously. "He's done that. Almost was indicted for it, but the girl's parents couldn't bring themselves to let their daughter testify in court."

"How did . . ." He let the thought trail off.

"How did I come to marry a guy like that?" Kay sighed so deeply it became a groan. "I was nineteen. Impressionable. At an age when I still took people at face value. Thanks to Phil, I am now three hundred years old. Can we talk about something else?"

"Feel like telling me what you know about Leon Donin?"

"Sure, if you're willing to tell me what you're really doing here. You didn't come to Texas to bid for the knife, Roy. And you aren't some kind of faceless bureaucrat. I saw how Ed Halley reacted to whatever it was you showed him from your wallet. A badge? I'll bet it was a badge."

"Don't look so smug. It wasn't a badge." Scanner dug out his wallet and flipped it open to a government ID card with his photo on it. "Department of the Treasury."

"Department of the *Treasury*." Kay made a face. "What a downer, I thought you were with the FBI or CIA or something exciting. Department of the Treasury sounds . . . well . . . to be honest . . . sort of boring."

"Oh really? Obviously you don't know that the Secret Service is part of the Treasury Department." Realizing he sounded a little testy, maybe even defensive. "That's right, the guys who guard the President himself. But that's not my job. I am in the Secret Service, though. It happens I'm chief investigator for the Secret Service Counterfeit Currency Unit. That's very exciting work, chasing down counterfeiters. Dangerous, too. If you want to know."

By the time he finished, Kay was giggling behind her hand. "I've known you less than a day and I'm already able to rattle your cage. Not bad, huh?"

"Very funny." Scanner feared his face had turned red. He put away his wallet and looked at a spot above Kay's head until he felt his mouth slipping into a smile. "Nice work, you scored a direct hit on my ego. You might as well know that I also batted .404 on my high school baseball team and I was the tallest boy in my graduating class. So there."

"My hero," Kay said in her highest falsetto.

"Don't push it."

Kay finished her wine and put down the glass. "Okay, I'm ready to be serious. You chase counterfeiters for a living. Does that mean someone connected with the auction has something to do with counterfeit money?" She leaned forward. "My God! One of our bidders plans to buy Jim Bowie's knife with counterfeit currency, is that it?"

"Maybe. I don't know that for sure."

"You're interested in Leon Donin. He's the one you're after, the one you suspect. Right?"

Instead of answering, Scanner stood and moved toward the door. "Let me get my paperwork. That'll help me explain my situation, which is sort of complicated. I'll be back in less than five minutes. I'll knock two times, then three times, then once. Don't open the door for anyone else."

He was gone only three minutes, returning with an oversized manila envelope with green hash marks along all four sides and the words REGISTERED CONFIDENTIAL—U.S. SECRET SERVICE stamped on the front.

The idea of looking at Secret Service documents gave Kay a tingly feeling. "Wow. Secret stuff."

"Secret stuff," Scanner agreed. They reseated themselves across from each other and he opened the envelope. The first item to slide out of the envelope was an eight-by-ten black-and-white photo of Leon Donin. An old photo. Maybe fifteen years old, maybe a little more. He was wearing some sort of uniform and he appeared to have twisted his face into an unusually stern expression for the camera.

"Leon Donin," Kay said.

"That's the name on the diplomatic passport he used to enter the U.S. When that photo was taken back in the eighties he was Major Nicolai Leontin, commander of a Russian battalion of infantry in Afghanistan." He showed her a sheaf of documents, some of which were in Russian and some in English. "Donin, let's call him that instead of Leontin because it's the name he's using here in Texas, is a graduate of the University of Moscow. He studied English and fine arts but on graduation went into the Russian Army as an officer candidate. He did well. Promoted to lieutenant quickly. By the time he became a captain, the war had started in Afghanistan. He was sent there. Earned himself a field promotion to major because he was absolutely ruthless. He led a battalion that probably killed more Afghans than any other Russian unit. Executions of suspected rebels. Torture. Burning of whole villages. There wasn't anything he wouldn't do. Didn't help, the Russians still lost that war because the Afghan rebels were just as ruthless. After the war, Donin left the army and joined a small merchant bank in Moscow, a bank that was soon bought up by the Russian mafia. With his earlier training in fine arts and his command of English, Donin was recruited to work the mafia's racket to loot national treasures and sell them abroad. Over the last couple of years they've combined that racket with pushing counterfeit U.S. currency. That's why I need whatever information you might have on Donin."

"Well, I met him a couple of weeks ago in Singapore." Since Roy was now willing to exchange information, Kay saw no reason to hold back what little information she had. "He was using his real name, Nicolai Leontin. I bought a Fabergé egg from him for an American client. The egg was genuine. In fair condition."

"Tell me about the transaction." Scanner took out a small notebook to make notes.

She recounted the circumstances under which she purchased the Fabergé egg, including her suspicions that Donin, or Leontin, whatever his name, might have obtained that particular antique from one of the old established Moscow museums. Perhaps even the Russian National Museum, which was known to have an impressive collection of Fabergé creations. "He was a tough bargainer, but he didn't use any unethical tactics. I didn't like him. I spotted him for a thug right away. I've heard of the Russian mafia," she said. "They're rumored to be looting the museums there with the help of highly placed government officials. I don't like to buy items that come on the market that way, but I had no proof that Leontin, Donin, is part of that racket."

"There's no question that he is. He's got two complementary rackets. He and his group sell some antiques to generate cash that helps finance his other operations, which include but aren't limited to counterfeiting. We think he came into the U.S. carrying a suitcase full of counterfeit hundred-dollar bills."

"Then arrest him!" Kay was irritated at what she saw as typical government slowness in taking action.

Scanner shaking his head. "The bum has a diplomatic passport. He can go where he wants, do what he wants, I can't touch him. Can't even search his luggage."

"All right. I've heard of diplomatic immunity, that makes things tougher for you." Kay sat up ramrod-straight. "And for me! If he can just print money, he can top anybody's bid for the Bowie knife! Damn him!" A further thought. "But you'll be at the auction, you can examine the currency and arrest him, or at least confiscate the counterfeit, if that's what he's planning to do. Can't you? That's why you're here, right?"

"Yeah . . . sure . . . except for one thing."

"What *thing?*"

"The hundred-dollar bills these people print can be so good that they're indistinguishable from genuine U.S. currency."

"You can't be serious." Kay laughed at the idea. "You must have experts, special tests, chemicals, ways of telling genuine paper from counterfeit paper. I mean, U.S. money is printed with special ink and paper, right?"

"Right. But technology has caught up with us. One reason Donin has been selling antiques like that Fabergé egg is to buy the best counterfeiting technology and talent on the world market."

"You mean the Russians can print genuine U.S. currency?"

"Not the Russians. It's the Syrians who are behind this scheme, the Russians are just their marketing arm. The Syrians hate the U.S. They've got a state-of-the-art printing plant somewhere in Lebanon's Bekaa Valley, which is controlled by Syria, the same region Syria uses to process drugs for the world market. The Syrians have been working with the Russian mafia to flood the U.S. with fake hundred-dollar bills. Really good product. Paper just like ours. Sequential serial numbers that match original bills. Ink that matches the special ink used by the Treasury to print our own currency. Great counterfeit, best we've ever seen. In fact, we called their product Supernotes."

Scanner took out two plastic pages, each of which held a hundred-dollar bill, one marked A and the other B. "A is genuine U.S. currency. B is fake. We were able to identify the fake only because the Syrians let a flaw slip by in this particular bill, a tiny speck of dirt in one corner."

Kay couldn't tell the difference between the bills, though she was certainly no expert. "How did you keep this out of the newspapers?"

"We've been lucky. There have been a few stories, but it's so bizarre that people don't seem to take it seriously. As long as the money in their own pockets is good at the supermarket or local bank, that's all most folks care about."

"What have you been doing to stop the counterfeiting?"

"A lot. Remember when the hundred-dollar bill was changed just a few years ago? A totally new design?"

Kay did remember. "Poor old Ben Franklin is off-center on the new hundreds."

"We had to introduce a newly designed hundred-dollar bill in order to ruin the scheme the Syrians had to destabilize U.S. currency. The problem had gotten so bad that banks in London, Tokyo, Paris and other capitals were refusing to accept U.S. hundred-dollar bills for fear of taking big losses. It's estimated that two hundred million dollars of bad currency was accepted by Hong Kong banks alone. We were pretty sure that Russian banks, many of which are now controlled by the Russian mafia, fed a lot of counterfeit into the world's financial system. So we changed our hundred-dollar bill.

"The change worked. The new hundred has driven the old bills out of the market. The new bill with Ben Franklin off center has a lot of other technical changes as well. A new watermark. A splotch of ink that shifts from green to black when it's viewed from different angles. A better paper that's really tough to duplicate because of the multicolored polymer threads built into it. We're using the same paper in our fifty- and twenty-dollar bills, too. That stopped the Syrians and the Russians, at least until now."

Kay had been following Roy's story as if it were a particularly well-told fairy tale. "You think they've found a way to beat our new hundred-dollar bill?"

"I think Donin is here to test-market a new counterfeit U.S. hundred-dollar bill. If he can pass his Supernote in this deal, and we know Stewart Ruddington won't accept cash as payment for the Bowie knife without running it past an Austin bank, then the Russian banks can begin feeding their new counterfeit into the economy."

"If he outbids the rest of us and hands over the money, you can confiscate it."

Scanner smiled ruefully. "Yeah, if I can prove it's counterfeit. But what if the new fakes are as good as the old? What if a banker can't tell the Supernotes from the real thing? I don't think the Russians or Syrians would put new fake U.S. currency on the market unless it's really good stuff."

"How? When you've got this new high-tech paper and all?" Kay was beginning to worry about the money in her own purse. If you couldn't trust U.S. money, what could you trust?

"Russian banks have bought up a huge supply of crisp new U.S. twenty-dollar bills over the past year. We think they're sending most of those twenty-dollar bills to Syria, where they're bleached so they can be reprinted as hundred-dollar bills. That's an old counterfeiter's trick, bleaching a low-denomination bill and reprinting it in a higher denomination. With genuine paper they're halfway home."

"Oh my. And to think that all these years I've only been worrying about fake antiques."

"I'm not saying the Syrians and Russians can bankrupt America with fake hundred-dollar bills," Scanner said. "Cash is only a minor part of our economy anymore. Most of the wealth of the country is in stocks, bonds and other financial instruments and most business is done through electronic transfers. But for a long time now the U.S. dollar has been the most trusted financial instrument in the world. These guys have the technology to debase U.S. currency, making our cash look suspect in the global economy, giving our whole economic system a black eye and at the same time enriching themselves at our expense."

"And maybe costing my client the ownership of the Bowie knife." Kay saw Scanner frown and added, "I know that's small potatoes to you, no big deal in comparison with *debasing U.S. currency*, but we're talking about what I do for a living. Donin could cost me a big commission and disappoint a client who's depending on me. That's a very big deal to me." Kay had a thought. "Why don't I go to Stewart Ruddington, tell him Donin is here under a fake name, I have evidence he's also part of the Russian mafia. I wouldn't even have to mention the possibility of fake currency. Stewart is very sensitive about his reputation. Any hint he'd let a Russian racketeer take part in one of his private auctions could cost him clients."

"That's why Donin's trying to drive you out of Austin. He sent Wolf to cut up your clothes, send you home crying before you could say anything to Ruddington that would get him dumped from the auction."

"Are you absolutely certain Wolf is the one?" Kay had been thinking that Melanie Wadsworth might be behind the vandalism, that she'd hired someone to do the job. Melanie was known to have pulled dirty tricks on competitors.

"This afternoon I called Washington to have Bud Wolf's criminal record pulled and faxed to me." Scanner slid a few more pages out of the envelope and showed them to Kay. They seemed to be pages of arrest records, each headed with a photo of Bud Wolf staring into a camera, sometimes with a grim expression and on other pages with a cocky smile. Several of the pages carried Wolf's fingerprints. "Wolf has a long history of arrests for all kinds of shit. Interstate hijacking. Murder. Extortion. Suborning a witness in a federal prosecution. Receiving stolen goods. Even plain old auto theft. But Wolf is smart, he's never been convicted of any crime. He was brought to trial only once, seven years ago in Missouri, for the murder of a trucking company executive. The trial was called off when the key witness had an 'accident' the day the trial started. The witness drowned in his own bathtub in about eight inches of water. That's Bud Wolf in a nutshell. Oh, he's known to like working on people with knives. Explains why he got so hot over that Bowie knife."

Kay shivered at the thought of a man like that standing in her room, probably grinning as he fingered her underwear and then cut it to ribbons. "Okay, you've convinced me. So where do we go from here? I should say, where do *you* go. I'm here to buy an antique, not to arrest anyone or to confiscate counterfeit money. I'd like to help you, but I can't see what use I'd be."

"I've been looking for a way to get hold of one of Donin's hundred-dollar bills before the auction. Thought you might be able to help. Any ideas?"

*He must be desperate,* Kay was thinking, *if he's looking to me for help.* "Not offhand." It came to her that Roy wouldn't ask such a question if he didn't have at least half an answer. "I'll bet you've got an idea, though."

Scanner stretched his long legs. "You could drop a little rumor in Stewart Ruddington's ear."

"What kind of rumor?"

"That if Donin wins the auction, he intends to pay for the Bowie knife with Russian rubles. Nobody wants rubles, they're almost worthless outside of Russia. If you dropped the rumor in the right way, you could scare the hell out of Ruddington. Get him to demand that Donin show him what kind of currency he brought in from Russia. That might give us a chance to get a hold of one of those new hundreds. Just one, that's all I need. I'd courier it to our lab in Washington. It would only take a few hours to find out whether there's a test that can tell Donin's new counterfeit from the real thing."

"What if Donin's bills are so good your lab can't say they're counterfeit? For that matter, what if Donin is using genuine U.S. currency? That's always a possibility, isn't it?"

"Doubtful." Scanner was reluctant to admit Donin could outsmart him. "I don't think he gives a damn about Old Bowie except as something valuable that he can exchange for a large sum of counterfeit."

"I don't mind talking to Stewart." Kay decided that Roy's agenda dovetailed with her own. If she could discredit Donin, why not do so? One less competitor in the auction. Nothing unethical about pointing out that Donin was a snake, a snake with two names. And Donin's bodyguard Bud Wolf was just as bad. A thug and worse yet—at least from her perspective—a desecrator of pantyhose! On the other hand, it might not be smart to let Roy drag her into such a dangerous game. "I just can't afford to get too involved."

"You already are involved."

"I don't see any reason to get in still deeper. This is just one auction. I don't want it to be my last."

"Suppose I throw in some bonus points?" He took a card key out of his pocket, tossed it in the air a couple of times. "I showed Ed Halley the backgrounds on Donin and Wolf and he offered to loan me a master card key. I've already used it to search Wolf's room, nothing incriminating there. Donin's asleep in his own room right now, so I can't get in there tonight. I am going to search that room first thing in the morning, while he's at breakfast. I doubt he's left any counterfeit money laying around, but I might find something of help. Here's my idea—how would you like to pay a visit to Bud Wolf's room with me? Bring along a pair of scissors?" Scanner lifted an eyebrow. "He had two pairs of pants in his closet, plus some boxer shorts."

Kay sat up straight. "Oh my." Visions of creating havoc in Wolf's room. "What a deliciously evil idea. When could we do that?"

"We might be able to slip in there right now. Wolf left the hotel about an hour ago. Halley's got people watching the two main hotel entrances for him, plus the elevator from the basement." He picked up Kay's phone and punched a four-digit extension. "Ed? Roy Scanner here. First of all, the meal was great, we both enjoyed it. Thanks again. Second, I'd like to get into Wolf's room once more for a few minutes. Is he still out of the hotel? No, I'll be inside the room less than five minutes. Okay. Sure. You will? That's great, I owe you a big one."

"Well?"

"Wolf hasn't come back to the hotel. If he returns within the next ten minutes, Halley'll keep him occupied long enough for us to get in and out of his room. Got a pair of scissors?"

"No." Kay's excitement was immediately dampened. "Just nail scissors. They won't work."

Scanner took out his Swiss Army pocketknife. "Use this."

She grabbed the knife and stepped into a pair of loafers. "Let's go, I don't want to miss this chance."

Before she could leave the room, Scanner took her firmly by the arm. "You'll make that call to Stewart Ruddington for me?"

"You're a darling man." She kissed him on the cheek. "I'll call Stewart as soon as we get back from making some *alterations* to Mr. Wolf's wardrobe."

# CHAPTER 14

K azuo Goto had arranged a pleasant evening for himself. At 7:00 P.M. he went to the suite on the fourth floor where his mistress, Kimiko, was staying. His own suite was on the seventh floor, which followed one of the many dictums of Goto's late father: *When traveling with both your wife and mistress, always keep at least a three-floor interval between the two.*

Although Goto's father had been dead for twenty-two years, Goto zealously followed his advice about business, sex, politics and the achievement of family harmony. It wasn't that Goto had no ideas of his own. On the contrary, his mind was fertile and his ego strong. He had used his own drive and ideas to build the medium-sized corporation inherited from his father into the second-largest insurance company in Japan.

When he joined Kimiko in her suite, she bathed him and then massaged his back and feet, poured warm sake, put out a small plate of sushi and read poetry to him while he enjoyed the food and drink. Finally they laid down for sex, which, as usual, Kimiko drew out for more than an hour through a series of sensual games and inventive uses of her tongue. Very exciting. At one point it became a bit too exciting. Angina pains struck Goto's chest and he had to lie back for a while with a nitro tablet under his tongue. Kimiko lay with him, keeping his forehead cool with a wet cloth and calming his worries with gentle kisses and caresses. Soon the pain subsided, but it would be back. One day in the not too distant future his heart would clutch up and cease to function. He did not fear that future day so much as regret it.

When the angina had definitely left him, he and Kimiko completed their sexual interlude. The sex was as good as ever. Goto was proud that despite his illness and his sixty-eight years he was still able to satisfy a beautiful girl like Kimiko. He wasn't fool enough to think that all of Kimiko's gasps of pleasure were genuine. She was, after all, a professional mistress trained by one of the best geisha houses in Kyoto, but Goto believed that her affection for him, and her pleasure in their sex, had a core of honesty.

By eight-thirty Goto was back in his own suite with his wife, Eiko, looking at a videotape that had arrived by DHL from their son in Japan of their grandchildren enjoying a day at the Tokyo Disneyland. They both laughed when little Risako kissed the statue of Mickey Mouse near the entrance to Frontierland. A light dinner was served. After dinner Eiko retired to her own room and Goto phoned Shimu Shibata, his executive assistant, and asked him to come to his suite.

"Good evening, Goto-san." Shibata bowed as he came into the suite. "You look well tonight. Even so, Dr. Watanabe would like to examine you this evening."

"Yes, yes." He didn't like to be constantly reminded of his precarious health. It was annoying, though necessary, to travel with a personal physician. More annoying to be examined at the beginning and end of each business day. "I'll see Dr. Watanabe after our meeting. Now let's get down to business. First, tell me how the project is going. Then we'll discuss the auction."

The project, as Goto was prone to call it, was the construction of what would be called the Kazuo Goto Museum of Antique Weaponry. The site of the museum was a square block in Harajaku, one of the most fashionable and expensive neighborhoods in Tokyo.

"Construction is on schedule and the interior designers are already at work painting the exhibition halls and setting up the display cases, video theater and library." Shibata showed him photos of the workmen's progress.

Goto beamed. "Excellent, very fine." Beautiful workmanship, no expense spared. Most of his personal fortune was going into the project. He wanted a museum that would be appreciated not only by the Japanese people, but by visitors from other countries, an international museum of the highest quality. "Any new acquisitions?"

Shibata took out a second batch of photos and spread them on the coffee table. "The Acquisition Committee has purchased the following pieces.

"A Soshu School long sword manufactured in the twelfth century in Kamakura, probably when Minamoto Yorimoto was the shogun. From the information that can be read on the *tang*, it appears to be the work of the smith who called himself Hoyuku.

"A collection of hilt ornaments from the fifteenth century.

"A shobu-suzuki short sword from the Muromachi period, probably forged around 1500."

"And from the West we have a very fine dagger with a buffalo horn grip made in San Francisco between 1890 and 1900.

"This is a boot knife made in France in the same period; note the beautiful spiraled blackwood grip.

"Here, a medieval short sword made in Sheffield, England. Iron, of course. Not very sharp, but so extraordinarily heavy that it was lethal against chain mail and even the armor worn by knights of the period."

There were several other pieces of equal interest to Goto, swords and knives from Arabia, Spain, Germany, Peru, Indonesia. "Good choice," he would say in a whisper as Shibata showed him a photo. "Excellent piece." "Yes, that will fit nicely into the collection." "Our first exhibit from Indonesia! Excellent."

Once they had finished with the new acquisitions, they moved on to this particular auction. "I want Old Bowie very badly."

"I understand, Goto-san."

"It will be the centerpiece of my museum. Jim Bowie is known throughout the world, the only man in history to be made famous by the knife he carried. So tell me what information you've gathered about our bidders." Goto personally poured a strong scotch for each of them. Shibata was a very hard-working executive assistant, he deserved some pampering.

"I used our business and government contacts to gather intelligence on the bidders. I've also paid bellmen and other staff at this hotel and the Driskill to feed anything they hear about the bidders to me. One development was just reported to me. Kay Williams changed her room earlier this evening—for a very interesting reason. It seems likely that Leon Donin's bodyguard vandalized all the clothing in her room earlier today in an effort to scare her out of the auction."

7

"Russians." Goto shrugged. "They have no subtlety. Why did Donin target Miss Williams? I would say she has only a small chance of success."

"It appears she had met Donin before. At the time Donin was using his real name. It seems he's a member of the Russian mafia. He may be planning to pay for the Bowie knife with new counterfeit hundred-dollar bills. Do you remember all the counterfeit U.S. hundreds that turned up in Tokyo a few years ago?"

"Indeed I do. Our banker friends were hard hit by them."

"These may be of equal quality."

"Ah, I see an opportunity to solidify our relationship with Mitsubishi Bank. If I privately warn them of the possibility of a new counterfeit Supernote showing up in the Japanese economy, they can take precautions in advance of their competitors. Then, if I need another loan, they can hardly refuse." This was good intelligence, the kind of information Goto was always happy to pay for. Building his museum had cost him a fortune and eroded his credit standing. Another loan would definitely be needed before the project could be completed.

Though Shibata made no comment, he was privately worried that Goto had overextended himself in his passion to build his museum. "Goto-san, I have never asked you this—why are you so determined to build the museum? What I should say is, what prompted your great interest in swords and knives?"

Goto didn't mind the question. It was a story he liked to tell. "You may have heard that I was one of the first businessmen in Japan to take a strong stand against the Yakuza. The Yamaguchi-gumi gang used to send *sokaiya*, extortionists, to demand protection money. They would threaten our salespeople, break up our corporate annual meetings, do anything they could think of to make us pay them. One day I just stopped paying them. I was young, my father had just died and I was determined to make the company more profitable than ever."

He sat back and sipped on his scotch. "I realized that was risky, so I began carrying a knife for protection. I wanted to carry a gun, but the local police wouldn't give me a permit. The police are in the pocket of the Yakuza, after all. One day I was leaving my house and walking towards my car when a man stepped out from behind a wall and shot my driver. I was rushing to my driver's side when the assassin ran up and tried to shoot me, too. I was the main target, after all. His first shot went wide. I jumped up, grabbed the knife from my coat pocket and stabbed the assassin in the chest. Then I stabbed him again. And again. And again. Stabbed him many times over until I was certain he was dead. I looked down at my hands, they were covered with blood. Do you know what I did? I kissed my bloody hands. That brush with death transformed me. Not one day since then has the prospect of death terrorized me." A thin smile. "All the newspapers ran stories. I was on television. The Yamaguchi-gumi was disgraced by the fact that a young insurance executive had killed their professional assassin. I was never bothered by the *sokaiya* again."

Shibata was truly impressed.

"I still carry that same knife." Goto lifted his right leg to reveal a ten-inch stiletto with an ivory grip strapped to his calf in a leather scabbard. "Since the day I killed the assassin, I've been very interested in knives and swords. Many say I'm obsessed with them. Probably true. Do I sound morbid to you, Shibata-san?"

Goto did sound morbid, but Shibata shook his head. "Did your driver survive?"

"No, he died right there on the sidewalk."

Shibata wasn't surprised. The employees of wealthy men are expendable.

"Now," Goto said, "tell me what you've learned from the listening devices. I'm especially interested in any clues as to how high each bidder is authorized to go."

Shibata gave a capsule report on each bidder:

Roy Scanner—Undercover Treasury Department agent . . . not a legitimate bidder . . . target Leon Donin . . . frequently on the phone to Washington. . . . Donin may be carrying large amounts of counterfeit currency . . . information obtained from Japanese embassy in Washington, D.C.

Leon Donin—Well-financed . . . Russian national . . . former army officer . . . real name Nicolai Leontin . . . bodyguard Bud Wolf . . . may be carrying as much as three million dollars in either genuine or counterfeit U.S. hundred-dollar bills . . . known member of Russian mafia . . . protected by diplomatic passport.

Kay Williams—Represents Billy Boy Watkins, prominent Louisiana oil man and collector of antique knives and guns . . . has dealt with Leon Donin before . . . may be authorized to bid as high as two million dollars . . . under harassment by Leon Donin . . . also under pressure by ex-husband . . . information obtained by private detective in New Orleans who learned that Mr. Watkins has withdrawn that amount from his bank in the form of bearer bonds.

Melanie Wadsworth—small but respected antiques shop in San Francisco . . . exclusive clientele . . . known to be a ruthless and sometimes underhanded competitor . . . may on occasion use sex as a business weapon . . . never known to pay more than eight hundred thousand U.S. dollars for an antique.

Arthur Ward—Independently wealthy collector . . . wide-ranging tastes . . . no specific interest in knives or other weapons . . . tends to overbid when drinking . . . original fortune severely reduced by several marriages and divorces . . . has never bid more than two million dollars for an antique . . . not expected to exceed that bid at this auction . . . drinks heavily.

When Shibata had finished his report, Goto nodded approvingly. "Very succinct. It appears I must be prepared to bid in the low three-million-dollar range to win this prize. I hadn't expected to go that high."

"Goto-san, please excuse me, I worry that you are overextending yourself. The latest figures indicate that costs for building your museum and acquiring a first-class collection may now exceed fifty million U.S. dollars. That does not include the trust fund for the museum's annual upkeep."

Goto waved his hand as if the figure were nothing. "I would say the final amount will be more than fifty million." He shrugged. "What if it is? My son will take over the company and is already well on his way to making his own fortune. I have put money aside for my wife and grandchildren. Let's be realistic, my health is so precarious I may not even live to see the museum open."

"No," Shibata argued. "The doctors say you may live for many years."

"It's in their interest to tell me that. Shibata-san, we are in the insurance business, are we not? Have you looked at our actuarial tables lately? Statistically speaking, I am a dead man already." He laughed. "Don't look so grim. I have come to terms with my approaching demise, why can't you?" Goto poured another scotch and paused to admire its smoky color. "Call the Mitsubishi Bank tonight." He looked at his watch. "It is now ten a.m. tomorrow morning in Tokyo. Talk to Furawa-san, tell him what you've learned about the possibility of a new counterfeit U.S. hundred-dollar bill coming on the market. Then tell him I may need another million U.S. dollars for this transaction. He will be reluctant at first, but the loan will be approved. Go ahead, do that. I'm going to retire for the evening."

When his executive assistant bowed and left the suite, Goto allowed his calm and confident manner to erode. Worry lines appeared around his eyes and his shoulders sagged. Fifty million dollars. Probably more. This was beyond his original dream. Building the museum was an incredible *ego trip*, as the young people liked to say, talking like the damned *gaijins* they admired so much. Shibata was right, the project would probably ruin him financially. However, it was too late to stop. Instinct told him that the Bowie knife would draw more people to his museum than the rest of the collection combined. His dream rested on its acquisition.

*I will have that knife*, he promised himself. *Or die trying*.

# CHAPTER 15

Chauncy walked up and down Sixth Street looking for easy money. The phrase "easy money" was one he often used, though he didn't really believe in the concept. *Nothing be easy about money*, he thought. *Not in this old cowboy town or anywhere else. Money hard. Hard to come by, hard to keep. The other phrase, "hard cash," more realistic.* "You got any hard cash on you?" He'd heard that all his life.

For once Chauncy wasn't wearing his white suit. Instead he was dressed in black pants, dark blue silk shirt, black shoes. With the .38 Taurus in his pocket. Looking for easy money, hard cash, whatever you wanted to call it.

The trouble was that these days everybody carried credit cards instead of cash. Spotting a mark with cash in his pocket takes a practiced eye. Chauncy knew he had the eye. But there weren't enough marks. Plenty people on Sixth Street. People by the hundreds. Bumping shoulders, most of them with a nice buzz on. Students, lot of them, from the University of Texas. Bars going strong, police had even blocked off the cross-streets so the crowd could overflow into the street itself. People yelling. Pickups cruising the side streets. Music drifting from the clubs. Country and western. Jazz riffs. Blues. Rock and roll. The avenue have it all.

Trouble was, college kids never carry much money. Chauncy looked at them, kids in T-shirts and khaki shorts, sandals too, or worn sneakers, or scuffed old cowboy boots. Fifty dollars a lot of money to most of them.

Chauncy brightened. Okay, so most kids have only a couple crumpled twenties in their pockets. How do they spend their piddling little bankrolls? Liquor, sure. But dope, too. Must be dealers on a street like this.

He stepped off Sixth Street onto Nueces and found a doorway to stand in. From the shadows he could see the flow of traffic on Sixth, watch the folks enjoy themselves. Plenty girls moving up and down the street, beer bottles in their hands, "longnecks" they called them around here. Lone Star. Pearl. Shiner Bock. Texas beers. Chauncy leaning against the door frame, liking the quiet he'd found for himself, smiling at the wolf packs of young guys hitting on the girls.

*One dealer be all I need. Not even a big-timer. Score five hundred, that be plenty. Just enough for Phil to impress Lady Melanie, maybe put a little money in my own pocket, too. No fun counting change all the time.*

After about twenty minutes he noticed three college kids scuttling up Nueces with their heads together. One tall, blond, broad-shouldered, wearing a HOOK 'EM HORNS T-shirt and jeans. The second small, rat-faced, dirty clothes, a born hanger-on. The third appeared sort of prosperous because he was fat as a hot air balloon, looked like he might explode. All three with their hands in their pockets, pulling out crumpled bills. Pooling their assets. A corporation looking for a connection.

He followed on his side of the street, staying in shadows when he could. No problem there, the neighborhood got darker and grungier to the south of Sixth Street. Warehouses. Machine shops. Garages. All of them closed at this hour.

Three blocks further on, the corporation slowed and finally stopped in their very own block of shadows. Chauncy knew this game, too—Waiting for the Connection.

Cars cruised down Nueces. One of them, an old dented Chevy primed to be painted one of these days, maybe, came by twice. Then a third time. Guy behind the wheel had long hair, early thirties maybe, great big nose shaped like a beak, hadn't shaved in a couple of days, head going round and round like the beam from a lighthouse. Man might as well wear a sign on his chest—I AM THE CONNECTION. Chauncy decided to call him The Nose Man.

On his third pass, The Nose Man slowed and pulled over to where the kids were waiting. They came out to the car, the big blond guy in the lead, stuck his head in the window, CEO of the corporation.

The deal went down, money exchanged, dope peddled, the blond guy pranced down the street with his pals in tow, all of them happy as pigs because they'd scored.

Chauncy stayed put. The Nose Man had the imagination of a dead flashlight battery, he'd keep on cruising, find customers along the side streets, work the streets until four or five in the morning. Chauncy knew because he'd done the same kind of work when he was younger. Liked to think he'd done it better than The Nose Man, that he'd had some flash, looked cool to the ladies, at least.

*Mon, the ladies. How many times I trade dope for a fast fuck?* Too many times, lucky to make his nut most weeks.

Chauncy moved to the next block and found another dark doorway. Chewed a stick of Juicy Fruit while he waited.

It took a half-hour for The Nose Man to make another run along Nueces Street. When he saw the beat-up old Chevy coming, Chauncy spit out his gum and staggered into the street. Waved his arms drunkenly and sang an old Harry Belafonte tune at the top of his voice: "Sad to say . . . on my way . . . won't be back for many a day . . ."

Got himself positioned, lurched into the front end of the Chevy before The Nose Man could hit his brakes. Screamed when the car hit him. Fell down below the hood line, too low for The Nose Man to see him.

"Hey, you. Nigger! What the hell you think you're doing?" The Nose Man jumped out of his car, looked around the dark street, not wanting any cops, not interested in trouble of any kind, no intention of reporting an accident. Just wanted to make sure the nigger wasn't hanging on his grill, hadn't ruined the front end. One quick check and he'd drive away, leave the nigger in the street for somebody else to run over.

He came around the car and was momentarily blinded by his own headlights.

"Don't move, mon." In that moment Chauncy put the barrel of his Taurus against The Nose Man's throat. "Don't say word one either. Let me get up slow, don't want twist my ankle."

"What is this?"

Chauncy was on his feet. "This a takeoff, Nose Man. Don't be antsy or I shoot you, take your money, drive away in your own car. Stay quiet and live. Got that?"

The Nose Man took a second to think it over, nodded.

Chauncy led him to the driver's side, shoved him in. "Keep your hands on dash. Move your hands, you dead. Got that too?"

The nod came more quickly, The Nose Man learning the drill fast enough. Chauncy went around the car with his eye on The Nose Man, who clearly wanted to make a fight of it but couldn't find the nerve to take his hands off the dash, reach for a weapon. "Keep the hands right up there." Chauncy slid into the passenger seat, patted him down, found nothing. "Where be your piece?"

"I don't carry a gun."

"Mon, don't lie to me." The Nose Man was wearing highly polished black cowboy boots with silver toes. "Which boot?" Dug the barrel of the Taurus into his side.

The Nose Man's eyes spun. "Shit, my right boot."

Chauncy reached into the boot and relieved him of a .25-caliber Beretta automatic. "Okay, start driving. Don't go too fast, don't jump any red lights, don't attract attention. Hear me?"

"I hear ya," The Nose Man grumbled.

"Big park nearby, Zilker Park? I walk up past there this afternoon. Head for the park, I let you go when we get there, Nose Man."

"What's this Nose Man shit? I got a big nose, so what? You don't have to make fun."

"Sorry." Chauncy hadn't meant anything by it. "You ought not say *nigger*, either. I got my sensibilities, too."

"My name's Harry."

"Okay, Harry. No more Nose Man, that be a promise."

"Lots of guys got bigger noses than me."

"Very true."

"People been making fun of me all my life, I hate it."

Chauncy nodded, tired of the subject. But the dealer was just warming up.

"You knew how it feels to have a honker like this, you'd be more sensitive. I went to see that play, *Cyrano de Bergerac*? Now that guy had a big nose, mine's a button by comparison. I catch people staring at my nose, I slap 'em down. Lucky for you that you've got that gun."

"I tell you . . . *Harry* . . . no more Nose Man talk. Now shut your mouth, drive. Stay between thirty and thirty-five."

Harry risked a sidelong glance at Chauncy. "You're crazy to do this. You know who I work for?"

"Don't know, don't care."

"I work for Ho Ho Gomez."

"That a real name or you laughing at me?"

"You know who Ho Ho is. Everybody from San Antonio to Waco knows Ho Ho Gomez."

"I be from out of town."

Harry's face shone with enlightenment. "You're just passing through Austin, needed some dough, decided to take me off."

"That about it."

"I know that accent. One of those Caribbean islands, right? Place with real white beaches? One of those voodoo places, they cut the heads off chickens and drink off their blood, kiss snakes, that kinda thing?"

Chauncy always marveled at how little people knew about his part of the world. "You be correct, Harry. That what we do. Matter of fact, I had myself some chicken blood couple of hours ago."

"Hey, no offense."

"Park right across the river?"

"Yeah, we're almost there. Look, buddy, this is a mistake. Ho Ho may sound like a funny name to you, but the guy's a total badass. Personally killed four people I know of. You take me off, he'll hunt you down. Hire guys to find you. Bad for business to let you get away with something like this, you see where he's coming from?"

"Sure, I been in your business myself."

"Then you know."

"I do. But I need the money."

"I'm not even carrying all that much."

"Not to worry, I get by with whatever you give me. Won't even take your product, just need some fast cash."

"I can get you a job with Ho Ho."

"Working for a mon named Ho Ho Gomez not exactly my life's ambition." They were into the park now and Chauncy was looking for a good spot. "Pull into the parking lot, stop over there where there be no lights. Near the playground equipment, see where I point?"

The Nose Man was starting to sweat and smelling bad from it. He smelled some of fear, but mostly he smelled from going his whole life not showering more than a couple times a week. Chauncy was looking forward to getting out of the car.

"You're going to let me go, you said. No way I can hurt you if you're on your way out of town."

"Mon, I know that. Don't worry so much."

They stopped in a dark spot, just enough moon for them to be able to see each other's face pretty well.

"Pass over your cash." Chauncy had checked the Beretta, found it loaded, round in the chamber, put it to Harry's head. "Do it slow."

"Got you." The Nose Man moved as slowly as a mime as he slid a hand into his shirt pocket and extracted a thin sheaf of bills, which he handed to Chauncy.

"Rest of it, too."

"Whaddaya mean?"

Chauncy smiled. "Twelve years old, I sell dope on the streets of Mo' Bay, great education. Boss tell me never carry cash in one bundle, split into three stashes. I know Ho Ho tell you the same. Pass it over real slow."

With a tortured sigh, Harry took his time to produce two more sheafs of bills, each one folded in half. "That's all of it."

Chauncy pulled the trigger. The .25 caliber round knocked Harry's head sideways into the window. He fired a second bullet into The Nose Man's brain just for insurance, causing the body to slide down the seat until it became jammed under the steering wheel. Nice little gun, the .25 Beretta. Not much noise at all.

With the money stuffed into his pants pocket, Chauncy slid carefully out of the Chevy and closed the door with his knee. The only place he'd touched with his hand was the door frame when he'd gotten into the car real fast in order to keep The Nose Man covered. He pulled out his shirt-tail and used it to wipe down that spot on the door frame.

You could hear the flow of water a few yards away, the Colorado River running right through the park. Chauncy walked quickly to the river's edge, wiping down the Beretta with his shirttail. He picked up a big leaf from the ground, wrapped it around the Beretta so he wouldn't leave any fingerprints when he threw away the gun, tossed the pistol along with the leaf into the center of the river.

He figured a two-mile walk back to the hotel, just a nice stroll on a pleasant night.

Wolf had left the hotel to have a couple of beers. While he was out, he called Emma to make sure Bud Junior was doing his chores. "You've got to stay on him every minute, Emma. The kid is lazy, you know that."

"He's not lazy," Emma said. "You give him too much to do."

THE TIME OF THE WOLF

"Bullshit, he doesn't work half as hard as I did when I was his age. How are the girls?"

"Just fine."

"They miss me?"

"Yes, I'm sure they do," Emma said mechanically.

"Tell 'em their daddy misses them, too."

"I will."

*I'll bet you will*, Wolf thought. "You miss me, Emma?"

She struggled for an answer, finally said, "When will you be home?"

"Few days." He never told Emma exactly when he'd be home. Better to let her worry he might pop in any time. "Tell Bud Junior he'll feel my belt on his back if he doesn't get those fences painted. Call you tomorrow."

"All right."

Wolf walked the streets for a while, went into one bar to listen to country music, drank another beer, then headed back to the Omni. As he approached the hotel entrance, a tall, husky black guy in dark clothes went through the revolving door ahead of him. *Familiar. Where'd I see that guy? Yeah, he was talkin' with Kay Williams's ex-husband outside the hotel. Wearin' a white suit then. They knew each other real good, too. Yappin' at each other like long-lost friends. Or like long-lost enemies, some kinda heat between them. Kay Williams's ex and a big black dude who's . . . uh-huh . . . that sag in his right-hand pocket has to be a gun Well, I'll be dipped in shit, we got us a whaddayacallit—conspiracy.*

For the hell of it, Wolf stepped into the elevator with the black dude and rode up with him, curious to find out what floor he was on. Guy pushed the button for the fifth floor, Wolf hit the eighth floor button. Looked straight ahead, no eye contact. No chitchat. He did sneak a peek at the guy's right-hand pocket, confirmed he was carrying a piece. When they reached the fifth floor, the black guy stepped out and Wolf stayed put until the elevator door was almost closed. He put his hand between the doors just as they were closing and they popped open again. He did that one more time, gave the black dude another few seconds to get ahead of him. Then Wolf left the elevator and followed him up the corridor. Good thing the floor curved, the black guy wouldn't see him following.

Wolf stopped and took a step backwards when he saw the black guy crouched in the hallway, pushing money under a door. Weird thing to be doing at midnight. Some kinda money deal going down with the ex-husband of one of the bidders and Wolf wanted to know what it was.

He stepped through the fire door and walked up two floors to his own room, pondering the connection. The moment he unlocked the door to his room, he knew someone had been in there. Not the maid to turn down his bed and leave a piece of candy on the pillow. Somebody who meant him harm. He wasn't depending on any kind of warning system except instinct, which was the only thing he ever depended on. He flexed the muscle of his right forearm and a seven-inch throwing knife slid down into his hand. Flipped on the light.

Oh yeah. He'd had a visitor, all right.

Wolf closed the door, put the knife back where it belonged. A slow, powerful anger began to boil up into his chest. He felt his face go red hot, his stomach knot up. "Goddamn that bitch!" He strode to his bed and picked up his two extra pairs of pants, or what was left of them. Cut to pieces, especially around the crotch. As nasty a job as he'd done on her things.

*Had to be her! Couldn't be anyone else! How the hell did she get into my room?*

He was shaking, his heart pounding so hard and erratically he feared he was having a heart attack. Sat down on the bed, a pair of vandalized pants crushed in each hand, took some deep breaths to clear his head. Tried to get control of himself. He felt dizzy and off-balance. "Bitch! Bitch! Bitch!" Never had a woman done anything like this to him, made him look a fool, feel outsmarted and small and humiliated. Not until Kay Williams. "She's gonna pay for this. *Really* pay. Little cunt thinks she can play games with Bud Wolf? She'll find out."

It took a good five minutes to bring himself under control, to begin thinking out the situation.

The pants were thrown into the wastebasket. He reached for the phone and dialed a number in San Antonio. "Hello, I'm lookin' for Kelly Watts. Is he there? No? Got a number for me?" He wrote down the number and called. "Kelly Watts," he said to the man who answered. "Is he there? Okay, got a number for me? No, I already called that one." Wolf wrote down another number and called. Still no Kelly. He had to call two other numbers before he tracked down Kelly Watts in some bar, loud music and breaking glass in the background. "Kelly? This is Bud Wolf."

"Hey, Wolfie! You in San Antone? Come on down here, I'll buy you a beer, fix you up with Fay the Fire Fucker, hottest thing this old town's ever seen. Pure nitro."

"I'm in Austin, Kelly."

"Steal a car, you can be here in ninety minutes."

"I've got a job for you. Tomorrow."

"Ah, so we're talking money instead of pussy. I'm listening."

"Stay where you are, I'll call you in ten minutes. I need to find a secure phone."

"That kinda deal, huh. Okay, I'll be here. Anybody tries to use this phone'll get a pool cue across his head."

Wolf went down to the front desk and exchanged a five-dollar bill for a fistful of quarters, walked up Eighth Street until he found a pay phone on Congress, called the number in San Antonio where he'd finally located Kelly Watts.

"Wolfie? Start talking, man. I've got a woman waiting for me, thinks I own a ten-thousand-acre cattle ranch called the Ponderosa. She ain't too bright, but she's willing."

"Well, don't fuck her all night, I want you sharp tomorrow. You'll need a second man, too. I'm not takin' any chances with this bitch."

"You got a woman problem, Wolfie?"

"No, *you* got a woman problem. She pissed me off and I want her dead. You don't have scruples about that, do you, Kelly?"

"I've got plenty of scruples but they're all for sale, you know that."

They both laughed, old buddies who've been in on some hard deals together, weren't worried about talking straight to each other.

"Why do you need two guys? This bitch a Wonder Woman?"

"Nah, just an antiques dealer. But she may be with a guy tomorrow, I'm not sure. You may have to do a two-for-one. That's why it's best if you bring along somebody reliable."

"When and where?"

"Not sure yet. You'll probably pick her up somewhere near the Alamo, that's where she's headed tomorrow morning."

"Do you want her disappeared or just stomped to death?"

"Either way, whatever's easiest. I'll come down tomorrow and point her out to you."

"Afterwards I'll buy you that beer. Now, what's the price tag on this bimbo? Gotta tell you, these days I get fifteen thousand for this sort of work."

"Kelly, this is probably comin' out of my own pocket. I'll pay you five thousand, plus twenty-five hundred for the second man."

"Okay, special price for you."

"What number can I reach you at tomorrow morning?"

Kelly gave him a number, which Wolf wrote down on the back of his hand with a felt-tipped pen. "I'll call you sometime between six and nine. Bring plenty of ordnance."

"Wolfie, you're starting to worry me. Never heard you get so uptight about a woman."

"This one's got more heat in her than most."

"Then we'll just have to chill her out."

# CHAPTER 16

K ay awoke before the alarm went off, took a moment to figure out she was entwined in someone's bare arms and then remembered how she and Roy had done a fine job of seducing each other the night before. "Mmmm." She snuggled up to his back as more extensive details of their lovemaking came back to her. Great night. It had been quite a few weeks, no, she should at least be honest with herself, quite a few months since she'd had a similar evening. Foolish to do it with Roy, of course. He was a federal agent, lived hundreds of miles away from Connecticut in Washington, D.C., and was operating on an agenda that had nothing to do with her. Sadly, this was probably just a hit-and-run for both of them.

She snuggled closer to him anyway. The good ones were always married, either to other women or to their careers. With Roy it was probably his career. He had that obsessed view of his job that she could spot pretty easily because she had the same intensity about her own work.

She stroked Roy's bare back and pressed her head against the pillow for a clearer view of his face. His features were very plain, some would say ugly, but imbued with a rugged honesty she found irresistible. Apparently found irresistible. Otherwise, she asked herself, why would I be here? Correction. Why would *he* be *here* in *my* room at . . . what? . . . six o'clock in the morning?

Apparently the question wasn't one to haunt her, because she soon slipped comfortably back to sleep, awakening later to find Roy awake too and looking at her with the same kind of silly smile she had earlier conferred on him.

"Good morning." He touched her cheek, then withdrew his hand.

"Morning. Now I know what the Secret Service means by an *undercover* agent."

"Means we're great under the covers?"

"You wish."

"I heard no complaints last night."

"Neither did I," Kay countered.

"No, our evening was, I have to say, one of the higher points of my life." They flowed quite naturally into each other's arms and kissed for a long time. Afterwards, Scanner said, "Last night I was totally smitten, completely satisfied, incredibly stimulated. I feel the same this morning."

"As a rule I don't like to feed the male ego, which I've found to be voracious, but I'm feeling very good about us, too."

"*Us* . . . that's a nice word."

"Are you saying there is an *us*? Or that you want there to be an *us*?"

Scanner rolled his shoulders. "You make the proverbial *us* sound like a mythical creature glimpsed only from time to time rising from a Scottish *loch*."

"A real *us* is even more rare than that." Kay did some artful snuggling. "I haven't seen one in years."

"Your cynicism is obviously a product of your marriage to Phil."

"Not entirely. Yes, Phil is a pig who'll sleep with any girl who admires his looks and his wardrobe, which I was foolish enough to do at the age of nineteen. Yes, it took me four years to find the brains and nerve to dump him. Yes, I would enjoy seeing Phil impaled on spikes at the top of some medieval tower, screaming himself to death with exquisite slowness. None of that has anything to do with my deep suspicion of the word *us*. Look around, Roy. You'll see very few couples who would qualify as an *us*. My mother and father certainly didn't. Did yours?"

Scanner shook his head. "Even in the Illinois heartland it's hard to find a genuine *us*. My father pretty much ignored Mom, and she despised him for it. I doubt anyone outside the family knew that, they put on a pretty good front."

"Yes, I do see a lot of pretty good fronts."

"What are you telling me?" Scanner was reluctant to put it into words.

"That there's no hope for . . ." He had to laugh. "Jesus, I almost said *us*. No real chance for you and I outside this auction, outside this intense little game we're playing against Donin and his pal Wolf?"

Kay was actually frightened. She'd never before revealed to a man her fears about the word *us*. To girlfriends, yes, as they sat around a fire with glasses of wine trading unpleasant truths and long-buried secrets, dipping into the dark creases of their souls. But never to a man, especially to a man she'd slept with and was actually willing to consider, seriously consider, as the other half of an *us*. "I didn't say that. Things have moved so fast, Roy. It's just fair to let you know I'm not as confident about how to make a relationship work as I am about, say, how to launch a nuclear missile."

"I know what you mean. A face like mine isn't exactly a confidence-builder."

"You're very handsome, in your own way."

Scanner felt the usual bruise to his pride. "Girls sometimes tell me I'm really very handsome, and then add that same qualifier you used: *In your own way*. Or *Unlike any other man I've met*. Another good one is *Like Abe Lincoln was handsome*. Let's face it, Honest Abe was one ugly dude and so am I."

"I'm sorry, Roy, I really do think you're handsome. Yes, in your own unique way, whether that's a cliché or not. Matter of fact, I woke up before you did this morning. Looked you over very carefully and decided I liked what I saw."

Scanner relaxing. "Did you peek under the blanket?"

"Of course I peeked, and I liked what I saw down there, too."

"You hear the one about Louise, the nurse who came back to her nursing station all flustered? She told Annie, the other nurse on duty, '*I just discovered that the man in Room 17 has the word Swan tattooed on his cock.*' That was rather intriguing to Annie. '*I've got to see that,*' Annie said. So Annie went down to Room 17 and was gone a long, long time. Louise was worried, she was about to go down to Room 17 herself. Just then Annie returned. Annie's hair was all disheveled, her skirt hiked up almost to her waist, her nurse's stockings gone. '*What happened to you?*' Louise asked. '*You were wrong,*' Annie said. '*He doesn't have the word Swan tattooed down there. He's from Canada. The word tattooed on his cock is the name of his home territory in Canada—Saskatchewan.*' "

Kay threw back her head and laughed. "I suppose you have the name of your hometown tattooed down there, too."

"You bet I do. I'm from a little town in Illinois called Catahootchee-on-the-Lake and I had no problem getting it all tattooed on there."

"You're a liar and a braggart. I've been to Illinois. I happen to know you're from the town of Hays and that you had a tough time making the tattoo fit."

"That's cruel. You've probably launched me into some kind of psychosis."

"You haven't seen anything yet." She reached under the blanket and pinched the place where Scanner claimed to be tattooed.

"Ouch!" Scanner shot up almost above his covers. "That really hurt!"

Kay seized him, kissed him, bit his lip until she tasted blood.

When he was able to pull away, Scanner said, "Jesus, I'm in bed with a vampire!"

"Yum." She licked her lips. "Type O-negative. My favorite."

"How'd you know my blood type?"

Kay was amazed that she'd guessed right. "I told you . . . the taste."

"This is scary. I'm not sure anymore that I want there to be an *us*."

"Ahhhhh . . ." With a thick Hungarian accent patterned after Bela Lugosi's. "But I can offer you eternal life."

"Does that include an eternal hard-on?"

"Men! You have no souls! That's what we female vampires like most about you."

They tussled for a while, Kay trying vampire-like to bite Roy's neck while he pretended to fight her off. Finally he let her sink her fangs into his throat and groaned with pleasure. "This is wonderful." He caught a glimpse of the clock and reluctantly sat up. "But I think we'd better get ourselves showered and dressed. I want to see Donin's face when Stewart Ruddington demands to see his money."

"And I want to see Bud Wolf's face." Kay jumped out of bed and ran into the shower. Over her shoulder: "The minute he looks at me, I'll know whether he got my message."

"Oh, I'm sure he got your message." The shower went on and Scanner arose from bed with a series of twitches and groans, observed his face in the mirror, groaned more expressively. "Got room for one more in there?" he called.

"What?"

"Never mind." He went into the bathroom, opened the shower door and stepped inside.

*     *     *

Donin had a difficult time suppressing a smile as he listened to Wolf describe the damage Kay Williams had done to his pants. The man was livid. Donin had to ask him to keep his voice down, people at nearby tables were frowning at him.

"I knew the Williams woman would be trouble." Donin took a bite of his toast. "What kind of preserves are these? Peach preserves? Wonderful!"

"Yeah, we grow the best peaches in the world here in Texas." In a very low voice, Wolf said, "I'm tryin' to tell you not to worry about Miss Williams, she ain't comin' back from her trip to the Alamo."

"Explain."

"All the bidders . . . and that includes Miss Bitch . . . are goin' down to San Antonio this mornin' to look at the Bowie knife on display at the Alamo. I've got a couple of guys on standby down there. I'll finger her. They'll make sure she never comes back."

"I see." Donin had no objection to Kay Williams's death, he only wanted to make certain it couldn't be connected to him. "What worries me here, Wolfie, is that you are taking this action for personal reasons. You vandalized her clothes. Being a smart young lady, she understood you were responsible and did the same to you. Check and mate. Like chess, a game not to be taken emotionally."

"You don't want her around, neither do I." Wolf smeared some of the peach preserves on his own toast. "We both get what we want."

"Just do your job dispassionately, that's all I ask. With no way to trace it back to you or me."

"The guys I'm hirin' don't even know you exist. Far as they're concerned, this is my play. I promise they'll never hear your name."

Donin saw Kay Williams approaching the dining room with Roy Scanner. Wolf's back was to them.

"At first I only wanted her frightened and driven out of town. I see now that she is in the game to the end. Just make sure it's her end, not mine and yours."

"Don't worry, this'll be handled professionally. And at no cost to you. I'll pick up the tab for the guys I hired. My idea, my expense."

"No," Donin said, "I will pay. You are working for me, Wolfie. Where I come from, murder is a legitimate business expense."

"Whatever you say." There were some things about the Russky Wolf did like. He made tough decisions fast and wasn't afraid to spend money to get what he wanted.

"Speaking of Miss Williams, she is about to join us for breakfast."

Wolf swiveled around. Kay was settling herself into a chair that Roy Scanner had pulled out for her. They were about four tables away. His eyes locked on to hers. Kay gave him a "fuck you" smile, as Wolf interpreted it. Wolf controlled himself and smiled back, thinking of what Kelly Watts would do to her later in the day. He returned to his breakfast. "Nervy bitch."

"I rather like her." Donin added more peach preserves to his toast. "Almost a shame she has to die."

They were finishing breakfast when Stewart Ruddington entered the dining room. He mopped his brow wildly with a huge red handkerchief as he came their way. Ruddington had forgotten to put the monocle in his eye, he was that upset. "Good morning, Mr. Donin. Mr. . . . uh . . . yes . . . Mr. Wolf. Please, may I sit down?"

Donin nodded coldly, intuiting some sort of trouble from this overly dramatic auctioneer.

Ruddington got right to his business. "I had a most disturbing evening. It's been suggested to me that if you win the auction you intend to pay for Old Bowie with either Russian rubles or dubious U.S. currency."

"That is a lie."

"The suggestion came from a reputable source," Ruddington continued. "I can't ignore it."

Donin picked the white napkin off his lap and threw it on the table, upsetting a glass of water. He ignored the soggy mess it created, the ruined food, his eyes drilling into Stewart Ruddington. "This is an outrage. I am a representative of the Russian government traveling on a diplomatic passport. My credentials are impeccable. I am in possession of legitimate U.S. currency, which is protected, as I am, by my diplomatic status."

Ruddington looked to most people like an absent-minded professor. He liked to create an atmosphere of gentle civility at his auctions and the monocle, tweed jacket, bow tie and other affectations helped. Underneath the pose was a strong sense of self. Auctioneers who could be intimidated by bidders didn't last long. "I don't deny what you say. However, your diplomatic status doesn't confer on you the right to take part in this auction. You're a bidder because the Koska Museum vouched for you. Even so, you aren't as well known to me as the other bidders and I have a responsibility to make sure your participation will be legitimate."

"You can do nothing to stop me from bidding. You're merely the auctioneer." He laced the word with contempt. "I intend to call the Russian Embassy in Washington and make a formal complaint about this treatment."

"You can call the President of Russia if you wish. Perhaps he'll be sober enough to speak with you, perhaps not. Either way, the Russian government can't help you. International politics are irrelevant to this situation." Ruddington's shrug was eloquent with disdain. "I'm the only person who can approve you as a bidder. Those are the rules of this auction."

"Who is spreading the ridiculous story that I intend to bid with counterfeit money? Or with rubles?"

"I'm not at liberty to say."

Donin looked across the dining room at Kay Williams and Roy Scanner, who were pretending not to be aware of his discomfort. "Never mind, I can guess who invented these lies. Another bidder who hopes to force me out because I am too well financed."

Wolf just sat and listened while he finished his coffee. *So that was the deal, the Russky was pushin' counterfeit money. And it turns out this Stewart Ruddington isn't an idiot after all, he just looks like one. Whatever he took in payment, cash or bearer bonds or whatever, would be checked through a bank twenty fuckin' ways from Sunday before the Bowie knife was passed over to the winning bidder. Donin must know that,* Wolf thought. *Which tells me he's got some damned good counterfeit in that big old heavy suitcase of his. No wonder people don't trust the Russians.*

Suddenly Donin was acting less hostile. He set the spilled water glass up straight, sopped up most of the mess on the table with the napkin and said in a mild voice, "I'm sure we can settle this matter to your satisfaction."

"Yes, we can," Ruddington replied. "If you'll bring your money to the Longhorn Bank, only four blocks away, I'll have the bank manager inspect it. He's the best currency man in Austin."

"I am going to the Alamo in San Antonio today, as are the other bidders. Would tomorrow morning be acceptable?"

"Well . . ." Ruddington clearly wanted to get it done. "I suppose so. Although that's cutting it very close to the auction hour."

"The auction doesn't begin until four p.m. The banks here open at ten a.m., is that correct? My funds are in a safety box at the bank across the street. I will take out the money at ten a.m. tomorrow and meet you in the lobby of the Longhorn Bank at ten-thirty. Surely that is reasonable. I would rather not walk around for very long with a suitcase full of cash in a country famous for its violent thieves. Mr. Wolf will accompany me to safeguard my funds. You will understand?"

"All right." Ruddington rapped his knuckles twice against the tabletop, an old auctioneer's signal that a deal is done. "Ten-thirty tomorrow morning at the Longhorn Bank." He stood up and bowed in his old-fashioned, patrician manner before departing.

"More coffee?" Wolf did the pouring. "How much counterfeit you got in that suitcase?"

Donin accepted the coffee, added a little sugar. "Three million dollars in hundred-dollar bills."

"Is your stuff good? Or was that just a bluff, you're really on your way out of town, back to Moscow and your fat wife?"

"My *stuff* is so good I am not at all worried about whatever tests the bank may apply."

"I'm fuckin' impressed." Wolf gave a sidelong glance at Kay, who was still chatting away with Scanner as if she had nothing to do with Ruddington's visit. "What about our lady friend? You're still payin' to put her away? I hope you know she's the one who set up Ruddington. Her and Scanner. He's some kind of cop."

"A federal agent," Donin agreed. "Secret Service, I would guess. Counterfeit Currency Division. Yes, they are the source of this morning's embarrassment. They slept together last night?"

"I couldn't say for sure, I wasn't in bed with them. Scanner did spend the night in her room. I paid a bellman to keep an eye on her room."

"They are lovers, look at them."

"Yeah."

"Scanner is her protector. They will go to San Antonio together."

"Sounds right." Wolf looked at his watch. "We'd best get on our horses."

"Horses?" Donin looked worried.

"Don't bite your fingernails, we're takin' the car."

Donin leaned forward with a stir of urgency. "I would like this Scanner to die, too. By the time his superiors hear of his death and send other agents to investigate, I will be out of the country."

"Whoa, Nellie. I wasn't hired to knock off a federal agent. My two guys in San Antone aren't geared up for that job, either."

"What you mean is that it would cost more money to add Mr. Scanner to your portfolio."

"You hired me to bodyguard your suitcase and your ass. Put down a federal agent? You bet that's more money."

"How much more?"

Wolf wondered how far he could push this Russky. Guy had a good front. Though Donin didn't show any anger, Wolf guessed he was massively pissed. He was the sort who lived by a minute-to-minute timetable. Now his timetable was in the toilet. He even had an auctioneer, old guy in a bow tie went out of style fifty years ago, tellin' him to get fucked. Yeah, Donin was pissed as hell at Scanner. *And he's worried about me killing folks for personal reasons.* "Fifty thousand for the two of 'em. I'll pay my guys out of that. Oh . . . the bodyguard work's a separate deal. You still pay for that."

Sarcastic laugh. "Every visit I have made to the U.S., three in the last five years, has been extremely profitable. I may lose money on this trip."

"I'll call the Contractor, tell him we've got this new transaction added to our agreement. You pay him, not me. He takes his commission and sends the rest to one of my accounts outside the U.S., that's the way it works. But I'll need money up front for my guys in San Antone."

"Not a problem."

"I'm also gonna tell the Contractor not to let you pay him in hundred-dollar bills."

A broader laugh from Donin. "Our minds are so much alike it is almost frightening."

# CHAPTER 17

"A ren't you going a bit fast?"

"They don't have too many speed limits in Texas," Phil said. "Besides, I've heard you're the kind of girl who likes to go fast."

"I do," Melanie agreed. "I daresay nobody's ever gone faster or farther than I have. But I like to get to know the driver first."

Though he hated to do it, Phil let up on the accelerator so the car slowed from eight-five to seventy. They were on Interstate 35 headed southwest toward San Antonio through countryside on the verge of heavy development but still pleasantly rural in places. He saw some of the old Texas longhorns grazing lazily on high grass, horses romping in a pasture, big rolled wheels of hay stacked up in fields.

The Mercedes Melanie had rented for the trip to San Antonio was a dream to drive. The faster he went, the smoother the ride became. It had been a long time, much too long, since he'd been behind the wheel of such a beautiful automobile. All his adult life Phil had felt he was born to drive luxury automobiles, to wear fine clothes, to eat in the best restaurants, to sleep with the most beautiful women.

For a few years, when he was a trader in stocks and bonds, all those dreams had come true. Then the damned SEC had moved in on him, canceled his trading license, threatened to throw him in prison. Prison! Just because he'd made a little money on what *they* called "insider infor- mation." At a time when *everybody* was operating on inside information.

He'd been lucky to avoid the humiliation of a public trial and the pain of several years in prison. What saved him was giving the SEC the names of some friends who'd cut a few corners with insider trading, too. His pals had taken it badly. One had yelled at him in the street, "You bastard, you ratted me out!" The others had been just as insulting. *Fuck them, a guy has to look out for himself.* Now he had a chance to get it all back—the money, the cars, the clothes, the women, everything. *I mustn't blow it,* he thought. *I've got to get back in the big leagues. Back where I belong.*

"What?" He realized Melanie was talking to him.

"Penny for your thoughts." She laughed at herself. "Pennies won't do for you, will they? A thousand dollars for your thoughts, is that better?"

"Sounds about right." Phil slid his hand onto Melanie's thigh, let it linger only a couple of seconds, withdrew it. "So how do you think you'll do in the auction?"

"I'll win. You know why? Because I've got a surprise up the sleeve of my best Oscar de la Renta."

"You're convinced the knife is the real thing? The original Bowie knife?"

"I'm ninety-five percent certain. We're going to the Alamo so I can take a good look at the knife on display there, make sure its not the one Jim Bowie was carrying when he died."

"Crazy, what those guys at the Alamo did. I mean, what'd they really accomplish except to throw away their lives?"

Melanie wasn't terribly surprised by Phil's take on the battle of the Alamo, she doubted that self-sacrifice rated very high with him. "The Alamo defenders pinned down Santa Anna's army for a couple of weeks to give Sam Houston time to organize the Republic of Texas Army. It worked. Houston brought an army of volunteer Texans together and defeated Santa Anna a few weeks later at San Jacinto. Don't you remember your high school history?"

"I must have been out sick the day they taught that one," Phil said cheerfully.

Melanie laughed, which caused Phil to chuckle along with her, thinking he must have said something witty. Witty. Not on his best day would Phil Williams be capable of wit. Phil was such an empty suit, so dense, so obvious in everything he said and did, such a liar, and almost impossible to insult because anything negative she said went right over his head.

Oh, sure, he was a hunk. As good-looking as any man she'd ever seen.

Partly for that reason, she intended to let Phil screw her before the day was out. She expected to be only mildly satisfied, Phil was probably a stud more in his own mind than in a warm bed. The number one reason to fuck Phil was not because she lacked for sexual partners, but simply to have something nasty with which to taunt dear Kay.

Dear Kay. Back to business.

"Tell me something, Phil. Does Kay really think she can win the auction?"

"Oh, absolutely." Phil had no idea what Kay thought, not about the auction or anything else. He did know her well enough to understand generally how she operated at auctions. First of all, she'd be representing a wealthy client. "She's well-financed, of course."

"By Billy Boy Watkins," Melanie said.

A new name to Phil. "Right. Watkins, he's the client. Kay'll just take a commission." That was how she usually worked these auctions. "Don't underrate Kay. People often do, then she swoops down and picks up all the marbles. I swear I don't know how she does it. She's smart, I always knew that. But it took me years to realize she could also be devious."

"Darling, that doesn't worry me. I'm the queen of devious. I am curious, though, about just how high dear Kay is prepared to bid. Do you have any idea?"

*Wish I did*, Phil thought. "This may sound like a reach, but I wouldn't be surprised if she bid as high as . . . uh . . . a million dollars?"

Melanie stifled a hiss of impatience. *The fool doesn't know a thing! A million dollars? The bidding will start there.* "Yes, that's a sizable sum. What's she got with her? Cash? Bearer bonds? Or will she do a bank transfer?"

"It'll probably be a bank transfer kind of thing."

*Doesn't have a clue about that, either.* Usually in an auction like this Kay got bearer bonds from her client in particular denominations, five thousand dollars or ten thousand dollars, depending on the auction. "Bank transfer. Interesting."

"Hey, look who just passed us." Phil pointed at the Cadillac that had just blown by them at a lot higher speed than the seventy mph they were doing. "That's one of your competitors, isn't it?"

Melanie caught a quick glimpse of the two men in the car. "Leon Donin and his bodyguard, the Cro-Magnon who calls himself Mr. Wolf."

"Bodyguard?" The word caught Phil's attention. "Why does Donin need a bodyguard?"

"Apparently he's carrying around a suitcase full of cash."

Cash. An even more interesting word. "Sounds like a dangerous thing to do." Phil pushed the Mercedes from seventy to seventy-five. "I mean, this is *Texas*, for Christ's sake. Anything can happen here. How much cash do you think Donin is carrying?"

"If I knew that, I'd know exactly how high he'd be able to bid. That's the kind of information I need." She looked quickly at Phil. "What's your interest?"

"None. Except I was just wondering if you'd like me to try and find out how much money Donin brought in? Got a little time on my hands, might be fun to do some detective work for you."

"Ahh." Melanie thought she understood. She had never bought into Phil's story that he owned a string of restaurants called . . . called what? . . . oh yes . . . *Seis Amigos*. That was bullshit designed to impress her. An original lie, though, showed a feeble spark of creativity. But Phil Williams as a successful businessman? No bloody way. Melanie had built a prosperous antiques business from scratch and knew what it took. Building a chain of restaurants would have required years of hard work and gritty determination, not the kind of activity Phil was up to. He'd probably come to Austin hoping to borrow some money from Kay. Smart girl that she was, she would have turned him down. Now he was scratching for a few dollars to pay for the trip. *Maybe,* she thought, *Phil could be useful for something other than a quick fuck.* "Do you really think you could find out how much money Donin brought in?"

"Possibly."

"It would be worth a thousand dollars to me if you could." She didn't want Phil to know she'd spotted his story about being a rich restaurateur as an obvious lie. "I realize that's a drop in the bucket to a man like you, a man with his own chain of restaurants. I'm embarrassed to offer you money, but I wouldn't want you to be out of pocket doing me a favor. I mean, you'd have to put your own business aside for a day."

"I wouldn't mind doing that. Not for money, of course. Just to help you win that auction."

"You're a doll. You won't be sorry you took the time to help me, Phil. I'm *very* creative when it comes to returning favors."

He let a few seconds pass. "So tell me what you know about Donin and his suitcase."

"Okay. He put the suitcase in a vault at the bank across the street from the Omni, I forget the name, there are so many banks in Austin. Donin had planned to leave the money there until just before the auction begins tomorrow afternoon. But Stewart Ruddington, our auctioneer, apparently got to wondering if Donin was really well enough financed to compete in the auction. I don't know why Stewart got antsy, I suppose because Donin is Russian and a nasty-looking piece of work besides. I've been suspicious of him myself."

"Makes sense," Phil said, just to keep Melanie talking.

"Anyway, when I passed by the phones in the lobby this morning I heard Stewart making an appointment with the manager at the Long-horn Bank. It seems Leon Donin is meeting Stewart there at ten-thirty tomorrow morning. Donin will bring in the money he intends to use in the auction. I couldn't catch the whole conversation, but I gather Stewart wants to make sure Donin is carrying legitimate U.S. dollars instead of those worthless Russian rubles."

"That's a smart move."

"Stewart is good at what he does."

Phil was tingling with excitement. "How much do you suppose Donin brought?"

"Umm, I'd guess a couple of million dollars. This is a major auction, he couldn't be a serious competitor for less." She squeezed Phil's leg and let her hand glide down around his cock. "It occurs to me that Donin doesn't know you. If you were in the Longhorn Bank tomorrow morning at ten-thirty, sitting somewhere near the bank manager's desk, you might be able to find out exactly how much money Donin's bringing to the auc-tion."

"All right, glad to do that." *But not for you, Melanie.* Phil felt elated at having so easily obtained the information Chauncy needed. His job was now all but done. Chauncy would do the rough work, taking the money away from Donin and the bodyguard. Chauncy wouldn't try to rob them right there in the Longhorn Bank, a place with guards and alarm systems. Probably do it somewhere on the street between the Longhorn Bank and the Omni Hotel. Or in the Omni itself when Donin returned to the hotel with the money. Coming up with a plan and doing the robbery was Chauncy's work. Two million dollars minimum! A million apiece, maybe more. No taxes to pay. Nobody else asking for a split.

He did experience a nervous flutter thinking about the robbery. On the one hand, he didn't want to be anywhere nearby when the robbery took place, there probably would be shooting or other violence. On the other hand, he had to be nearby to make sure Chauncy didn't just take off by himself with all the loot. You couldn't trust a Jamaican, they were all crooks. And worse.

When he'd come awake that morning, Phil found that Chauncy had made good on his promise to finance his trip to San Antonio with Melanie. Four hundred and fifty dollars in cash had been pushed under his door. He hadn't wanted to know where the money came from. Unfortunately, the bellman had left a free copy of the *Austin American-Statesman* outside his door, and he couldn't miss the front-page story about a drug dealer found robbed and murdered just a few blocks from the hotel. Chauncy had often bragged to him about his days as a "take-off man," a specialist in robbing low-level dealers for whatever cash and drugs they happened to be carrying. The killing in the newspaper had Chauncy's signature all over it.

Phil shivered. Made a resolution to never again work with a hard case like Chauncy Alexander. Well, he wouldn't have to. Not with a million dollars in the bank.

"Darling, look at that!" Melanie pointing ahead to a motel called The Naughty Sagebrush. Its sign advertised BEDS THAT GIVE YOU THAT TEXAS TINGLE! Place looked clean and modern, too.

"Like to find out what the Texas Tingle is?" Phil didn't have time to wait for an answer, they were almost opposite the motel, so he swung off the highway and cut across the frontage strip into the motel's parking lot.

"I really have to get to San Antonio." Melanie glanced at her watch. "Umm, I guess we can spare an hour or so."

"Sure, the Alamo isn't going anywhere." Phil swung out from behind the wheel. "I'll get us a key, be right back."

Melanie took a cosmetics bag from her purse and, with the aid of the rearview mirror, applied fresh lipstick, telling herself that the Texas Tingle had better be good.

# CHAPTER 18

"This is it, sir." The driver's voice twangy with pride. "The Alamo."
Arthur Ward peered out the window of the hired limo in which he'd been driven to San Antonio. In Austin the driver had introduced himself as Hooter Willis. "My goodness, Hooter. The Alamo's much smaller than I'd pictured."

"The men who died here were plenty big enough."

"From that remark I assume you're a native Texan."

"Born in Deaf Smith County," Hooter said proudly. "Deaf Smith was another Texas hero, helped old Sam Houston kick General Santy Anny's ass." He hopped out of the car and came quickly around to open Arthur's door. "I'm fixin' to put the limo in that garage over there, Mr. Ward. When do you want me to pick you up?"

Arthur looked at his Rolex. "I may or may not stay in town for lunch. Depends on whether I run into any of my friends. I suspect I will. Why don't you meet me right here at noon. Don't get the car out of the garage beforehand. I'll be able to tell you then if I'm staying in town for lunch."

"Yessir. Plenty of good restaurants down on the River Walk, right across the street. Tex-Mex is great here, you can't go wrong with it."

"I'll keep that in mind. Thanks, Hooter. See you right here at noon."

Arthur didn't immediately go onto the grounds of the Alamo. Instead he walked across the street and took another look at the old mission that bore so much of Texas history. The structure looked even smaller and more fragile from that vantage point. He tried to imagine more than 180 men holed up inside the pitifully low walls with not much food, not enough weapons or ammunition, surrounded by thousands of Mexican troops, fighting them off several times before the Mexicans prevailed.

Hard to imagine today that a massive battle had even taken place here. Arthur did a leisurely 360-degree turn, observing the way San Antonio had changed from 1836 when it was just a lazy village on a small, meandering river. The Alamo was dwarfed by the downtown high-rise buildings, bumper-to-bumper traffic and the stadium where the Spurs play basketball. The nondescript river had been reengineered into the now-famous River Walk—both banks of the river heavily but creatively overbuilt with bars, restaurants, hotels and trendy boutiques. Crowded tourist boats went up and down the river itself, not a foot of space wasted.

Arthur sighed and turned his gaze back on the Alamo's old mission building. A small but lovely structure with sand-colored walls. Behind it, a large garden that during the battle had been used to hold the cattle the defenders depended on for food. In the years leading up to the battle, the Alamo had been a mission and a stockade for Mexican army troops. For some time before the battle it had been more or less abandoned because the roof on the chapel building had fallen in. The walls had not completely enclosed the mission, which made the Alamo difficult to defend. Hastily built palisades had been thrown up in bare places, but there was no way they could have halted Santa Anna's army.

Arthur Ward loved history. He dealt in antiques because they embodied more history than anything else, even more than the thousands of well-read books on history that lined the walls of his library. His estate on Long Island was close to Teddy Roosevelt's historic home on Sagamore Hill and his collection of Roosevelt memorabilia was extensive. The furniture in his home consisted of carefully chosen antiques, many pieces with their own unique histories.

This knife of Jim Bowie's fascinated him. Of all the artifacts of American history, this one stood near the top. He was determined to have it, had gone so far as to make a deal with the devil to assure that the knife would be his. Strangely enough, he almost hated the thought of prevailing at this particular auction. What disturbed him was the look of disgust Kay was bound to give him when she learned about the deal he'd made. Well, it was done. A deal is a deal. He was committed to his silent partner.

He walked into the chapel and shook his head. Terribly small interior. He imagined it crammed during the siege with wounded and dying men, probably some livestock, too, the disgusting aroma of open wounds prevalent despite the caved-in roof.

The roof now on the chapel building was solid and tight, the interior clean, the stone floor well scrubbed. Glass display cases held scores of antiques from the battle of the Alamo—everything from old weapons to some of the clothing and other personal possessions of the defenders.

The display case attracting Arthur's immediate attention held a Bowie knife that did not greatly resemble the one Jim Bowie had described in his letters and that journalists and friends of Bowie had written about. It resembled a butcher knife more than a weapon made for hand-to-hand fighting. Engraved on the grip were the words *R. P. Bowie/H. W. Fowler USD.* Inscribed on the blade was the cutler's name: *Searles—Baton Rouge.* No first name. No date.

"They don't actually claim this is Old Bowie—Jim Bowie's knife."

Arthur turned to find Kay looking over his shoulder, Roy Scanner at her side. She was dressed in a green blouse, jeans, sneakers. Scanner was equally casual in a knitted sports shirt, khakis and Rockport hiking shoes. Arthur suddenly felt overdressed in his blue Brooks Brothers blazer and gray slacks. Casual attire was something he didn't do well. "No," he agreed. "They don't *say* this is Jim Bowie's original knife. By simply displaying it here without any explanation they *imply* it's Old Bowie and that it was found here at the Alamo after the battle. Clever."

"Who was H. W. Fowler?" Scanner asked.

"A friend of Rezin Bowie, Jim's brother." Arthur had done a lot of research on the Bowie family. "Rezin evidently presented this knife to Fowler at some sort of ceremony."

"Rezin's an unusual name."

"The patriarch of the Bowie family couldn't spell too well. He had meant to name his oldest son R-e-a-s-o-n. Missed by quite a few letters. They say he never knew his mistake. Nobody ever told him about it because he was known as a tough old Indian fighter who'd crack your head open in a minute."

They left the display of Rezin Bowie's knife and strolled out of the chapel building into the garden that had been built around the old Spanish well. Once a cattle pen, it was now beautifully landscaped.

Their walk took them back to the plaza in front of the chapel, where

they found Leon Donin and Kazuo Goto looking at the mission and discussing the subject that seemed to occupy everyone's mind—the small-
ness of the Alamo and the fragility of its walls.

Goto bowed in turn to Kay, Scanner and Arthur and gave them a formal smile. "Good morning." He was wearing a beautiful cashmere jacket
and tailored slacks. "I am pleased we are all here today. Have you seen the
Bowie knife on display inside?"

"Yes, we have," Kay answered Goto, then looked pointedly at Donin.
"Did you both have a pleasant evening?"

Thinking of his mistress, Goto said, "I felt extreme happiness last
night."

"My flight from Moscow left me very tired." Donin returned Kay's
stare with an innocent smile. "I went to bed early. Slept very well. You
have this wonderful tablet in the U.S—melatonin?—the best sleeping
pill I have ever used. Do you think I could buy the franchise for Russia?
Does anyone know how I should go about that?"

"I'd be glad to help put you to sleep," Scanner drawled. "In fact, I'd
consider it an honor."

Donin threw his arms open. "Generosity! It is the hallmark of Americans. Thank you, Mr. Scanner, I will keep your offer in mind."

There was a rustle of confusion as Arthur and Goto tried to understand
the undercurrents between Donin on one side and Kay and Scanner on
the other.

To break the mood, Arthur said, "I've arranged for us to use a room in
the library. I think the presence of Rezin Bowie's knife is worth a discussion. A lot of people do believe it was Rezin, not his brother Jim, who
invented the Bowie knife. I, for one, would feel pretty silly if I bid on a
knife that wasn't the original."

"Then let's all sit down and talk about that," Kay agreed.

She waited until Donin had walked ahead to the library by himself
before starting out to join the others in the small library building managed by the Daughters of the Republic of Texas. Someone called out:
"Hey, there!"

Melanie came running up, panting but not really out of breath, just
uncomfortable from running in high heels. Phil jogged along at her side.
They both grinned at Kay, who felt an uncomfortable tightness in her
throat but managed to maintain a vaguely friendly expression.

Kay immediately saw that Melanie and Phil had just enjoyed sex together. The tipoff was Melanie's hair. She didn't let her hair get tousled for anything except sex. *She wants me and the others to know it. So does Phil. Well, I know it. They know it. Everybody knows it.*

"We're just going into the library to talk about the knife that's on display here. Have you seen it yet?"

"No . . ." Breathlessly. "Phil and I just got here. We took a little, uh, *rest stop* on the way down from Austin." Melanie smiled sweetly at her colleagues. "If you know what I mean."

Kay took hold of Melanie's elbow. "Then you'll want to see Rezin Bowie's knife before we talk. Come on, I'll show it to you. You come with us too, Phil. You might find this interesting." To Arthur: "We'll join you in five minutes."

Melanie let Kay steer her into the mission and up to the glass case holding Rezin Bowie's knife. Phil trotted along behind. He and Melanie exchanged glances, both disappointed with Kay's nonchalant greeting. Melanie thought it very cold of Kay not to care that she'd slept with her ex-husband.

"This is it." Kay wheeled on them. "But I didn't really come in here to talk about Rezin Bowie's knife. Melanie, I've always respected you as a professional. I've got to tell you that sleeping with Phil in the middle of this auction is very unprofessional. I imagine you hoped to shake me up the day before the auction. Sorry, that won't work."

"You are jealous." Catlike smile. "You're covering up well, though."

"No, I'm not the slightest bit jealous."

Phil snorted. "I saw that pulse jump on the left side of your neck, Kay." In truth, Phil hadn't seen Kay's pulse twitch even though he'd been looking for it. Expecting it. He had to say he'd seen it happen, just to goad her. "That only happens when you're upset."

"I don't care if you think you saw my heart leap out of my mouth and do the tango. What the two of you do together is of no interest to me." *Am I telling the entire truth?* Kay wondered. *I think I am.* "Melanie, this story is going to spread through the business because Arthur will tell Stewart Ruddington. Stewart is a talkative old fellow who dines out on gossip like this. I may appear a bit pathetic in the story of this auction as Stewart will tell it, but you'll come out worse. What bothers me is that you're harming your professional reputation for the likes of Phil. I made the same mistake years ago and he just wasn't worth it." She crossed her arms. "Tell me the truth, how long was he good for? A couple of minutes?"

Melanie couldn't resist a smile. "Let's say I once enjoyed a longer erection in a man of eighty."

"Jesus Christ, Melanie. Why would you say a thing like that?" Phil couldn't understand why Melanie had suddenly turned against him. It was as if she were using him. As if she'd gotten what she wanted and didn't even give a damn about him anymore. Huh! It came to Phil that Melanie probably didn't give a damn about him any more than he did for her. "You women are disgusting! You're all alike, total bitches."

"Darling . . ." With a little-girl smile designed to appease, Melanie twisted one of the buttons on his shirt. "Would you mind terribly going back to Austin on your own?"

"On my own! How?"

"Hire a limo. Take a bus or a taxi. Walk?" She gave up on the button. "For heaven's sake, it isn't all that far!"

"You can't just dump me here." Phil shifted his weight from his left foot to his right in a threatening manner. At least, it was threatening when Clint Eastwood did it. "I won't stand for that."

"Oh really?" A hundred-dollar bill appeared in Melanie's hand. She stuffed it into his shirt pocket. "That should get you home."

"You're a worse bitch than this one." Gesturing angrily at Kay.

"Oh, I know that already." Melanie planted a kiss on Phil's cheek, grabbed Kay's arm, dragged her away. "Bye-bye, darling."

They left Phil standing alone inside the chapel, a tower of frustrated anger.

On the way to the library, Melanie asked Kay, "How long were you married to that one?"

"Four years, give or take a couple of months."

"Oh dear, why did you stay with him that long?"

"I was a lot of things then. Young . . . stupid . . . impressionable . . . broke . . . loyal . . . confused . . ."

"Enough. I've got the picture." Melanie plucked at her hair. "My tresses look like hell."

"You appear well bedded, exactly the look you were after."

"Phil was right, I am a terrible bitch." She sounded pleased with her flaw.

Their arms were still linked, so Kay patted Melanie's hand in a sisterly way. "Compared with Lucrezia Borgia, you're a saint. Pity we can't be friends. I really do admire the way you've built your business." Kay quickly revised what she'd said. "I mean, that could never happen, could it? You and I becoming friends?"

"I'm afraid not." Melanie's sigh was—for once—sincere. "We're too much alike."

"I don't even want to hear that, much less think it." Kay hoped Melanie was just giving her another dig. "Don't say that to anyone else, okay? They might believe you."

"Kay, wake up! You're in a state of total denial about your own high level of bitchiness. I mean, it was obvious to everyone at breakfast that you jumped into bed with Roy Scanner last night after knowing him for how long—six hours? A genuine bitch-in-heat move. On top of that, I just heard you ruthlessly ridicule your ex-husband's sexual prowess. At yesterday's pre-auction meeting you publicly insulted me in the cruelest way, so cruel I took poor old Phil to bed just to get even with you, which didn't exactly work. And even Phil just commented on how much alike we are. Most important, you're prepared to pull whatever low trick is necessary to win Old Bowie for your client, don't tell me you aren't. Doesn't all that add up to a first-class bitch?"

Kay's spirits sank. "You may be right."

"Of course I am! But don't go all gloomy about it. *Exult* in your bitchiness. *Revel* in the way you use and abuse your men. Every one of them would do the same to either of us, for God's sake."

Melanie sounded so gloriously free of any form of guilt that Kay found herself laughing along with her longtime enemy and even hugging her arm. When they strolled into the Alamo's small library with linked arms, conversing in fits of giggles like old chums, their colleagues were astonished. Arthur's jaw dropped almost to his chest and even Kazuo Goto lost his inscrutability long enough to look surprised.

"Now I can die," Arthur pronounced. "For I have truly seen it all."

"Oh hush," Melanie snapped. "This is a temporary truce that means nothing, just like the ones in Bosnia and horrible places like that. Kay and I are still implacable enemies. Am I right, dear?"

"I intend to scratch out Melanie's eyes at the earliest opportunity," Kay confirmed.

"They have been drinking," Donin surmised. "I do not appreciate female drunks."

"You . . . do not appreciate . . . females . . . period," Kay said in a passable imitation of Donin's stiff, unpleasant voice.

"Let us get to business." Donin glared at Kay before going on. "I am concerned there may be a chance that Rezin Bowie was the real inventor of the Bowie knife. How do we settle that issue?"

Arthur had selected a number of old books, letters and publications from the Alamo library. They were stacked on the table. He picked up one of the publications and leafed through its pages, looking for passages he'd read before. "There are a lot of theories about the original knife. Rezin Bowie claimed he manufactured the knife, not James Black. Ah, here we are." Arthur tapped the page he'd been looking for. "In 1838, two years after the fall of the Alamo, Rezin Bowie wrote a letter published in the *Planters' Advocate*, a Louisiana publication. The letter was written to counter a story in the *Baltimore Transcript* to the effect that Rezin Bowie should not be trying to take credit for achievements of his brother James. In this letter Rezin asserts that . . . well . . . let me read out loud what Rezin Bowie said:

" 'The first Bowie knife was made by myself in the parish of Avoyelles, in this state, as a hunting knife, for which purpose, exclusively, it was used for many years. The length of the knife was nine and a quarter inches, its width one and a half inches, single edge, and blade not curved, so that "the correspondent" is as incorrect in his description as in his account of the origin of the Bowie knife. The Baltimore correspondent must have been greatly misinformed respecting the manner in which Col. James Bowie first became possessed of this knife, or he must possess a very fertile imagination. The whole of his statement on this point is false. The following are the facts: Col. James Bowie had been shot by an individual with whom he was at variance; and as I presumed that a second attempt would be made by the same person to take his life, I gave him the knife to be used as occasion might require, as a defensive weapon. Sometime afterwards (and the only time the knife was ever used for any purpose than that for which it was originally destined) it was resorted to by Col. James Bowie in a chance medley, or rough fight, between himself and certain other individuals with whom he was then inimical, and the knife was then used only as a defensive weapon, and not till he had been shot down—it was then the means of saving his life. The improvement in its fabrication, and the state of perfection which it has since acquired from experienced cutlers, was not brought about through my agency. I would here assert, also, that neither Col. James Bowie nor myself, at any period in our lives, ever had a duel with any person. Signed, Rezin Bowie.' "

Arthur sat back. "So Rezin categorically claimed to have invented the Bowie knife, not his brother James."

"The *rough fight* he talks about," Melanie put in, "sounds like the famous duel on the sandbar at Natchez."

"Does indeed," Kay agreed. "Bowie had been shot, as Rezin said, by a Major Wright and used his knife to kill Wright."

"Tell me more about this incident," Donin said.

"All right." Kay took out a pocket notebook and referred to the notes she'd made a week earlier on the duel. "Two groups of people in Natchez had been in a long-running feud. Their arguments were basically over land deals, plus personal animosities. Plainly put, the two groups hated each others' guts. On September 19, 1827, two of the parties, Dr. T. H. Maddox and Samuel Wells, met on a sandbar on the Mississippi River opposite the town of Natchez. About a dozen other people were present as witnesses or supporters, plus a couple of physicians. Jim Bowie was there as a supporter of Samuel Wells. Maddox and Wells did the usual macho bullshit, walked away from each other, turned around, fired their pistols. Turned out they were both lousy shots. They missed each other. Twice. At that point sanity briefly prevailed. Maddox and Wells agreed that their precious *honor* had been satisfied and put down their guns.

"Then one General Cuny, a Wells supporter, unhappy with the lack of bloodletting, drew a gun and began firing on members of the other party. A Colonel Robert Crain, who hated Bowie, drew a gun and killed General Cuny, then shot Jim Bowie through the hip. Bowie limped toward Colonel Crain with his knife drawn. Crain hit Bowie over the head with his empty pistol, a terrible blow that almost killed Bowie on the spot. Dr. Maddox intervened, holding back Crain from finishing the job on Bowie. By the way, everyone on the sandbar seemed to have a title of some sort—General . . . Colonel . . . Major . . . Doctor . . . whatever. I guess that's a Southern thing. There was a Major Wright present who also hated Jim Bowie and fired at him even though Bowie by then was lying against a log on the sandbar, hardly able to move because of the bullet in his hip. Bowie had a gun, too. He fired back, hitting Major Wright in the stomach. Major Wright dropped his pistol, drew a cane sword and rushed at Bowie intending to run him through. According to eyewitnesses, Major Wright shouted, 'Damn you, Bowie! You've killed me!' Jim Bowie made sure of that, gutting Major Wright with his knife, killing him instantly. Others on the sandbar were fighting with knives and guns, too.

One of them, Edward Blanchard, shot Bowie through the body, then had his own arm shattered by a ball from someone else's gun. Of the dozen men on the sandbar, Wright and Cuny were killed, Bowie, Crain and Blanchard were very badly wounded, others had lesser wounds or escaped injury."

Donin laughed. "I have seen the same on Saturday night at a Moscow bar."

"I might add," Arthur said, "that there was terribly bad blood between Jim Bowie and Major Wright long before the duel on the sandbar. The year before, Major Wright had walked up to Jim Bowie on the street, pulled a pistol and shot Bowie. The pistol ball was evidently deflected by a silver dollar in Bowie's waistcoat pocket. Bowie was in the process of beating Major Wright to death with his bare hands when passersby pulled him off. All this because Major Wright and Jim Bowie were competitors in a land venture."

"Sounds to me," Scanner said, "like Rezin Bowie insisted he invented the knife out of jealousy over his brother's fame from that duel and the battle of the Alamo. And that the sandbar duel turned into a good way for Bowie and some others to settle their old arguments."

"I agree," Goto said. "I too have read the history of James Bowie. Rezin Bowie's statement that his brother never engaged in any other knife fight, or duel, is clearly untrue. James Bowie fought a well-known Natchez gambler, for one." Goto bowed his head. "I apologize, I cannot pronounce that man's name."

"Bloody Jack Sturdevant," Melanie said. "Jim Bowie and Jack Sturdevant had a knife fight in Sturdevant's saloon in Natchez-Under-the-Hill, which was the red light and gambling district of Natchez. Bowie let Sturdevant live, but deliberately cut up Sturdevant's right arm so badly he was never able to use it again. Ruined Sturdevant as a gambler, he couldn't deal from the bottom of the deck anymore, and as a killer."

"I'd say Bowie had a pretty strong mean streak." Scanner wasn't even sure he liked Bowie. "How many others did he kill or maim?"

Goto supplied the number. "Twelve to fifteen. That does not include military ventures."

Everyone around the table seemed to have an example.

"In Galveston," Kay said, "when James and Rezin were doing business with the pirate Jean Lafitte, Jim Bowie got into an argument with one of

Lafitte's men. To settle the argument, Lafitte tied both men to a log floating in the water of Galveston Bay. They were tied only at the waist and legs, their arms were free and they both had knives in their hands. They were facing each other at a distance of about three feet. The fight apparently lasted less than a minute and ended with Bowie cutting the pirate's throat."

A queasy murmur went around the table.

Melanie had a similar story. "Bowie killed a man on a Mississippi riverboat, that's been documented, too. The riverboats were infested with gangs of crooked gamblers who cooperated to fleece passengers. Two of those gamblers separated a young businessman from five thousand dollars in Twenty Card Poker, a popular card game of the day. The young man was on a combination business trip and honeymoon. Jim Bowie felt sorry for the youngster and his bride, who were in tears over the loss of so much money. Bowie demanded that the gamblers return the money. They refused. The gambler pulled a gun and Bowie promptly killed him. He took the five thousand dollars off the gambler's body and returned it to the young man, who swore he'd never gamble again."

"Yes, I've read about that killing," Arthur said. "But Bowie killed that gambler with a Derringer pistol, not with his knife."

"True," Melanie said. "My point is that Jim Bowie wasn't the quiet, rational man his brother Rezin often claimed. After Jim Bowie died in the Alamo, Rezin made it his business to take credit for a number of his dead brother's exploits."

"Including the manufacture of the Bowie knife?" Donin looked around the table. "Are we all agreed on that?"

Everyone did agree that the knife on display in the mission was not the original "Old Bowie."

They spent another half-hour discussing the relationship between Rezin and Jim Bowie and talking about other cutlers and smiths who had tried to take credit for manufacturing the Bowie knife. In the end they agreed that James Black was the manufacturer, as Jim Bowie had always claimed, and that Antonio de Baraga was indeed offering them "Old Bowie" itself.

The meeting ended and the bidders broke into small groups to stroll the gardens or further explore the old mission.

Kay was curious about the building called the Long Barracks, where the Alamo defenders bunked and people could find shelter during the bombardments from Santa Anna's artillery. She drifted out of the garden while Scanner and Arthur were deep in a conversation about the weakness of the Alamo's walls.

"It's a miracle the Mexican troops didn't wipe out the defenders in the first attack," Arthur was saying.

"I've seen Fort McHenry," Scanner said. "I've been to Gettysburg. Other battle sites. I've never seen a defensive position as hard to defend as this one."

The Long Barracks lived up to its name. It turned out to be a long stone building containing a series of small rooms, dimly lighted and sparsely furnished, with extremely low ceilings. Kay went through each room in turn. There were few doors in the building. Instead, most of the rooms were entered through a common passageway running all the way along the building's longest wall.

Kay looked into the last room and saw that a slide projector, screen and about twenty chairs had been set up. From the disarray of the chairs, the slide show had already taken place and the audience had departed. She was wondering what the presentation had been about when she felt a hand on her back and was shoved roughly into the darkened room.

"How y'doin', Miss Williams?"

It was too dark to see the speaker's face, but the voice sounded a lot like Bud Wolf's. He had moved into a pocket of shadows next to the door. No use trying to get out that way.

"Mr. Wolf?"

"Naw, my name is Mr. X. Though I do know Bud Wolf. Helluva guy. But I gotta tell you, last time I saw him he was pissed as hell."

"Stand aside and let me leave."

He put his hand out like a school crossing guard. "Cuttin' up Wolfie's clothes was real bad shit, lady."

"Same as you did to me!"

"Me? Naw, that might have been Wolfie. Okay, maybe he did play with your head. That didn't give you the right to cut up the man's clothes, fuck up the natural order of things."

"What natural order?"

"Man gives orders. Woman obeys them."

Kay almost hooted at his Neanderthal thinking, but held her laughter because of the tension in the man's voice. Wolf's voice, she was fairly certain. He was mad as hell. She'd hit the bastard right where she'd wanted—in his big, fat male ego. *What does he want? Kill me? Hurt me?*

*Humiliate me? All of the above?* She had a feeling he wasn't going to do anything right now. Not here in the Alamo, lots of people outside. Someone might have seen him come into the Long Barracks or might see him leave. Wolf wasn't a psycho. He was doing a job for Leon Donin and having what he thought of as fun at the same time. This was just another of his head games, like the vandalized clothing.

"You may not realize it, but that's a very old-fashioned point of view. You're trying to live in another time and it won't work."

"Mr. X is an old-fashioned kinda guy. He'll make it work."

"Here's another thing that won't work, Mr. X—you can't scare me."

"Anybody can be scared, lady. I've been scared shitless a few times myself. One time, this was years ago when I was maybe twenty or twenty-two, I got so scared I actually peed in my pants. Thought I was a dead man at a young age, seen as much of life as I was ever gonna see. Turned my bladder inside out. So don't get to feelin' all smug and peppery. I set my mind to it, you'd never get a full night's sleep again, you'd be so fuckin' terrified."

"Mr. Wolf, I know it's you by the way, no need to call yourself Mr. X, it's time to put your hand down and let me pass."

"I'll say when it's time."

"No." Kay used the cover of darkness to slip a hand into her purse. "I'll say when it's time, Mr. Wolf."

"I told you to call me Mr. X. Can't you do nothin' you're told?" His open hand came flying out of the darkness and slapped her across the face.

Kay staggered from surprise and pain.

"You're gonna learn to give respect when respect is due, or you're gonna . . ."

She yanked the can of Mace from her purse, flipped up the protective cap with her thumb and sprayed the chemical in the general direction of her attacker's head.

"Shit, whassat?" He flailed his arms and jumped sideways, away from the cloud of chemicals. "Goddamn you . . ."

Kay dodged for the doorway, then shied back as something silvery white swished through the air not more than two inches from her throat. She broke into a sweat and retreated a yard or two, stopped to again spray the air with Mace. A huge cloud of the stuff. More profanity from the darkness. Kay ducked and ran full speed through the door. Her left shoulder cracked against the stone sill. The pain from the collision was so sharp she almost screamed. The next room was also dim. Kay felt disoriented. Her own eyes were all teared up from the Mace. The direction of the passageway wasn't clear to her until she burst into still another room, one that was more brightly lighted, and pushed past a startled couple touring the Long Barracks.

She saw sunlight to her right and ran through the door. This time her forearm banged into a doorjamb, knocking the Mace from her hand. The hell with the Mace. Kay just wanted out of the Long Barracks.

When she reached the plaza, Kay had to stop and rub at her eyes. She'd done a job on herself with the Mace, but at least she was out in the open now. When her vision cleared, Kay spun around to see if Wolf had followed her. He was nowhere in sight. At least, she didn't think he was near; she could see figures only as fuzzy, indistinct objects.

"Are you all right?" A woman in a yellow dress was holding her arm in a steadying way. "Do you need help?"

"No . . . thank you . . . something got in my eyes, that's all." Kay blinked rapidly to rid her eyes of the last traces of the Mace. "I'm all right. But thanks for asking, I appreciate it."

"Do you want to sit down? There's a bench over there by the mission doors."

"No, really, I'm fine now." She could see again without pain and with clarity. No more frightening, fuzzy images that might be Bud Wolf. A moment of panic swept over her as she saw a man coming towards her, followed by relief when she was able to recognize him as Roy Scanner.

As Scanner approached, he could see that Kay was disoriented and frightened. She kept rubbing her eyes and seemed to need the help of the woman holding her arm in order to stand up. "Kay, what's the matter?"

"She was terrified, rubbing her eyes, couldn't see," the woman in the yellow dress said.

Scanner gripped her by both shoulders. "Are you hurt?"

Kay shook her head.

"Thanks very much," Scanner said to the woman who had helped Kay. "You were very kind."

"I'd take her to a hospital if I were you." The woman smiled and left them.

"What happened?"

"I went into the Long Barracks," Kay explained. "Bud Wolf shoved me into a dark room, at least I think it was Wolf. I never saw the man's face and I don't know his voice very well. He called himself Mr. X and told me I shouldn't have messed up Bud Wolf's clothes."

"Must have been Wolf. How'd you get away from him?"

"I had a can of Mace in my purse. I sprayed him, myself too by accident, and ran past him out the door."

"You Maced him? Then he may still be in there. Kay, can you show me where this happened?"

She nodded. "Sure, right over there inside the Long Barracks."

Scanner took her arm in a protective grip and let her lead him towards the doorway near the end of the Long Barracks. When they stepped inside, Scanner reached down and drew a short-barreled revolver from an ankle holster. The main passageway was occupied by a few tourists looking into the rooms, so Scanner held the pistol down at his side and mostly out of sight. "Which way?"

Kay took him to the room where the projector, screen and chairs had been set up.

"Wait here." He went cautiously into the room and came out ten or twenty seconds later. "Wolf is gone. I'll find him, though. He'll be under arrest before dinner."

"Roy, I can't really swear that the man who threatened me was Bud Wolf. I told you I couldn't see his face in the dark, and his voice and accent are too much like a million other Texans."

"Bastard was here." Scanner returned the revolver to the ankle holster and straightened up with a loud wheeze of frustration. "We can't let him get away with this."

"It's Donin who's responsible."

"Yeah, that's true. Maybe I should bust up Donin, give him an internal hemorrhage to worry about. That'd stop him from sending Wolf to harass you."

"Bust up a Russian national with a diplomatic passport? That doesn't sound smart. You'd probably be out of a job. And you'd be passing up the chance to put your hands on one of Donin's fake hundred-dollar bills."

"Then I'll bust up Wolf instead." Scanner was simply in the mood to hit somebody, almost didn't care who that person might be. "He doesn't have a goddamn diplomatic passport."

"Roy, don't blow your chance to take Donin's money away from him. That would be bad for you and bad for me, too."

It hit Scanner that Kay wanted Donin out of the auction, one less bidder, even more than she wanted revenge for being threatened. "You amaze me, Kay. This is all just *business* to you, isn't it?"

"Not totally business." Trying to downplay Roy's rebuke. "But yes, I do hope what you're doing will force Donin to drop out." Kay didn't appreciate his sudden sullenness. "For heaven's sake, you're in the business of catching counterfeiters and I'm in the business of buying antiques for my clients. As it happens, our interests coincide. That's why you approached me in the first place, isn't it? Not wholly because of my girlish figure and well-turned ankle."

Scanner, exasperated, could only give himself a bearlike shake. "Kay, I'd hate to think what would happen to me if our interests didn't coincide. If I were really competing for that knife, you'd probably have me hogtied and set out in the alley with the garbage by now. Are you sure you aren't Melanie's younger sister?"

"You're the third person this morning to compare me with Melanie." The comparison irritated Kay, but didn't gravely hurt, which surprised her. *By the time I reach Melanie's age, will I have become Melanie?* "I suppose there must be some truth in it."

# CHAPTER 19

Wolf met Kelly Watts and his number-two man, Jimmy Loomis, in a bar across from the Alamo. They had a window table, a beer in front of each of them, a bowl of salted peanuts, the makings of a satisfactory meeting.

"That's the girl." Wolf pointed her out. "Her name is Kay Williams. She's an antiques dealer from back East. She has to go. The guy with her has to go, too." Kay and Scanner were still talking in the plaza in front of the mission's old chapel. Wolf believed they were discussing what to do about the threats he'd laid on her. What Wolf didn't like was the expression on Kay Williams's face, still full of piss and vinegar. Goddamn Mace, his eyes wouldn't stop burning. He pulled out a red bandanna and wiped them for the sixth or seventh time.

"They don't look like a problem," Kelly Watts said. "You agree, Jimmy?"

"Consider it done." Jimmy Loomis wore a cowboy hat set low over bloodshot eyes. He was lean, in his late twenties. His hair was longish and greasy, held together in a ponytail by an old rubber band. His shirt and jeans were dirty, too, but his boots were highly polished. He had a jailhouse pallor, having spent time in county and state lockups in Texas, Oklahoma, Arkansas, West Virginia, Kentucky and Alabama on mostly minor offenses. Only one felony rap to his name. "So long as I get paid in cash," he added.

Watts looked puzzled. "What's wrong with your eyes, Wolfie? You been crying? Hate to do the girl, is that it? Didn't think you was sentimental." Watts had a guttural laugh that shook his belly, which hung out dramatically over a silver belt buckle.

No way Wolf was going to admit that the girl had Maced him. "I got allergies. Kelly, you have to know that the guy, his name is Roy Scanner, is a federal agent. I'm sure he's armed. Nothin' heavy, probably a standard-issue .38. You can tell by lookin' at him that he's not packin' a Glock or any other nine-millimeter, his clothes are too tight. I'd guess he's got the .38 in an ankle holster or tucked under his shirt."

"Whoa there, hoss." Watts reared back in his chair and ground out his cigarette on the tabletop. "Federal agent? You didn't mention that little detail on the phone. Federal agent is a whole other deal." Watts was almost as big as Wolf. Like Wolf, he was in his early forties. He'd been in prison twice, once for murder and the other time for setting a black church on fire, a crime he called 'urban renewal.' The arson job had put him in a federal prison and he'd sworn never to go back inside a federal joint again. "The feds don't like to see their little gray men killed."

"Makes a difference," Loomis muttered. "Bigger risk."

"Sure it makes a difference," Wolf conceded. "The difference is the amount of money you collect to put one down."

Watts and Loomis exchanged interested looks.

"How much more money are we talking about?" Watts's eyes glittered. "And when do we collect?"

"I've got the money with me. Thirty thousand dollars, the split is up to you."

"I get half." Loomis directed his demand at Watts.

"Jimmy, no offense, but you've never seen fifteen thousand dollars in one piece and you never will." Watts picked up a longneck beer and drank deeply. "I take twenty and you get ten. That's a fortune for you. I mean, your job is only to back me up. I'll do the work."

It was hard to tell what Loomis was thinking, he seemed to have only one sluggish, unimaginative expression. "All right, you do the work. I'll be there if you need me, but you do it."

Wolf had the cash Donin had given him in a manila envelope under his shirt. He passed the envelope to Watts under the table. Watts counted it down there, his lips moving with the numbers. *Greedy eyes,*

Wolf thought. *Even greedier than mine.* He drank his Lone Star and waited until Watts completed the count.

"You're as good as your word, Wolfie. That's what I always liked about you." He passed a stack of cash under the table to Loomis, who accepted it in his cowboy hat and quickly put the hat on his head.

*Money's gonna get all greasy,* Wolf thought.

"This has to happen today?" Watts asked.

Wolf nodded. "Today. You got your Winchester with you? I know that's your favorite."

"I brought the Winchester, a Remington shotgun, an M-16 and two handguns. Thought I'd take the Winchester and let Jimmy use the M-16. He's a damned good shot with a rifle, we do some hunting together."

"What kind of wheels did you bring?"

"Cherokee. Four-wheel drive. Stole it last night after you called."

"Good. I've got it all planned out for you. The two of them came down from Austin this mornin' in a rented red Ford, license number SFH-70C. Scanner drove. They'll be goin' back to Austin on Route 35 right after lunch."

He paused while Watts wrote down on a napkin the license number and description of the car.

"Lot of commercial development along Route 35 these days," Wolf went on. "But there's a stretch between San Marcos and the little town of Budda that's pretty much empty."

"I know the stretch you mean," Watts said.

"I'll be with you in the Cherokee. When Scanner and the bitch leave town, we'll be right behind them. Stay on their tail for maybe thirty miles. Well before we reach San Marcos, we'll pass them and run a good five or six miles ahead of them. Have you seen the billboard near Budda with the two blondes half-naked? Ad for a sunscreen? You pull your Cherokee off the road, park it behind the billboard. But first you drop me off a hundred yards up the road by an old abandoned car I can use for cover. I know their car already, you'll be able to recognize it by then, too. I'll watch for them to make absolutely sure we target the right car and signal you when their car passes me. From the cover of the billboard, you shoot out their right front tire. With luck, they'll go off the road and crash. Maybe even flip over if they're goin' fast enough. If the crash kills them, that's dandy. Nice and simple. Even if Scanner avoids a crash, he'll have to stop to change his tire thinkin' it's just a blowout. They'll have to stop close to you, not more than forty yards away. You step out from behind the billboard, shoot them both, jump in your Cherokee, pick me up, we hightail it. There may be some other traffic passin' by. If you have to shoot a witness, I won't complain. But you don't get paid more for witnesses, so show a little restraint. I don't really expect anybody will interfere with us, identify us, nothin' like that. The day of the Good Samaritan is long gone."

"What's a Good Samaritan?" Loomis asked. "And what am I supposed to do all this time?"

"A Samaritan's some asshole who butts in where he doesn't belong," Watts explained. "I already said you back me up. Be ready with the M-16 in case they get a clue to what's happening and try to run for it."

"I hope they do run," Loomis said. "I don't like to just stand around when there's sport to be had."

For the first time since he'd met him, Wolf saw Loomis smile. It wasn't a pretty sight. Loomis only had about half his teeth. The gaps made him look like a jack-o'-lantern in a cowboy hat.

"I want this done clean and fast," Wolf emphasized. "Afterwards we'll all have plenty of time to slide out of sight. There won't be any real heat for at least a week."

Jimmy Loomis had a second expression after all—skeptical. "How do you know that?"

"It'll take the local cops a day to figure out who they've got on their slabs," Wolf predicted. "Another day, maybe two, for Washington to react, get in the picture. Then lots of confusion. Lab guys from different agencies all over the place steppin' on each other's toes. Forty federal cops, different agencies again, they'll argue over jurisdiction. Local cops'll get disgusted, throw up their hands, let the feds go ahead and fuck up the case. Believe me, I've had the feds investigate stuff I've done, they've always fucked up the investigation. That's why I've never done time. One good local cop can make a case, forty federal cops do nothin' but argue with each other. I've seen it over and over."

"You paint a beautiful picture, Wolfie." Watts picked up a handful of peanuts and tossed them into his mouth. About half the peanuts went where they were intended. The rest bounced off his chin, then his shirt front, then the table, then the floor. Watts washed the peanuts down with beer. "I hope the car flips, that'd make all our lives simple. Where'd they park the Ford?"

"The underground garage at the Marriott."

"I'll move the Cherokee to the street-level lot across from the Marriott. What time do you think they'll leave for Austin?"

At the Alamo plaza, the entire group of bidders had gathered to decide where to eat lunch. There was a lot of pointing in different directions as they tried to make a decision. Arthur's driver came up to the group and evidently made a good suggestion, because they all trooped across the street and went down the steps to the River Walk.

"They'll be down there for an hour minimum." Wolf looked at his watch. It was noon. "One-thirty, that's about when Scanner and the bitch will be ready to leave. I'll keep an eye on them. Find you at the parking lot when they go for their car."

"We'll be ready."

Wolf felt he should check in with the Contractor, let him know about the changes he and Donin had made in the contract. He got the usual pocketful of quarters and went through the rigmarole of multiple computer-controlled phone transfers before he reached his party.

"Sales department."

"Mr. Spring calling."

"Good to hear from you, Mr. Spring. Having a good road trip?"

"A few problems, nothin' I can't handle. I'm callin' to let you know I've picked up a subcontract from our client."

"Just a second while the computer does a background scan."

Wolf waited while the Contractor's computer retraced each phone link to check that no one was listening in anywhere along the chain. "All right, what's the subcontract for?"

"Two cancellations. One's a woman, the other works for the federal government."

"Is that wise?"

"No, but it's necessary. The contract's for fifty. Thirty goes to the mechanics doin' the job for me. That's been paid already. The balance will go through your books."

"Sounds like this contract has become more difficult to fulfill than expected. I probably should have asked a bigger fee."

"You still can. The client can afford whatever price you ask, he literally prints his own money."

"Are you serious?"

It gave Wolf a pleasant lift to have actually surprised the Contractor. "Don't take any hundred-dollar bills from him."

"Foreigners are so untrustworthy. Thank you for the warning. Would it be helpful for you to take a contract in Mexico when this job is completed? About six weeks work down there, two removals? The client is the same gentleman you serviced a year ago February. He'd like to use you again."

That would be Eduardo Jayez, the drug kingpin of the Guadalajara area. "Yeah, this would be a good time for me to do some work out of the country."

"I'll arrange it."

After the conversation Wolf jogged across the road and looked down from the street level at the River Walk below. Didn't take five seconds to spot the group from the auction, Kay Williams and Roy Scanner among them, going into a Mexican restaurant famous for its *huevos rancheros*. He leaned against the rail and settled down to wait and watch while they had their meal.

The wait gave him an opportunity to think seriously about Old Bowie. The knife was never far from his thoughts. He needed that knife, had to have it. Jim Bowie's own blade, the most important weapon in the world. Wolf believed he was born to possess it. *There can't be anyone in this whole country who's killed as many people with a knife as me*, he thought. *Yet I can't afford to outright steal Old Bowie from Donin. The Contractor would never stand for that. Bad for business. He'd have to send someone to cancel me out. If Donin wins out at the auction—and why wouldn't he win with a suitcase full of great counterfeit cash to throw around?—he'll take it back to goddamn Russia and I'll never see it again.*

*Shit!*

Another option came to him. *What if I fixed it so Donin* didn't *win the auction? What if I talked to one of the other bidders, let them know Donin is carryin' three million? It would have to be someone who could scratch up enough dough in one day to beat Donin in the bidding.* He thought about each of the bidders and decided on Arthur Ward. *Perfect choice, bastard so rich he probably farts money. I'll bet he could raise enough cash in one phone call to beat out Donin. He'd haul his suitcase back to Russia without any idea I'd double-crossed his arrogant Commie ass. The Contractor? He wouldn't care if I ripped off the knife from someone who wasn't a client. And I could take Old Bowie off*

*Arthur Ward with two fingers of my left hand. I might not even have to kill him.*

*Hot damn . . . that's the answer!*

The first thing Phil did when Melanie brushed him off was to head for the open-air bar at one of the restaurants on the River Walk. He drank two scotch and waters very fast, settled down with a bottle of Heineken for some pensive drinking. The bartender was Mexican, had a heavy accent. Phil pretended he couldn't understand him so the manager would have to come over and take his order. Bartenders were Phil's favorite punching bags. They couldn't afford to give customers any back-talk, they might lose their jobs. Whenever he was feeling down he went into a bar and needled the guy mixing the drinks.

"A pair of bitches," he kept saying to himself. Melanie was even worse than Kay. Melanie must have forgotten she'd asked him to spy on Leon Donin at the bank tomorrow morning. Well, he planned to be at that bank at ten-thirty tomorrow anyway. Check out Donin's bankroll for Chauncy. Then let Chauncy take it away from Donin.

Fuck Melanie, let her get her auction intelligence from somebody else.

Fuck the auction, too.

For that matter, fuck the Alamo.

"What the hell did you say?"

Phil realized he'd uttered those words aloud. The man on the stool next to him, a big rough type in expensive jeans and starched blue shirt and cowboy hat and boots, face all creased from the sun, hands as big as hams, was glaring at him.

"I didn't say anything," Phil insisted.

"Hell you didn't." The stranger leaned in close to Phil, giving off the curious mixed aroma of a strong aftershave and cattle herds. He was wearing a badge that identified him as Walter Penny, a delegate to the Western Cattleman's Convention headquartered at the Hyatt. "You get profane about the Alamo again, I'll dump you in that river outside and wash out your durned mouth with my fist. You unnerstan?"

"Yeah . . . sure . . . don't worry about it."

"You move down the other end of the bar," Walter Penny commanded. "I don't wanna sit by you."

Phil considered protesting his treatment to the manager, but didn't like the stubbornness in Walter Penny's eyes. So he picked up his Heineken and moved down the bar as he'd been ordered to do. What really pissed him off was catching the bartender in a private grin. If he hadn't just ordered the Heineken, he'd have walked out of the place.

Realizing he was a touch too angry for his own good, Phil tried to concentrate on his surroundings, soak up some sun, enjoy the afternoon. And after a few minutes he was indeed able to put Walter Penny, and even Melanie and Kay, out of his mind.

One way to look at it was that Walter Penny had actually done him a favor. From his new barstool, Phil had a more panoramic view of the boats gliding up and down the river, the tourists gawking and taking pictures of each other and the quaint restaurants and shops on the opposite side of the river. Shoppers strolled along the winding walkways and climbed the arched bridges that spanned the river, small bridges but built high enough so the flat-bottomed tourist boats could float underneath. Many of the shoppers paused to look at the menus displayed at the front door of each eatery, trying to pick a place for lunch. They were in no hurry, the atmosphere was so relaxed. You could hear guitar music coming from several directions, even some piano jazz from a New Orleans–style restaurant down the way.

Phil decided he'd move to another restaurant after he finished his beer, give some other bartender a hard time while he had an expensive lunch. Midafternoon he'd take a taxi to the airport and catch a commuter flight to Austin.

But he simply wasn't destined to enjoy the day. Across the river a party of six—Kay, Melanie, Scanner, Arthur, Donin and Goto—stopped to look at the menu of a Mexican restaurant. As luck would have it, Melanie looked across the narrow river and noticed Phil at the outdoor bar. Raised her hand and waved as if they were still best of friends. Then her expression changed in the space of two seconds from a smile to a question mark to a sort of grimace. In those two seconds she'd evidently remembered how she'd cajoled him into spying on Donin tomorrow and realized that Phil no longer had any incentive to do her that particular favor.

"Bartender, bring me a telephone."

The manager happened to be standing behind Phil. "I'm sorry, sir, We don't provide phones for the bar or the tables in the restaurant. You'll find pay phones next to the restrooms."

Phil turned around, gave him a disbelieving squint. "No phone here at the bar? What kind of place is this?"

"I'm sorry we disappoint you so consistently, sir. Why don't you pay your bill and take your business elsewhere."

"Sure, when I've finished my drink."

"You have finished it."

Turning back to the bar, he saw that his Heineken and glass had been taken away. A bar bill lay in their place. "Hey, I wasn't done with that beer!"

"Oh, yessir." The bartender lifted the check, wiped the surface underneath with his bar rag, pushed the bill closer to Phil's hand. "I take your money now, sir."

"This is a clip joint!"

"You will pay your bill," the manager whispered into Phil's ear. "You will leave. You will not return."

"I'm being eighty-sixed? I don't believe this."

"Lower your voice, sir."

Phil wanted to tear up the bill, throw the pieces in the manager's face and storm out of the place. Decided that move would probably blow back at him, all these restaurant managers were wired into the cops. He studied the bill, then left exactly the amount he owed for two scotches and a Heineken. No tip, that was the only protest he could manage. He was trembling when he left the restaurant. One goddamned insult after another today.

He found phones in the Hyatt lobby and called Chauncy at his room at the Omni in Austin.

"Chauncy Alexander here," came the mellifluous voice.

"This is Phil."

"About time. What you got?"

That was just about the last goddamned straw. Even his partner treating him like shit. "Don't give me that *about time* crap. I've been working while you've been taking your afternoon beauty nap."

"I be resting, I was up late raising money so you do your playboy number for Melanie. You not want to know where that money came from."

"Okay, this is the deal. The auctioneer started to worry that Leon Donin—the Russian?—didn't have enough cash in dollars instead of rubles to pay off if he topped everybody else's bid in the auction. Donin has to bring his suitcase full of money, whatever amount he has in there, to the Longhorn Bank tomorrow morning. Ten-thirty. Prove he isn't just carrying around old phone books or Montgomery Ward catalogs."

"Huh. That's good. He be out on the street with his money. Exposed for once. *If* he really got money."

"That's where I come in." Phil felt compelled to prove he was more than what Chauncy had called him—a playboy. "Donin wasn't around this morning when I got to the Alamo, and I ditched Melanie fast so she couldn't introduce him to me. He doesn't know me, get it? So I'll be in the bank myself tomorrow morning, scope out what's going on."

"Hey mon, how you gonna peek into that suitcase? You think they invite you over, ask you help them with the count?"

"I don't have to look into the suitcase. I just have to see the auctioneer's face, whether he's satisfied or not. If he's satisfied, that means Donin really is carrying a lot of cash."

Chauncy thought that one over. From what he'd seen of Ruddington, the auctioneer didn't exactly have a poker face. "Listen, I don't like talk about these things over the phone. Come back to Austin, we figure out how and where to take off Mr. Donin."

"And that tough-looking bodyguard of his."

"Mon, don't worry so much, I handle dumb crackers like him all my life."

But the bodyguard did worry Phil, he had a feeling Chauncy was underestimating both the Russian and Wolf. He thought he'd better get back and help Chauncy with the planning. "I'm catching the next commuter flight to Austin."

# CHAPTER 20

Driving north on Interstate 35, Kelly Watts felt compelled to point out every Ruby's Cafeteria they passed. "That's the fourth Ruby's we've seen just on this one road. It's a good one too, they give you lots of gravy on your grits. Huge glasses of iced tea."

"I don't eat at Ruby's anymore," Loomis said from the backseat. "All those wetbacks on the serving line. Any time the immigration cops want to punch up their numbers, they raid a Ruby's. I've been there when that happens. Who needs all that noise and aggravation when you're eating, servers being dragged away to busses with prison wire on all the windows. Makes it hard to digest."

Wolf said, "I haven't eaten at a Ruby's since they stopped putting the little pieces of banana in the Jell-O."

"Food's still good," Watts insisted. "And cheap."

"Man with twenty thousand in his pocket shouldn't worry how much a cafeteria meal costs," Loomis grumbled.

Watts and Wolf exchanged a look that said it was time for Loomis to shut up about his cut, concentrate on the job.

"Keep them in sight," Wolf ordered. "I don't want to lose them."

"I never lose anyone." Watts's eyes never left the Ford except when he noticed a Ruby's out of the corner of his eye. "I never asked, where's your car, Wolfie? You coming all the way back to San Antone afterwards to pick it up?"

"A friend's bringin' it down to Austin for me." He didn't mention Donin's name.

The red Ford carrying Kay Williams and Roy Scanner was a good dozen car lengths ahead of them. "I'd like to see that Ford go fifteen miles an hour faster," Watts said. "Then they'd be sure to crash and maybe even overturn when I shoot out the tire."

"One way or another," Wolf replied, "a crash or a couple of bullets, those two are on their way to becomin' historical figures."

"Like George and Martha Washington," Loomis said, and immediately thought of a second pair. "Or Franklin and Eleanor Roosevelt."

"Jimmy likes to show off his education," Watts explained. "Graduated tenth grade. What are you driving these days, Wolfie?"

"I change cars every three weeks or so, same as you. I drove a Caddy down here. Handles nice. Boosted it from a parking lot in Dallas."

"Yeah, I get mine mostly at airports and shopping centers, too."

"Sometimes I pick up a car in the parking lot of a church on a Sunday mornin'. I'm partial to Episcopal churches, those folks have the best cars."

"Stealing cars from a church lot is probably a sacrilege," Loomis said, showing off his education again.

"No, it isn't." Wolf didn't appreciate being called sacrilegious by the likes of Jimmy Loomis. Wolf's mother had raised him as a strict Southern Baptist. He liked to think he still was even though he hadn't been to church since he was seventeen.

In the back seat, Loomis straightened up and tapped Watts on the shoulder. "Kelly, they're turning into that Conoco station."

"I see them. What do you think, Wolfie, should I pull in the other side of the station or just pass them by?"

Wolf looked at the odometer. "Keep drivin'. This is as good a place as any to get ahead of them, set our snare."

"You got it." They passed up the Conoco station and Watts increased his speed by five miles an hour, anxious to reach the spot between San Marcos and Budda where they'd set the ambush.


After they filled the gas tank and got back on the highway, Kay turned to the subject of Arthur Ward.

"I'm telling you, Arthur was acting funny today."

"I don't know him well enough to understand what *funny* means in his particular case. I did notice he only had one drink at lunch. That surprised me. In the bar last night, he had four or five drinks, I thought that was his style."

"Only one drink at lunch? I didn't pick up on that, I was too preoccupied with the way he was sweating."

"Sweating? Was he? Maybe he has the flu."

"I've known Arthur for years," Kay explained. "Today at lunch was the first time I ever saw him sweat. I always thought he had too much blue blood to sweat. I thought that was strange, that's all I'm saying."

"Those of us with normal sweat glands are obviously an inferior breed. I'll throw myself from the highest battlement tomorrow. If I can find a battlement."

"Stop it, Roy." Kay gave Scanner a playful punch on the arm. "You know how I meant that. Arthur has a unique bearing. At first people tend to think he's a snob because he doesn't seem to sweat and his clothes hardly ever wrinkle and he insists on paying for everyone's drinks, but he's really a dear."

"That's how I think of him, too," Scanner said. "As a dear. Actually, I do like Arthur. Can't relate to him very well, a guy with all that money and an estate crammed to the rafters with antiques, but he's likable. Generous. Nice dry humor. What my father would have called a sport."

"Only one drink at lunch? And all that sweating? And he seemed nervous whenever he talked to me? I'm wondering what all that has to do with the auction."

Scanner groaned. "Silly me, I thought you were genuinely worried about him. Turns out it's just business."

"I *am* worried about Arthur. Whatever's wrong has something to do with the auction, that's what I'm trying to tell you."

"If you ask me, it's our friend Goto-san who's worried. During lunch he made two trips to the telephone. Right after lunch he slipped a nitroglycerin tablet under his tongue when he thought nobody was looking. Didn't you pick up on that?"

"Yes, I did. I suspect he was on the phone to raise more money for the auction and that the pressure's getting to him. The price on Old Bowie is going up, can you sense that?"

"Everybody believes it's the real thing," Scanner agreed. "Including me. That's bound to drive up the price. Are you beginning to think you can't win this one? Is that what's making you so nervous?"

"I suppose so." Kay hated the idea of losing, always had. As soon as they reached Austin, she planned to call Billy Boy Watkins and ask if he was willing to increase the limit on his bid. Too late to get more bearer bonds delivered to Austin. However, Billy Boy could transfer money straight to her account. If he'd be willing to do it, commit himself to as high as three million, which Kay now thought would be the high range in the bidding. God, that would be a lot of money to commit to one antique. Kay feared she was doing exactly what she'd always warned her clients about: *Never get emotionally involved in an auction. You'll overbid if you do.*

But how do you put a price on Old Bowie?

"There it is." Wolf pointed out the abandoned old wreck at the side of the road. "And that's the billboard I told you about, a hundred yards or so farther on. Be sure you park behind the billboard. I don't want your car seen from the road. You get the occasional sheriff's car patrolling the highway."

Watts stopped to let Wolf out. "Pump your arm twice when they pass by."

"You'll only have a few seconds' warning, so be ready to fire."

"I know my business," Watts snapped. "That's why you hired me."

Wolf left the Cherokee, walked around the abandoned old auto and dropped to one knee. He watched to make sure Watts followed instructions. As soon as Watts pulled the vehicle around back of the billboard, he and Loomis jumped out. Loomis slammed a clip into the M-16 while Watts went down into a prone position underneath the billboard and racked a round into the Winchester's chamber. Wolf approved of the position Watts had chosen, a piece of ground a little higher than the roadway. Forty-yard shot at most. No question he'd hit the right front tire.

Loomis took up a similar prone position about five yards away from Watts. Neither was likely to be noticed by other drivers on Interstate 35. And the Cherokee was well out of sight, too. Wolf felt a surge of confidence in his people and his plan.

He estimated ten minutes for Scanner to gas up the Ford, maybe another five minutes to take a leak, both him and the bitch, say twenty minutes until they reached this spot. But if they'd pulled into the Conoco station only to use the rest room or get a cold drink out of the soda machine, the red Ford could appear at any moment. So Wolf settled down behind the abandoned car and kept his eyes on the road.

"You and Melanie were as cozy as sisters today," Scanner was saying. "Really surprised everyone."

"Melanie was just playing one of her head games." Kay couldn't always explain Melanie's motives, but in this case she thought she understood Melanie well. "First Melanie tried to rattle me and cause a sensation among our auction group by going to bed with Phil. When that didn't work out, she went in the opposite direction—gave my darling ex-husband a hard time out of pure spite. Insulted him, paid him off with a hundred-dollar bill as if he were a male prostitute, sent him away. Then she put on 'her best friends' act with me to give our auction group something else juicy to talk about. The thing you have to know about Melanie, she isn't happy unless she's at the center of attention. *Did you hear what Melanie did this time?* That's the way she wants every conversation to open."

Scanner laughed at his own naiveté. "I always thought of antiques as a dry and dusty business. How wrong I was."

"No business is dull when there's a lot of money at stake and the competition is intense."

Kay was aware of a loud noise, a *bang* of some kind, as their rented car suddenly lurched to the right.

"Hold on!" Scanner shouted.

She grabbed a handhold on the door with her right hand and braced her left arm against the dashboard. The car was skidding wildly. It went across the next lane, bounced off the concrete divider, veered back to the right lane again. Scanner was fighting the wheel, first left, then right, with quick snapping motions, his foot pumping the brake rather than stomping down on it.

They did an unplanned 360-degree turn. One moment Kay was looking down the road, the next moment gaping in the direction they had just come from, then looking back down the road in the right direction. The movement was like a rollercoaster ride and did to her stomach what those rides usually do. She swallowed hard. Fought the urge to throw up.

"Motherfucker!"

Despite the danger, Kay was surprised by Roy's language.

They were off the road, onto the bumpy hardpan shoulder, dust flying everywhere, but at least the car was slowing down. They went sideways and stopped hard with a great shriek of metal as something tore into the Ford's bodywork. Kay's head jerked and her right temple hit the window glass on the passenger side.

"Get out! Fast! My side!"

Scanner hit the buttons for both of their seat belts, kicked open his door with his left foot.

Kay felt herself being dragged across the driver's seat, her rib cage painfully colliding with the gear shift. "I can walk, for God's sake!" Though she felt dizzy from the blow to her head.

"Stay low! Stay low!"

"I'm all right." When she tried to stand, Scanner jerked her off her feet. "What are you doing?"

Scanner was peering over the hood of the Ford. The cloud of dust created by their skid onto the shoulder of the road was still rising, you couldn't see more than five yards past the car. He looked to his right, saw another car approaching, lifted his arm and waved wildly, but the car passed them up.

"Bastard!" he shouted at its driver.

Things were coming back into focus for Kay. They were several yards into what looked like rural countryside. Perfectly safe now. "I don't understand. We're all right, aren't we? I mean, we survived the blowout, we're off the road, nobody's going to run into us."

Another car passed them, the driver slowing somewhat to look at their predicament with interest but with no inclination to stop. By the time Scanner lifted his arm in a plea for help, the car was well past them.

"That wasn't a blowout, someone shot out our tire."

"Are you sure?"

"I saw the muzzle flash. Somebody shot at us from under a billboard." The cloud of dust was beginning to settle. In a few seconds the gunman would have a clear view of them. Scanner wished he could hunker down here and wait until someone finally saw they were in trouble and stopped for them, but he couldn't afford that. "Whoever shot out the tire was using a rifle, must have been waiting for us, knew my rental car when he saw it. And he's still there. We've got to get out of here."

"Who was waiting for us?"

"I don't know. I just know we're liable to be dead in a couple of minutes if we don't move."

"Where to?" Kay looked around at an unbroken vista of empty countryside relieved only by some patchy grass, stunted trees and a lot of low cactus plants shaped like Ping-Pong paddles.

"That way." Scanner grabbed her hand. "Come on, we have to move before the dust settles."

Kay was glad she'd worn jeans and tennis shoes. They ran across the highway, jumped the concrete divider, and fled into the desert. Several cars came down Interstate 35 in the direction of San Antonio. Scanner stopped to shout and wave, but again he was ignored or not seen at all now that they were off the highway. He hesitated. So much traffic on this highway. Somebody would stop for them.

The dust had cleared, leaving the rented Ford sitting on the shoulder at a peculiar angle, right front fender lodged in the dirt. From behind the billboard came two men, trotting toward the Ford, holding rifles in a port arms position.

"Two of them!" Kay said.

"And a third over there." Scanner saw the third man emerge from the cover of an abandoned car and converge with the other two. "Let's go."

They ran hard and fast toward nothing, interested only in putting distance between themselves and their attackers. Kay's mind had cleared, she knew this attack must have been engineered by someone connected with the auction. Probably Leon Donin. Which meant that one of the men behind them might be Bud Wolf. The thought chilled her. *Anyone but Wolf*, she prayed. *Anyone but him.*

"Goddamn it! You fucked up!" Wolf was furious.

"Your plan was bullshit," Watts shouted back. "First off, that fed handled the blowout as slick as a Formula One driver. Plus which you didn't anticipate all the fucking dust that would be raised. I couldn't get a second shot, couldn't see a damn thing until the dust cleared. By that time they were across the highway. We didn't fool that fed, he knew it wasn't a blowout from minute one."

The three of them were crouched behind the Ford, trying to stay out of the sight of passing traffic, wondering what to do next. No one was stopping because once the dust had settled back to the ground the Ford looked like it might have been parked on the shoulder for some time, the owner off to get help from the nearest garage.

"They were smart to go to the other side of the highway," Loomis pointed out. "Because of that concrete divider, we can't use the Cherokee to cross the highway and chase them with our wheels."

"We'll have to follow on foot." Though Wolf didn't like it, that was the only option. "Finish it out there."

Watts heaved a weary sigh and rubbed his large belly. "A nice long foot chase on a hot day, that's exactly what I don't need."

"You're being paid enough to run the whole length of Texas if I tell you to." Wolf snatched the M-16 from Loomis. "I'll take this, you go back and get the shotgun. And pass over your extra clips, too. Any water in the Cherokee?"

"A canteen under the front seat," Watts said. "Maybe half-full."

"Bring it," Wolf told Loomis.

They waited for Jimmy Loomis to pick up the Remington shotgun and the canteen. When he returned, Wolf said, "I don't want some rubbernecker to see us cross the highway with guns, figure out we aren't hunters, mark what we look like. Wait till the road's clear, then we all go across together. Move fast, we'll pick up their footprints on the other side."

"I'm a good tracker." Loomis had become more animated, moving around as restlessly as an eager young hunting dog. "I'll go ahead of you guys. Take the point, like they say."

"That's great," Wolf said drily. "I was worried about how we were gonna find our way through that vast wilderness the other side of the interstate." He saw that the highway was temporarily clear in both directions, a few cars just dots on the horizon. "Hump it!"

They got across the interstate and quickly found footprints. Loomis, acting as if he'd discovered the Northwest Passage, took off in pursuit.

"Kid can run," Watts said.

They followed at a trot. Within fifteen minutes Watts was breathing heavily even though they'd only traveled a mile. Wolf wasn't worried that he'd give out. Watts looked like a tub, but he had a lot of muscle and even more determination. A dozen times over the past ten years Wolf had worked with Kelly Watts and had never been let down by him. Watts had a style Wolf liked. For openers he was dependable . . . without conscience . . . mean as a snake . . . greedy . . . tough as an old army boot. The fuckup on the highway was, Wolf had to admit, his own fault. Watts had done his part, shot out the tire at the right time, right place. Everything went to hell after that, no fault of Watts.

Lot of other things Wolf liked about Watts. He had four wives in three different states, they all knew about each other and didn't seem to care. He hand-loaded his own ammo. He could drink all night and have a clear head for business in the morning.

From somewhere ahead, the hollow boom of a shotgun rang out across the empty countryside.

Wolf stopped in his tracks, so did Watts. They looked at each other and smiled. Maybe Jimmy Loomis had earned his ten thousand after all.

They came over a ridge and saw a dirt road leading to a house, a bungalow really, half a mile ahead. Loomis was standing in the road, the shotgun thrown up to his shoulder. He fired. No hit. Scanner and the bitch were out of range of the shotgun. They'd reached the front door of the bungalow and Scanner was pounding on it, yelling to be let in.

"They're in range of your Winchester. Take 'em, Kelly."

Watts unslung his rifle as fast as he could, chambered a round, brought the stock to his shoulder and the scope to his eye. Before Watts could flick off the safety, Wolf saw Kay Williams kick out the glass panel in the front door. She put her hand through the hole, unlocked the door, dragged Scanner inside.

" Shit!" Watts lowered the Winchester. "Almost had them."

"Jimmy!" Wolf cupped his hands around his mouth and yelled again. "Jimmy! Get back here!"

Loomis, still running toward the house, halted in the road. He didn't want to retreat, he wanted to bust into the house and kill them both. Then Watts would have to split the money down the middle. He'd have done that except that Bud Wolf intimidated him. So Loomis reluctantly turned and jogged towards his partners, the shotgun sagging in his right hand.

When Loomis joined them, Wolf said, "Kelly, I don't want anybody usin' the phone in that house. Can you shoot down the telephone wire where it connects to the pole?"

"Sure enough."

Watts took aim and fired. There was a flash of light at the connector and the wire fell gracefully, almost snakelike, towards the barren ground.

"Why didn't you let me go after them?" Loomis started to reload the shotgun.

"Guy's carryin' a pistol, remember? And he's got cover for now. You tried to go in there cold and he would've put you down."

"I could have taken the fed. The girl's nothing, it's the fed who's got the gun and I could've taken him."

"You'll have your chance. Let's get behind that ridge."

"What the hell for?" Loomis's frustration was boiling over. "We're three hundred yards from the house and he's only got a handgun! He can't touch us!"

The kid was getting on Wolf's nerves. "He went in with a handgun, we don't know what he might find inside. Somethin' with more range and firepower than a revolver, maybe? A rifle? A shotgun? How many rifles? This is Texas, for Chrissake. Everybody keeps guns, ever think of that?"

"Oh."

"Yeah . . . *oh.*"

They went behind the ridge and dug in to watch the bungalow. It was a decent position. They were looking down on the place from enough height to see all four sides, even the backyard, which consisted mostly of weeds.

"So what do we do?" Loomis asked.

Watts had gone into a prone position again. He was building a six-inch-high sand bridge on which he rested the barrel of the Winchester. Sighting through the scope, he replied, "We wait to see if that fed makes a mistake."

Wolf was down on the ground, too. He passed the canteen up to Loomis. "Get your head down. And drink some water, we might be here for a while."

Scanner was tearing the little bungalow apart, opening every cupboard and drawer, dumping the contents on the floor.

"Roy, what are you doing? This is somebody's *home* you're wrecking."

"Looking for another gun. We need all the guns we can come up with. Keep watch out the window, Kay. Let me know if those guys move."

"They're up behind a little hill."

"All three?"

"Yes, I can sort of see their heads and shoulders. I think they're lying down, they've got guns pointed at this house. I can't tell how far away they are, I'm no good at distances."

"They're three or four hundred yards from the house. One of them shot down the telephone wire from that range, which was nice work." He stopped ransacking a chest of drawers and looked solemnly at Kay. "I didn't thank you for saving my life. If you hadn't kicked in the glass and forced the door open, they would have shot us down outside the house. I guess my training as a lawman kept me from housebreaking."

"You're certainly making up for that now."

"I'll see that Mr. Marvin is compensated for all this damage."

They had found some bills on the kitchen table in the name of Henry Marvin. Owner of the house. There were old family pictures on shelves and on the walls, a couple photographed, sometimes with kids, at many different ages over many decades. A lot of dust had accumulated on the furniture and the place had a musty aroma. Because there were no women's clothes in the closets, Scanner surmised Henry Marvin was a widower in his sixties or seventies living alone.

Kay thought Mr. Marvin was very lucky to have gone out for the afternoon.

Scanner had pulled a chair out from the kitchen table and was standing on it to search the higher cupboards in the kitchen. "Hey! Found something!"

Above the stove was a long horizontal cupboard from which Scanner pulled an awkward-looking rifle, more wood to it than any rifle Kay had ever seen. She couldn't imagine a hunter using such a rifle. Though hardly an expert, she thought it had more of a military look.

"Jesus, an old M-1." Scanner was clearly excited by his find. "My dad owned one of these back on the farm in Illinois. When I was seventeen he used the M-1 to teach me to shoot. He liked the peep sight on it better than the open sights on most rifles." He also found a plastic sack holding ten loaded eight-round clips. "We can hold them off with this until dark, then slip away."

"Until dark! I need to get out of here before then!" Kay knew Roy would start complaining about her priorities again, but she had to say what was on her mind. "I've got to talk to my client this afternoon, get him to send more money for the auction."

She might as well have been talking to the wall. Roy was absorbed with the weapon. Several times he opened and closed the bolt on the rifle— the bolt and trigger and barrel, those were the only parts of a rifle Kay could identify—to make sure it was in working order. He looked satisfied. Put a clip into the whaddayacallit where the bullets go, Kay couldn't think of the word for that. Pushed the clip down. Let the bolt slam home.

"This rifle has to be forty years old, maybe even World War II vintage, but Mr. Marvin's kept it in prime condition. Well-oiled. No pitting in the barrel. Bless him for it."

Scanner went to the window and looked through the crack in the curtains, careful not to show himself or make the curtains rustle. He noted the silhouettes of the three men up on the ridge, their heads and shoulders barely showing.

"What are they doing?" Kay was getting anxious. It wasn't her style to sit back and wait for disaster. She wanted to do something. Take action. She looked over Roy's shoulder through the crack in the curtains. "Why aren't they shooting at us? Or trying to get in the house?"

"They know the habits of people like Mr. Marvin who live way out in the country. Figure the owner probably keeps guns in the house, a rifle or a shotgun at a minimum, and they were correct. So they're showing just enough of themselves to maybe draw some fire, which would tell them we're now better armed than when we broke in here."

"We didn't *break in*." Kay wanted to make it clear that she respected Mr. Marvin's property. "We were in danger and took shelter."

Scanner chuckled over that, Kay worried somebody would think badly of her for avoiding a bullet in the back. "However you want to put it."

"Did you hear me before? I don't want to sit here all afternoon, I have business to do."

"Tell them that." Pointing the rifle in the direction of the ridge.

Kay picked up the phone and tried clicking the receiver with her thumb.

"They shot down the telephone wire. Remember?"

"When we get back to civilization, I'm buying a cellular phone for my purse."

*When* we get back, not *if* we get back. What Scanner liked most about Kay was that she never doubted she'd prevail. He leaned down and took a hammerless .38 revolver with a two-inch barrel from his ankle holster. "I want you to carry this. You ever fired a gun before?"

"Never."

"This one is as easy to use as a hair dryer."

"That's a sexist remark."

"No, it isn't. Men use hair dryers, too." *Why did I even respond to that?* "Just aim and fire. The range is low, you probably wouldn't hit anything farther away than fifteen yards, so use it only in the event one of those guys on the ridge gets in real close to us. Here, take these extra rounds, too." He slipped six additional bullets into the left-hand pocket of her jeans. Then he showed her how to reload the revolver and suggested she stow it in her jeans' right-hand pocket. "Keep your hand away from the trigger while you're putting the gun in or taking it out of your pocket. Okay?"

Kay put the revolver in her pocket, took it out. Put it in, took it out. "I can do that. But I'm not sure I can shoot someone."

"I'm sure you can, if you have to." Kay was the strongest woman he'd ever met.

"Oh damn!"

"What's wrong?" Scanner slid his finger inside the rifle's trigger guard and pushed the safety switch to off.

"We left the car so fast that I left my purse behind. I don't have any makeup with me, not even a lipstick."

"Makeup . . ."

Kay stared in disgust at her reflection in a wall mirror. "Look at me, I'm going to be a total mess at the auction tomorrow. Big bruise on my forehead. Scratches on my cheek. And my skin's become *parchment*." She gently probed the spot on her forehead that had gotten banged when the car skidded off the road. "I've got to do something about *this* right now, otherwise it'll swell up and turn bright red by tomorrow morning."

"Look, please, we're in a dangerous situation here." Scanner couldn't believe he had to explain that. "We have to concentrate on keeping those three guys up on the ridge well away from us."

"You can handle that, you know you can. I'm going to see if there's any ice in Mr. Marvin's refrigerator. Ice is the only thing that might keep this bruise from swelling up and turning red." She went into the kitchen.

"Kay . . ." There was some movement on the ridge, he turned his attention back where it belonged.

Jimmy Loomis was totally sick of lying in the sand, looking down on a crumbling old bungalow. He stood up and strutted back and forth, daring the federal agent in the house to shoot at him. "Let's get this show on the road, guys. Let's make it happen. Here's an idea, we could set the house on fire, burn 'em out."

"That's goddamn brilliant." Wolf nodded sagely. "Lots of fire and smoke risin' up to the sky. Pillar of smoke, let's say that. What do you think, Kelly, how long would it be before the San Marcos fire department arrived on the scene?"

Watts pretended to give the matter serious thought. "We're pretty far out, might be fifteen minutes before we saw the first fire truck."

"What's your take on this, Jimmy? Do we want to draw the fire department out here or not?"

"I guess not." Loomis kicked the ground with the toe of his boot. "But shit, Wolfie, we have to do *something*."

"You haven't known me long enough to call me Wolfie." Wolf did have an idea of how to break this stalemate. The more Jimmy Loomis talked, the better it looked. "I do have a brainstorm. Sit down before you get shot, I'll tell you about it."

Loomis sank to the ground, shotgun cradled in his arms. Pulled his cowboy hat down over his eyes Clint Eastwood style.

Wolf turned away from Loomis, gave Kelly Watts a *go along with this* wink. "Jimmy, that shotgun of yours won't do much good from way up here. I'd like you to work your way down to that rocky outcrop about sixty yards from the house. See it?"

Loomis nodded.

"Open up on the place from there with the shotgun. Stay under cover, but blow at least a dozen holes in that old shack. If Scanner found a rifle, sooner or later he'll fire back. Don't worry, we'll cover you from here. He tries to return your fire, Kelly and me'll riddle the fucker with thirty-calibers."

"Okay . . . right." Loomis eagerly checked the loads in the shotgun's chamber, then went down the hill in a zigzagging crouch.

"Like I said, Jimmy's a good shot." Watts lined up the front window of the bungalow in the crosshairs of his scope. "Not too bright though, tenth-grade education or not."

"Fuckin' understatement of the century. We may get a clear shot at Scanner after all, Jimmy does his job."

"He'll do it. But Wolfie, you know we're probably gonna lose our pal Jimmy."

"I'll send flowers."

They lay there with their rifles trained on the front window, waiting for Loomis to begin firing.

Scanner saw the guy coming down the hill like some gung-ho actor in a commando movie. All hunched over. Zig left. Zag right. Zig left. Zag right. Shotgun clutched to his chest. Finally plopped himself down behind a narrow rock ledge, which didn't make sense, not enough cover for real safety. He called: "Kay? They're making a move."

"What?" She came out of the kitchen with a plastic bag full of ice held to her forehead.

"One's come most of the way down the hill." He took Kay's arm and led her to the dining room, where he'd piled up the heaviest furniture in the bungalow—the dining room table and breakfront, bedroom dresser, big oak table from the kitchen, anything else he could find that was thick and solid. Right in the middle he'd left a hollow space large enough for two to hide. Scanner pushed Kay inside the makeshift fort and wedged himself down beside her. "Let him blaze away for a while, waste some ammo. See what they're really up to. We're pretty safe here."

"What about the other two? Won't they move around behind us?"

"I don't think so. I get the feeling they sent this one down to test us. Stupid move, he's so exposed."

They heard a blast and the whole bungalow rattled. Kay peeked out and saw at least twenty holes the size of nickels in the living room wall.

"Buckshot," Scanner said.

"Roy, those walls are so thin. The buckshot went right through."

"That's why we're hiding in here."

Another blast and the living room window shattered, sending the curtain flying.

They sat in silence, Kay holding tight to Roy's arm.

Another blast, more holes in the wall. Plaster and dust all over poor Mr. Marvin's living room. Another blast. Another. Kay covered her head, fretting over what all the falling dust was doing to her hair. Silly thing to worry about, she knew that, but it helped take her mind off the gunshots. Which kept coming. The old bungalow practically disintegrating around them. The occasional piece of buckshot reached their hiding place, thunking into the breakfront or oak kitchen table, but not penetrating.

She glanced sideways at Roy, who seemed unconcerned. Almost at peace. The M-1 rested across his knees and the bag of ammunition clips lay on the floor between his feet.

After a time the blasts tailed off, as if the gunman had become physically tired by his chore.

"They stopped shooting." Kay had lost count of exactly how many shots had been fired. "He must have shot at us a dozen times."

"Fifteen times. Now he's wondering if he killed us, probably thinks he did. This is a good time to show him that he's wrong."

Scanner left their hiding place with the M-1, going across the living floor at a crawl. He stopped six feet short of the window, raised up slowly, brought the rifle to his shoulder, took aim and fired.

His shot was answered immediately by two others. Scanner cried out and spun around.

"Roy!"

Kay crawled across the floor and grabbed his arm, pulling him towards the safety of the little fort he'd built for them. His neck was bleeding. He was conscious, she believed. Groggy, though. She would have gotten to her feet, it would have been easier to drag him if she were standing, except that more shots were peppering the walls. These sounded different, sharper and somehow more dangerous. Rifle shots. With each shot a little shaft of light appeared in the living room wall.

"I'm okay." He hadn't dropped the M-1, it was held tight in his left hand. "At least I think I'm okay."

When they were safe, Kay examined him. "Your neck is bleeding. No . . . that's wrong . . . oh dear, there's an ugly gash along your jaw. And I'm afraid you've lost the tip of your earlobe."

"Better my jaw than my neck." Scanner sat up and let Kay press the tail of her shift to the wound to stanch the bleeding. He rather enjoyed her nursing.

"I should get some water."

"No, you shouldn't." He took her arm to restrain her.

Rounds continued to crackle through the bungalow. Three of the rounds hit their barricade, rocking pieces of furniture in a much harder fashion than the shotgun pellets had done.

"I don't hear the shotgun anymore," Kay said.

"No, I hit the guy with the shotgun. The way he dropped, he's dead or dying. The other two sacrificed him, sent him down close to the house hoping I'd fire at him, give them a target. I should have seen that coming, I guess I'm not used to dealing with people who throw away the lives of their friends." He was disappointed in himself. If that was Bud Wolf up there, he wouldn't hesitate wasting a friend or two to get what he wanted. *Bastard's tougher than I am, or meaner anyway, I have to keep that in mind.*

\*        \*        \*

Up on the ridge, Wolf was asking Kelly Watts if he thought he'd hit the federal agent.

"Oh, I hit him. How solid? I dunno. He went down, but I got the impression through the scope that I didn't exactly knock him off his pins."

Wolf didn't want to hear that. He looked at his watch. Two o'clock already, he couldn't afford to spend all day killing just two people.

They shifted their attention from the bungalow to the body of Jimmy Loomis, who lay on his back, arms thrown out, blood pooling all around him. His cowboy hat had come off, the breeze already had blown it twenty yards away.

"Jimmy did a nice job, far as it went." Watts sighed. "The kid could be a pain in the ass, but I'm thinking I'll miss him."

*The fuck you are,* Wolf thought. *You're thinkin' about the ten grand in the hat that's blowin' around down there.* "So we're still at square one."

"Nah, they're in a lot worse shape now. They're pinned down, no way out, the fed is hit, the girl's got to be tearing out her pretty hair by now, crying and screaming for help."

"You don't know that bitch. I've been tryin' to tell you she's got more sand than most."

"Ah, women always cry and throw fits when they see the butcher coming." Watts took a swig from the canteen. "She ain't gonna be no different about that."

"We can't sit up on this ridge all afternoon. Night comes, they'll slip away."

"My suggestion, wait a half-hour. Let the fed bleed for a while. Weaker he gets, the harder it'll be for him to take a steady aim with that rifle he found. In half an hour we'll go in for them through the back and through the left side of the house. Do them in a crossfire."

That was agreeable with Wolf. "We'll need to coordinate our fields of fire. I plan to set my M-16 on automatic. Don't want to shoot you by mistake and I sure as hell don't want you to shoot me."

Watts grinned. "Wouldn't be friendly. We'll work that out before we go in."

Kay was trying to force three Tylenols into Scanner's mouth. "Take these, Roy!"

"I don't like to take pills."

"Don't be such a baby." She finally got the capsules into his mouth and jammed a water glass between his lips. "Drink them down."

After he'd taken them, Scanner said, "I'm not a baby. I just don't like pills of any kind. Never have. A lot people are like that."

"Well, you were a good boy this time." She patted him like a mommy placating a spoiled kid. "Now eat your strained peas."

"Strained peas? Well, I guess I'm glad you haven't lost your sense of humor. Even if it's at my expense."

"So what do we do now?" Kay had been using humor to fend off the terrible anxiety centered in her chest. At one point she'd actually wondered if she was having a heart attack. "We can't stay here much longer, can we?"

"No, they'll come after us pretty soon. I think they're hoping we were hit, one or both of us, and that we'll be weak, or maybe even dead, by the time they come in. They won't wait very long, though."

"Again, what exactly do we do?"

"I'm afraid we have to burn down Henry Marvin's little house."

"What?"

"Got to do it. For two reasons. First, I let the guy with the shotgun bang away at us for a long time in hopes there were other houses nearby, one at least, and somebody would call the police. Didn't happen. We're on our own, we have to make our own luck. Second, we need a fire and a lot of smoke to cover our run. From up on the ridge they can see all around the house. They might even be able to hit us out back of the house with rifle fire from the ridge. Four-hundred-yard shot, I'd say. Three-fifty maybe. That's a hard shot. But one of the two on that ridge is a sharpshooter with a scoped weapon, the one who did this." He ran a finger over the face wound that Kay had dressed with a bandage from Mr. Marvin's medicine cabinet. "Also, the smoke from the fire will draw the fire department. The police, too. They'll find the guy with the shotgun dead out front. After that they'll search the area."

"Poor Mr. Marvin. This is his *home*. Will you be able to get the government to repay him?"

"I doubt it." Reacting to Kay's distress. "Look, he has to have fire insurance on this place."

Kay was looking at the pictures on the walls. "You can't replace the history of his life." She jumped up.

"Kay, stay down!"

She'd begun running around the house, pulling pictures off the wall, throwing them out the back windows. Tossing out of the house anything else that looked like a family memento.

"You're crazy!"

"Start the fire!" she snapped. "I'll save as much as I can."

Scanner dragged himself up, stuffing loaded clips of ammo into his pockets. Staying away from the front windows, he went into the kitchen where he'd seen a big can of starter fluid for barbecues and a box of kitchen matches. He shook the can, found it to be more than half-full. Still avoiding windows, he began squirting the fluid on anything at the front of the house that looked flammable.

"Look out, I'm starting the fire. When there's enough smoke, we'll leave through the back door. Hold my hand, we'll run like hell."

Kay had found a big box of old photos and trinkets. She opened the back door, leaned out, threw it as far as she could. "I'm ready." There was an old vase, not an antique or a very valuable-looking piece, but placed on a shelf as if positioned by someone who really cared for it. Somehow it had survived the shotgun blasts. She wrapped it in a towel and threw the vase out the back door too, towards a sandy patch to soften the fall.

"Goddamn it, we aren't trying to save inanimate objects!" *Didn't the woman ever give up on her damned antiques?* "We're trying to save ourselves!"

"Start the fire."

He was already striking matches and tossing them around the living room like a crazed pyro. The flames jumped high and spread quickly through the front of the wooden bungalow. Scanner kicked forward the curtains that had come off the window. They burned harder than anything else and in turn ignited the front door and frame, the front window molding, a coffee table, the couch, everything they touched.

Scanner retreated to the kitchen.

"Shall we go?" Having done what she could for Mr. Marvin, Kay was anxious to get out.

"Not yet, we need more smoke and flames."

Suddenly the living room virtually exploded, went up in a fireball. Kay and Roy were rocked backwards, their faces singed by the heat.

"Is that enough flame for you?"

"Yeah, that should do it."

Scanner used his left hand to grab her arm, the other hand holding tight to the M-1. "Let's go!" They went out the back door and ran from the house in lockstep without looking back.

Kelly Watts hit Wolf on the shoulder. "The house is on fire!"

"I see it." Wolf lifted his rifle. "They set the fire themselves, they'll go out the back door. Lay down some goddamn fire, Kelly."

"I can't see anything!"

"Shit, neither can I. But we know they'll go out the back door. Lay down some fire back there, for Chrissake! Maybe we'll get a lucky hit." He began to fire through the smoke into the backyard, his rifle set on automatic, bursts of three or four rounds at a time. Watts was firing, too, frustrated because he couldn't make the best use of his scope.

"There!"

Two forms glimpsed in flight, then the smoke swallowed them up. They fired in tandem, trying to estimate the speed and direction of their targets.

"The fuck they go?" Watts wondered.

Wolf lowered his rifle. "They're gone." He jacked himself up to his feet. "Come on, we have to follow."

Watts was slow to get up. "Christ, Wolfie . . ."

"I said we'll follow 'em. We're gettin' this done, one way or another. Come on, Kelly, move your ass. We have to be out of here before the fire trucks arrive."

They jogged down the hill towards the house. Wolf went to the body of Jimmy Loomis and signaled Watts to join him. "We'll throw Jimmy in the fire. I know that sounds cold, but I don't want his body found in front of the house, bullet hole in him, that'll draw a lot of cops out here. I want them to think some guy, maybe the owner of the house, died in the fire. Be a day before some medical examiner discovers he was shot."

Wolf took Jimmy Loomis under the arms and Watts grabbed his legs. They got as close to the fire as possible, heaved the body through the front window.

"We'd better toss his hat in there, too." Watts ran over and retrieved the hat, slipped the ten thousand dollars out of the lining while his back was to Wolf, stuffed the money under his shirt. Then he added the cowboy hat to the fire.

Didn't bother Wolf, he expected as much. "Let's move, we can't afford to give them a good lead."

# CHAPTER 21

need to pee."

"What?" Scanner couldn't believe what he was hearing.

"I have to *pee*," Kay repeated. "What's so unusual? Are you going to tell me I should have peed before I left the house?"

"Yeah, I guess that's what I'm thinking."

"The house was *on fire* when we left. Here's a place." Kay dodged behind a little rise and dropped her jeans. "I'll only be thirty seconds."

Scanner looked behind, saw no one following. Not yet, anyway. He examined the horizon and saw no buildings either. No roads. No sign of life or property of any kind. Texas is too goddam *big*. It bothered him that the one thing he could see was a definable set of their tracks. Their luck wasn't good on that score—evidently it had rained out here a day or so earlier and the ground in most places was still soft.

Kay popped up, drawing her belt tight. "Okay, I'm ready."

They started off at a fast pace, but Scanner reached over and put a hand on Kay's arm. "We'll double-time it for now, save our energy in case we do have to run flat out."

"Where are we headed?"

"Northeast. I've got no idea what's ahead. If we can find some hard ground, a place where it hasn't rained and they can't track us, we'll try to circle back to Route 35. The crazy thing is we aren't all that far from the highway. If we didn't have those guys behind us, we could find someplace safe in forty-five minutes."

"Is Bud Wolf one of them?"

"I couldn't tell."

"At first I wasn't all that much afraid of Wolf. Now, I guess it's all right to admit it, he's got me completely terrified."

"It's all right to admit it." Scanner didn't let on that Wolf was beginning to intimidate him, too. The guy had a relentlessness you didn't run into very often. Not that there was any solid proof Wolf was behind them. All he had was the crawly feeling he got when the guy was nearby. He found himself saying, "Tell you the truth, he scares me too."

Kay was surprised. She'd been thinking of Roy as Bud Wolf's superior in every way. If Roy was genuinely scared of him, Kay thought it wise to be doubly scared. She tried to find something positive to say. "Well, if it is Wolf, then he must be scared of us by now. We escaped from the car, we escaped from the house, and you even killed one of his men. So far, he hasn't had a very good day."

"Neither have we. But you're right, he must be at least mildly discouraged by now." Scanner didn't point out that one of their pursuers was carrying a scoped rifle with an effective range of at least five hundred yards. The ability to make the long shot was usually the trump card in this kind of game.

Despite their situation, Kay couldn't help admiring the great blue Texas sky. The sky wasn't just *above* them. It was all *around* them. The biggest, bluest sky she'd ever experienced, she couldn't recall coming across that particular shade of blue anywhere else. Here and there pink stripes, a subtle salmon pink, gave relief from the solid blue. *If I get back home,* Kay decided, *I'm going to redo my bathroom in that exact pink even if I have to fly a painter out here to copy that color.* She corrected herself— *When I get back home.*

They'd been moving at a steady double time for almost half an hour when Kay said, "Now I'm thirsty."

"First you had to pee, now you're thirsty." Scanner was grateful for something to laugh at. "This is like a nightmare family vacation."

"We should have picked up a bottle of water before we left the house."

"I had a choice between carrying food and water or ammunition for the rifle. Guess which I chose."

"I could have carried the water," Kay grumbled. "We should have thought of that."

"You were busy saving some of Mr. Marvin's personal possessions, I was busy burning down his house."

"When Mr. Marvin sees what happened to his house, he's going to be devastated."

"I'm tired of hearing about Mr. Marvin." *You'd have thought Bud Wolf was after him instead of us.* He tried to change the subject. They were traveling at a good clip, double-timing in lock step, working up a healthy sweat. "You look real good when you sweat."

"Women don't sweat, we perspire."

"Women say they want to be treated as equals, then object when common words like *sweat* and *fart* are applied to them."

"Women don't fart either, we fluff."

"See what I mean!"

"Women are adorable, men are grungy. That's the basic difference between us."

"Somewhere along the line you people have developed a superiority complex."

"We are superior. Just ask God, She'll tell you."

"You think God is a woman?" He laughed. "God is a man, His first name is George. Everyone knows that."

"What's his last name?"

"God. His name is George God, it's written down somewhere. On an ancient Sanskrit tablet or something." Scanner was almost enjoying himself. The rifle in his left hand felt light as a feather. "Don't try to change things like that. You'll make Him mad at us."

"She must already be mad at us or we wouldn't be in this mess."

"Good point."

Kay had been trying to ignore the stitch in her side, but it was growing worse. Every other breath she took was painful. "My side hurts, I have to stop for a minute."

"All right."

They stopped and Kay threw herself on the ground and lay with her arm thrown across her eyes. "Now I'm *really* thirsty."

"When I was in the army, they sent me to desert warfare school at Fort Huachuca, Arizona. We learned to lick our own sweat for moisture. Oh, sorry. I forgot you don't sweat."

"That's disgusting. It probably doesn't work either."

"It works." He gave his right arm a long lick to prove his point.

"Ugh. Where did they send you after desert warfare school? I know. You must have been in Kuwait—Desert Storm."

"No, after desert warfare school they sent me to Fort Richardson, Alaska." He shrugged. "That's why I didn't stay in the army. Nothing made sense there."

"And what we're doing today makes sense?"

He searched the countryside and still saw nothing that could be of help to them. On the other hand, the two gunmen weren't in sight, either. Maybe they'd turned back, given this up as a bad job.

Kay sat up, then rose to her feet. "That helped, I'll be all right now."

"I think it's time to change direction." Scanner was examining their surroundings. "The ground's harder out here, they'll have a tougher time following us."

"That crease in your jaw is bleeding again. Let me tighten the bandage." She loosened the dressing, then rewound it. "Nasty, you'll probably have a scar."

"With my face, a scar'll be an improvement. Come on."

They took off on a tangent from their previous direction.

"Fuckin' people travel like goats, never stop." Kelly Watts was panting hard. "I gotta have some more water."

They stopped and Watts unslung his canteen, drew a long swig of water.

"Save some," Wolf warned. "We may be on their trail for a long time. They're headin' farther out into the country, nothin' but a few head of cows and a lot of cactus out there."

Watts offered the canteen to Wolf, who shook his head. Though he was thirsty, he knew he'd feel better in the long run if he drank sparingly.

"I could use some food, too," Watts said.

"Eat some of that ten thousand you took out of Jimmy Loomis's hat."

Watts didn't reply. Instead he dragged a big red kerchief out of his back pocket and wiped his face and neck. "They're moving pretty good, better than I thought they would."

"Yes, they are." Wolf was looking at the soil. "And they changed direction slightly, too. Gone to harder ground."

"Think they'll try to circle back to the highway?"

"That's what I'd do." He was considering the idea of splitting away from Watts. They'd have a better chance if one followed tracks and the other tried to cut their trail. Scanner and the bitch weren't traveling especially fast, just steadily. Saving their energy in case they needed to crank up some real speed. Wolf approved of their strategy. "Kelly, I want you to follow their tracks. I'll go to the southeast, try to get ahead of them. An ambush would finish the job."

"All right." He offered the canteen a second time. "If you're going off alone, you'd better have that drink of water."

Wolf took the canteen. "I'll do better than that, I'll take the whole damned canteen."

"Wolfie!"

"You've already had enough water to float a fuckin' houseboat. Stay thirsty and you'll move faster."

Watts glared at him.

"When you spot them, fire a shot. I don't care if you're firin' in the air, I just want to know if they're headed my way or not."

"I'll fire all right, straight into their backs."

"Better yet." Wolf put the canteen strap over his shoulder. "Let's hump it, pardner. We can finish this in two hours if we keep movin.' "

"Oh, I'll hump it," Watts promised. "I'll just think of those two as a couple of tall, cold beers. That'll keep me on their trail at double time."

Wolf grinned and slapped Watts on the back. "See you soon."

The ground stayed hard, which helped Kay and Scanner move at a faster pace. Gradually they changed their direction until they were making a semicircle in the general direction of Interstate 35. Several miles off to their left the smoke from Mr. Marvin's burning house could still be seen, though it was becoming whiter and more dispersed as the fire department brought the flames under control.

"Wish we could get to Mr. Marvin's house." Double-timing wasn't as easy as Kay had thought, her breath was now coming in heavy gasps. "There's bound to be a police car at the fire."

"No way we'd make it," Scanner said. "Our friends are between us and that house."

"You don't think we've lost them?"

"No, they're nearby."

"Roy . . ." Kay's voice was choked. She'd just looked over her shoulder. "I thought I saw them, one of them anyway."

Scanner looked back. "I don't see anyone."

"It was just a glimpse, something brown moving way back there. On that hill we came over."

"A cow, maybe? We've seen a few."

"I hope it was a cow."

"I wish we'd run into a whole herd of cattle, we could lose ourselves among them." Scanner took another quick glance over his shoulder and still saw nothing back there. He suspected Kay was just jumpy. "Might as well wish for a herd of zebras. We could catch a couple, ride off into the sunset."

"Zebras wearing saddles," Kay added. "Might as well wish for the ultimate."

Even though they saw no one following, a feeling of immediate danger settled over them. Kay picked up her own pace and Scanner matched her step for step so that they were soon jogging quite fast. The M-1 was no longer a feather in Scanner's hand, more like an anvil. As Kay had said, it would have been smart to bring along a container of water.

*Can't go back and start over again,* he thought.

A single rifle shot, like the crack of a giant whip, echoed across the empty terrain.

Kay flinched, ducked her head instinctively and came to a halt. "They're shooting at us!"

"No." Scanner grabbed her arm and pulled her along in a flat-out run. "They must have split up. One of them signaled the other that he spotted us. We're still out of range, but they'll be on us as soon as they join up again."

"Oh, no."

"Don't talk . . . run . . . just run hard . . . for five minutes. Push yourself."

Kay hadn't pushed herself like this since running the mile on her high school track team. Back then she didn't break the four-minute mile. Or the five-minute mile. And she wasn't going to break any records today. But they did cover a substantial stretch of ground over the next five minutes without any more shots being fired.

"There! That little rise." Scanner was desperate to reach the cover of the hill, it was their only chance.

They did reach it safely, a piece of ground that rose about ten yards in the shape of an anthill. They dropped flat behind the modest rise and sought to regain their breath.

When he could again breathe easily, Scanner said, "The shot we heard came from the scoped rifle. Different sound from the other rifle. We've got to stop that guy before his partner gets here."

"How?"

"I'm not sure."

"That's encouraging."

"Well. Okay. They split up, we have to split up."

"No!"

"I want you to keep moving." He pointed in the direction of Interstate 35. "Believe me, I'll have a better chance by myself and so will you. Get to the highway. Flag down a car. Get yourself to a sheriff's substation."

"I'm not going to leave you here to be shot!"

Scanner pushed her away. "I have no intention of being shot. I'm going to double back and take that guy. Once I have his long-range rifle, the second man won't give me any trouble. Now get going! Run like hell! Don't stop for anything! In thirty minutes you'll be safe."

"I won't leave!"

"Damn it, you have to do things *my way* for a change!" He shoved Kay, stepped forward and shoved her again. Shoved her once more until Kay was finally moving away from him, picking up her feet on her own. "That's it, go! Hurry up!"

She finally turned her back on him, blinking back some tears, terribly fearful of being alone, but moving faster, letting herself separate from Roy until she was running hard and crying even harder.

Kelly Watts had caught a glimpse of them and fired the shot that would draw Wolfie back in his direction. Then he lost sight of the fed and the girl as the ground around him lowered a bit. By now they'd be running like a pair of goddamn white-tailed deer. Watts knew they couldn't keep up that pace for long, but neither could he run hard himself. Best he could do was to jog a couple hundred yards, walk a hundred yards, jog again. Fucking Wolfie shouldn't have taken the canteen.

He went forward as fast as he could manage, eyes moving left to right and back again. What Watts lacked in speed he made up for in thoroughness. He'd started his career in the army, knew how to flush out an enemy and protect himself while doing it. Pretty soon now the fed would make a move, either try to double back for an ambush or dig in and try to draw him in close. Either way, Watts was ready.

"Come on, Wolfie." It would be easier with two of them, they could catch the fed and the girl in a crossfire.

Watts had a sixth sense, or simply a powerful survival streak, that had served him well over the years. Whatever you called it, he felt a galloping unease that told him the fed had made the move he'd expected. He dropped prone behind some mesquite, looking and listening in his own unique style. The wind had dropped off. Earlier it had brought the aroma of smoke from the house the fed had set on fire. Now the air was clearer and sweeter. Watts sniffed, caught the aroma of something else. The fuck was it? Sweat? Yeah, the smell of sweat and fear. He saw the branches of a mesquite bush tremble. Christ, somebody was moving over there to his right.

He dropped to his knee and fired a shot two yards to the left of the mesquite bush. Jacked another round into the chamber. Fired another shot three yards to the right of the mesquite.

Fire and move, that's what they'd taught him in the First Infantry Division and that's exactly what he did, ran about twenty yards south and threw himself prone in the dirt.

A rattle of rifle fire made him flinch. The ground close to where he'd just lain was suddenly pocked by rifle bullets. If he'd stayed where he was, he might have been hit.

Watts grinned. The fed had made his first major mistake, firing off seven or eight tightly spaced shots, probably a whole clip or magazine depending on what kind of rifle he had. There'd been enough shots fired so that he could see the muzzle flashes. The fed had been maybe four hundred yards away when he fired, probably rattled by the two bullets sent his way. *The fed'll pull back now*, Watts reasoned. *Try to come at me from a different angle.*

Watts rose. Keeping his head well below the level of the mesquite and brush, he scuttled a hundred yards to his left. When he reached the cover of a small scrub oak, he dropped to one knee and listened intently, wondered if the fed and the girl were still together. He had a sense they'd split up. The fed was probably one of those heroic types, sent the girl on ahead and stayed behind to fight it out. Watts loved heroes. Their actions were easy to predict.

*Let's flush him out some more,* he thought. The fed would have moved southeast for maybe fifty or sixty yards, still trying to cover the girl's retreat. Watts picked another mesquite and again fired a shot a few yards to the left of it and then a few yards to the right.

He was rewarded with the faint sound of panicky movement, the fed pulling farther back but still determined to stand and fight.

Where the fuck was Wolfie?

Never mind. He could handle this sucker all by himself.

Wolf heard a number of shots fired and stopped to determine the direction the sound had come from. Hard to tell out here in such flat country, the echoes rolling around and careening off each other like marbles. He was confident the sounds wouldn't reach the burning house and the fire crew that would be trying to put out the fire. The *snap snap snap* of rifle fire was too thin to carry that far. And he doubted anyone else was close enough to hear the gunshots from this little firefight.

Watts had to be about a mile, maybe two miles from here, but in exactly which direction was harder to determine. If possible, Wolf wanted to come at Scanner and the bitch from their blind side. Catch them in a crossfire. Between them, he and Watts could just waste the hell out of them.

Another shot was fired, the familiar sharp crack of Watts's favorite Winchester.

*Either Kelly's got his targets zeroed in,* Wolf thought, *or he's keepin' up a steady fire to make sure I track in the right direction. Or both.*

Confident now of the direction he should go, Wolf gave his pants a hitch, tightened the sling of the M-16 against his shoulder, and took off at a strong trot towards his targets.

Kay heard all the shooting too, a confusing and ragged *rat-tat-tat* that brought her to a complete halt. Her heart rose to her throat. All that rifle fire, and she was sure the sounds came from at least two different guns, meant Roy was in terrible danger, that he was very close to at least one of their pursuers. He was *engaging the enemy.* Wasn't that what they called it? *Engaging the enemy* sounded so antiseptic in the newspapers. She'd never again be able to read another dry news account of a battle without thinking of the terror of this moment.

*What should I do?*

She knew Roy would want her to ignore the gunfire, keep going, get to the highway, save herself.

The rebel in her refused to do it.

*Men always think they know what's best. Well, they don't.*

Her hand moved almost of its own will, digging into the right-hand pocket of her jeans and carefully dragging out Roy's heavy pistol.

She stared at the pistol and grew angry at the recollection of Roy's words: "As easy to use as a hair dryer."

What a sexist remark! She should have chewed him out properly at the time he said it. *You can't let men get away with such remarks, they'll just continue talking to women in their same old thoughtless way.* Kay turned and started back in the direction she'd come. Now was as good a time as any to take him to task.

Okay, this is it. Whatever *it* is, this is definitely that thing they call *it.* Damn, but I'm scared of *it.*

Scanner's old drill instructor at Fort Huachuca, Sergeant Powell, had taught him how to use the butt of a rifle to dig a quick and dirty foxhole. He was down on his knees, digging hard with the butt of the M-1, dirt flying. Sergeant Powell was right, you could scoop out a pretty fair hole with one of these things. Been a long time since he'd done it. Hard god-damn work. It was Scanner's desperate goal to create a foxhole from which he could fire with relative safety. Reduce the shooter's advantage and maybe . . . hopefully . . . please God . . . create one for himself.

In three minutes he created a trench about two feet deep, two feet wide, four feet long. Sergeant Powell wouldn't have approved of his effort. Scanner could almost hear his screams: "NOT GODDAMN DEEP ENOUGH! NOT GODDAMN LONG ENOUGH! FUCKING SLOPPY JOB! YOU'RE A FUCKING DISGRACE TO THE UNIFORM OF THE UNITED STATES ARMY, PRIVATE SCANNER!"

All probably true, but he didn't have time to do more. Crude as the hole might be, he felt a lot safer lying on his stomach in it. Scanner looked through the M-1's peep sight and tried to locate the shooter, who'd probably be approaching any minute. He conceded the guy was a pro, Sergeant Powell wouldn't yell at *him. The guy's already boxed me in and put himself between me and Route 35. One of his shots almost took my leg off. My only chance is to make him come to me, come close enough so the M-1 is as effective as what he's using.*

He wondered whether Kay had made it to the highway yet.

Something moving out there.

Scanner started to wipe the sweat off his brow, keep it out of his eyes so he could see better, froze his hand. Stupid! Stupid! Stupid! Don't move! You see something moving and you move yourself. Stupid!

Before he even heard the crack of a rifle shot, there was an explosion of dirt not six inches from his elbow. The sound of the shot followed, rang in his ears like a bell. For a moment he couldn't see or think. Dirt in his eyes and hair. The hole had saved him. If he'd been higher, the bullet would have taken his head off.

There!

He spotted the shooter up on one knee, looking to see if his round had hit home.

Scanner quickly looked down his own rifle sight and began squeezing the trigger. Seven shots left in the clip. He fired all seven. Fired them too fast. What the hell, let somebody else dodge bullets for a change. Let somebody else go sick with fear.

The empty clip popped out of the receiver, fell with a metallic *clink* off to the right. He pulled a loaded clip from his pocket and shoved it into the rifle, felt better when the weapon was reloaded. He was swinging it around to take aim, trying to see whether he'd scored a hit, when the M-1 exploded in his hands and hit him in the face with the force of a baseball bat.

Scanner's head fell forward. His nose was bleeding and he couldn't see out of his right eye. It seemed to take an hour to raise his head, which throbbed with pain. "Jesus . . ." He coughed until all the dirt plugging up his mouth was cleared. Gradually his sight returned, he could see the M-1 lying nearby in three or four broken pieces. At first he thought he must have fired the rifle, that the damned barrel had exploded in his face.

Not quite right.

The shooter had fired a second time, hit the M-1, tore it apart.

Scanner realized that was why his hands ached as badly as his head.

He tried without success to get up, managed only to part way sit up.

"Nice try, fella." Big guy with a round, drooping belly stood in front him. He was drenched in sweat, licking at dry lips. The scoped rifle was in his hands.

"The girl got away." Scanner wanted to go out with a feeling of accomplishment. "You're too late to stop her, she's probably caught a ride on the interstate already."

"My partner'll get her," the big guy said. "Not today, maybe. But he'll nail her sooner or later. He hates the bitch. What'd she do to him, anyway?"

"If you let me go, I can make it worth your while."

"Federal agent? You wouldn't have enough dough to interest me."

"I'm with the Treasury Department. I have access to unlimited federal funds." That was a lie, the best Scanner could come up with. Nothing to lose in pushing the lie, making it as strong as possible. "What would you say to a million dollars in cash? Delivered wherever you say?"

Watts raised his rifle. "I'd say you had a good run, now it's time to wave bye-bye." Wicked grin. "Didn't expect you to dig your own grave, but I appreciate it. Saves me some work."

The snaps of rifle shots led Kay right to them. She approached as silently as she could manage, on the balls of her feet, ready to bolt like a deer. A voice, loud and brassy and arrogant, helped to pinpoint their location. She hoped both their pursuers weren't there. One she might be able to handle, two would be a stretch. She especially didn't want to meet Bud Wolf face to face, not today. But the brassy voice wasn't Wolf's.

Through luck or some primitive instinct, Kay had come up behind the rifleman. She approached with the pistol held way out in front of her in both hands. All she could immediately see was a wide, sweatstained back. He was looking down as he talked. When Kay came within ten yards of the man, she could see Roy sitting in some sort of trench, face smeared with blood and eyes glassy, leaning first this way and then the other. He was making a rational, low-key argument about why he shouldn't be killed. Offering money. The M-1 rifle Roy had been carrying lay on the ground in several pieces.

The rifleman raised his weapon, pointed it at Roy. My God, Roy was about to be executed!

"Stop!" Kay hadn't planned to say anything, the word just popped out. The rifleman spun around, surprised but not frightened. It took precious seconds for him to swing the barrel of the Winchester far enough around to shoot Kay. The man had a huge, drooping belly. She aimed Roy's pistol at it. "Don't!" Kay had already pulled the trigger once when she said the word. She fired three more times. The rifleman disappeared. Just vanished from sight. At first Kay thought he'd run away. Then she realized he was on the ground, practically at her feet, bleeding from several wounds.

"Oh . . ." She stood and watched the man buck and jump with pain. "Oh . . . I'm sorry." His body twisted itself into a strange shape as he gasped for air. He reached towards her with trembling arms. Then his eyes rolled up under their lids, his arms fell, and he stopped moving altogether. "Dear God, I killed him!"

Scanner staggered to his feet. "Where the hell did you come from? I told you to get yourself over to the interstate. Don't you *ever* do what you're told?"

His words were like a bucket of cold water thrown in Kay's face. "Not if I don't want to! And I didn't want to because . . . because . . . I had to tell you what a *stupid* remark you made!"

"What remark?"

"When you said this pistol"—she waggled it in his face—"is as easy to use as a *hair dryer*. That was a thoughtless, stupid, sexist, insulting thing to say. Typical *man talk*, which is the absolute lowest form of communication!"

"That's the reason you came back? To tell me off?"

"Absolutely."

"Lucky for me that you did." Scanner bent over with an arthritic groan and retrieved the dead man's rifle. "We'd better get down, this guy's pal is going to be here anytime now."

"Did I hear you say you were actually glad I came back?"

"You saved my life. And you were right to bawl me out, the hair dryer remark was stupid. I knew that as soon as I said it."

"You did?"

"Sure." They each sank slowly to the ground on their knees. "But that wasn't really why you came back. At least I hope it wasn't."

"I heard the shooting and just couldn't leave you here alone."

"Good thing you're not Chinese. Having saved me, you'd be responsible for me the rest of your life."

"I am Chinese, on my Uncle Woo's side."

"Uncle Woo?"

Kay shrugged. "Everybody's got an Uncle Woo."

"I don't."

"No matter, you're my responsibility now." She peered around at all four corners of the compass, suddenly afraid that Bud Wolf might be close by. "But we aren't safe, are we? Not with that other man around, especially if it is Bud Wolf."

"You keep lookout, I want to see who this fella is."

Kay averted her eyes while Scanner searched the body of the man she'd killed. The memory of him bucking and jumping as he died caused her to shudder.

"Found his wallet. Hell, he's got Texas driver's licenses in the names of Walter Boyd and Kelly Watts and a Florida license in the name of John Haley. Credit cards in more names than that. This guy had more identities than an escaped Nazi war criminal."

"A hired killer?" Kay said

"I doubt he did this sort of work for free. Hey, he's got a lot of cash on him, too. Some hundred-dollar bills. I'd better take them, have them tested."

"I see something!"

Scanner rose and readied the Winchester. "Where?"

"Out there, where I'm pointing."

Looking through the scope, Scanner did locate a figure way out in the bush. Five, maybe six hundred yards away. Carrying a rifle. Had to be the partner. "I've got him. Let's see if I can back him off." He fired the Winchester once and saw the bullet kick up dirt at least twenty-five yards short of his target. The rifle was powerful, but you'd have to know the weapon intimately to be able to hit a man with it at six hundred yards.

Even so, the bullet had the right effect. The guy turned and jogged off into the distance.

"He's clearing out, giving us a wide berth."

"Was it Wolf?"

"Couldn't tell. He looked big, could've been Bud Wolf, but I wouldn't be able to swear to that." Scanner jacked another round into the Winchester's chamber, just in case the guy still had some nasty ideas.

"What should we do now?" Kay was anxious to get out of this desert and doubly anxious to leave behind the body of the man with the multiple identities.

"It should be safe to cut straight across to Mr. Marvin's place. The firemen should still be there, probably the police, too."

"Will they have a phone?"

"We could patch into the phone system from a police car."

"I need to call my client right away to find out whether he's willing to put up more money for tomorrow's auction."

Scanner gave her a pinched-nose frown. "Between us we've killed two people this afternoon and you're still focused on the auction?"

His judgmental tone annoyed Kay. "That's the business I'm in. And what about you? Weren't you just rooting around on the body of a dead man looking for counterfeit hundred-dollar bills? What makes your priorities more noble than mine?"

"You've got to see that the currency of our country is more important than an antique. I mean, there's something bigger at stake here than Old Bowie."

"Yes, I'd say your testosterone is at stake. You've been sent down here to find fake hundred-dollar bills and you're by God going to find them no matter how many people you have to shoot."

"That's not fair! I didn't start this fight, they did."

"Oh, shut up. Which way is Mr. Marvin's house? I'm going there, you can stay if you want, look for more hundred-dollar bills, take off this poor man's shoes to find them, I don't care."

"Since when did this hired killer become a *poor man*? And by the way, have you noticed that you and I seem to go back and forth between arguments and love talk?"

"Yes, I've noticed that. From now on we'll stick to arguments or to discussions about hundred-dollar bills, I'm sure you'll feel more comfortable with that arrangement." She saw what was now a thin pall of smoke from the fire drifting in the air to the south. "Is that the direction I want? I'll see you there." She stuck the pistol back into her right-hand pocket and began walking in the direction of Mr. Marvin's house without looking back.

Scanner stuck the killer's wallet and wads of currency into his own pockets. He also tossed away the useless clips of M-1 ammo he'd been carrying and took some extra rounds for the Winchester off the body. Then he trudged along in Kay's wake, trying to keep his eyes peeled for trouble and his temper in check.

Wolf was jogging as fast as the rough ground would allow, headed for the highway and the Cherokee parked behind the billboard. It was a stolen car, so there were no keys, but Watts no doubt had left the van hotwired.

Kelly Watts had to be dead. The only way Scanner could have gotten hold of that long-range Winchester would be to pry it from Kelly's hands.

Wolf counted Kelly's death as his own fault. He'd underestimated Scanner and the bitch. Together they made a respectable team. Shouldn't have sent Kelly off on his own. Not with Scanner in possession of a decent rifle and Kay Williams with him. Not that he cared about Roy Scanner any longer. When you came right down to it, the federal agent was Donin's problem, let him sweat it.

And he still had to make sure neither Donin nor Goto would win the auction and take Old Bowie out of the country where he couldn't get his hands on it.

He also cared about Kay Williams. She'd stuck her thumb in his eye too often. The bitch had to die and Wolf planned to do the honors himself. Today obviously wasn't gonna be the day. He'd wait two months, three months, whatever it took. *She'll put this bad day out of her mind, let down her guard. That's when I'll pay a visit to Kay Williams*, he thought.

*But first I have to get myself out of this goddamn place.*

# CHAPTER 22

"Y ou did good, mon." Chauncy Alexander was in a restless mood, pacing his hotel room and talking in bursts to Phil about the coming day's work. "Now we got to *execute* on this thing. *Execute*. I don't worry about that bodyguard, I worry about Leon Badass Donin. Russians nuts, you know. They got something in their genes, what I think, make them mean and troublesome. I see Russians on holiday down in Jamaica. They party all night and go out sport fishing next morning, fight big marlin for hours. All day they drink rum or vodka, fight with each other over nothing at all. Donin one of those, be trouble unless we handle him just right."

Phil had just arrived in Austin on a commuter flight from San Antonio feeling more relaxed than he had in weeks. The monkey was off his back and onto Chauncy's. He'd provided the idea and the information. Chauncy would have to handle the *execution* he was making so much noise about. Phil sometimes watched Chauncy pace the floor talking out a problem, but today the Jamaican was almost manic. Phil decided that was how Jamaicans acted when they smelled a lot of money.

"Good thing you call me from San Antonio. I had time go into the Longhorn Bank, look it over." Chauncy rubbed his hands together as he paced. "Lots of places in and around Longhorn where we could move in on Mr. Donin. Lobby. Staircase. Sidewalk right outside. But that be poor *execution*. Donin and his pit bull be on their guard in the bank.

Closer to home they get—home right here at the Omni—more relaxed they be."

"What if they don't come back to the hotel?" Phil felt obliged to contribute something to the plan, if only a few questions. "What if they take the money back to the vault in that other bank across the street from here?"

"I doubt they redeposit the money. Just have to take the cash out again few hours later for the auction. I think they go Donin's room here and sit on their precious suitcase till auction time." Chauncy smiled. "When they step into their room, I be there waiting to take their money."

"What if they go to Wolf's room instead? Or sit in the lobby bar? Or go somewhere else until the damned auction starts?"

"I guarantee they not do that." Chauncy's confidence was at high tide. He brought out a yellow legal pad on which he'd been scribbling when Phil arrived. "You see here, this sketch of the bank lobby? You be in lobby when Donin and Wolf and auctioneer arrive, okay? Keep your eyes open, make sure they got cash in the suitcase." He saw Phil's objection coming. "Mon, you not go soft on me now. I know you can't sit in their laps, just get as close you can. All I ask, you catch one flash of beautiful green money. How much? A few million be lovely. If it be less, no quibble. I mean, two of us flat broke, right? Whatever we take off Donin gravy. Has to be a nice bundle, nobody bid on expensive antique with nickels and dimes."

Everything Chauncy said made sense. Even so, Phil's nerves began to jump. "I don't want to call attention to myself, make them suspicious."

Chauncy agreed. "Look here at my sketch. You see three little squares north wall of the bank lobby? Three pay phones. Once Donin there, you go to phone and call switchboard of the Longhorn Bank. Ask operator put you through to Mister Leon Donin, tell operator he a customer of the bank, probably with bank executive. Operator find Donin for you."

"What then?" Phil didn't like the idea of talking to Donin, even on the phone. He feared being sucked into the robbery itself.

"I write out what I want you say." Chauncy handed Phil a sheet of paper on which he'd written the Longhorn Bank's phone number and a couple of paragraphs of text. "Go ahead, say out loud. You need rehearse this anyway."

Phil cleared his throat. "Mr. Donin, this is Dave Wingate at the Omni

Hotel. I was told you were at the Longhorn Bank. I'm sorry to bother you when you're doing business, but a parcel just arrived for you from Russia, of all places. First package I've ever seen from there. It was delivered by DHL and marked *Urgent*. I thought you should know as soon as possible that the parcel had arrived. I had a bellman take it up to your room. Again, sorry to bother you."

"Pretty good delivery." Chauncy nodded like a movie director about half-satisfied with a rehearsal. "You say that, hang up. No dialogue."

"What if he asks how I knew he was at the Longhorn Bank?"

Chauncy looked exasperated. "That's why I tell you hang up right away! Don't give him no chance ask questions! Sure he have questions on his mind. What's in parcel? How they find me at Longhorn Bank? Why they put parcel in my room? Other questions, too. What I bet on is plain old curiosity. He want see what the parcel is, why it sent by DHL courier. You ever see anybody who *didn't* open a surprise package?"

"And you'll be in his room waiting for him." Phil wanted to be certain his role ended right there in the bank with the two phone calls.

"That's it. When they leave the bank, you call me in Donin's room. See here in the corner, I write down number of Omni, too. And Donin's room number."

Phil was beginning to breathe easier. "How do you plan to get into Donin's room?"

"Mon, I sneak into hotel rooms all my life. These electronic locks easier to beat than key locks."

"When do we meet and split the money?"

"Slow down. First you come up Donin's room, help me take care of our two friends."

Alarm bells went off in Phil's head. "What do you mean by *take care of* them? I didn't sign on to kill anyone."

"I don't want no killing either." Chauncy was talking to Phil with elaborate patience. "Two 'businessmen' found murdered in first-class hotel? That raise the heat too high. The dope dealer I put down last night something else, nobody give a damn about him. Donin, he travel on diplomatic passport. We kill him, we got thousands of cops after us. Best thing—take their money, leave them alive."

So Chauncy did kill a dope dealer last night. "Why do you need me?"

"Harder to do it alone. You got to be there. You come up to room right after they do. I have them covered by then, probably down on floor. You tie them." He showed Phil a length of rope and a serrated kitchen knife bought from a nearby hardware store. "This be in the room, too."

"They'll see my face! They'll figure out who I am and track me down!"

"Don't whine," Chauncy snapped. "No matter what we do, we have *somebody* on us. Better it be just two guys, not thousands of cops."

Phil sat on his hands so Chauncy wouldn't see they were shaking. "You'll have to find another way, Chauncy. I don't think I can do this."

"Fine." Chauncy had expected Phil to play the weasel. "I guess I try do it myself. Of course, you don't share in money."

"What are you talking about? That's not fair, this whole thing was my idea!"

"Mon, you expect me take out Donin and Wolf all by my poor self? You want your cut with no risk? Don't talk about fair."

"I'm not good at that kind of work."

"Christ, you don't cut any throats. All you do is tie hands together!"

"They'll find us."

"I probably go back Jamaica, buy myself a house in Mo' Bay. Two white dudes come look for me down there, I hear about it before they clear customs."

"They'll find *me!*"

"You go New York, Miami, San Francisco, any big U.S. city. That your kind of turf, mon. You hunker down someplace rich and quiet, change name. I got friends in New York set you up with driver's license, Social Security card, credit cards in new name. A Russian and some kind of shit-kicker Texan? They never find you. What they do, stand on corner Seventy-second and Lex all day, watch for your face? Don't make me laugh."

Phil desperately wanted to believe Chauncy. The money was the thing he had to focus on. Nothing else mattered. Without money, he was finished anyway. "All right . . . I'll do it."

Big grin from Chauncy. Let Phil think he'd be rich and safe, a big man with the ladies again, King of New York. "Good decision. Now you my partner again."

Kay sat in the backseat of a sheriff's car parked near the charred remains of Mr. Marvin's home. Only one fire engine and a small crew of firemen remained on the scene. They were hosing down the smoking embers of the bungalow while a medical examiner and arson investigator studied the charred body found inside. Meanwhile Kay tried to get through on the car phone to Billy Boy Watkins in New Orleans.

Outside the car, Roy was having a spirited argument with a sheriff's deputy named Bubba Pinchet. Kay had never met anyone named Bubba. She wondered how his parents could have done that to him. She kept darting glances his way, testing the reality of Bubba Pinchet. The guy was in his mid-twenties, as big and blubbery as a Bubba should be, with a wide quizzical face and eyes like ball bearings painted blue and white.

Suddenly Deputy Bubba Pinchet spun around and opened the door next to Kay. "Mam, I'm sorry, yew'll have to get out of the car? I have a few questions to ask yew? We have a very strange sicheation here?"

"I can't talk to you right now, I'm trying to get through to New Orleans. Here . . ." She took Roy's pistol out of her pocket and handed it to Deputy Pinchet. "This is the gun I shot a man with. You should probably have that for now. But it's Roy's pistol, see that he gets it back."

"Mam, we have a dead body in this here burned-out house? And Mr. Scanner tells me that yew killed a man about three miles away, another dead body lyin' out there in the brush? We have to get to the bottom of this sicheation?"

"Not now!" Kay grabbed the door handle and slammed the door closed.

Deputy Bubba Pinchet's broad face went scarlet. This woman was talking to him as if he worked for her. She had introduced herself as Kay Williams and had confessed to killing a man. She'd even handed him the murder weapon, which he didn't know she was carrying because he'd been vaguely afraid to search her. This man Roy Scanner carried the ID of a Treasury Department agent and had admitted to killing a man and burning down a house. The victim's body had been found in the ruins of the bungalow, as crisply done as a side of bacon. It seemed to Deputy Bubba Pinchet that both these people should be detained on some charge, if he could think of one, even though both acted as if they'd done nothing wrong. He wished Sheriff Hunnicut hadn't gone fishing down to the Guadalupe River today.

"Miss Williams and I need a ride into Austin," Scanner said. "Can you handle that for us?"

Now the killer wanted a ride into Austin! Deputy Pinchet didn't know what to think of that. "Sir, yew'll have to come into San Marcos with me? We haven't even started to get to the bottom of this sicheation?"

"I've explained that I'm conducting an investigation for the United States Treasury and time is important to me. Miss Williams has to come with me, she's a material witness. You can reach both of us at the Omni Hotel in Austin." Scanner looked impatiently at his watch. "It's four o'clock already, we need to get on the road within fifteen minutes."

"Sir, we'll get this sicheation straightened out in due time? Meanwhile, I must advise yew that anything yew say may be taken down and held against yew in a court of law? Yew are entitled to an attorney? If yew cannot afford an attorney, one will be provided for yew?"

"Oh, for Christ's sake. You put in a call to the Texas Rangers' headquarters in Austin, didn't you? Buck Colter's the liaison with the Treasury Department and he knows why I'm down here, he'll tell you to let me go on about my business."

"Sir, Captain Colter was out the first time I called? I cain't talk to him right now because Miss Williams is using my phone and I cain't seem to get her to put it down?"

Scanner jerked open the door. "Kay, get off the phone! We're waiting for the Texas Rangers to tell Deputy Pinchet we're not a couple of criminals so we can get the hell out of here!"

"Sshhh! I'm almost through to Billy Boy Watkins." Kay closed the car door again.

"Sorry, Deputy. She's not the kind who takes orders. I'll tell you something else—every hour I've spent with her has been an adventure. Not always fun, but always an adventure. Sometimes I want her more than any woman I've ever met." Scanner shrugged. "Other times she makes me so mad I hope I never see her face again. We seem to argue a lot, you see what I mean? Do I actually love her? Will I ever see her again after this is over? How deeply does she care for me? Does she care for me at all? I don't know the answers to those questions and it's driving me fucking crazy!"

Hearing a fellow law enforcement officer unburden his soul about his personal love life came as a shock to Deputy Bubba Pinchet. He remained silent and his face remained scarlet.

Inside the car, Kay was tapping her foot as she talked to a third secretary, probably the one secretary in the office Billy Boy wasn't sleeping with because she seemed to know what she was doing.

"Mr. Watkins is out in the Gulf, Rig Number Eighteen. I've patched you through to the rig, Miss Williams. It'll be a minute before Mr. Watkins can pick up. Please hold."

"Will do, and thanks very much."

Kay listened to intermittent static for maybe thirty seconds, then Billy Boy Watkins's booming voice came on the line. "Kay honey! Good to hear from ya, how's the auction shaping up?"

"Very competitive."

"Yeah? Then the knife must be the real thing."

"It's Old Bowie, all right. Everyone in the auction agrees on that. Nobody's pulled out and the price is going up."

"That's why you're calling me, huh? Lookin' for more money?"

"That depends on how badly you want the knife. I'm afraid the bid may go to three million, maybe even higher. Do you want to put up another million dollars? I'm afraid that's what it's going to take."

"Holy shit! Excuse my French, but that's a lot higher than I'd reckoned."

"I want you to have that knife."

"Hell, I want it! You know I want it! But I gotta tell you, this comes at a bad time for me. I'm sitting on a dry rig here. I got fifteen million tied up in this rig, mostly borrowed money, of course. Figured on twenty years' production and I've only been pumpin' for two. What you call your basic financial disaster."

"I'm awfully sorry to hear that."

"Million in cash? I could talk to my banker, he might give it to me or he might laugh in my face. Word travels fast in the oil business when your luck goes sour."

"Do you want me to drop out? Sounds like you need to conserve your cash right now."

Some silence. Some sighing. "I do want Old Bowie. I hear my pal Goto-san's after it, too. He's got some nice blades over there in Tokyo."

"Yes, I'd say he's the toughest competition."

"Don't be too sure. I been told Goto's buildin' a whole museum in Tokyo for his swords and blades and it's driven him damn near broke."

"Really?"

"That's what my banker says. My banker's a lyin' polecat, wouldn't even trust him with my spinster sister, but he may be right about Goto. Honey, I don't like that scratchy sound in your voice. You sick? What's goin' on out there?"

"Long story. The bottom line is that some people tried to kill me and another of the bidders today."

"What? Tried to kill you? Was that about Old Bowie?"

"Yes, in a way. We were coming back from a visit to the Alamo and three men tried to ambush us. Chased us out into the countryside. We got away. I ended up killing one of them myself. A rancid thing and I suppose that's why my voice is scratchy."

"You killed a man? Kay honey, I warned you about Texas. You did get yourself a gun after all?"

"Yes, I killed the man with a pistol."

"I'll be damned. You gonna be all right?"

"It was an awful experience, I can't say I'm feeling guilty. Basically, I feel lucky to have survived."

"You're something special, honey. Look, at the moment I'm broke, but I been broke a lot of times. Haven't been poor since I was a kid, poor's a different deal altogether. Thing about being broke is you can still raise money if you can talk bullshit. I pride myself that my bullshit's as strong as ever. I think I can tell the right lies to raise a million from the bank this afternoon, have it sent to your hotel as a bank draft. Will that do it?"

"Another million will give you a real shot at Old Bowie. I'll do my best for you in the auction."

"Well, I want Old Bowie so bad I'd almost give up cheatin' on my taxes to get it. And after what you've been through because I sent you to get that knife, you deserve all the backup I can give you. Just wish I was in a position to write you a blank check."

"Thanks. I'll look for the draft."

"Honey, I got a security director for my rigs. Name's Cody Smith. Former New Orleans policeman, fired a few years ago for takin' bribes. Not too honest, but tough as they come. Smart, too. I can put him on a plane, he'll be in Austin tonight to watch over you."

"You don't have to do that. Roy Scanner, the man I was with today, is at least as tough as your Mr. Smith. He's a federal agent."

"Federal agent? Not the IRS, I hope. I hate those bastards."

"Roy's a Treasury agent. One of the bidders may be trying to buy Old Bowie with counterfeit money. That's what all the shooting was about today."

"Counterfeit? Well, everything you tell me confirms what I've always known. Texas isn't a state, it's a high crime zone with its own flag."

Kay was grateful she could still laugh.

"Take real good care of yourself, honey. I count you as more important than Old Bowie."

"Thanks, Billy Boy."

"Good luck at the auction." Billy Boy Watkins rang off.

Almost immediately Scanner yanked the door open. "Are you *finally* through with the phone?"

"Yes, I am."

He took the phone from her, called Texas Rangers headquarters in Austin and got through to Captain Buck Colter. He and Colter had known each other for years, going back to a course they both attended at the FBI Academy in Virginia. Scanner explained the afternoon's events to Colter, who asked the appropriate questions. When Colter fully understood what had happened out in the countryside near San Marcos, he told Scanner to put Deputy Pinchet on the phone.

"Texas Ranger wants to talk to you." Scanner offered the phone.

The deputy accepted the phone and listened intently, saying, "Yessir, I understand yew?" more than once and nodding his head often throughout the one-sided conversation. "Yessir, I will comply?" were Deputy Pinchet's final words before he put down the phone.

He looked at Scanner and Kay as if they were creatures from an alien planet. "I been ordered to escort yew safely to Austin? First, I have to send somebody out to the brush with a pair of dogs to find that other dead body? Don't want to lose it to the turkey vultures? Yew don't mind if I do that, I hope?"

"Just make it fast." Scanner slid into the backseat of the sheriff's car next to Kay and gave her a sidelong look. "Still sore at me?"

"I should be, I don't have the energy." She slipped her hand into his and they laced fingers. "Did you find out where Mr. Marvin is? Has he heard about his house?"

"Deputy Pinchet says Mr. Marvin is in a nursing home in San Antonio with a stroke. He isn't expected to last long. He has a son who's said to be living down around El Paso, nobody knows where to find him. Nobody except Deputy Pinchet seems to care what happened to the house. Or to Mr. Marvin."

Kay's eyes went wet. She thought about the family pictures on the walls of Mr. Marvin's bungalow, the scant visual history of his stay on earth. "We take life for granted. Why don't we appreciate it more? And why do we do things that hurt ourselves, even throw away our lives, like those two men did this afternoon?"

"Nobody's ever been able to explain that." Scanner had his own opinion. "Tell you the truth, I think the human race is just plain crazy."

Kay's reviving spirits suffered a relapse, sliding off a cliff into what felt like a bottomless pit. "This may be the worst day I've ever had."

"Hey, it wasn't all bad." Scanner searched for a bright spot. "You got to meet a genuine Texas Bubba."

# CHAPTER 23

Wolf felt better with a shower and a change into clean clothes. Only thing that rankled was having to call the hotel men's shop to send up a couple of new denim shirts and two pairs of jeans in his size, replace the pants the Williams bitch had cut up. Well, sooner or later little Kay would pay for that. And not just in money, either.

Once he felt clean and rested, Wolf sat down at the desk in his room and used the hotel stationery and ballpoint pen that came with it to write his note. He wrote in big block letters that bore no resemblance to his own handwriting: LEON DONIN'S TOP BID WILL BE THREE MILLION CASH. YOU CAN BEAT HIM!

*That oughtta do it,* he thought. *Keep Old Bowie out of Donin's hands and out of Russia, where I'd never have a shot at it.*

Didn't want to think about what Donin would do if he found out he was being double-crossed by his own bodyguard. *Well, fuck Donin and fuck Mother Russia. That knife belongs right here in Texas. Bad enough a family of Mexicans owned it for all these years.* If the Mexicans were near the ass end of the human food chain, the Russians were even farther down.

Wolf carefully folded the sheet of paper in half and took the elevator to the third floor. Arthur Ward's room was 355. As he passed Ward's room, Wolf bent and slipped the paper under the door. Then he walked briskly to the nearest stairwell and returned to his own room.

He was sure Ward would put the information to good use. Only other question was how to stop the Jap from winning the lottery. People said the Japs had more money than God, so Goto could possibly come out with the high bid. If the knife went to Japan, it might as well be in Russia. Wolf recognized his own limitations, and operating in some dingbat country the other side of the world was one of them. He had to stop both Donin and Goto from winning the bid.

How to stop Goto? He had no idea how high the Jap was liable to bid, what kind of resources he could draw on. Guy might have five million to spend. Ten million. Who could tell?

Wolf remembered the Jap doctor who accompanied Goto to the preview meeting. The talk around the table, when Goto wasn't nearby, was that the doctor went everywhere with Goto because he had a bad heart, liable to conk out on him anytime. Had a doctor nearby twenty-four hours a day, they said, especially when he was traveling. Shouldn't be all that hard to kill a guy with a bad heart.

Wolf's phone rang. "Hello?"

"Wolfie, this is your esteemed employer. I'm in the hotel bar. Join me for a drink, I want to hear all about your exciting day. I trust it was exciting?"

"Like they say about Arnold Schwarzenegger movies—action-packed."

"Splendid."

"No, I wouldn't call it that."

"Oh?" Note of worry in Donin's voice. "What went wrong?"

Had to tell him sometime. "Order me a beer, I'll be right down."

Donin took bad news well, Wolf gave him that. Donin frowned occasionally, never showed any heavy anger while Wolf, sipping now and then from a glass of Shiner Bock, gave Donin a complete review of the fucked-up ambush and the chase through the desert. Wolf didn't try to prettify what had happened or lay off the blame on two dead guys, Kelly Watts and Jimmy Loomis. He told Donin he'd made the two key mistakes. First, not anticipating that Scanner and the girl would survive the car wreck and be able to charge off into the countryside under cover of all that dust. And, later, splitting up with Watts, sending him off on his own to track down Scanner and the bitch.

"I should've kept Kelly with me," he concluded.

"Yes," Donin agreed. "Your story reminds me of a patrol I led in Afghanistan. I was commanding two companies of Russian infantry. Very fine troops, utterly ruthless. We ambushed a force of partisans, killed some, drove the rest into the foothills. I had the bright idea of sending one company north to intercept the rebels while I followed hard on their heels with the second company. We had armored personnel carriers, the rebels were on foot. Should have been a classic pincer movement." He smiled wryly. "They anticipated my strategy. Set a trap for the lead company and cut them to pieces with American-supplied machine guns and antitank missiles fired from handheld launchers. Total slaughter." He moved around in his chair to shake off the memory. "That was the only serious blemish on my military record."

"Yeah . . . well . . . this is one of the few total fuckups on my record, too."

"I believe that." Donin reached into his coat pocket. "Oh, yes, here are the keys to your Cadillac. I drove it back from San Antonio, it's in the hotel garage. I still prefer quality German automobiles over your fabled *Detroit iron*."

"I'm in no mood to argue about that." Wolf felt he had to talk money. "You shouldn't have to pay for today's fuckup, either. The thirty thousand you advanced me? I'll see you get repaid through the Contractor, my personal expense. The thirty k was on Kelly Watts when he died, so I hope there weren't any of your *special* hundred-dollar bills in there, Scanner probably searched Kelly's body."

"No, I gave you legitimate currency from the expense money I'm carrying." Because they were sitting in a public bar, Donin looked around to assure himself they couldn't be overheard. There was nobody at the nearest table and music from the piano bar provided additional privacy. "The federal agent and the Williams woman probably assume you and I are responsible for the attack. I carry a diplomatic passport, so the authorities cannot touch me. You are more exposed. Is there any chance you might be arrested for today's activities? Did either of them see you?"

"I never got near enough for either of them to see my face. That was the problem. If I'd been able to close on them, they'd be dead." Wolf wasn't deluded that Donin cared if he went to prison. The Russian only wanted assurances that he'd have a bodyguard tomorrow when the money had to be moved. "I didn't leave any evidence layin' around, nothin' they can use to haul me in."

"Good. I am still concerned about this Roy Scanner, of course. He may try to spoil my plans, but my diplomatic passport is a trump card."

"Let's say you win the bid," Wolf said. "Pay the money over to the auctioneer. Once the money doesn't have any diplomatic protection, Scanner can do whatever he wants, even seize all those counterfeit hundreds and have them examined. Doesn't that worry you?"

"I expect Scanner to do just that." Donin's eyes had a triumphant gleam. "Let him. Believe me, the merchandise I brought with me is superb. Whatever tests he wants to make will take hours or perhaps even days. Even then, I doubt they'll be able to tell my merchandise from the real thing. By that time I'll be on a plane back to Moscow with one of America's greatest pieces of history in my possession."

*Don't fuckin' count on it*, Wolf was thinking.

What he said was, "What if somebody beats you in the auction? I heard the other bidders talkin', they say the Jap is loaded, got yen to burn."

"He'll be the toughest bidder. However, I doubt that he can go as high as three million, my sources tell me he is overextended."

"What's that, a fancy way of sayin' he's broke?"

Donin hesitated. "Not exactly."

"Then this Goto can still raise cash?"

"Ah . . . perhaps."

"So he's a threat to your master plan, am I right?" Wolf saw a hairline crack in Donin's confidence, the Russian not quite ready to admit he might have underestimated Goto. "I mean, the Jap owns a whole insurance company, I'm told. He could dip into the till, take what he wants?"

Donin let out a long breath. "When I was considering how much of my merchandise to bring, I thought three million dollars was the outside number. I did not believe a knife could possibly be worth more than that. Now I wonder."

"This is the Alamo we're talkin' about, Ivan. Jim Bowie's knife. The price is goin' up on Old Bowie. I can smell it. Can't you?"

"I believe I can," Donin agreed. "You have a suggestion?"

"Fact is, you can't go back to Moscow with all that money still in your suitcase, am I right? You came here to unload the money. Test it out with a U.S. bank. Bring back somethin' valuable in exchange. Goto could screw that up for you."

"I asked if you had a suggestion."

"Digitalis."

"What?"

"The Jap's got a heart condition, he must take all kinds of medicine. My brother-in-law had the same problem. Took stuff with names that sounded like cities over in the Middle East. Kumadin? Calan? I don't know what medicine Goto's takin', but I do know that a heavy dose of digitalis on top of it will send his ticker into outer space."

"Kill him?"

Wolf shrugged. "Might kill him, might just send him to the emergency room for a nice rest. Or a ten-year coma. What do you care so long as Goto can't bid?"

Donin stroked his chin. "How? Where?"

"You see how much coffee Goto drank at the preview? They say Japs drink even more coffee than Americans, coffee so strong it doesn't need a cup. You can bet he'll be slurpin' it down at the auction."

"We slip digitalis into Goto's coffee during the auction." Donin was smiling. "He collapses, everyone believes it was the tension of the moment. A sound idea. Where can we get digitalis at short notice?"

Wolf winked. "I know a pharmacist here in Austin who's about as honest as I am."

"Call him. Be sure to find out how big a dose we should give to Goto-san in order to put him in the hospital. Better than killing him. An actual death during the auction would look suspicious."

"You never know what might happen with a heart case," Wolf said. "The Jap could buy the farm even if the dose is right."

"What farm?"

"I meant he could die."

"That is a risk I am prepared to take."

"I figure we both go into the auction with nice big doses on us. I'll get a pair of whaddayacallit, vials, from the pharmacist. Whichever of us has the first chance to pass a cup of coffee to Goto slips him the digitalis."

"Agreed."

Wolf was satisfied he'd just stopped Old Bowie from leaving the country. *It isn't going to Japan and it sure as hell isn't goin' to Russia.*

Donin was looking over Wolf's shoulder. "We shall soon know whether Scanner or the woman caught a glimpse of your face. They've just returned from their desert adventure and they've brought some sort of policeman with them."

Scanner and Kay had come into the lobby in the company of a round-faced deputy sheriff. Their clothes were dirty and singed in places from the fire at the bungalow, their hair unkempt, their backs and shoulders slumped from fatigue. Someone had applied a fresh bandage to Scanner's jaw. Scanner noticed Donin and Wolf sitting at a table in the bar area and nudged Kay. Wolf expected hostility. Instead they just looked at him as if he were a particularly ugly frog perched on a rock.

Deputy Bubba Pinchet tipped his hat and shook hands with Scanner and Kay. "If yew come into any more facts about that sicheation out there, I'd appreciate a call?"

Scanner considered telling Deputy Bubba Pinchet that the man who could tell him all he needed to know was sitting less than twenty yards away. But that wouldn't accomplish a thing. There was no way to prove Bud Wolf had been one of their pursuers. "I'll do that, Deputy. Thanks again for the ride."

"You've been a big help." Kay gave him a genuine hundred-watt smile of gratitude for getting them out of that hard country and back to a first-class hotel. When the deputy left, the smile slid from her face. "Look at Wolf, the smug bastard's enjoying our grunginess, he especially likes that crease along your jaw. Donin looks pretty amused, too. They probably think we've been scared off. I know you felt you couldn't have Wolf charged with anything, but I'd like to at least go over there and slap his grinning face."

"A kick in the balls would be a better idea."

"Should I? Will you back me up?"

Scanner felt too tired to deal with Wolf right now. "Toughest thing in the world is to kick the balls of a man who's sitting down. Besides, that'd just keep us from the shower. I really need a shower."

"I could still slap his face."

"That's about on a par with *Let's ring his doorbell and run.*"

"Deputy Bubba gave you back your pistol. Walk over there and shoot him!"

"I'm not authorized to shoot citizens just because I think they're slimeballs."

"This country is going to the dogs," Kay grumped. "Let's go take that shower. In fact, let's take a shower together."

They walked past Donin and Wolf as if the pair didn't exist.

Some of Scanner's juices had begun to flow again. "Are you serious about the shower?"

"I doubt I'll go anywhere alone until you've found a way to have Bud

Wolf locked up tight. That means you'll have to sleep in my room tonight, or I'll sleep in yours."

They got into the elevator.

"Are you talking about just sleeping, or does the arrangement include making love?"

"If you play your cards right, you can have both."

Scanner felt a trifle delirious. "We're not going to argue anymore today, are we? I'm too tired."

"There won't be any arguments," Kay promised. Then she had a second thought. "So long as you stop disagreeing with everything I say and do."

A groan from Scanner. "This is why I'm still a bachelor."


"It appears that you wounded Mr. Scanner along his jawline."

"Watts was pretty sure he got a piece of Scanner with one of his rounds. Guess he was right. Six inches higher and the bullet would have gone between Scanner's eyes, your problem with that guy would have been solved."

"You had better go find that digitalis," Donin said. "Bring the drug and the vials to my room, we will work out a system for slipping it into Goto-san's coffee."

"Whatever you say."

Wolf's eagerness to please seemed out of character. "I am impressed with your dedication to my cause, Wolfie. And somewhat surprised. I hope you have no agenda of your own."

"Ask the Contractor what my 'agenda' is. He'll tell you Bud Wolf does the job and collects his money, that's all I'm about."

At the preview meeting Donin had noted Wolf's great interest in Old Bowie. He hoped Wolf hadn't developed a desire to own the knife himself. "I will prevail at this auction and take Jim Bowie's knife back to Russia. In two or three years I will resell it at a healthy profit. Meanwhile, your duty is to help me accomplish my task. I would regret having to tell the Contractor that you have lost the ability to remain loyal to your clients. Am I understood?"

"Don't threaten me. And don't worry about me doin' my *duty*. I've been in this business a long time and never had a single complaint on that score."

"Splendid." Donin waved away the subject. "Then I will see you this evening."

⁂          ⁂          ⁂

The note Wolf had slipped under Arthur Ward's door was found by him at about five o'clock that afternoon. He immediately placed a call to another room in the hotel and said, "Are you alone? I need to talk with you right away." Look of relief. "Good, I'll be right up."

He took the elevator to a higher floor and knocked on the door of a suite.

Melanie opened the door with a glass of wine in her hand, which she passed to Arthur. "Come in, darling. And try this chablis, it's wonderful."

Arthur accepted the wine with an absentminded smile and walked around the suite's aggressively modern couch three times while drinking the wine. "Not bad," he commented, and handed the note to Melanie. "Read this."

After reading the one-line message, she asked, "Who do you think wrote it?"

"I don't know. Do you believe what it says?"

Melanie shrugged and read it a second time. "This could be some sort of trick. Perhaps Donin can commit even more than three million and wants to throw us off guard."

"Possibly. But Donin is such an abrasive character that I think someone really wants to do him harm."

"How did you get this note?"

"When I came back from San Antonio I found it slipped under my door."

"Why your door, I wonder?" Melanie was miffed that Arthur had received this message instead of her. There were so many crosscurrents and double deals taking place she could hardly keep track of them. Melanie found the double dealing stimulating except when she wasn't at the heart of it. "Let's suppose the note is true and Donin's limit is three million. Somebody wanted to make sure you'd be prepared to bid higher than that. Could Señor de Baraga be trying to drive up the price of Old Bowie? What about Stewart Ruddington, could this be his doing?"

"Not Stewart." The wine hadn't satisfied Arthur. He went to the bar and poured a real drink. "I wouldn't put it past de Baraga, except that he doesn't seem smart enough to have come up with such a strategy."

"Someone could have helped him."

Arthur seated himself and crossed one leg over the other. "Do you think someone knows we've gone into partnership on this bid?"

"I don't believe so." Melanie could not accept the idea that someone had figured out their plan. "We've been extremely careful. Came to Austin on separate planes and made a point of insulting the hell out of each other for the past couple of days."

"And of course you've been sleeping with other men." Arthur's tone became acid. "That certainly convinced everyone you have no interest in me. Convinced me, too."

"Oh, Arthur, don't go Victorian on me. No, I feel certain our colleagues are going to be very surprised when we announce that you and I have pooled our assets and are bidding together." A winsome smile. "Especially dear Kay."

Arthur cringed as he foresaw the shock in Kay's expression. He liked to believe Kay thought a lot of him, perhaps she had even considered a romantic interlude with him. Certainly she'd always admired his knowledge and taste. His association with Melanie would diminish him in Kay's eyes.

Arthur both regretted and delighted in his rather complicated relationship with Melanie. He'd known Melanie for fifteen years. During the first thirteen years of their acquaintanceship they'd had occasional liaisons in hotel rooms from New York to Miami to Paris. Their lovemaking, if you could call it that, had meant nothing to either of them. Sexual exercise, nothing more. Then, a year or so ago, Melanie's feelings for him apparently underwent a change. She developed an insatiable need for him. She called him on the phone almost every day, sent him expensive gifts, once even gave him a bath in a tub full of champagne. Not domestic, either. Good French champagne, thirty dollars a bottle.

It took Arthur a few months to realize what Melanie wanted. She'd built her own business as far as it would go. A fine business. High-gross revenue per square foot and a satisfactory profit margin. She was respected if not well liked by her peers. But the shop in San Francisco was still only a shop. Little more than a boutique, really. What she wanted, Arthur deduced, was something much grander. She wanted him . . . Arthur Ward . . . and all that came with him—old family name, tons of money, estate on Long Island, friends in high places. Most of all she wanted his collection of antiques. Not to own, to sell. The woman put marrying him on the same plane as buying into an NFL team, a great investment opportunity that also offered a chance for celebrity.

Arthur decided to take advantage of Melanie's rather transparent ambitions by dangling himself and his collection in front of her. At first the strategy worked. For six months Arthur had let Melanie provide him with one perverted sex act after another. Depraved things. The morning after one of their couplings, Arthur often arose shuddering in disgust at what he'd allowed Melanie to do with him. Melanie was hardly the youngest or most attractive woman he'd ever bedded, but she was certainly the most innovative. He often wondered whether Melanie got her ideas for sexual games out of books or if she actually invented them herself.

The strategy backfired on him. Without realizing what was happening, he found that in gradual increments he had surrendered his free will to her. When it dawned on Arthur that he'd come to need her perversions, *desperately* need them, he attempted to break away. A couple of months ago, during a visit to San Francisco, he worked up the nerve to tell her he was through with her. Melanie just laughed. "I have to be in New York on Tuesday. Call me at the Pierre." She said she had to leave, she had a date with a young man who waited tables at a coffee house in North Beach. "His cock is ever so much longer than yours," she taunted as she went out the door.

Arthur breathed easier. His dalliance with Melanie was over. He flew back to New York on a Saturday and began to go about his business. Sunday was all right, he stayed busy examining, cataloguing and estimating the current prices of the rare editions in his library. Monday he felt nervous and out of sorts. His mouth was dry and his palms sweaty and he couldn't work. On Tuesday Arthur awoke too early, showered hastily, cut himself shaving. He knew Melanie's arrival in New York was causing his nervousness. He wasn't a fool, after all. No matter. Many years ago he'd quit smoking with the same kind of brief aftereffects. He went back to his examining, cataloguing and pricing determined to get through the Jane Austens and William Makepeace Thackerays by the end of the day.

It didn't happen.

Instead Arthur found himself hovering next to the telephone in his library, trying with creeping desperation to keep his hand from reaching out for the receiver. He drank a strong scotch, single malt, which raised his spirits and stiffened his backbone for fifteen minutes. A second scotch didn't help. Reverse effect, he became maudlin. Most of the flights from the West Coast arrived in New York between 5:00 and 7:00 P.M. By five-thirty he was blubbering into a third scotch and asking the information operator for the number of the Pierre.

Melanie had just checked in. She said, "What kept you?" and invited him to come into the city. "Dinner at Sparks and sex afterwards. I brought my special black case. The one with all the perfumes and rubber animal parts and other things. How's that sound?"

Arthur closed his eyes. "I'll be there in an hour."

They'd been together ever since. Few people yet knew of their alliance, but that wouldn't last long. After they bid together at this auction, word would soon get around. Melanie already had dropped hints that they should "formalize" their relationship in some way. She'd never mentioned the word *marriage* or *partnership*, she was too clever for that. Instead she'd drawn him into this deal for Old Bowie. Made him a de facto partner. After the auction she'd want a "formalized" agreement of some sort. He was in bed with Melanie in more ways than one.

"You're very pensive, Arthur. Thinking about us?"

"As a matter of fact, I was."

"Good thoughts?"

"Not necessarily."

"Sexy thoughts, then." Melanie slid into his lap and kicked off her slippers. "On my way to San Antonio this morning I stopped at a motel with Phil Williams. We had some quick but ferocious sex."

"I realized that when you showed up at the Alamo," Arthur said. "*Everybody* realized it."

"Does that turn you on?"

"Apparently it does." Arthur felt hollow inside.

"Phil's got nothing between his ears and he isn't even a very good fuck. Poor Kay had a terrible marriage."

Arthur changed the subject. "I take it you choose to believe the anonymous note I was given about Donin topping out at three million."

"Yes, I think I do believe it. Either way, there's nothing we can do now, the auction's tomorrow. If the note is true, we have an advantage."

The phone rang and Melanie picked it up. "Yes? Ah, that's just fine. Come up right away, we've been expecting you."

"Who's that?" Arthur asked.

"Tonight's entertainment. I thought we'd have our fun early, then go out for a quick dinner. We should be asleep by eleven. Tomorrow will be a busy day."

The hollowness inside Arthur filled with a sweetly sickening fear. "I'd rather just finish this drink and go to my room."

"Nonsense, this will be fun."

"Really, I don't feel like any . . ."

"Wait till you see what I've arranged for us." She slithered out of Arthur's lap and looked herself over in the mirror while she waited for her guests to arrive. A minute later there was a knock on the door.

Melanie opened the door with a flourish. "Welcome! Please come in." She stepped aside for three handsome young people, two girls in their early twenties and a somewhat older young man who might have been thirty, all three dressed in gym workout suits. Despite the loose clothes, it was obvious that each had a spectacular body. The blonde was short and had a cheerleader's perkiness. The other girl's hair was long, dark and tied back in a ponytail. She was quiet almost to the point of sullenness.

"I'm Mandy," said the blonde, shaking Melanie's hand with enthusiasm. "This is my friend Anita."

Anita nodded without offering her hand or saying anything.

"Anita hardly talks at all, but she's so good at her work nobody minds," Mandy explained. "Once they get to know her. And this is Henry. A few years ago he was on the U.S. Olympic gymnastics team. Would've won a medal except he pulled a muscle two days before competition."

"Hello, Anita . . . Henry." More handshaking. Melanie smiled in Arthur's direction. "This is Arthur. He's my darling, I want you to be very good to him."

"That's why we're here." Henry had dark, curly hair and the outrageously V-shaped body of a gymnastics freak. "What kind of *exercise* are you up for tonight, Arthur?"

Arthur looked away from him. "Did you bring your trampoline?" He felt uncharacteristically unfriendly. "I've never done it in midair. Though I'm sure Melanie has."

"I choose the games." Melanie spoke with a hard-edged authority.

"Fine with us," Henry said. "We just need a couple of minutes to get ready."

"Go ahead."

Melanie walked around the room dimming lights while Mandy, Anita and Henry took off their gym suits. Underneath they wore nothing at all. Their bodies were hard and beautifully proportioned. Anita took a plastic bottle of oil from her gym bag. They passed the bottle around, oiling themselves until their bodies glistened in the low light. Henry did knee bends to warm up and the girls began loosening up with stretching exercises. Anita went into a long stretching motion that brought her head back and down all the way beneath her spread legs.

From the couch, Arthur watched their fluid contortions as if in a trance. Melanie thrived on coming up with new people. This time it was gymnasts. Once it had been a circus freak with amazing genitalia. He had despised himself for days after that one.

When their warm-ups were completed, they gathered around Melanie and Arthur in an eager semicircle.

"What's the game?" Mandy asked in her sparkly voice.

"Tonight," Melanie announced, "we're going to play Simon Says."

"Great!" Mandy clapped her hands. "Who goes first?"

"I do the Simon Says," Melanie informed them.

"I get it," Henry said. "Arthur's on the bed and we do to him whatever Simon Says."

"No, it's you three who are on the bed." When they just kept looking at her, waiting for more instructions, Melanie herded them forward as a group. "Get with it, troops. Okay, here's the way the game is played." The three spread themselves out on the bed and listened intently. "I tell one of you by name to do something. If I tell you what to do without first saying Simon Says and you do it, that person has to do the same thing to me, too. Got that, people?"

"We understand," Mandy chirped.

"Okay. Arthur, Simon Says take your clothes off."

Melanie began to shed her own dress. Arthur followed her lead, though without her buoyant enthusiasm. The three on the bed smiled admiringly as if Melanie and Arthur had bodies as good as their own, which told Melanie they were professionals who were going to give top value for what they were being paid.

When they were as naked as the three gymnasts, Melanie told Arthur, "Simon Says hop into bed, dear. You'll be welcome there."

Arthur climbed into the middle of all that firm, well-formed flesh and allowed himself to be fondled, kissed, cooed over, caressed. His erection began. He half closed his eyes and let himself sink into deep but troubling ecstasy.

Kay and Scanner had showered together, made love and now lay in each other's arms on the lounge in her room wearing white terrycloth robes provided by the hotel. The warmth and softness of the material had lulled them into total inactivity.

The knots of fear in Kay's stomach were finally unraveling. She hadn't realized how deeply the events of the day had shaken her until, coming up in the elevator, she noticed her hands still trembling all these hours after she'd had to shoot that big, burly man out in the countryside.

"Hungry? Interested in some room service?" Scanner asked. "Chicken-fried steak? It's a Texas specialty."

"Maybe later. First I want to see how long we can lie here without either of us moving even a single muscle."

"The way I'm feeling, we could set a new world's record for laziness." Scanner yawned. "Usually I can't sit still. If it weren't for you, I'd be on the phone to Washington. Or talking to my crickets, see what's happening out in the big wide world."

"Crickets?"

"Informers," Scanner explained. "People who stay in the dark corners and only make noises when they've got info to sell—like where a counterfeiter is getting his paper or who's just bought a new high-speed press. Most of my crickets work for printing supply houses, paper mills, press manufacturers. Some deal counterfeit themselves; they rat out their competitors in order to put them out of business."

"Nice people you work with."

"Hey, they're not much different from your friend Melanie."

Kay asked if that was how he got onto Leon Donin, through a cricket.

"Sure. I've got a cricket in Moscow who feeds me leads in exchange for real U.S. dollars, rubles being essentially worthless outside Russia. Donin's name came up two or three times. After a lot of legwork, and some leads from my other crickets, I finally tied him into the Moscow–Syria syndicate."

"What happens after tomorrow? After you ruin Donin's deal?"

"I'll head back to Washington, I suppose." Scanner spoke slowly. "Listen to my crickets. Chase down other counterfeiters. You know, play the game. What about you?"

"Same thing. Back to Connecticut, play my game."

"It's not that far from Washington to Connecticut. We'll go on seeing each other."

"Yes . . . of course."

"You sound doubtful. What's wrong?"

"I don't know. I was thinking about Mr. Marvin again."

Scanner groaned.

"Yes, I was! I was thinking about that poor man dying in a hospital with no one to sit beside him, nobody to care. His house burns down, all his worldly goods destroyed, doesn't matter to anyone. Sometimes . . . well . . . I wonder if I'm going to end up like that."

"Mr. Marvin is an extreme case."

"No, he's not! That sort of thing happens to people every day. They just sort of slip out of their lives without anyone in the world to notice."

"It won't be that way with you," he assured her. "And we will go on seeing each other."

She'd had this conversation before. Other times. With other men. It never seemed to work out, no matter how much she wanted it or how hard she tried. Kay wondered whether the fault lay more with herself or with them. It should be possible to hold a relationship together despite the gap of a few hundred miles. Shouldn't it? My God, there were phones . . . faxes . . . the legendary trains, planes and automobiles. Scanner was obviously as committed to his career as herself, but he didn't seem as obsessed with it as most of them. *This time,* she promised herself, *I'm going to make it work.*

# CHAPTER 24

At two minutes past 10:00 A.M. on auction day Donin walked into the bank across the street from the Omni and showed his identification to an assistant manager. Wolf was at his left side, a pace to the rear, armed with a Colt Python concealed beneath his jacket and the usual assortment of knives distributed about his person. His boots had been shined. The newly purchased jeans he was wearing looked neat enough but were tighter in the crotch than he liked, causing him to once again curse Kay Williams. A little discomfort wasn't about to keep him from doing his duty, though. Nobody was going to touch Donin's suitcase, he could goddamn well promise that.

Donin was escorted to the vault, where he signed some papers and retrieved his suitcase. Before leaving he checked the contents and smiled in satisfaction. "Everything correct," he told Wolf.

"Lemme check the street before you come out." Wolf went out on the sidewalk and studied the pedestrian traffic before assuring himself there were no suspicious cars in sight. He signaled Donin to come out and hailed a taxi from the line in front of the Omni.

"It's only three blocks to the other bank," Donin said when they were in the taxi. "A beautiful morning like this we could have walked."

"You could've painted a bull's-eye on your back, too." Wolf looked out the taxi's rear window. "We're okay, nobody special behind us. Just for fun, when the taxi stops at the Longhorn Bank I want you to hustle across the sidewalk and inside the doors as fast as you can."

"What's going on?" Donin's head swiveled around. "Are we being followed?"

"No, I said we're okay. I just got to feelin' this funny itch between my shoulder blades. Don't know what it means, except I want you inside the Longhorn Bank in a jiffy."

Donin took Wolf's precautions seriously. "During the Afghan war I sometimes felt a certain tingling sensation between my own shoulder blades. Invariably there was a sniper lurking nearby."

"No snipers on Congress Avenue." Wolf continued to study the street. "Might be a snake or two underfoot."

"Well, snakes are usually easy to kill."

"So long as you don't let 'em get too close."

"That's your job. I won't worry about it."

Wolf appreciated the confidence Donin showed in him. Even though Donin was your basic foreign termite, Wolf had gotten closer to him than he did to most of his clients. Wolf almost regretted having to spoil the auction for Donin. Couldn't help it, though. He wasn't about to let Old Bowie go to a country full of godless fuckin' commies.

They rolled up in front of the Longhorn Bank a few minutes before 10:30. Wolf paid off the driver and hustled his client across the sidewalk and into the bank.

Stewart Ruddington was waiting in a chair at the head cashier's desk. He rose when Wolf and Donin came in, his eyes skittering to the suitcase in Donin's hand. "Good morning, Mr. Donin. Thank you again for coming here."

Donin ignored the auctioneer's outstretched hand. "Let us get this over with."

"Certainly." Ruddington glanced at Wolf, not liking the man's looks any more than the first time he saw him, but accepting his presence. "A room has been set aside for our use. This is Henry Hopwood, a currency expert from the local office of the American Banking Association. He'll examine your funds. Mr. Hopwood, this is Mr. Donin and his . . . uh . . . assistant, Mr. Wolf."

Donin didn't shake hands with Hopwood, either, merely nodded to him. To Ruddington he said, "You understand that you cannot be present when Mr. Hopwood examines my funds. If you knew how much money I have in this suitcase, you would know how high I am prepared to bid. An obvious conflict of interest."

"Yes, of course," Ruddington said stiffly. "That's why Mr. Hopwood is here."

Donin fixed Hopwood with a severe stare. "It would be equally unfair for you to tell Ruddington how much money I am carrying after we have left this bank."

"I give you my word I won't say anything about that." Hopwood was a lean, scholarly-looking man with stooped shoulders and straight black hair touched at the temples with gray. The American Banking Association was not his employer. Hopwood was a close-up magician who specialized in doing sleight-of-hand magic tricks at nightclub tables. Roy Scanner had hired him to pose as a banker. Hopwood had never taken a job like this before. Wouldn't have taken this one if the money hadn't been so good. Hopwood didn't like the looks of this guy Donin or the beefy cowboy type with him. They made him edgy, but a magician who worked right up close to his audience needed steady nerves, so he looked straight into Donin's eyes and said, "Can we do this now? I have another appointment in half an hour."

He left Ruddington in the lobby and escorted Donin and Wolf to a private paneled room just off the lobby.

As soon as the bank opened, Phil Williams had settled himself into a chair on the far side of the lobby with a copy of the Austin American-Statesman. Donin and Wolf came into the bank on schedule, conferred with the auctioneer, then spoke with another man who took them into a side room.

Phil got up and went to a nearby pay phone. He called the Omni and asked for Leon Donin's room.

"Hello?"

Chauncy Alexander's deep voice was unmistakable. "This is Phil. They're here. Some banker type took them into a private room. Donin's carrying a suitcase and he's got that headbreaker Wolf with him."

"Settle down, Phil. Follow the plan. We about to score, y'unnerstand? Score big. Wait five minutes, make your call to Donin. Then you call me again soon as they come outta that room. Take note, mon, what mood they in, y'see? Donin's money look fine, everybody be happy. Everybody be relaxed. Call me right away, then get up here to Donin's room. Don't follow right on their heels! They be watching. That Wolf's a champion watcher, I bet on that."

"How did you get into Donin's room? Nobody saw you, did they?"

"Never mind that! I be here, that what counts. Call me when they on the move."

Phil put down the phone, returned to his seat, picked up his newspaper. He was sweating under his arms. He didn't want to go up to Donin's room, but what choice did he have? If he didn't show up, Chauncy would simply take Donin's money and split without him. Between a rock and a hard place, that's where he was this morning. And it didn't feel too damned comfortable.

The room was furnished in a typical bank's idea of comfort—oak paneling, teak table, uncomfortable chairs, a couple of dull oil paintings on the walls.

"Let's see what you've got." Henry Hopwood had been thoroughly briefed by Scanner on how to appear to be examining a piece of U.S. currency. If it turned out that Donin was carrying rubles instead of dollars, which was Stewart Ruddington's concern, the whole exercise would become pointless, at least from Scanner's view. Scanner was expecting Donin to be carrying counterfeit hundred-dollar bills. Hopwood's assignment was a simple switch of several of Donin's hundreds for genuine hundred-dollar bills provided by Scanner.

Donin opened the suitcase to reveal stacks of U.S. hundreds. Hopwood swallowed hard. He'd never seen so much money. "Okay, you're carrying U.S. money instead of rubles. That satisfies Mr. Ruddington's first concern. He also has it in his mind, or someone suggested to him, that you may be trying to buy some sort of antique with counterfeit U.S. dollars. I'll have to examine some of these notes, Mr. Donin. A spot check will satisfy me."

"I would like to know who suggested to Mr. Ruddington that my funds are irregular," Donin said.

"Can't help you there," Hopwood answered. "All I know is that I've been asked to authenticate your funds. I hope you understand that counterfeiting has become a serious problem and that hundred-dollar bills are an especially attractive product." Hopwood was using the spiel Scanner had provided. "The legitimacy of U.S. currency is of profound concern to . . ."

"Spare me the civics lesson." Donin began taking stacks of hundred-dollar bills out of the suitcase and tossing them almost carelessly onto the teak table. "Help yourself, Mr. Hopwood. A spot check, you say? Would samples from six stacks of bills be agreeable? You select the stacks to be tested, of course."

A secretary knocked on the door, then put her head into the room. "Mr. Donin? We have an urgent call from your hotel. I'll put it through to this office."

Donin, frowning, picked up the phone.

"Mr. Donin, this is Dave Wingate at the Omni. I was told you were at the Longhorn Bank. I'm sorry to bother you when you're doing business, but a parcel just arrived for you from Russia, of all places. First package I've ever seen from there. It was delivered by DHL and marked *Urgent*. I thought you should know as soon as possible that the parcel had arrived. I had a bellman take it up to your room."

"I was not expecting a package." Donin still frowning.

"Well, it's in your room. Excuse me, sir, I have people at the desk." The connection was broken.

"Somethin' wrong?" Wolf, standing with his back to the wall, arms crossed, nothing much to do right now, wondered how the Omni had found Donin here.

"No, a package delivered to the hotel for me, that is all." Donin turned his attention back to Hopwood.

Wolf had to admire the Russian's gall. The money was no good. All of it fake. Yet Donin had thrown around stacks of counterfeit as if they were good as gold, challenging a goddamned banker, of all people, to prove it was phony. Must be damned good counterfeit.

Hopwood loosened the rubber band that held together one stack of hundreds and held a bill up to the light as Scanner had coached him to do. He snapped the bill as if testing the authenticity of the paper. Then he went to the end of the table and turned on an ultraviolet lamp equipped with a magnifying glass under which he gave the bill a more careful scrutiny. Jesus, you could really see all the little flaws under this lamp. Particles of dust stood out like boulders. The tiny "black window" built into the new hundred-dollar bill loomed large. Old Ben Franklin's nose looked as huge and veined as a drunk's.

That was about the extent of Hopwood's observations. He had no real idea of how to tell a counterfeit bill from the real thing. Nor was that his real job. To reinforce the idea that he was a banker, he took a jeweler's loupe from his pocket and put it to his eye. As he did so, his agile hands slipped the hundred-dollar bill of Donin's into a special pocket sewn into the left sleeve of his coat and switched it for a crisp new hundred supplied by Roy Scanner. The switch took only a nanosecond. He'd done this sort of thing thousands of times at nightclub tables, but the people he entertained in clubs didn't carry guns.

Scanner had warned him that the guy leaning against the wall, Bud Wolf, did carry a gun. And maybe carried some knives too. Wolf looked mean enough to do a lot of damage to anyone he got sore at, but Hopwood also knew Roy Scanner was in the next room monitoring everything going on in here. If he made a slip and Donin realized bills were being switched, Hopwood only had to say the single word "Help" and Scanner and two other Treasury agents would come crashing into the room.

So far, that didn't seem necessary. Hopwood said, "This bill looks all right," and picked up another stack of hundreds.

Donin, looking on smugly as Hopwood went through his routine, winked at Wolf as if to say, "This is too easy."

Hopwood examined another bill. As he did so, he coughed loosely into his hand. That was a cover for switching another of Donin's hundreds for a legitimate hundred provided by Scanner. Again, neither Donin nor Wolf caught the swift movements of Hopwood's talented hands.

Hopwood began to relax as he saw how much this assignment resembled his nightclub act. Direction and misdirection. A game he loved. The only difference was that these two guys, the Russian and the thug, thought he was a banker instead of knowing he was a close-up magician. That was almost a shame, because there'd be no applause at the end of this gig. Hopwood loved applause as much as he loved the money he made playing his little games.

He examined four more bills from four stacks of currency chosen at random. In each case he successfully switched a Donin hundred for a Scanner hundred. The whole gig took only ten minutes. Hopwood was just getting warmed up. His nightclub act ran fifty minutes and he wanted to keep on working, really earn his fee.

But Donin said, "You've examined six bills at random, Mr. Hopwood. Isn't that enough?"

Regretfully, Hopwood tossed back a seventh stack of bills. "Yes, that should do it." Tossing money around made him feel like a real banker.

"Wolfie, pack up my funds and we will be on our way."

Wolf packed the stacks of hundreds into the suitcase as neatly as he could. The money sure as hell looked real to him. The fact that it had fooled a banker made Wolf wish he could get access to Donin's printing press for a couple of days, make himself rich for life. His fake license plate racket was beginning to look kind of penny-ante by comparison.

"Thanks for your cooperation," Hopwood said in his version of a banker's rumbling voice. He held out his hand, but once again Donin chose not to honor that particular American custom.

"Good-bye." Donin left the room without uttering any niceties.

In the lobby, Stewart Ruddington rose from his chair with a questioning look.

"I found no irregularities with Mr. Donin's funds," Hopwood told him.

Ruddington looked relieved. "That's very good news! Mr. Donin, I regret you had to be put through . . ." Donin had already walked wordlessly past Ruddington with the suitcase in his hand.

Phil was on the phone before Donin and Wolf reached the sidewalk. "Chauncy? Donin and Wolf are leaving the bank right now."

"What's the story? Everybody look happy?"

"The auctioneer looks happy, that's for sure. Donin doesn't look happy, just very satisfied with himself."

"Bingo!" Chauncy was exultant. "That means Donin be carrying a heavy load of good cash. Phone call worked? He think he got a package waiting in his room?"

"Seemed to work."

"Get your ass up here, Phil. Party time!"

Phil wanted to make one more argument for his absence from Donin's hotel room, but Chauncy had hung up.

Henry Hopwood went upstairs to the office of the bank's president. The CEO was out of town and Scanner had taken over the office for the day. Scanner was waiting for Hopwood along with another, more soberly dressed Treasury agent and a young shirt-sleeved technician with longish hair who had set up an array of portable testing equipment on the CEO's desk. There was also an attractive young woman in a business suit, looking even more tense about all this than the Treasury geeks. He hoped Scanner would introduce him to the girl, maybe let him take the girl to lunch. That wasn't about to happen. Scanner was too focused on his job.

"Henry! You got the goods?" Scanner rubbed his hands together. "We could hear everything, but we couldn't tell whether you were able to make the switches."

Hopwood began pulling Donin's six one-hundred-dollar bills out of his left sleeve. "I copped six hundreds. Nothing to it. Neither of your friends noticed a thing."

The Treasuries all grinned at each other.

"Outstanding!" Scanner said.

"It was easier than my usual act. I mean, these guys looked tough and all, but they weren't expecting any kind of switch. My usual audience knows I'm a magician, so they're *always* looking for a switch. Even so, they can't tell what I'm doing or how it's done."

"You've got great hands, Henry. Everybody told me that. I'll catch your act one of these days. Meanwhile, we've got work to do. The Treasury Department appreciates your cooperation." Scanner took out a wad of bills and counted out two thousand dollars, which he put in Hopwood's hand. "Here's your fee. In cash. As agreed upon."

"You're sure these hundreds are good?" Hopwood recoiled when the Treasuries gave him nasty looks. "Just joking, gang. Hey, are the bills I got for you counterfeit? They looked to me like every other Ben Franklin bill I've ever seen."

"As soon as they've been thoroughly tested, we'll know." Scanner gave Hopwood an "attaboy" pat on the shoulder. "Just a reminder, Henry. Don't tell anyone about this morning's gig."

"I understood the rules going in." Hopwood was annoyed without quite knowing why. As he left, the Treasuries and the attractive girl were gathering around the desk and the hundred-dollar bills he'd lifted for them. His act was over, they weren't interested in him anymore. No real goodbye. No applause. That's what was bothering him. The two-thousand-dollar fee for fifteen minutes work was just fine. Going offstage to no applause sucked.

Kay was fascinated by the testing process that the technician had already begun. It looked to her like a form of alchemy.

"Andy, you can work on two of these bills right here, we've got this office for the day," Scanner told the technician. "I'm sending the other four bills to the big lab in Washington."

"The auction starts in less than six hours," Kay reminded him.

"There's a plane standing by at Austin airport." Scanner slipped four of the bills Hopwood had palmed into a see-through plastic envelope. "It's a three-and-a-half-hour flight to Washington. Terry, you'd better get moving. Tell the lab I need results ASAP. Call me on my cellular phone when you've got some news for me."

"Will do, Roy." The agent left for the airport.

Scanner turned to Andy, the technician. "What can you tell me, Andy?"

Andy was looking at the bill under a microscope. "Not much right out of the chute. Paper's great. Washington'll have to tell you whether it's the right percentages of cotton and linen, but the paper looks and feels authentic. Bleached one-dollar bills? Wouldn't be surprised. The serial numbers are in the right range for new bills. Ink? I can't tell you anything until I put it through the spectrometer. Again, the ink looks legitimate. Printing's the easiest part, but again it's a first-class job. There's not one damn thing in this bill that *appears* phony. I have to tell you, at first glance this piece looks A-okay. If I were a bank teller, I'd take the hundred and give you five twenties in change."

Kay wondered if Donin might be carrying genuine currency. She resisted the notion that Roy might be wrong, that Donin might be only a nasty-tempered hustler with no connection to the Russian mafia after all. But the possibility had to be examined, so she asked the question. "Could Donin's money be good?"

"Donin is a counterfeiter," Scanner said without any hint of qualification. "The currency he's carrying didn't come out of a U.S. Treasury printing plant and either Andy or the Washington lab will find the flaw. There *must* be a flaw."

"I used to think every piece of counterfeit had lots of different flaws," Andy murmured, his eye to the microscope. "Even the best product had a *tell* of some sort. Now I'm not so sure. The technology's getting ahead of us, Roy. Anybody with a computer, good paper and a high-speed press can print their own money these days. If this bill is queer, I can't see it. Are you sure Hopwood made the switch? That he didn't just go through the motions and give you back the hundreds you gave him? Then collected his fee and split?"

"These are the serial numbers on the bills I gave to Hopwood." Scanner showed his technician a list of numbers. "He gave us back a set of bills with a different series of numbers. Convinced?"

"I guess." Andy put one of the other bills under the microscope. "Don't worry, Roy. If this stuff is queer, we'll find the weak spot."

"We need to find it fast. If we don't, Donin will unload it at the auction and be on his way back to Mother Russia on the first plane."

"I won't find it faster with you looking over my shoulder, big fella."

Scanner eased away from the desk. "Message received and understood. Come on, Kay. Andy thinks he can do a better job without my hot breath on the back of his neck. Let's go for coffee."

"You've got a pretty girl with you, so take your time," Andy suggested. "Have two coffees. Go to that Starbucks down the street and bring a container back for me. Black, no sugar."

"Stay with it," Scanner urged.

"Go away." Andy cut a small piece out of the corner of one of Donin's hundreds and fed it into the spectrometer. "Come back in an hour, and make sure my coffee's hot."

Going down the steps to the lobby, Scanner said, "Andy's kind of cranky, but he's a great tech. I hope to hell he can find a flaw."

"What if he doesn't?" Kay was beginning to think of that as a real possibility. "What if your lab in Washington comes up blank, too? Would that mean Donin's money is legitimate currency?"

"No, it would mean Andy's right, the technology for printing money has become too advanced for the U. S., or any other country, to print money that can't be counterfeited."

"That's scary. I'd want to invest whatever money I've got in something solid. Real estate, for example. Or more antiques." A thought struck her. "Hey, if enough people came to mistrust paper money, they'd begin to buy things like gold coins and rare books and antiques and other collectibles. That could create a real boom in my business."

Kay's take on the problem disturbed Scanner. "I wish you'd stop equating the undermining of the U.S. Treasury with good times for people who sell antiques. That's a very selfish view."

"It's a realistic view. What are people supposed to do if they begin to distrust paper money? Bury their heads in the sand?"

"If the currency becomes debased, what would you take in exchange for your precious antiques? You wouldn't want to take U.S. dollars. Or any other currency, for that matter. We'd all have to go back to a barter system."

"Sometimes you don't look at a situation from every . . . wait a minute . . ." As they emerged from the bank, Kay thought she saw her ex-husband. "There's Phil!"

"Where?"

"Phil just got into that taxi. Didn't you see him?"

"No."

"Do you suppose he was in this bank?"

"I don't know why he would be." Scanner didn't like the idea of Phil Williams hanging around the Longhorn Bank. "Unless he was keeping an eye on Donin. Or on you. Why would he do that?"

Kay had no idea. She only knew that wherever Phil went, trouble inevitably followed.


"No need to put the suitcase back in the vault." Donin was feeling expansive after having beaten the banker's silly little tests. "We will return to my room and have a late breakfast sent up."

"Brunch," Wolf said. "That's what we call a combination of breakfast and lunch."

"Brunch." Donin repeated the word approvingly. "A pleasant word. Did you see how easily the banker accepted my product?"

"Yeah, yeah." He was tired of Donin's bragging, which had started the moment they got into the taxi. "He was a little too easy on you, you ask me."

"What do you mean?"

"Most bankers have tight assholes. Hopwood didn't." Donin stared at him blankly. "I'm talkin' about the way he acted. Too loose."

"You are an expert on bankers?"

"I wouldn't say that."

"If you have a specific concern, I would like to hear it. Something more substantial than a . . . what was it? . . . *tight asshole?*" He chuckled. "Some Americanisms are quite colorful. I shall make a list of them for my friends in Moscow."

"You got friends? I'm amazed."

The taxi arrived at the Omni and Wolf abandoned the conversation. Donin was probably right, his product was high-quality and the banker bought it. Nothin' very complicated about that.

They went up in the elevator, Wolf still in attack mode. He felt antsy. Ready to tear off somebody's head. The scratchy sensation lingered between his shoulder blades, he couldn't shake it off. *Fuckin' Russian is makin' an old lady out of me,* he thought.

Wolf went into the room first, swept it with his eyes. Looked okay. He motioned Donin to come on in.

Donin put down the suitcase and stretched, looked around for the DHL package. "Jet lag has finally overtaken me. I may take a nap before lunch. You don't mind just sitting and guarding my funds while I nap?"

"Take a dozen sleepin' pills if you want, what the fuck do I care?"

"You are in a nasty mood, Wolfie. Nastier than usual, I should say."

"Got an itch I can't scratch."

"I will write down that one too. I wonder where they put . . ."

The closet door swung open and an enormous black man in a white suit stepped out, his gun pointed directly at Wolf's heart. "Easy, mon, don't give me no trouble. Just chill out for two minutes and I be gone from your life." Chauncy saw he'd been wrong, Wolf was the one to worry about. The Russian was tough enough, but Wolf had that look. "Down on floor. Stretch out your legs. Hands behind your heads."

Donin looked at Wolf. "Wolfie?"

Wolf surprised both of them by smiling. "Do what the man says, Ivan." He dropped slowly to his knees. He was satisfied now, almost happy, his worries had been real, he wasn't an old lady after all. With deliberate slowness, Wolf lay down and put his hands behind his head as the black guy had directed. Donin hadn't yet moved. He was looking hard at the black guy, on the verge of being stupid. "Don't do it! He'll fuckin' shoot you!"

"Good advice, mon. I be ready to shoot both of you, it come to that."

With a savage glance in Wolf's direction, Donin lowered himself to the floor, stretched out, put his hands behind his head. His expression was one of massive disappointment in Wolf. For his part, Wolf didn't give a shit about the Russian's expression.

"That be the right idea. Don't move, don't even twitch."

Wolf noted the rope dangling from the black guy's left hand.

"Yeah, that's right, you gonna be tied up. Better than being shot, am I right?"

"What are you waitin' for?" Wolf asked, genuinely curious.

"Reinforcements." Chauncy kept his eyes on Wolf, on the Russian, too, but mainly on Wolf, while he opened the snaps on the suitcase and lifted the lid. "Hey, mon, I win the Wheel of Fortune! Where the blond girl, kiss my cheek?"

The black guy had a booming voice, biggest voice Wolf had heard in a long time. West Indian, he'd heard that accent before. Had a nice lilt to it.

In another situation he would have enjoyed the guy's talk. Wolf stayed put and waited. Sooner or later the guy would use the rope, try to tie them up.

"You be uncomfortable a few hours," Chauncy said. "Won't last too long, maid come to turn down bed later tonight." He grinned at them. "Better than be dead, that true?"

"True enough," Wolf said agreeably.

"Wolfie . . ."

"Shut up," Wolf told Donin in a mild voice, careful not to make the black guy nervous. He noticed the guy was jumpier than a minute ago, kept looking at the door for those *reinforcements*. Wolf hoped he was expecting only one more man. He could handle two. Three would be a stretch. He'd bet there was only one more guy, though. Dudes like this one didn't like to split a take more than two ways. They probably didn't know how much money Donin had in his suitcase, only that he had brought a bundle into the country. A bundle that required a whole suitcase. Guy was practically havin' an orgasm, so much dough in the luggage. What would he do if he knew it was counterfeit?

Two quick, nervous raps on the door made the black guy happy. He went to the door, careful to keep Wolf covered, opened it.

Wolf got a small surprise when Phil Williams walked in and hastily closed the door behind him. "Hey, I know you! You're that cunt's husband!" Wolf laughed. "Didn't think you had this sort of deal in you, Goldilocks."

"He knows me." Phil looked stricken. "Chauncy, he knows who I am!"

"And now he know my name, too." Chauncy wanted to kill Phil right this minute. One shot to the gut, watch his face go all pale and twisted while he died. Couldn't do it. A gunshot might bring someone running. Besides, he needed Phil to tie up the two whiteys. "The big one got a gun under his arm. Lift it, Phil. Be real careful, don't put yourself between me and him."

Phil folded back the flap of Wolf's jacket, took the gun, tossed it onto the bed.

Wolf was pleased. *Now they think I can't hurt 'em.*

"Tie them up," Chauncy ordered. "Big one first. Wrists and ankles. Be a Boy Scout, make the knots tight. Can't let them . . . I said don't come between us!"

When Phil bent over to tie Wolf's wrists, he made the mistake of putting himself between Wolf and Chauncy. Wolf rolled onto his left side. A flat, nine-inch throwing knife slid out of his shirt sleeve. His hand flicked out as if he were swatting at a fly and the knife flew.

Chauncy staggered when the blade pierced his throat. His mellifluous voice, of which he'd always been so proud, was no longer available to him. His cry for help came out as a feeble croak. His knees felt shaky. He looked down and saw blood flowing like water onto his white suit. The pistol dropped from his hand. It took superhuman effort to reach up and pull the knife from his throat, but he couldn't hold onto it. He took a step and fell onto Wolf, who was coming swiftly to his feet.

"Shit . . ." Chauncy's weight knocked Wolf backwards. It was pure reflex that made Wolf draw a second knife from his boot and drive it into Chauncy's liver. Chauncy's eyes went wide, then the life in them flamed out. Wolf pushed Chauncy's body off of him.

Phil, who had been frozen by fear, bolted for the door. Yanked it open. Ran as if all the hounds of hell were on his trail. He found an exit that took him down a flight of stairs. He took three or four steps at a time, falling, tumbling forward, not even feeling the bruises from the fall. His heart beat at triphammer speed.

It came as a shock to realize he'd reached the ground floor. He yanked open another door, ran through the lobby to startled stares from hotel guests and staff alike, reached the street and ran blindly away from the hotel.

Chauncy was dead and the killer knew his name. Phil wished he'd never left Jamaica. Never heard of Chauncy Alexander. Never had the notion of using Kay to get rich. He had only a few bucks left in his pocket and he didn't even care. All he wanted was to get out of Texas alive.

Wolf closed the door and got four big towels from the bathroom to put under Chauncy's body. He didn't want the carpet soaked with blood, be too hard to clean.

"The other one might go to the police," Donin said calmly.

"No, he's a lightweight, no guts at all. He'll just keep on runnin'. I mean, what's he gonna tell the police? *Me and my partner tried to rob this honest businessman and my partner got killed.* No way he's goin' to the cops. Couldn't you read that in his eyes?"

"From my position on the floor, I could not see his eyes or much of anything else." Donin had completely regained his composure. "I apologize for doubting your commitment to your job, Wolfie. I should have known you were only waiting for a chance to make your move."

Wolf collected his Python from the bed. "Apology accepted. I don't have time for you to kiss me, I got to get rid of this body."

"How?"

"I'll run over to a sporting goods store, buy a sleeping bag and a big duffel. Put the body inside the two bags. Clean the carpet good. Carry him down the service elevator to the garage. Load him into the trunk of my Caddy and take him out in the country, dump him somewhere quiet." He anticipated Donin's question. "Don't worry, I'll get it done and be back way before the auction. While I'm gone, I want you to wait downstairs in the bar with your suitcase."

"In the bar?"

"Have yourself a good lunch, drink a Shiner Bock for me. Nobody else is gonna bother you, I'd be feelin' it between my shoulder blades."

"I have come to trust your shoulder blades more than I trust my wife."

"You probably got good reason for that."

"Such a wicked man you are." Donin looked down on the body of Chauncy Alexander. "This one puzzles me. How did he come to know that I am carrying a great deal of cash?"

"His partner was Kay Williams's ex-husband."

"Do you think she was part of the robbery attempt?"

"I doubt it. She's just an all-around troublemaking cunt who's gonna pay with her life for messin' with the Wolf."

# CHAPTER 25

While his mistress, Kimiko, gave him a massage, Kazuo Goto thought about his wife, Eiko. Loyal wife. Good mother. Devoted grandmother. Goto felt guilty about his treatment of her. Not because he had a mistress who traveled with him, Eiko long ago had accepted his need for a mistress. His guilt arose from another quarter. When Shibata-san, his executive assistant, informed him that the banks would not extend him even one more yen in credit, Goto telephoned Tokyo and transferred one million dollars to Texas from the account he had set aside for his wife's security after he was gone.

Goto, lying facedown on the bed in Kimiko's suite, said, "I have become a dishonorable man."

"Never." Kimiko was massaging Goto's shoulders. Seeing his inner pain, she moved her hands down to caress his sexual organs.

"Not now." Goto had sworn not to touch the money set aside for his wife no matter how desperate his financial situation became. Having broken that pledge by removing the one million dollars from the account, he feared he wouldn't be able to stop himself from stripping the account bare. Five million dollars had been set aside for Eiko to live on after his death. After taking one million to help him win Old Bowie in today's auction, there was still enough to keep his creditors at bay for about two months—if he went into the account again. He didn't want to do that, but his options were narrowing every day.

"Your muscles are so tight," Kimiko sighed.

"I have many problems. Many difficult decisions facing me."

"You will solve them. You are brilliant man."

*Not what my bankers would say,* Goto thought.

Shibata came into the bedroom carrying his usual heavy stack of papers and wearing his customary studious frown. Accustomed to seeing his employer being massaged by the mistress, he took no particular note of Kimiko. "I talked to three more banks, Goto-san. None would extend additional credit."

"I have arranged for one million dollars to be transferred to my temporary account at First Texas Bank. That should assure a successful bid for Old Bowie." Because Shibata-san tended to be judgmental, it gave Goto a small pleasure to contradict his executive assistant.

"So . . . excellent news . . . from what account did you draw the funds, if I may ask?"

"A private account." Let him wonder.

Shibata didn't have to speculate about the source of the new money. The only account his employer had not tapped was the one set aside for his wife. Shibata felt like the executive officer of a sinking ship. On one hand, he owed Goto an enormous personal debt. Shibata had attended a mediocre university, which doomed most young Japanese men to low-level jobs in second-rate companies. Goto had recognized his keen mind, ignored that humble beginning and rewarded him with a well-paying and prestigious position. On the other hand, now that he had something of a reputation in Tokyo's business circles, Shibata had no desire to go down with Goto's ship. If the man wanted to ruin himself by building an insanely expensive monument to his obsession with knives and swords, let him. Shibata had plans to move on. Meanwhile he would keep Goto-san happy. "I picked up some additional intelligence about the other bidders."

"Go ahead." Goto closed his eyes and gave himself over to Kimiko's nurturing hands.

"It seems that Mr. Ward and Miss Wadsworth have pooled their resources to bid against you."

Goto's head came up. "How high are they prepared to bid?"

"They haven't been specific." Shibata consulted his notes. "I estimate their combined assets could be more than three million dollars."

"Ha! I can beat that!"

*And drive yourself deeper into debt,* Shibata thought. "Miss Williams has also received another million dollars in backing from Mr. Billy Boy Watkins. Nevertheless, I don't believe she's a serious contender."

"Neither do I. What about Mr. Scanner? Still a toothless tiger?"

"Yes, I am sure of that."

"Donin is another story. He may be well financed. What else have you found out about him?"

"Not much more. Except that Mr. Ruddington is satisfied the U.S. dollars Mr. Donin is carrying are genuine. If so, Donin may be your most dangerous competitor."

"I will have slightly more than four million dollars at my disposal. With that backing, I don't believe anyone can beat me." Kimiko began to knead at an especially sensitive spot between his shoulder blades. "Yes, right there, Kimiko. Ahhhh . . ."

"Do you have any Alka-Seltzer?"

"Poor darling, tummy all upset? I'll get you some." Melanie went into the bathroom and returned with a glass of bubbling water. "Here you are. Can you eat anything? We could go downstairs for a nice brunch."

"I don't want food. As soon as my stomach settles into a more rhythmic churning action, I want a drink." In reality, Arthur wanted more than one drink, he craved an entire pitcher of martinis. The night had been both exhausting and degrading. The three young people Melanie had hired were too enthusiastic about their work. Arthur could scarcely believe the contortions they'd achieved, or the positions they'd lured him into. His legs ached. His spine felt like a corkscrew. There were contusions along his rib cage. His stomach was shaky. He may have aged as much as three years over the past eight hours.

"Come on," Melanie urged. "Let's have brunch."

"Simon Says go away." Arthur closed his eyes and slipped under the sheet until only the top of his head showed.

"Those kids were great at the game, weren't they?"

"They could be arrested for what they did to me," he said through the sheet.

Melanie laughed. "Darling, we *all* could have been arrested for what went on here last night. That's the fun of it.

"Being twisted into a sexual pretzel is *not* my idea of fun."

"Of course it is. You know, our relationship would be more fruitful if you dispensed with the holier-than-thou attitude." Melanie had grown quite weary of Arthur's condescension. "You like kinky sex as much as I do. You eat it up, and I mean that literally. If last night's action truly disgusted you, why didn't you just put on your clothes and walk out the door?"

"I wanted to do just that. Came within an ace of leaving, as a matter of fact."

"No, you only like to say you wanted to leave."

Arthur supposed she was right. Melanie could read him perfectly, that was how she'd gained this terrible hold on him. *I could break away from her if I really tried*, he thought. *But I never really try. She's a black hole in space and I'm a planet being sucked towards my destruction.* The sheer bleakness of the metaphor was oddly cheering. *At least my brain hasn't yet turned to jelly.* He felt marginally better about himself, well enough to admit that Mandy's sexual contortions had indeed been welcome and, to be *completely* honest, rather delicious.

With his eyes closed and the sheet sealing him off from Melanie's vision, Arthur mentally revisited one of the Simon Says games he'd played out with Mandy. Her blond hair had fallen into his face at the same moment she forced him to strenuously arch his back in order to fix his mouth to that sweet spot between her legs. He could almost relive the powerful orgasm that rippled through her athletic body. He could envision the strong thighs closing on either side of his head. Yes, delicious. As a younger man, these kinds of high jinks had been forbidden to him by his severe New England upbringing. Melanie had become a master at fulfilling his unfilled desires—damn her. He feared it was only a matter of time before she maneuvered him into marriage.

"Come on, darling. Get up, go to your own room, shower and shave, dress for the auction in your tweed jacket and charcoal gray slacks, and meet me in the lobby in an hour for brunch. As a reward for getting up, I'll see that you get a large quantity of dry martinis with your shrimp salad."

How she knew he wanted a shrimp salad for lunch was a mystery to him. She also seemed to know whenever he was in the mood for martinis. And somehow she even knew he had planned to wear the tweed jacket this afternoon, simply as a thumb in the eye to the irritating *casualness* of everything Texan. The goddamned woman was *surrounding* him.

"Oh, all right." Arthur threw back the sheet, sat up, stretched. A flash of pain streaked along his groin, a legacy from Mandy. As he put on his clothes, he wondered what Melanie's next surprise would be. Something even more lurid and tacky than last night's game of Simon Says, no doubt. He flailed himself for looking forward to it.

Scanner came into the office of the president of the Longhorn Bank carrying the bag with his technician's coffee. "Watch out," he told Andy, "it's really hot."

"Hot's just what I like." Andy sipped his coffee while surreptitiously ogling Kay's legs, then pushed himself back from the jumble of instruments on the desk.

"Can you prove the money's counterfeit?" Kay knew it was really Roy's place to ask the question, but she couldn't help blurting it out.

The technician shook his head and directed an "I'm sorry" smile at Scanner. "Roy, this stuff is *good*. I mean *GOOD*! I'm still wondering if that fucking magician didn't pull some kind of switch on us. I can't find one point of irregularity on either of these two hundreds."

"There has to be something," Roy said grimly.

"The big lab may find something wrong with the ink. Or the paper. But the print job is just fabulous."

"You sound like you want to go to work for the Russians." Scanner's mouth felt sour. "Shit, this is a disappointment."

"Hey," Andy said, "you know I can't do a full-points test with this portable lab. Be a little patient, the big lab in D.C.'ll find a flaw."

"By that time Donin will be back in Moscow."

"You couldn't arrest him anyway," Kay reminded him. "He's carrying a diplomatic passport."

"Yeah, but I could impound his currency and personally kick him to hell out of the country. Even rough him up a bit on the way to the airport."

"Roy!"

"A couple of sharp elbows to his ribs, like an NBA player under the backboard, that's all I'm talking about."

"Still . . ." Kay wondered why she'd bothered to object, Donin certainly deserved to be roughed up.

Scanner looked at his watch. "Five hours till the auction. How long does an auction take?"

A shrug from Kay. "With so few bidders in the room? I'd be surprised if it ran longer than thirty minutes."

"The plane'll arrive in D.C. at about two-thirty our time. Say twenty minutes from National Airport to the big lab. That gives the techs about an hour to find a flaw."

"They're good, Roy." Andy felt the need to stick up for his colleagues back home. "They can move fast when they have to and they'll have four of Donin's hundred-dollar bills to work with."

"With all the tests they have to do, they probably won't have any news for us until midnight."

Andy came to a decision. "Why don't I call D.C. right now, tell 'em when they get their hands on the bills Terry's bringing to concentrate on the paper and ink. That'll save some time. You aren't gonna find any holes in Donin's printing process, I'll stake my rep on that."

After thinking for a few seconds, Scanner said, "Do it."

Wolf had found an ID that identified the body as that of Chauncy Alexander, a citizen of Jamaica. He had rolled Chauncy first into a sleeping bag, then into a huge duffel bought at a nearby Oshman's Super Sporting Goods store. He cleaned up the remaining blood on the hotel room floor with a combination of Mister Clean and Arm & Hammer baking soda. "Baking soda's great for cleanin' up blood," he told Donin. "I've used it for that lots of times."

"Baking soda," Donin mused. "Does *Yankee know-how* have no bounds?" He let Wolf do the cleanup alone, he was obviously practiced at it.

"See you soon." Wolf hoisted the bag by the shoulder strap and went down to the garage through the service elevator. Chauncy's inert form sagged and felt as if it weighed at least half a ton, but Wolf managed to get Chauncy into his Caddy trunk without incident. One bellboy, smoking a cigarette near the elevator doors in the garage, saw him with the heavy bag over his shoulder but showed no curiosity.

The drive out into the countryside was pleasant. He headed east towards Pflugerville, one of the many little German towns dotting central Texas. The sky was a vivid blue. Wolf wished he could stop and spend a few minutes just enjoying it, he always liked a bluer-than-blue Texas sky. But the auction was only a couple of hours away.

Out past Pflugerville he spotted an old rundown farmhouse, obviously unoccupied, shingles scattered on the ground, the chimney mostly collapsed, the gravel drive so weed-ridden it was proof no one had come by in a long time. Best part was that the old farmhouse had a well.

Wolf drove slowly up to the house, ready to give a friendly "Pardon me, I guess I turned into the wrong drive" if anyone did appear. He parked near the well. Got out of the Caddy. Knocked on the door.

Nobody answered. He didn't think anyone would. Just for caution's sake, he walked around the house and looked over the property to make sure nobody was taking a shit in the bushes or fishing in the little stream out back. Satisfied that he was alone, Wolf opened the trunk of the Caddy and wrestled Chauncy Alexander's incredibly heavy body up and onto his shoulder.

Six steps to the well. He let the big duffel fall off his shoulder and into the well. Listened for the splash. No splash. Just a big *thunk*. Dry well. *Fuck it*, he thought. *The body'll raise a stink for a few weeks, but there's no one around to smell it. Even if somebody did notice a smell, they'd think a critter was down there. That's what I'd think, anyway.*

His Caddy had left tracks, but it was a stolen car he planned to ditch when this job was over anyway. *Nothin' to worry about, just have to remember to take the plates with me.*

*Nothin' here to tie me to a dead nigger in a well, either.*

The shape of the house brought him to a standstill. *Goddamn, just like the house I was born in. Dog run through the center, give you some breeze in the summer. Shallow well probably goes dry every July through September. I think I spotted an old kettle hangin' in the fireplace, too. Pure central Texas.*

Wolf drove off in a nostalgic mood, whistling.

Before returning to the hotel he made a quick stop at a gun and knife show at Palmer Auditorium only a few blocks from the Omni. He browsed the show more quickly than he would have liked, ignoring the vast displays of pistols, rifles, shotguns, automatic weapons and specialty guns such as Derringers and other "pocket pistols," to concentrate on the trays of used knives.

At a booth in the back of the auditorium he found what he was looking for—an old Bowie-style knife that somewhat resembled the original Old Bowie, at least in size and general design. The old knife's steel was pitted from having done heavy duty over the years and the grip had been worn down by steady use to a soft brown hazelwood color. Probably owned for years by someone who hunted and spent a lot of time out-doors. Nothing like a Bowie for skinnin' deer. Wolf bought the knife for a few dollars.

Driving back to the Omni, he noodled over his plan to use the worn-out old blade he'd just bought to help him acquire Old Bowie.

# CHAPTER 26

The auction was due to begin at 4:00 P.M. By 3:45 most of the bidders had come up to the Driskill Hotel meeting room where the auction would take place. Before being admitted to the room, the participants' IDs were scrutinized by thick-necked security men. Though dressed in suits, the bulges of the security guards' weapons were evident, as they were meant to be. Two armed men were posted outside the door, three more inside the auction room. Stewart Ruddington was taking no chances.

All those who come as bidders to a major auction bring with them some degree of nervousness. With his practiced eye, Ruddington could see jittery nerves everywhere. He saw it in the rather hysterical eye makeup of Melanie Wadsworth. In the flushed-from-drink cheeks of Arthur Ward. In the way Kay Williams drummed her fingers on the arm of her chair. In Leon Donin's gritted teeth. Even the customarily hooded eyes of Kazuo Goto showed pinpoints of emotion.

Most nervous of all was Ruddington's client. Señor Antonio de Baraga clutched the walnut box containing Old Bowie as if fearing one of the bidders would rise and snatch it from him. Ruddington didn't blame de Baraga for his concern. Of all those in the room, only the auctioneer knew how far into debt the de Baraga family had fallen. Selling Old Bowie was the only way the de Baragas could pay off their most pressing debts and retain title to their estate in Mexico. This was to Ruddington's advantage. Señor de Baraga had given him *carte blanche* to run the auction as he saw fit. The Mexican had given Ruddington only two instructions. First, he wanted the auction run in a way that would draw no attention from tax authorities on either side of the border. Second, payment must be in liquid assets such as cash, bearer bonds or gold.

Hence the auction was being held in a quiet hotel conference room instead of in the glare of lights at Christie's or Sotheby's.

Ruddington glanced at his watch. Three-fifty p.m. He could start the auction right now instead of at four o'clock. The absence of Roy Scanner, whom he did not consider a real bidder anyway, would be no loss. However, another ten minutes of waiting would heighten the tension, always a desirable element at an auction. So the auctioneer merely smiled placidly at the bidders and said, "Please help yourself to coffee. There are some cookies and little cakes, too, if anyone is interested."

Everyone wanted the coffee; the cookies and little cakes were left untouched.

Wolf had taken a seat at the back of the room in a chair directly across the table from Kay's. She forced herself not to draw back from his presence. No way she'd give the bastard the satisfaction of showing fear. She wished Roy would get here, though. He was on the phone to the lab in Washington, pushing for results. Interesting to watch him badger people, a whole different side of him at work. Roy could be rude, demanding, impatient—everything she usually disliked in a man. "You'd better move your asses back there or I'll be putting an ad in the trade journals for a whole new crew of techies," she'd heard him tell someone. Not exactly the way to inspire your staff, she'd thought.

She was aware of Wolf leaning across the table towards her. Heard him say in a low voice that no one except herself could hear, "I'm real sorry you and me got off on the wrong foot. I'm a rough old cob, but I'm not the horned devil, y'know." His smile was folksy. "Whatever's been goin' on to make you antsy, I'm not the guy responsible. I just wanted to tell you that."

Kay gave him back an equally false smile. "I know better. You threatened me at the Alamo and you were pursuing Roy and me out near San Marcos yesterday. I can't prove it, Mr. Wolf. But I know it was you."

"Call me Wolfie, everybody does." His eyes as crinkly as Santa Claus. "Except my wife, she calls me Bud. Nice gal, you two would get along real well. Emma's a down-home sort, but like you, she enjoys artistic things.

Got an eye for it. Just last year she bought a print by that fag painter, what's his name, Picasso? Looks like somebody kicked over a can of paint on a canvas? But Emma liked, it so I didn't say shit when she hung up the damned thing in the dinin' room, just let her do it. I knew she was just tryin' to help me appreciate the finer things. Lost cause, most likely."

"What's the point of this conversation, Mr. Wolf?"

"No point at all, just makin' small talk till the auction starts. You don't think you're too good to talk to the likes of me, do ya?"

"Don't play class warfare with me."

"I'm not." His voice still low but urgent. "I'm just tryin' to find some common ground between you and me, get the hard feelins out of the way."

"That's not possible."

Her reply seemed to antagonize him, the way his eyes flared. "Don't be too sure. Like they say—never say never."

"I say *never* whenever I choose. For example, you and I can *never* put what's happened this week behind us." Kay was now out to antagonize him, the big thug with his boots and rancher's clothes, trying to make people think he actually worked with his hands for a living. To hell with him. She wanted Wolf to understand she didn't buy any part of his good-old-boy act. "For one thing, I don't care to put it behind me. Roy and I are going to see that you pay for what you've done this week, Mr. Wolf. Pay one way or another."

"Is that right? You and Roy? I don't think so."

"Don't underestimate your enemies. And make no mistake, I am your enemy."

"Sorry to hear it."

"No, you're not."

Wolf chuckled. "You're not an easy person to talk to, y'know? Guess that's why you're not married, you must scare off a lot of guys with that butch attitude."

"I only scare the people I want to scare."

"You think I'm scared? Of you?"

"By now you should be. I've beaten you at every one of your own vicious games this week, haven't I? Come on, admit it."

"Tell you what, Kay. Mind if I call you Kay? Doesn't matter, I'll call you what I want to call you." Wolf couldn't believe she actually thought of him as beatable. "One of these days you will think better of me, Kay. I'll call on you some time when you're back home, when you least expect me. We'll go out and have a cup of coffee at whatever kind of diner you got back there in . . . where is it? . . . Connecticut? We'll talk things out, you'll be surprised to discover how much you like me. How much you want me, even."

Kay's skin began to crawl. "Is that some kind of threat?"

"Hell, no." Wolf contrived to look hurt. She had the idea, let her run with it. "I'm just sayin' you will look at me differently when the time comes."

"*When the time comes* sounds like a threat to me."

"You're just too sensitive is all." She had the idea real good now, her face had a yellowish tinge. He sat back in his chair well satisfied. Let the bitch sweat. And wait. And sweat. And wait a long time. And sweat some more. Then one day he'd be there, right in her own damned bedroom. "If you're gonna take every little thing I say the wrong way, there's no use talkin' to you." He turned away and drank off some of his coffee with a slight slurping sound.

Kay looked around, hoping that Wolf's threats had been overheard. Not likely. There were two or three conversations going on around the table, people preoccupied with their own thoughts. Only Donin had taken note of her conversation with Wolf, his humorless smile telegraphing his hope that Wolf would carry out whatever threats he'd just made against her.

"It's four o'clock, the auction will begin," Ruddington announced.

The conversations ceased, people leaned forward.

"As I said at the preview meeting, the bidding will begin at one million dollars. Other ground rules—further bids will be accepted in a minimum of five-thousand-dollar increments. Payment must be made immediately following the bidding in cash, gold, bearer bonds or other liquid assets." With a glance at Donin. "Only U.S. dollars will be accepted. Gold will be assayed by the local firm of Higgins and Clark before Old Bowie is passed to its new owner. Financial instruments such as bearer bonds will be vetted by the brokerage firm of Delaney, Reese, Powers. Is everything clear?"

Murmurs of assent.

"Any questions?"

Kazuo Goto raised a hand. "I would like to examine the knife once more before the auction begins."

"I think all of us would," Melanie said.

"Certainly." Ruddington separated the walnut case from Antonio de Baraga's arms, opened it, took out Old Bowie, presented it to Goto.

The Japanese examined the knife with an expression of complete satisfaction. "The most famous knife in the world." Though not normally a talkative man, he found himself voicing his thoughts. "As a boy I read of this knife and the battle of the Alamo. Japanese youngsters who don't know where Texas is, or what it is for that matter, know of the Bowie knife. Whoever wins this auction will own an important part of history. Not just Texas history. Or American history. World history." He gazed around at his competitors. "I am privileged to be here."

*Long speech for a Jap,* Wolf thought.

Goto handed the knife to Donin, who gave it a cursory inspection before passing it on to Melanie.

Wolf was disgusted. *The Russky doesn't give a damn about the knife, it's just a hot investment to him, plus a way to pass a shitload of phony hundreds. Fucker should pay for the privilege of touchin' Old Bowie. The Jap at least understands that much.* No one offered the knife to Wolf for inspection, a tacit message that at this party he was just a hired hand. Didn't bother him. Whoever won at this auction, Wolf expected to be the one who'd ultimately possess Old Bowie.

As the knife went from hand to hand, participants also paused to reread passages from the technical documentation and the letter written by de Baraga's ancestor. There were no doubts about the knife's provenance. That was almost a drawback; the price for Old Bowie was bound to reflect the bidders' certainty they would be buying an absolutely authentic and exciting object.

When each bidder had exercised the opportunity to examine the knife, Ruddington placed it on display in the walnut case.

Melanie had been awaiting the perfect moment to make her announcement. She wanted attention and lots of it. "Stewart, you and the bidders should know that Arthur and I have decided to pool our resources and bid on Old Bowie together."

Kay felt her jaw drop. "Arthur, is this true?"

Arthur nodded in what Kay thought was rather tepid agreement. "Yes, Melanie and I have gone partners in today's auction." He licked his lips. "This is a one-time arrangement."

*He's kidding himself,* Kay thought. One glance at Melanie's glittering cat's eyes convinced her the hook was set pretty deeply into Arthur's mouth. Another two months and she'd reel him in, have him flopping around at her feet just like a landed fish. Poor Arthur.

Melanie's news had the effect she'd wanted.

Donin came to his feet with a red face. "I must object! These two people have given themselves an unfair advantage in the bidding."

Ruddington was as startled as everyone else by the partnership between Melanie and Arthur, but not displeased. Their combined funds would guarantee a healthy bid. "I have no objections, so long as Señor de Baraga is satisfied."

Though his steep debts stamped him as an incompetent businessman, de Baraga did recognize this consolidation presented an opportunity for a very high price for Old Bowie. "I have no objections."

Ruddington shrugged off Donin's furious glare. "Mr. Goto? Miss Williams? What are your thoughts?"

"Let the bidding begin," Goto said.

"I have no problem with two bidders going in together." Kay now doubted that she had enough financial backing to win, but an objection wouldn't change anything except to reveal that her position had eroded. Actually, she feared for Arthur more than for her own fortunes. Might not hurt to give Melanie a jab in the ribs, though. Roy had just come into the room and sat down next to her. "In light of Melanie's announcement, you should know that Roy Scanner and I are also combining our resources and will bid together. You all know that I represent Billy Boy Watkins and that Roy is bidding for former Treasury Secretary Wallace Wright. Our principals are in agreement on this."

Scanner had heard Melanie's announcement and vaguely understood what Kay was trying to accomplish—puncture Melanie's balloon, worry her, generally keep her off-balance. He had to back her up. "Yeah, that's right, we're together on this. I talked to Secretary Wright this morning and he agreed to commit his funds in a joint bid. Said he'd rather own half of Old Bowie than be shut out. Since Kay has more experience than I do at auctions, she'll do the actual bidding."

*Better and better*, Ruddington thought.

The other bidders were well confused. They'd written off Scanner as some sort of auction *voyeur*. Was he actually speaking for Secretary Wallace Wright? If so, he had to be taken seriously. Secretary Wright was a wealthy man, something of a collector, a person of substance.

Goto wondered if Shibata's intelligence people had failed him. He felt a burning sensation in his chest, another attack of angina, took a deep breath as he waited for it to pass. No, he decided this was just a wild bluff by Miss Williams. She and the Wadsworth woman were natural competitors. The angina was slowly fading. Some coffee would help. He turned toward the coffee service, but Leon Donin's bodyguard waved him back.

"Let me get that for you." Wolf had placed himself near the coffee urn with the small vial of digitalis palmed in his hand. He'd figured the dose carefully. Fairly small dose. Take a while to work, his pharmacist connection had promised. *Don't want the old Jap to keel over right after I give him coffee, that'd look suspicious as hell.* "Here you go."

"Thank you."

Wolf poured himself a cup, too. He admired the fine old Driskill Hotel. It was quiet and comfortable, everything about it spelled class. Like this damned good java. You couldn't beat old Texas for the real goods. Wolf caught a surreptitious wink from Donin, who plainly appreciated his help in getting rid of the Jap. *Glad to be of assistance,* Wolf thought. *One less foreigner in the game.* The news that Melanie Wadsworth and Arthur Ward had pooled their bucks was satisfying, too. Wolf figured the note he'd slipped under Ward's door must have scared the hell out of him, forced him to make a pact with old Melanie. *There's a pair for you, a prime bitch and a blue-blooded wimp.*

Donin didn't raise an objection to Kay Williams's so-called alliance with Roy Scanner and his patron because he gave no credence to it. *Scanner is out to get* me, Donin thought. *Not some damned knife.* This was just a ploy by Kay Williams to counter the partnership between the Wadsworth woman and Arthur Ward.

"If there are no other issues," Ruddington was saying, "the auction will begin." He moved to a lectern set up in front of the room and offered up a benign smile. "The bidding will begin at one million dollars."

"One million," Donin said, anxious to get on with it.

"One million fifty thousand," Goto countered.

A couple of gasps and a cleared throat. No one had expected the bidding to move in increments of fifty thousand. Goto had taken part in many auctions, knew that serious buyers liked to feel each other out with cautious bids in the early stages. Goto was deliberately breaking an unwritten rule. Almost flaunting his disregard for their conventions. Only Ruddington was pleased to see a bump of fifty thousand so early on.

"The bid is one million fifty thousand." He spoke into the silence in order to prompt the next bid.

"One million sixty thousand," Melanie said.

*Oh dear,* Kay thought. *If Arthur is letting Melanie bid for the both of them, he has truly lost himself to her.* "One million sixty-five thousand." Kay was trying to bring the increments back down to five thousand. A runaway auction would be a disaster.

"One million eighty-five thousand," Melanie shot back, letting everyone know she was going to push Kay to the wall.

*This isn't an auction,* Donin thought. *This is a cat fight.* "One million ninety thousand." A runaway auction wouldn't work to his advantage, either.

Scanner put his mouth close to Kay's ear and whispered, "This is more exciting than I expected. Can I make a bid?"

Despite the tension eating away at her insides, Kay almost laughed. "Go ahead."

"One million one hundred thousand." Scanner immediately experienced a surge of panic. Suppose everyone suddenly stopped bidding? He'd owe de Baraga more than a million dollars! *What's the matter with everyone? Why have they suddenly clammed up? Jesus God! Somebody else bid!*

"One million five hundred thousand." Goto had decided to bring this auction to a swift and favorable conclusion through simple financial intimidation. He kept his voice firm even though he was feeling a bit dizzy and his throat had gone dry. A bitter taste permeated his mouth. This wasn't angina.

Letting out his breath, Scanner promised himself that he'd never do such a stupid thing again.

Kay felt as if she'd been punched. Goto must be better financed than anyone had expected. Even Donin looked shocked by the huge bump Goto had given the bid. She saw Donin shoot a questioning look in Wolf's direction. Wolf responded with a *Damned if I know* shrug. What was *that* all about?

Arthur and Melanie were engaged in a furious whispered conference, Melanie saying, "We can't let Goto control this auction."

"You shouldn't have gone up twenty thousand just to spite Kay," Arthur whispered back. "That only gave Goto the impetus to bid even higher. Get control of yourself or I'll have to take over our bidding."

"Forget that idea," Melanie hissed. "Just forget it. This is *my* time in the sun, Arthur. Don't try to spoil it for me or I'll make you sorry every day for the rest of your life."

Melanie's threat had an unintended effect. Arthur felt as if a fog had lifted from around his head and shoulders. He could see more clearly and his senses once again felt vital despite all the martinis Melanie had fed him at lunch. It occurred to him that he'd been drinking much more than usual lately, Melanie making sure there was always a glass of something alcoholic near to his hand. His own fault, he seldom turned down a drink and was usually looking for one. But was Melanie's pleasure at seeing him with a drink in his hand a part of her strategy to control him? If so, the control was about to end. "I'll stand by our agreement," he whispered into Melanie's ear. "You do the bidding, I'll add one point five million to your funds. But following this venture our *partnership* is dissolved." He enjoyed watching her blink several times in confusion.

While Arthur and Melanie argued in whispers, the bidding had continued.

"One million nine hundred and ninety thousand," Donin was saying.

Kay had not offered a bid for several minutes. "Two million," she countered with a decisiveness she didn't feel. She'd just committed two-thirds of the money Billy Boy Watkins had provided and the auction felt like it was heading above the three million plateau. This was already the highest she'd ever bid for any antique. A panic attack made her feel she was out of her league and that everyone in the room knew it.

Goto raised his hand as if to offer another outrageously high bump to the bid. Instead he said, "Please . . . my physician . . . I'm not feeling well." Goto sat back in his chair and loosened his tie. His head lolled to one side and his eyes went glassy. Suddenly he slumped over and would have slid onto the floor except that his head and shoulders fell across the table.

Shibata and the quiet Dr. Watanabe had been sitting far back against the rear wall. They leaped up and rushed to their patron's side. Dr. Watanabe loosened Goto's tie and felt his neck for a pulse. "Atrial fibrillation," he said. "This is a new problem, very serious." He spoke to Shibata in a rattling stream of Japanese that sent Shibata running from the room. "Shibata-san has gone to call for an ambulance from Brackenridge Hospital. Please do not crowd around the table, give Goto-san some air. In fact, I believe you should all wait in the hallway until an ambulance has taken Goto-san away."

The bidders withdrew from the room in twos and threes, looking back over their shoulders as Dr. Watanabe efficiently stripped off Goto's coat and prepared to treat this attack with Isordil.

Ruddington lingered. When Shibata returned from calling for an ambulance, the auctioneer caught him by the arm. "What should we do about the auction? Your employer was obviously determined to be the winning bidder, but I don't see how I can postpone when there's no way to tell when Mr. Goto might be well enough to participate."

"You should continue the auction without Goto-san," Shibata said. "It's the terrible pressure of this bidding that brought on this attack. He won't be well enough to do any kind of business for many days. Am I correct, Dr. Watanabe?"

"I am afraid so."

"I must inform Mrs. Goto and Kimiko about this."

"Go ahead and speak with them. Bring both of them to Brackenridge Hospital," Dr. Watanabe urged.

Shibata rushed away.

Ruddington closed the case holding Old Bowie and assigned three of the armed guards to stay in the room close to it, then turned to deal with de Baraga, who was wringing his hands and on the verge of a breakdown of his own. "What will happen here? Goto was the high bidder, will the auction collapse?"

"Not at all." Ruddington spoke in his most soothing voice even though his own nerves felt stretched. "Goto didn't even put out the last bid, it was Kay Williams who went to two million. I think we'll probably go on with the auction after Mr. Goto has been taken to the hospital."

"Will he die?"

"I don't know."

"There would be a story in the newspaper if he died," de Baraga complained. "The tax authorities would learn of the auction."

Ruddington was repelled by de Baraga's selfish concerns. "We'll monitor Mr. Goto's condition very closely, of course. If he should die, I will cancel the auction. It wouldn't be seemly to continue."

"No? Even though these people came a long distance?" De Baraga sensed Ruddington's disapproval. Because the auctioneer was his only ally here, he felt compelled to agree. "Yes, I see you are right." He pulled a white silk handkerchief from his pocket and pressed it to his brow. *If that Japanese dies*, he thought, *I will kill him.*

Because no one cared to chat with Donin or Wolf, they were able to stand alone at the end of the corridor.

"Fuckin' digitalis hit the Jap like a truck, didn't it?"

"Yes, but not until the bid went to two million." Donin narrowed his eyes. "I am extremely displeased that you did not put Goto out of action sooner."

"Hey, don't get on my ass about that. Stuff takes time to work. I put Goto down early in the auction, that's all I promised."

"The bidding will be picked up at two million. One of the others may be able to top me."

"You aren't really pissed at me," Wolf observed. "You're worried about the partnership between old Bang-Bang Melanie and that asshole Ward. They're gettin' it on together, you ask me. Guy's pussy-whipped, won't be any good to himself or anybody else till he gets her out of his system."

"I hope Goto doesn't die, Ruddington probably would postpone the auction. You didn't put too much of the drug in Goto's coffee, did you?"

"What am I, the digitalis expert of the fuckin' universe? I hit him with a low dose, like the pharmacist told me." Wolf chuckled. "You heard the Jap's head bounce off the table? Sounded like a bowlin' ball scorin' a spare."

"I don't understand half the things you tell me," Donin complained.

"Listen up better, you'll get an education."

With a great sigh, "I will be so happy to be back in Moscow."

"Yeah, I'll bet you miss all those good turnip dinners and the babes with bodies like sacks of potatoes."

"Like all Americans, your worldview is limited. That's what will bring down your country in the end."

Wolf just sneered. "Don't hold your breath."

Scanner was down in the lobby, on the phone to the Washington lab. He had a cellular phone in his pocket, but he made confidential calls from land lines so no one could listen in. "How long does it take to do the scan? I've got maybe half an hour, Terry. Then the auction'll be over and Donin'll be on the move. I'll have lost my shot at him. Get those guys *in gear!*"

"They're working, Roy. Not their fault this product is high-quality."

"Yeah, I hear you. Know what? *I don't care* how good the product is. Our techies are always bragging they're the best in the business. It's time they lived up to their rep. Make them live up to it."

"Will do, Roy."

The agent on the other end had a *Get off my back* strain to his voice, which Scanner ignored. He didn't enjoy leaning on his people, but sometimes it had to be done. "Buzz me on my cellular as soon as you get anything." He'd said that half a dozen times, too, and would keep saying it until he got results.

"Will do, Roy."

"Terry, do me a favor. Stop saying *Will do* and get it goddamn done!" He slammed down the receiver.

Kay had come up to him in the middle of the conversation, heard the way he treated the agent on the other end. "You can be pretty hard on your people."

"I hear that a lot." Scanner made a deliberate effort to soften his voice, get himself under control. "Sometimes I think I wasn't born to be part of an organization as big as the U.S. government. I'm too impatient. I don't follow rules very well, don't accept *It can't be done*, don't worry much about how the things I do and say affect other people."

"Like burning down Mr. Marvin's house."

"Sure, that's an example." She'd never forgiven him for doing that, he realized, even though burning down Mr. Marvin's house had saved both their lives. "I get the job done. That's what counts with me." He gave her a crooked smile. "You're the same way and you know it."

"Yes, and I'm beginning to question my own priorities. You know, do I care more about antiques than about people? That sort of thing."

"I understand." He was nodding along with her words, trying to empathize, worried he'd lose her if she came to think of him as a total hardass.

"When someone like Kazuo Goto falls out of his chair, I couldn't help thinking that he actually drove himself to a heart attack in a frenzy to buy a *thing*. And that my life is all about buying *things*."

"He was sick to begin with," Scanner pointed out. "He brought a doctor with him all the way from Tokyo."

"I'm just wondering if Old Bowie has claimed another life."

"Goto's not dead yet." Scanner inclined his head towards the front doors of the Driskill. Kazuo Goto, lying on a gurney with an oxygen mask attached to his face and a small cylinder of the precious air lying next to him, was being expertly maneuvered under the guidance of Dr. Watanabe to the ambulance waiting at the curb. Two equally well-dressed women, Scanner presumed they were Goto's wife and mistress, followed in the gurney's wake, accompanied by Shibata. Seconds later the ambulance doors slammed shut and the vehicle drove off with its siren blasting.

"Terrible sound," Kay said. "I always shudder when I hear it."

"Me too," Scanner said, even though he didn't. "We'd better go back upstairs, see what Ruddington's going to do about the auction."

"Unless Kazuo Goto dies in the next ten minutes, the auction will continue." Kay knew Stewart very well. "There's too much money at stake."

"I'm sorry, Arthur. I didn't mean to snap at you before."

Their whispered argument had moved into the hall outside the auction room.

"I'm not angry. I'm just . . . relieved . . . that's all."

"Relieved about what?" Melanie didn't like Arthur's new attitude. She knew all about control and sensed she'd lost it. "What did you mean when you said you were going to dissolve our partnership?"

"What part of *dissolve our partnership* don't you understand?" Arthur realized he really was angry. He put the emotion aside, it would keep until another time. "Melanie, I'm glad we're going together for Old Bowie. It's such a unique piece, nothing like it in the entire world. This deal doesn't have any parallels, so it's going to take both of us to win. The bid is obviously going over three million. That's a threshold neither of us anticipated when we got into this."

"I don't know. Without Goto, the auction could collapse."

"Donin has a lot of money in that suitcase. Three million, according to the note someone shoved under my door." Arthur wished he knew whether the note was accurate. "He'll be hard to beat, he's that kind of person."

Melanie wasn't intimidated. "We're not exactly underfunded ourselves. It would be a hell of an auction with just Donin and us."

"What about Kay? Do think her partnership with Scanner is real?"

"No, I don't. Kay was trying to rattle me."

And succeeded. Arthur tended to agree that Kay had been gaming them. "Donin's the one to beat. We must be reaching towards his upper limit, his bids have only been in five-thousand-dollar increments."

"Agreed." Melanie ran the tips of her fingers up and down Arthur's arm. "This is the craziest auction I've ever taken part in. What about you?"

"Definitely."

"Kind of sexy, though. Goto being here with both his wife and mistress and then collapsing at the two million mark. That big, important knife looking so deadly in its case. All of the Alamo history. The involvement of thugs like Donin and Wolf. Kay and Scanner becoming lovers. I mean, you couldn't ask for more in an auction, could you? Doesn't all of it turn you on?"

Arthur was relieved at how easily he was able to ignore Melanie's blatant seductions. "Let's go back inside, see what Stewart has in store for us."

"The auction will continue." Ruddington looked at the participants over the rims of his glasses. "There is one caveat. I've sent someone to the hospital to monitor Mr. Goto's condition. If he succumbs to this illness, the auction will be postponed for one week."

"What does it matter if Goto dies?" Donin felt that Goto was now nothing more than a historical footnote. "The auction should go ahead regardless."

"My auction . . . my decision," Ruddington said.

Donin pointed at Antonio de Baraga. "Shouldn't this be the decision of Old Bowie's owner?"

Having a finger pointed at him startled de Baraga. "Please, I defer to Mr. Ruddington."

"Oh, very well." Donin settled for shooting hostile glances around the room.

"The bidding will resume at two million dollars." Ruddington raised an eyebrow. "That bid came from Miss Williams. Do I hear two million five thousand?"

"Two and five." Melanie was determined to take charge of the auction.

Without Goto, the bidding became much more conservative. In five-thousand-dollar increments, the price crept slowly up to two million and eighty-five thousand dollars over a ten-minute period.

The slower pace was a relief to Kay. She sensed nobody was anxious to hit the three-million-dollar plateau, which meant she still had a chance.

The irritating electronic sound of a cellular phone ringing was suddenly heard in the room. Heads turned toward Scanner, the sound came from his pocket. "Excuse me, I'm sorry." Scanner stood, went out into the hallway and answered the phone. "Hello . . . Terry? . . . That you?"

"Yeah! We got it, Roy! It's the ink, just like Andy said!"

"Slow down." Scanner was listening intently. "What did the techies find?"

"Too much acid in the ink. Five percent differential, enough to blow away the chems. Here's the best part, Lundgren says we can provide every bank that wants one with a simple ultraviolet device that'll verify any hundred-dollar bill in two seconds. Simple to use. If the bill is okay, you get a blue reading. If it's counterfeit, you get a red reading. Lundgren says it'll cost every bank that wants one about twenty bucks. That's a lot of money for maybe a hundred thousand devices, but peanuts when it comes to stopping a flood of fake hundreds. We'll hire a vendor to make them, they can be on the market in six weeks."

"Wait, let me understand. The device will give a red reading unless the ink has exactly the same chemistry as the ink used by the Treasury presses?"

"That's it. The device is set to recognize legitimate currency only. Some guy passes a hundred-dollar bill at a bar, no device there, he'll get away with it. But when that hundred hits the bank, it'll be spotted and taken out of circulation."

"So we can stop Donin, plus anyone else who prints their own hundreds."

"Right. Lundgren says nobody is gonna be able to match our ink exactly."

"Why the hell didn't he come up with this solution before? It sounds so simple."

"He says a year ago a device like that would have cost almost a thousand bucks. All of a sudden infrared technology's become cheap, like computer chips."

"This is great news, Terry. Okay, I'm going to confiscate Donin's currency right now and kick his ass back to Russia."

"You got the State Department guy there?"

"He's down in the coffee shop, just waiting for the word. Two federal marshals with him."

"Have fun."

"I will," Scanner promised. "Tell Lundgren and his people they lived up to their reps, we owe them a big one."

"Will do," Terry replied, not afraid to say that now.

Scanner punched the off button on his cellular and hurried down the steps to the coffee shop. He found the trio drinking coffee. The two U.S. marshals were from Tulsa, hard-faced men with big, rough hands and suits a little tight for their frames. The State Department guy was better dressed, suit and an old-fashioned white oxford shirt and striped tie. He was from State's passport verification section, which handled people with diplomatic passports. His name was Philip Holly.

"Mr. Holly, thanks for waiting." Scanner shook his hand enthusiastically. "I just got a call from Washington confirming that a large amount of cash in the possession of Leon Donin is counterfeit."

"And we just found out," one of the marshals said, "that Mr. Holly here is related to Buddy Holly. Can you believe that? A State Department guy related to Buddy Holly?"

"We asked him to sing a Buddy Holly song, he couldn't do it," the other marshal said, clearly suspicious of Philip Holly's claimed heritage.

Philip Holly took the suspicion good-naturedly. "It's true, Buddy Holly was my mother's cousin." Philip Holly had his cousin's thin face and reedy voice, but the family resemblance ended there. "I once tried to memorize one of Buddy's songs, thought I might sing it at family parties or whatever, but I couldn't keep the lyrics straight in my head. I guess I didn't get very many of Buddy's genes."

"That's interesting." Scanner was not interested at all. "Look, we need to deal with Leon Donin right now. He's about to unload a pile of counterfeit upstairs, we have to stop him."

Holly tapped the brown briefcase lying next to his coffee cup. "Too bad you can't arrest him. Next best thing, I've got the extradition order right here. Signed by a federal judge. Witnessed. Approved by the State Department. Let's go."

Scanner led them up the steps to the room where the auction was taking place. The two security guards outside the room moved to block the door when they saw a bunch of men, two of them hardcases, headed for the auction.

"These are U.S. marshals and this gentleman is from the State Department," Scanner explained. "We're here to deport Leon Donin, one of the bidders. He's a foreign national with a diplomatic passport. You'd better stand aside or these marshals will arrest you for obstructing federal officers in the performance of their duty."

The marshals showed the security guys their badges.

"We'd enjoy arresting you," one of the marshals said. "Because we're kinda pissed that all we can do with this Russian is to throw him out of the country."

The security guys backed off and Scanner led his party into the auction.

"Two million three hundred and twenty thousand," was Kay's bid as Scanner and his party entered the room.

Stewart Ruddington glared at Scanner and the other bidders looked at him in astonishment.

"I'm sorry, Mr. Ruddington, you'll have to stop your auction again."

"I will not do that!" Ruddington slammed his open hand down on the lectern. "You have no right to barge in here with . . . disrupting . . . who are these people?"

"These two are U.S. federal marshals and this is Philip Holly of the State Department." Scanner couldn't keep a smile off his face as he zeroed in on Donin. "We're here to remove Leon Donin." Ruddington started to object again and Scanner cut him off. "You should be glad I'm here. Mr. Donin is trying to buy Old Bowie with counterfeit U.S. currency."

"That is a lie." Donin remained calm. "My funds were examined by a local bank this morning."

"That's true," Ruddington said.

"The man who looked at your money wasn't a banker." Scanner was having some fun, felt he deserved to. "He was a magician from Dallas who specializes in sleight-of-hand tricks. He *borrowed* a few of your hundred-dollar bills, switched them for genuine currency. Your phony bills were flown straight to Washington, where our lab could test them extensively. I just got confirmation that your currency is counterfeit. Serve your papers, Mr. Holly."

"You acted illegally! I'm the victim of a crime and because I'm Russian nobody cares!" Donin wasn't calm anymore, he couldn't believe he'd allowed himself to be tricked by such a frowzy gimmick. "You stole some of my money!"

Philip Holly stepped forward. "Mr. Donin, you've been declared *persona non grata* by the State Department. This is an extradition order. A copy will be delivered to your embassy in Washington within the hour. These marshals will drive you to Houston and put you on a flight leaving late tonight for Moscow."

"I'm also confiscating the counterfeit U.S. currency in your possession." Scanner reached under the conference table and dragged out the suitcase of cash Donin had placed there.

Wolf had his own personal sense of right and wrong and it seemed wrong for him to just sit here while his client was being arrested, regardless of what they called it, and his money taken from him. Wolf also didn't see how he could go up against two armed U.S. marshals and Roy Scanner, all of them carrying guns. Especially here and now, in front of all these people who'd testify against him in a heartbeat. But it wasn't in him to just sit and watch. "Hey Ivan, what do you want me to do?" Wolf half rose from his chair, his hand lingering near the gun under his jacket.

"Don't get involved," Scanner warned. "Watch that guy," he told the marshals. "He's armed."

"Yeah, I'm Donin's bodyguard. Legitimate work, I've got a state permit to carry a gun, so don't try to bust me."

Donin waved Wolf back into his chair. "Forget it, Wolfie. Even you don't have a chance with these people." He looked at the extradition order in his hand. "And besides, if there were a gunfight in this room I'd surely be hit by a stray bullet. That seems to be my luck today." Donin turned his attention to Philip Holly. "Suppose I wanted to defect to the United States as a political refugee? My life will be in danger if I return to Russia without either my currency or Old Bowie, that is the truth."

Philip Holly's reply was quick. "The State Department doesn't consider counterfeiters to be among the world's politically oppressed people."

"I see." Donin let his gaze travel the room. Among the shocked faces he saw only Kay Williams smiling. He drew himself up. "Do not count me out, Miss Williams. I survived Afghanistan, I will survive my return to Moscow, too. Good-bye, Wolfie. You were the one bright spot in this miserable adventure. Though I must tell you, I do not like this Texas of yours."

Philip Holly shook hands with Scanner and left. The two marshals took Donin away.

"Good-bye," Kay called after Donin. "Sorry you can't stay for dinner, they're serving *borscht* tonight!"

"Sorry for this interruption. I think you'll agree it was necessary." Scanner hefted the suitcase, biggest single counterfeit haul of his career. His return to Washington would be Conquering Hero time. "Please go on with your auction, Mr. Ruddington. Kay, I'll call you later."

When the shock of Donin's arrest and the enormity of the Russian's crime began to dissipate among those who were left in the room, the subject of whether to go on with the auction became a clamorous debate.

"We must go on!" De Baraga leaped up and punched the air with his fist. "I will not have this auction ruined! My family . . . my fortune . . . another delay would be too much to bear!"

"I agree," Melanie said. "We must go on."

"I don't know." Ruddington's hands flapped helplessly at his sides. "I've never been in a situation like this. Whatever happens will be without precedent. There could be lawsuits, court battles over the true ownership of Old Bowie, anything."

"You guaranteed Donin's funds were legitimate," de Baraga wailed.

"Yes, I did." Stewart Ruddington looked for a hole to crawl into. However this auction ended, his reputation would take a terrible drubbing. "I was deceived, we all were."

Kay didn't like de Baraga, the man was a born whiner. "Señor de Baraga, you just escaped a silver bullet, be grateful for that. My last bid was two million three hundred and twenty thousand. I suspect that was more than you expected to realize from selling Old Bowie, be grateful for that, too. Even though there are only two bidders left—Melanie and Arthur against myself—I agree that the auction should continue."

"I'll make it unanimous." Arthur was certain he and Melanie could prevail over Kay. Though he hated to win out over her in this strange fashion, Arthur was a devout believer in winning. "Old Bowie is in play, let's get on with the bidding."

"One thing." Kay looked across the table at Bud Wolf. "I want this man to leave."

Wolf had been sitting quietly, hoping to be forgotten or ignored. "Hey, I've been here all along. I'm not a bidder, but I'm doin' you folks no harm. I'd just like to see how your auction comes out." He *needed* to know who'd be leaving the room with Old Bowie.

"Wolf is Leon Donin's hired thug. Over the last few days he's done vile things, hurt people, threatened, and even tried to kill me. I won't stay in the same room with him." Kay felt her voice rising in the direction of pure hysteria. "And if I walk out, that *will* end this auction!"

Though nobody knew what to think of Kay's accusations, they didn't want the auction to end.

With the specter of lawsuits and a reputation in shambles haunting him, Stewart Ruddington did his best to rise to the occasion. "You'll have to leave," he told Wolf in the sternest voice he could summon. "There are five security men who will *help* you leave if you resist."

Wolf stood and buttoned his jacket, determined to be remembered as a peaceful sort later on when the police asked their dozens of questions. Let 'em have their fun. He ambled out of the room saying, "Sorry y'all feel that way. Good luck to you folks."

As soon as Wolf was out the door, Ruddington revved himself up to regain control of the auction. "The last bid came from Kay Williams, it was two million three hundred and twenty thousand. We'll pick up at that point." He looked to Melanie. "Do I hear a bid from this side of the room?"

"Two million five hundred thousand."

Old Bowie was slipping away, Kay could feel it. *Damn Melanie! Without Donin in the game, she'll push me over my limit.* "Two million six." No point to bidding in five-K increments now.

"Two million seven."

Kay wondered if one big bump might scare off Melanie. If not, she was lost anyway. Time to bet the ranch. "Three million dollars."

Melanie's and Arthur's heads went together in another of their interminable whispered conferences. That was encouraging. Maybe they hadn't planned to bid this high. *Maybe I really scared them,* Kay thought. *I know I'm scared. Is Old Bowie really worth three million?* Kay wondered if Billy Boy Watkins really wanted the knife this much. *Will he thank me if I win? Will everyone in the business say I overbid?*

The conference ended. Arthur had gone pale and was squirming in his seat. Melanie looked straight at Kay and said, "We bid three million one hundred thousand dollars."

The bid left Kay weak and nauseous. She hated to lose, just despised herself on those terrible occasions when someone got the best of her. To be beaten by Melanie was almost too much to bear. Gradually she became aware of all the eyes fastened on her.

"Do we have another bid?" Ruddington had watched Kay deflate and sensed the auction was over. "Kay, can you top three million one?"

Kay shook her head. "No, I'm out."

Melanie screamed in delight, jumped up, spun in a circle, clapped her hands. "Arthur, we won! We did it! Old Bowie is ours!" She grabbed his face with both hands and kissed him sloppily. Arthur responded with a sheepish grin.

"Congratulations." Kay could speak, she couldn't move.

Ruddington added his congratulations and de Baraga fairly danced around the room. Three million one hundred thousand dollars! His family was saved. His estate would survive.

The auctioneer let the celebration go on for a minute before bringing Melanie and Arthur back to business. He did some quiet celebrating himself, the commission would pay his bills for a long time to come. "Incredible auction. Unorthodox, but quite a stunning event. Before you take possession of Old Bowie we'll have to complete the financial transaction."

Briefcases were opened and everyone except Kay sat down at the far end of the conference table to finalize the sale. She forced herself up and out of her chair and left the room.

When the auction ended, Wolf was sitting downstairs at the bar having himself a cold beer and a bowl of pretzels. The pretzels were too salty, but the beer was pretty good. Lots of microbreweries in Austin, he wished he had time to visit a few. He remembered going to one of those joints with Kelly Watts, a little place over on Lavaca Street, they got shitfaced on local brew, later found a couple of girls and took them to a motel to suck their dicks. One of them didn't want to do it, Kelly slapped her around until she changed her mind. Poor old Kelly. The girls were safe from him now.

He put his beer on the bar when Kay Williams came down the steps. As she walked through the lobby, the slump of her shoulders said it all. *Ha! You lost out to Melanie and her boyfriend! You got beat! They kicked your ass!* He wanted to shout all that stuff at the bitch, make her jump out of her skin, but this was no time to cut a high profile.

Twenty minutes later Wolf was working on his second beer when Melanie and Arthur came down the steps arm in arm. She was laughing and throwing her hair around, he was grinning. He was also holding the walnut case tightly under his arm. *Fucker thinks Old Bowie is his, he's gonna get an education.* Melanie leaned into Arthur and planted an impulsive kiss on his cheek. Wolf finished his beer and put a ten on the bar. Slipped off the stool and followed the happy couple out the door of the Driskill at a discreet distance.

# CHAPTER 27

Kay asked Scanner to take her out to dinner at the best Tex-Mex restaurant in Austin. He asked around and was directed to Fonda San Miguel, a place out near Burnet Road that was all tiled inside, with lots of hanging plants and a fountain right in the middle of the dining room. The food was as good as advertised. They practically inhaled the nachos before moving on to their entrees. After they'd gorged themselves for a while, the conversation revived.

"Did you talk to your client?"

"Billy Boy Watkins took the loss pretty well. He wanted Old Bowie very much, on the other hand he's pressed for money right now, so I couriered his cashier's checks right back to him. Seems one of his oil rigs just *tapped out,* as he puts it. What's worse, he seems to be in some kind of ongoing battle with the IRS."

"Who isn't?" Scanner said.

The way his mouth turned down at the corners, Kay knew he'd been audited recently. "You too? I didn't think the IRS would go after Treasury agents."

"IRS auditors go after their own mothers. They also eat their young and shit in their own beds. That's the way they are."

"Oh, dear, you must have gone through a really bad audit."

Scanner shuddered. "It wasn't an audit, it was a ritual killing."

"Have another Dos Equis, you'll forget about it."

"I'll *never* forget." Scanner wanted to change the subject. "Well . . . hell with that . . . what do you do now?"

"Back to my shop in Connecticut. You know, I've lost out at other auctions. It hurts, but you get over it. What I'm not going to get over is Bud Wolf."

"Tell me about the threats he made."

"I'd never be able to prove he was threatening me, it was all innuendo." Kay repeated to Scanner exactly what Wolf said and described how he said it. "You know how he talks, like a good old boy who's really happy to be with you. Hides his real meaning behind a lot of tricky grins and nods."

"We can't let it drop." Scanner was more worried about Kay than he wanted to let on. "The guy is dangerous."

Kay was worried herself. "So what can be done?"

"First thing is to put as many law enforcement agencies onto Wolf as we can, keep him too busy to think about you. When I get back to Washington, I'll start with the U.S. Attorney's office. Wolf was working for Donin. The U.S. Attorney may be able to build an aiding-and-abetting case against him. I'd love to see Wolf in a federal lockup."

"You've got my vote, I'd do anything to keep him from popping up in Connecticut." Kay's eyes shifted around. "And I mean *anything*."

Scanner not liking her tone of voice, "What's on your mind? You want to go after Wolf yourself?" A worse thought. "What, you want to *hire* somebody to take care of him? Jesus, Kay. Don't get yourself jammed up that way."

"Roy, he could turn up at my shop in Ridgefield any night next week. Or next month. Or next year. I live alone above my store and I'm way out on a country road, Route 35. No houses within five hundred yards. The guy *scares* me. I can't wait around for the U.S. attorney to solve this problem for me."

"You know a hit man? Is that what you're telling me?"

"Of course not." She'd been thinking about someone else, an auto mechanic she'd known when she lived in New York. Vinnie Alesio. He was a great mechanic, kept her car running perfectly in the toughest winters. Big guy in his early thirties. Mid-thirties now. Not married, always flirted with her when she brought in her car for servicing. People in the neighborhood said Vinnie Alesio sometimes used his biggest lug wrenches for other things than taking wheels off cars, that he was a part-time collector for a mob loan shark. A legbreaker, when that had to be done. Kay believed the rumor. Vinnie drove a Jaguar that he kept all shiny and bright, wore expensive clothes when he wasn't working under a car, had once offered to take her to Sparks Steak House for dinner, a notorious mob hangout also known for superb food. "I do know someone who might be able to put Bud Wolf in a hospital bed for a few months. For a price."

"Don't even think about it."

Kay gave an elaborate shrug that indicated she'd think about his objections, but in the end do whatever was necessary.

"People who hire thugs always get caught along with the hard cases they hire."

"Oh really? Then why is Bud Wolf still running around doing terrible things to people? Why is Donin in a first-class seat on a flight to Moscow, instead of in jail where he belongs? Do you have any doubt that it was Wolf out there in San Marcos yesterday shooting at us?"

Scanner knew Wolf had been out there. He was a federal agent, he didn't need an antiques dealer to tell him. "It took a few days to understand just how dangerous Wolf is. Now we know. Kay, believe me when I say I'm going to make Wolf's life so miserable he won't have two seconds to think about hurting you."

"That's good." Kay nodded along to what he was saying. "I'll count on that." Thinking, *I'll keep open my Vinnie Alesio option, too.*

Wolf checked out of the hotel, put his things in the Caddy, moved the Caddy to a parking lot a couple of blocks away. He walked back to the Omni and went up to the floor where Melanie's suite was. She and Arthur the Wimp were in there having dinner, he'd seen the kid from room service wheel in a table with covered dishes. Wolf was about to knock on the door when he had a worrisome thought—*Suppose old Melanie looks through the peephole, sees me, won't open the door. Shit, she might even call Security.*

He backed off and rode the elevator up and down for about five minutes while he worked out this wrinkle in his plan. *Sure, that's it. A simple fix.*

There was a stamp machine in the lobby newsstand. He bought a little cardboard thing with three stamps in it, highway robbery what they charged for that, and went back up to Melanie's floor.

At Melanie's door, he licked one of the three stamps and pasted it over the peephole. Then knocked three times and said in a voice more friendly than his own, "Room service."

Heard nothing for a while, then Melanie's voice saying through the door, "Our dinner has already been served."

"I have a bottle of champagne and two glasses for you, compliments of a Mr. Stewart Ruddington."

"Oh! How nice."

The security bolt was pulled back and a second later the door opened. Melanie, a robe thrown over her nightgown, was smiling over her shoulder as she opened the door. "Arthur, guess what. Stewart sent up a . . ."

Wolf hit the door with his shoulder, knocking Melanie backwards into the room. She pinwheeled, bounced off the couch, landed in a clumsy heap on the floor. Before she was down, Wolf had closed the door and thrown the security bolt back into place.

"Sit right where you are," Wolf told Arthur. Probably didn't have to say anything, Arthur was too surprised to act. He was sitting at the room service table where they'd just finished dinner, also in a robe and slippers, nothing under the robe, glass of wine in his hand.

"What are you doing here?" Realized he should do more than talk, Bud Wolf had just knocked Melanie down. Arthur rose, the drink still in his hand but.forgotten. "You'd better leave right now, before I call Security."

"I told you to sit still." Wolf reached Arthur in three strides, pushed him back into his chair. The glass fell, staining the carpet with red wine.

He turned and helped Melanie to her feet. She was out of breath and angry as a nest of hornets. "You moron! You can't get away with breaking into my room!"

"You sure about that?" This was fun, her thinking she could send Bud Wolf running by calling him a name. He put his face about an inch from hers. "You want to live through this? Shut your mouth and go sit by your boyfriend."

Her eyes, so close to his own, widened. "Don't threaten me." Melanie realized her voice was too shaky to frighten him and decided to try buying him off. "Look, you can have whatever money we have, our credit cards, whatever. We won't give you any trouble. Just leave us alone."

"What if I want Old Bowie?"

"No!" Arthur started to stand, sat back down when Wolf leveled a murderous gaze at him.

"So that's it." Melanie feeling better now that she knew Wolf's game. Best thing, she thought, get him out of the room. "All right, take it and go." She gestured at an end table where the walnut case lay.

"Hey, that's a mighty cooperative attitude, Melanie." He winked at her. "You wouldn't think of callin' the law, would you? About ten seconds after I leave this suite?"

She glanced swiftly at Arthur to get his agreement with her charade. "We won't call the police until tomorrow morning. Six a.m. tomorrow. No! Make that ten A.M. Okay, Arthur?"

"Yes . . . I agree." He couldn't think well, too much merlot. Melanie was trying to get Wolf out of the room, he understood that much. "We'll keep that bargain, I swear it."

"Okay," Wolf said. "But first you have to cross your hearts and hope to die."

They just looked at him.

"Do it! Cross your hearts!"

They looked at each other dumbfounded. Joke? Not a joke? You couldn't tell with this man.

"I mean it!"

They crossed their hearts with their index fingers, like a pair of kids pledged to a secret.

*Sheep*, Wolf thought. *I'm dealin' with sheep.* "You forgot to say *I hope to die.* Oh, fuck it, you did fine. Melanie, sit down with your boyfriend." They sat.

With the two sweethearts intimidated, Wolf turned his attention to the walnut case. He opened it slowly, drawing out the moment. There it was, Old Bowie. *I'm not a man to cry*, he thought. *But this could do it. Old Bowie belongs to me now.* "Beautiful weapon, huh?"

Arthur and Melanie nodded, humoring him.

"I was born to own Old Bowie." He looked at them slantwise. "You want to laugh? Help yourselves. It's true, though. I'm as much Texas as the Alamo. If today was 1836, you know where I'd be? Up on the Alamo walls with Bowie and Crockett and Travis and the others. Where would you two be? Runnin' for your lives. That's why this knife belongs with me."

He put the case down carefully and took a large pill bottle from his pocket.

"Now listen up, folks. I don't believe for a minute you'd wait till

tomorrow mornin' to call the police. So I'm givin' you some sleepin' pills
to take, put you out like a light for about six hours. That's all I need." He
shook some pills into the palm of his hand. "Here's four for each of you.
Use the wine, they'll go down easier."

Nobody reached out.

"Do it!"

"How do we know those are sleeping pills?" Melanie was afraid Wolf
was trying to poison them. "Those pills could be anything."

"You're right, they're BIRTH CONTROL pills!" Wolf laughed. "What
the hell are you worried about? If I wanted to kill you, I wouldn't use
sleepin' pills." He drew his Colt Python. "I'd use this, or a knife, or what
they call a blunt instrument."

They remained apprehensive.

"Jesus, you just can't be nice to some people. Here, give me any one of
those pills, you make the choice."

Arthur hesitantly picked one of the pills out of Wolf's palm. Wolf
opened his mouth and Arthur popped it in. At a gesture from Wolf,
Melanie gave him a wineglass and Wolf swallowed.

"Y'see? Just sleepin' pills, that's all. I'll sleep good later on tonight
myself thanks to the pill, but not as good as you after you take four. Not
to hurt you, just right for a long night's sleep. Come on, swallow 'em."
He added another pill to those in his palm to make up for the one he'd
taken, then prodded them with the gun barrel to drink up. "That's
good," when they were done. "Now just lie down on the bed, I'll scoot out
of here as soon as you're asleep."

"This is bizarre," Arthur muttered, moving towards the bed. Melanie,
still suspicious, went with him. They lay down and Wolf took the nearest chair.

"Close your eyes. And don't try to fake goin' to sleep, think you'll call
the cops. That would piss me off." He looked at his watch. "Sleep tight,
don't let the bedbugs bite. That's what I tell my little girls when I put
them to bed. I've got two girls, did I tell you that? Sweetest little things
you ever saw."

Arthur and Melanie put their heads down, closed their eyes, self-
conscious about the whole thing and unwilling to trust Bud Wolf. Not
that they had much choice.

At first they lay rigid, unable to relax at all under his watchful eyes.
Half an hour passed. Against their wills, their minds began to drift into

sluggishness. A yawn escaped from Melanie. Arthur turned onto his side. They fought against sleep, but four powerful sleeping pills were more than enough to do the job. They whispered a few words to each other, Wolf didn't seem to notice or care. But they were both too drugged to stay alert, they felt themselves slipping into darkness with no defense against their own terrible sleepiness. Their heads nodded. They let themselves get comfortable.

Forty minutes after taking the pills, Arthur was snoring heavily and Melanie lay totally inert, her arm thrown across Arthur's chest.

Wolf waited another thirty minutes before standing and checking both to make sure they were genuinely sleeping, not out to pull some stupid stunt on him. Some pokes and prods drew no reaction, convinced him they were deeply asleep. He'd gotten the pills from the same pharmacist who'd sold him the digitalis. "Four of these'll knock out a horse," the pharmacist had promised. Wolf couldn't say what they'd do to a horse, but they'd sure done the job on these two.

Time to go to work.

First he put a chair under the smoke detector, climbed up, loosened the leads to the battery just enough so the alarm wouldn't go off.

Then he took out the old, beatup knife he'd bought at the gun and knife show and exchanged it for Old Bowie, which he tucked into his belt. He wanted the scabbard and walnut case, too. Wanted them so much it gave him a headache. But greed could get you killed, or at least arrested, so he settled for taking just Old Bowie and the letter from the de Baraga boy who died at San Jacinto, proof that this was Jim Bowie's original knife.

Melanie was a smoker, Virginia Slims her brand. Wolf rarely smoked, had nothing against it except that cigarette smoke usually bothered his eyes. Wolf rummaged in Melanie's purse and found her cigarettes and lighter. He lit a Virginia Slims, wiped his fingerprints off the lighter on his jeans. Bent over and pressed the burning tip of the cigarette against the sheet near Melanie's head. Took a while, but the sheet finally charred and then began to burn. Too much smoke, though. What Wolf wanted was lots of fire and not much smoke. He blew on the hot spot, fanned it with his hand, lifted the sheet so it had plenty of air top and bottom.

Finally the sheet burst into a real hot flame over an area of about six square inches. He dropped the sheet and stepped back, flipped the burning cigarette onto the bed near Melanie.

Damn, look at the fire spread! Within a minute, half the sheet was on fire on Melanie's side of the bed. The tip of the belt on her robe went up, too, then the robe itself began to burn.

Melanie didn't even move.

Wolf thinking, *Those pills'll make a zombie out of you.*

It took another two minutes for the flames to engulf the bed so thoroughly that Wolf could hardly see Arthur and Melanie.

*Shit,* he thought. *If they haven't moved till now, they aren't gonna move at all.*

He edged towards the door but didn't intend to leave too soon. What he wanted was to make sure at least one whole side of the room went up in flames, especially the table where the walnut case and the cheap old Bowie knife lay. *Got to make sure that old blade gets charred real good.* He no longer had any worries about Arthur and Melanie, they were toast already, the smell of burnt flesh about to make his stomach heave.

The curtains behind the bed caught fire with a *whoosh.* Wolf had to jump back, the flames leaping out at him. Couldn't risk staying any longer, he might get burned himself.

Wolf opened the door a few inches, checked the hall in both directions, left the room and closed the door solidly behind him. He took the stamp off the peephole and strolled down to the elevator. Not a trace of smoke in the hallway yet. Not even a sniff. Soon there'd be clouds of smoke coming out from under the door, alarms ringing, sprinklers going off, panicky people shoving each other in the hallways. He stepped into the elevator and rode down to the lobby, patting now and then at the comforting feel of Old Bowie hidden there under his jacket.

# CHAPTER 28

After dinner they went to the Broken Spoke, a country and western dance hall recommended by the waiter at the restaurant. "You could learn to dance the Texas Two-Step," the waiter said. Turned out to be a barnlike place with a scruffy-looking but talented band, beer in long-necks the accepted drink.

"Place like this, you could get punched in the mouth just for ordering a martini," Scanner said.

Kay laughed, feeling good about being able to laugh again. "Come on, I want to learn the Texas Two-Step." Dragging Scanner out onto the dance floor.

"I don't dance very well," he warned, and proceeded to prove it.

They danced for about half an hour anyway, Scanner doing better on the slow numbers. "I do have some dance training," he said. "I played Harry the Horse in *Guys and Dolls*, a college production, my senior year."

"I don't recall Harry the Horse being a dance part."

"Well, I had to sort of sway to the music now and then, like during the 'Sit Down, You're Rocking the Boat' number."

"Sounds like . . . ouch! . . . fun."

"Did I step on your toes again?"

"That's okay." She didn't want to embarrass him, even though her left foot was getting mangled. "Let's finish our beer."

They stayed a while longer, then took a taxi back to the Omni. The driver couldn't get to the entrance, Eighth Street was blocked off by fire engines, police cars and ambulances.

"What's going on?" Kay wondered.

"Beats me." Scanner paid off the driver and helped Kay out of the taxi.

The emergency, whatever it was, had just about played out. Guests were being allowed to go up to their rooms in the elevators and service had been resumed in the lobby level bar and restaurant. Outside, two bodies under white sheets were being loaded into ambulances. Firemen were still trudging in and out in their heavy rubberized suits and helmets, gathering up their equipment. Kay and Scanner moved through the mess.

"Look," Kay said, "there's Stewart."

Stewart Ruddington sat alone in a high-backed chair in the corner of the lobby with a balloon-shaped glass of brandy in his hand. His shoulders were hunched and his eyes red. He looked absolutely miserable.

Kay patted his back because he appeared to need comforting. "Stewart, what's wrong?"

The auctioneer looked up in an unfocused way. "You haven't heard? The fire was in Melanie's suite. Melanie and Arthur, both dead."

"Dead?" Kay grabbed Ruddington's arm. "How did it happen?"

"Don't know." Ruddington tipped his head way back for a long pull of brandy. "Dead, that's all I've been told."

Kay's immediate thought: *What happened to Old Bowie?* She hated herself for it, but Old Bowie was what had brought them all to Texas.

It didn't bother Scanner to put the thought into words. "Is Old Bowie still in the suite?"

A weary shrug from Ruddington.

"Awfully coincidental," Scanner went on. "Arthur and Melanie buy Old Bowie, a few hours later they're dead. You know what I wonder—where's Bud Wolf and where's Old Bowie?"

"You think Wolf had something to do with this?" The idea had been in the back of Kay's mind, too. "That he's stolen the knife?"

"He wanted it bad enough, you saw how he looked at Old Bowie." Scanner was remembering Wolf's cold eyes going hot whenever the knife was displayed. "Let's find Ed Halley."

The desk man paged the hotel's security chief. Halley was up in the suite where the fire had occurred and would be down soon. They paced around the lobby, rehashing the auction and Wolf's strange actions, trying to tie it together with this tragedy.

Ten minutes later Halley came out of the elevator brushing soot from his pants legs. "Hello, sorry to make y'all wait. Helluva mess up there." It clicked in Halley's mind that Arthur Ward and Melanie Wadsworth were part of the auction party staying at the hotel. "I'm sorry about your friends."

"How'd it happen?" Kay asked.

"An old story, they fell asleep in bed while one of them was smokin'."

"Neither woke up? The smoke alarm didn't wake them?"

Halley grimaced. "Apparently the smoke alarm was inoperative. The fire marshal just checked, the leads had come loose."

"This might sound cold." Scanner didn't see any other way to say it. "At the auction this afternoon Arthur and Melanie bought a very valuable antique knife. We're wondering if it's still in the room."

At first Halley was disgusted, thinking they had only money on their minds. Then he turned it over a few times and saw they were driving at something else. "What are you sayin'? This wasn't an accident?"

Kay jumped in. "The same man who cut up all my clothes wanted that antique knife very badly."

"Y'all come upstairs." Halley ushered them to the elevator. On the way up he said to Kay, "I hope you can take a nasty scene."

She nodded curtly.

The wall around the door to Melanie's suite was blackened from smoke, but the rest of the hallway was intact, the fire evidently contained within the suite.

"Careful where you step," Halley warned.

The fire marshal, still in the suite and making notes on a long form fastened to a clipboard, scowled at them.

"It's okay, Frank," Halley said. "These are friends of the fire victims."

"Don't let them touch anything," the marshal said.

Kay's nostrils filled with a stench worse than seared wood and plastic. She supposed it was flesh she smelled and tried to keep horrible images out of her mind. The side of the room where the bed was located had gone up in flames. Nearer the door the damage was less severe, though smoke had left everything a mess. Water damage, too, from when the sprinklers had switched on and stopped the fire from spreading.

"Hadn't been for the sprinkler system, this fire would have spread to the other rooms," Halley said. "Too bad the sprinklers didn't switch on sooner, would have saved their lives."

"Look." Kay touched Scanner's arm. "Isn't that the case Old Bowie was in? Or what's left of it?"

The case was on the floor, partly covered by the remains of a collapsed end table.

"Frank, we'd like to look at this item. Okay with you?"

"All right, Ed," the marshal said. "Nothing leaves the room, though."

"You've got suspicions about this fire?"

"Not really, I just haven't figured out why the leads came loose on the smoke alarm."

"Could someone have disconnected them?"

"Possible. No evidence of that, though. What I do know is the fire was definitely started by a cigarette. Burned a hole in the sheet, reached the mattress and blanket, sent this entire side of the room up just before the sprinklers went on."

Halley squatted and worked the remains of the walnut case out from under the collapsed table. The case had been left open. The lid had burned down to cinders, most of the case destroyed, too. "There's a knife in here all right." He lifted it out of the mess with two fingers, held it up for Kay and Scanner to see. "I don't know what made it a valuable antique, but it's not worth much now."

He was right. The grip was burned away, the rest of the knife charred beyond recognition.

"Dear God." Kay couldn't believe things were ending this way. "Arthur and Melanie dead, Old Bowie turned to junk." She turned away. "I just want to get out of this state as fast as I can."

So did Scanner. "But first I want to know whether Bud Wolf is still in the hotel."

"Let's go check on him," Halley said.

They went down to the front desk and learned that Wolf had checked out about 6:00 P.M., well before the fire in Melanie's suite. "I know y'all have Wolf down as a suspect, but the fire looks to everybody like an accident," Halley said. "Nothin' missin' from the room so far as we can tell. Miss Wadsworth smoked, I checked on that, too. Mr. Ward didn't smoke. The fire started on her side of the bed, which is also consistent with what happened. Nothin' about the bodies indicates they'd been robbed, beaten, whatever. Another item, the maid who does the room made a note on yesterday's room report that Miss Wadsworth left a big cigarette burn mark on the dresser. Sounds like she was all-around careless with her smokes."

Kay wasn't quite ready to agree that the deaths were accidental. "Wasn't it awfully early for them to turn in for the evening? Melanie was a night person."

"Folks go to bed for other reasons than sleep," Halley pointed out. "Fire marshal figures they had sex, afterwards Miss Wadsworth smoked a cigarette and they both dozed off before the cigarette caught the bed on fire. I'd have to go along with that."

Scanner had to agree there was no evidence that the deaths were anything but accidental. If Old Bowie were missing, that would have been another matter. "Let it go, Kay."

"I'm mighty sorry." Ed Halley was afraid Kay was going to faint, her face gradually had gone ashen and she seemed unsteady. "You all right?"

"No, I'm more depressed than I can ever remember." Kay got herself under control. "Delayed reaction, I suppose. Arthur and I were good friends, I'll miss him. Melanie and I were usually bitchy with each other, there was no kind of friendship there, but we competed so hard we were close. Do you know what I mean by that?"

"Sure," Scanner said. "Like a couple of tennis pros who play to kill in the big tournaments."

That wasn't quite it, but Kay nodded in agreement anyway, too tired and upset to go on with the conversation. "I need to lie down."

"I'll take you up to your room." Scanner shook Halley's hand. "Thanks for your help."

By 1:00 A.M. Scanner had stopped tossing and turning and drifted into sleep. About that time he came awake to the aggravating sound of somebody's knuckles rapping insistently at his door.

"Who is it?"

"Me." Kay's voice. "We need to talk."

He staggered to the door in his shorts. Kay was standing there barefoot and in hastily thrown-on jeans and T-shirt, her eyes wild and angry. "I've been thinking about this so-called accident."

"Oh, sure." He yawned, scratched his head, stepped back from the door. "Come in."

She crossed the room and planted herself on the edge of a chair. "I think Wolf did steal Old Bowie."

Scanner yawned again, tried to shake the sleep out of his mind. "We saw Old Bowie right there in Melanie's room."

"We saw a knife that *might* have been Old Bowie."

"How do you know it wasn't?"

"How do you know it was?" Kay countered.

"It was in the case."

"So what?" Kay leaned forward. "Wolf is vicious, not stupid. If the knife were missing, the police would come after him. Isn't it possible he took Old Bowie and left another knife, a Bowie-style knife, in its place?"

"The fire marshal says it was an accident. How could Wolf have forced Arthur and Melanie to just lie there while the bed went up in flames?"

"I don't know. He's too smart to have battered them unconscious. Maybe he smothered them."

"There'd be evidence of that, no smoke in the lungs."

"We need to have an autopsy."

"In this kind of death an autopsy is usually done." Scanner thought of his friend in the Texas Rangers. "I'll make sure it is done and get the results."

"How long will that take?"

"I'll try to get it done first thing in the morning."

"Another thing." Kay was so worked up she felt lightheaded. "I didn't see any ashes from the de Baraga boy's letter."

"There were ashes all over the place." Scanner thought she was too wound up to think straight. "The letter probably burned right away, old parchment like that."

"I think Wolf took it with him. He'd want the letter, it proves the knife belonged to Jim Bowie. The case and scabbard weren't as important." She snapped her fingers. "Wait! The knife was out of the scabbard! Why?"

"Melanie and Arthur may have been looking at the knife before they went to bed."

"Or Wolf left the fake Old Bowie out of the scabbard so the fire could get at it more easily!"

"That's a reach."

"I don't think so."

Kay wasn't about to let it go, Scanner could see that. "Let's get an autopsy report first, then decide what we're going to do."

"Yes," she agreed. "Call your friend in the Rangers right now."

"Calling Buck Colter at one a.m. would guarantee we *don't* get an early autopsy."

"Then call him at seven a.m. Will you do that?"

"Yes . . . Yes . . . sure." Anything to be able to get back to sleep. "I've got his home number."

"I'll call you at six forty-five."

"I've already left a wakeup call for six-thirty."

Kay still wasn't satisfied. "Then I'll call you at ten after seven to find out what he said."

"Okay. Can I go back to sleep now?"

"Yes." She hopped up and kissed him on the cheek on her way out the door. "You're a darling."

"I'm cute, too." Scanner yawning. "Tell your friends."

Kay was as good as her word. At nine minutes past seven, Scanner sat with his hand hovering over the phone. The phone rang thirty seconds later and he picked up before the second ring. "Good morning, Kay."

"Did you talk to Colter?"

"I did. He'd just gotten back from his morning jog and was in a good mood. He promised to call the medical examiner and make sure the autopsy on at least one of the victims is completed before noon. I can pick up a copy of the results from Buck's office at one o'clock."

"Not till then?"

"Kay, that's very fast for an autopsy, especially in a case where there's no immediate evidence of foul play."

"We have to move fast here, before Wolf can stash Old Bowie someplace safe."

"We can't do anything without an autopsy that indicates some sort of crime occurred. You want to have breakfast?"

"Okay. After breakfast, let's find out where Wolf lives. I think he mentioned he was from the Panhandle, wherever that is."

"Up around Amarillo."

"We need to know exactly where he lives. He has a ranch, I believe, bragged about it. Somebody has to know where it is."

"Breakfast first." Scanner believed he'd better have a big breakfast, Kay was going to be pushing him hard all day.

The autopsy report came in half an hour late. Kay seethed in frustration while Scanner tried to hold her down with calm words. "We'll have it soon, stop fidgeting."

"I'm not *fidgeting*. I expect people to hold to their schedules, that's all. I don't miss my deadlines, I don't expect other people to miss theirs."

Scanner was thinking, *Do I really want to go on seeing this woman?*

"I'm getting on your nerves," Kay said.

"No," he lied. "I'd just like to see you calm down a bit. You want the ME to do a thorough job, that takes time."

"I could have built an atomic bomb by now."

Scanner thinking, *You are an atomic bomb.*

As if she could read his thoughts, Kay said, "Sooner or later my relationships always break down. Men say I'm driven or too intense, those kinds of words. Are you beginning to think that?"

"No way." Second lie. "Let me check again, see if the autopsy's come in."

They were using a conference room in the Austin federal building. He called across the street to the Rangers' headquarters and asked Buck about the autopsy.

"Just came to my desk," Buck Colter said. "I skimmed it, nothing suspicious. Come on over and pick up a copy."

"Thanks, I'll be right there." He put down the phone. "It's ready, I'll go over and get it, be back in ten minutes."

"What did he say about the results? Anything to indicate Arthur and Melanie were killed?"

"I didn't ask." Third lie, wanting to postpone the inevitable argument with Kay over the results.

Scanner went across the street, made some small talk with Buck Colter, returned within fifteen minutes to the conference room, where Kay was pacing. She snatched the autopsy report from him and laid it out page by page on the conference table.

"Buck looked it over while I was going across the street. He didn't see anything to indicate they were killed."

Kay was concentrating on the way the autopsy was done. "Looks like the coroner was dictating into a tape recorder during the examination, then somebody transcribed his findings. Okay. This is Melanie's autopsy, I guess he hasn't gotten around to Arthur. No apparent trauma, I guess that means no broken bones. Both smoke and toxic chemicals present in the lungs. Third-degree burns along the right side of the body, legs, back, hips. But death was from asphyxiation rather than the burns. Oh, that's terrible! I can't read this part out loud. Okay, here's something. They'd just had dinner and there were traces of sleeping pills in Melanie's stomach! That's how Wolf did it, he forced them to take sleeping pills and then set the bed on fire!"

Scanner had been reading along at the same pace. "Also food and wine in her stomach. Nothing terribly suspicious about any of this. Did Melanie regularly use sleeping pills?"

"I have no idea. Suppose Arthur's stomach shows traces of sleeping pills, too. That would be suspicious, wouldn't it?"

"Maybe. Not proof of foul play, though. People take sleeping pills all the time."

"What if there's no pill bottle in the room?" Kay said. "That would prove somebody gave sleeping pills to both Arthur and Melanie."

Scanner was shaking his head. "The hotel's got a cleanup crew working on the room already, I saw them go in there after breakfast. We'll never know whether there was a pill bottle in that room or not."

"Why would they do that?"

"The deaths were an accident, the fire marshal signed off on it."

"This was no accident." Kay could feel Bud Wolf's fine hand at work. "We have to find Wolf right away."

"How?"

"Fly up to his ranch. You see, we didn't waste our time this morning with all those phone calls. We found out he lives outside the town of Quito. We'll fly up to Amarillo, rent a car, drive out to his ranch."

"No judge will give us a search warrant for Wolf's house, we don't have any evidence of a crime."

Kay wasn't about to be put off by a tangle of legal mumbo jumbo. "No law against going to Wolf's house and talking to him. I don't expect him to just hand over Old Bowie, but he needs to have his cage rattled hard."

"What good would that do?" Scanner had no intention of bracing Wolf at his home with no backup. "If he didn't kill Arthur and Melanie, he'll just laugh at us. If he did do it, we could be next. Think about it, we'd be on his turf, nobody to back us up, he'd have every advantage."

"You don't have to come along, I'll go up there by myself." Kay knew he'd never stand for that, it was a guy thing. "Don't think you can stop me, you'd need a judge's warrant for that, too."

"You can be a total pain in the ass, d'you know that?"

"I've heard it before, remember? *Driven? Too intense?*"

"You're all of that and worse." Scanner threw up his hands. "All right, God help me, I'll go with you."

"I knew you would," she cooed.

# CHAPTER 29

A mile from Wolf's place was a hill from which you could see the road leading to the house and the house itself. Wolf had built into the side of the hill a sort of bunker that he kept covered with camouflage netting stolen from a survivalist nut who lived on the other side of Amarillo. *Guy thinks he knows about survival, he should take lessons from me,* that was Wolf's attitude. Nobody knew about the bunker, especially his family. He'd built it while Emma and the kids were visiting Emma's idiot sister in Omaha.

When he thought somebody might be on his trail, Wolf would lay up in the bunker for a few days and watch his house, his pickup truck parked on the other side of the hill in case he had to get out fast. Good place to keep an eye on Bud Junior, too, make sure he did all his chores.

In the bunker he'd stashed a metal surplus U.S. Army ammunition box filled with cash, a sleeping bag, soap and a razor, binoculars, a couple of pistols, a rifle, ammo. He didn't expect the law to come after him today, but neither did he feel like taking chances. Not with Old Bowie.

Stretched out on the sleeping bag, his place down below looking like a doll's house, he took out Old Bowie and hefted it as he'd done a hundred times since taking it from the hotel suite in Austin. Nothin' but fine. Perfectly fine. He moved the blade in a cutting motion, wishing he had something solid on hand to work with. No matter. Soon enough he'd have all the time in the world to play with the knife. His plan was to build a secret space into the wall of his workshop, partly a hiding place and partly a shrine. Line the space with silk. Mount Old Bowie on the wall behind shatterproof glass, put the letter from the de Baraga kid in a series of museum-mounted frames. Picture of Jim Bowie, too.

His thoughts were interrupted by the sound of a car coming up the long road to his ranch house. Frowning, Wolf parted the camouflage netting enough to see who might be calling on him.

Plain old Ford sedan, had rental car written all over it.

He got out the binoculars, trained them on the front of his house. The car stopped in the turnaround, Kay Williams and Roy Scanner got out. Wolf processed this information and smiled. Just the two of them. No cops with them. That meant Scanner and little Kay had guessed what he'd done, had a vague idea maybe, but no proof to get a warrant for him. "I'm home free," he chuckled.

They knocked on the front door. Emma opened the door halfway and began talking to them.

"Slam the door in their faces," Wolf said aloud, "like I taught you."

They talked for less than a minute when Emma opened the door all the way and invited them in.

"Stupid thing to do." Wolf made a note to talk with Emma, teach her a lesson in reverse hospitality. He thought he might go down there, throw them out of the house himself, changed his mind. *Not with Old Bowie on my person*, he thought. *And I can't leave it up here, a place so exposed to the elements.* "Fuck it, I've got a date with little Kay back in Connecticut, I can wait till then."

He wondered what they were telling Emma about him.

"Do you know when Bud will be back, Mrs. Wolf?" Scanner had shown Emma Wolf his Treasury ID and introduced Kay vaguely as an "associate."

Emma shook her head violently. "He never says when he's going to be home, just shows up." She was scared. "Do you think he's on his way here now?"

"We don't know, thought he might be." Kay had been watching Emma Wolf closely. She was a pretty woman, or had been until recent years. Today she was too upset to think about how she looked. Her hair was uncombed, her hands and shoulders trembling. "Something wrong? Can we help you?"

"Nobody can help me. I have to help myself."

Kay couldn't guess what she meant by that. "Can we at least come in and talk?"

Emma stuck her head out the door and looked both ways as if this might be a trick. Bud might have sent these people to test her and be lurking nearby to watch her reactions. No, they weren't Bud's type of friends at all. Too nice. Too well-dressed. Too polite. The man a Treasury agent. "All right, come in for a minute."

They entered a house that didn't seem to have Bud Wolf's personality. It was quiet, well-decorated, neat, clean. Standing in the background, staring, were a boy in his early teens and two small girls.

"These are my children. Bud Junior. Charlene. Mary."

The little girls actually curtsied when their names were mentioned and Bud Junior came forward to awkwardly shake hands with Kay and Scanner.

"How nice to meet you," Kay said, charmed by their old-fashioned manners.

"Bud taught the kids to always be polite." Emma spoke with sadness rather than pride. "That's how Bud was raised. He's a good father, in his own way."

Kay noticed four suitcases in the hallway. "Are you taking a trip?"

"We're getting out for good." It was Bud Junior who spoke up, his voice a shade higher but otherwise as harsh as his father's. "He hits Mom all the time, I finally convinced her we can't live like this anymore."

"Bud!" Emma wasn't accustomed to having strangers know her problems. Once it was out, she found she wanted to add to the story. "We've been talking this out for days, I just made the decision this morning."

The girls nodded solemnly, saying nothing but looking intently at whoever was talking.

"The girls want to leave, too." She sounded defeated, as if she'd been arguing to stay and lost the argument to her kids. "We're going to my sister's house in Nebraska. She's been at me to get away from Bud, too. When you drove up, I like to died thinking it was Bud."

"I've met your husband," Scanner said. "What you're doing doesn't surprise me. Can we help you?"

"I can take care of her," Bud Junior said. "Nobody's going to hurt my mom ever again." He had a pugnacious way about him, too young to realize how hard it was going to be to keep that promise.

"Has your husband called within the last day or so?" Kay hoped to get some sort of information out of her. "Do you know where he might be?"

"He might be anywhere, Bud travels all the time." Emma bit her lip. "What really made up my mind to leave, I think a couple of weeks ago Bud killed an old friend of mine and her husband up in Montana. Sharon and Jimmy Walters. You're with the law, I'm telling you this in case anything happens to me."

"You're terrified." Kay came to Emma and put an arm around her. "We'll wait and leave with you, drive behind you until you're well out of this county."

"No, thanks." Emma detached herself from Kay. "I can't lean on people the rest of my life, I have to make my own way. That's one thing I've learned."

"And you have no idea where your husband is?" Scanner thought she could be withholding information out of pure fear. "When he might be back?"

"No. Please leave now. We've got to get on the road."

They made their good-byes and left. In the car, Scanner said, "That boy hates his father."

"And the women in the family are all afraid of him. I hope they get out before Wolf shows up." Kay looked at the countryside around Wolf's house. "Why don't we pull up in that grove of trees? We can watch the road to the house from there, make sure they get out safely before Wolf comes home."

"All right." Scanner was worried about the family, too. He turned left at the road and drove a hundred yards before pulling into the grove of trees. "Oh, shit," he said after the car was stopped and the engine turned off.

"What's wrong?"

"These are cedars. I'm allergic to cedars."

"I'm sorry. Do you want to leave?" She knew he wouldn't do that.

"No," he groused. "I just wanted you to know you've found another way to make me uncomfortable."

Wolf scratched his chin, realized he needed a shave. Ought to look better than this comin' back home.

He wondered why Scanner and Kay had only driven a little ways down the road and then turned into that stand of old cedars. *Catch me comin' in? What do they expect to accomplish? Without a warrant and a police-man to serve it, they can't do shit to me.* Curiosity ate at him until he decided to circle around on foot to where he couldn't be seen from that stand of cedars, and then just walk into the house through the back door.

He didn't want to leave Old Bowie up here, so he stuck it into his belt. *Have to make a new scabbard for it.*

It took almost twenty minutes to walk down the opposite side of the hill, around the base, and through the field at the rear of his house. Back door wasn't locked, he walked right in. Made a note to remind Emma and Bud to keep the house locked up during the day, you had to take precautions against all the weirdos around these days.

First people he saw were Mary and Charlene playing jacks on the living room floor. "Daddy?" Mary spoke up first. "Mama, Daddy's home!"

Emma came into the living room right away. She was holding a stack of the girls' sweaters and jeans in her arms, clutching them to her as if they were gold. "Where did you come from? I didn't hear your truck drive up."

"Came in the back door so those two folks down the road wouldn't see me."

"What folks?" Emma suddenly understood. "Oh, those two people who came looking for you. They're still nearby?"

"Parked close." Wolf sensed a different brand of fear on Emma. "What's goin' on here? Why'd you let them in the house?" He advanced on her. "I told you to keep people out. They didn't have any kind of warrant, did they?"

She shook her head. "No warrant. They just came into the hall for a few minutes."

Bud Junior entered the living room without a greeting and stood shoulder to shoulder with his mother.

"Not even a hello for your old man?" Wolf sniffed the same brand of fear on the boy. "What is goin' on, Emma? Spit it out."

"We're leaving," Bud Junior said. "We're going up to Aunt Jean's for a while."

"For a while?" Wolf felt easier now that he knew what they were up to. "You wouldn't think of stayin' in Nebraska, would you?" He strolled past them, looked into the hallway. "That's a lot of luggage for a quick trip to Omaha."

The color drained from Emma's features.

"We're going away for good," Bud Junior declared, flinching at his own audacity.

"The girls too?"

His son nodded.

"Leavin' me without anyone? That doesn't seem right." Wolf was enjoying this. Every couple of years Emma got antsy, wanted to run off to her sister's. The fun part was to convince her to stay. "Who's gonna cook? Who's gonna clean?"

"Hire somebody." Bud Junior still talking for his mother, who had practically become a statue. "You're always bragging about how much money you've got."

Wolf gave his son a backhanded slap that sent him reeling and made the girls start to cry. "Get outta here, Junior. Take the girls with you. Make them shut up, that's all you're good for. I've got things to discuss with your mother."

"Don't you hit Mom! You can slap me all you want, but I'll never let you hit her again!"

"Go do your chores, you're the laziest damned kid I've ever seen."

Bud Junior took away the girls, still crying and hiding their faces from their father.

Wolf closed the double doors to the hallway and turned to Emma. He put his arm around her, which made her cringe. "Now, now . . ." Off to a good start. "You know you aren't goin' anywhere, Emma. I want you to take all those suitcases out there and empty them, put all the clothes and other stuff back where they belong." He closed his arm around her until his wife was held in a painful vise, pinned so tightly the clothes in her arms fell to the floor. "I'd hate to do like last time, beat you real hard. Didn't get dinner for two days, you were in such miserable shape. Remember?"

With her eyes fixed on the floor, Emma said in a quiet voice, "I have to go."

"What?"

"I have to go. Don't you see? If I don't leave you, Bud Junior and the girls won't be able to get away, either. They can't stay here. You've become a terrible man, Bud. You went up to Montana and killed Sharon and Jimmy, our oldest friends, I know that in my heart."

"Jesus, are you crazy or just stupid?" Wolf dropped his arm from around Emma's waist and faced her. "Talkin' like that'll get you hurt." To prove his point he slapped her hard, drove her back a couple of feet, slapped her again.

"Bud, please! Just let us go! You don't love us! Just let us . . ."

Wolf hit his wife with his fist and she windmilled backwards against the wall, knocking a picture to the floor.

The noise brought Bud Junior running. "I told you to leave her alone!"

"Close that door!"

The boy rushed at Wolf, who slapped him down with the back of his hand. Bud Junior scrambled to his feet, saw the grip of Old Bowie above his father's belt and pulled the knife free.

"Put that down!" Wolf roared.

Bud Junior plunged the blade into Wolf's midsection. Wolf felt the searing pain, took a long breath, had trouble maintaining his balance. He stumbled backwards, turned, hit a wall. "Hey, Junior . . ."

"Bud!" Emma threw herself down and put her arms around Wolf. "My God, look what you've done. Call an ambulance!"

Wolf thinking, *I've been stabbed by Old Bowie, ain't that a hoot?*

It didn't occur to Wolf at once that he might actually die, Bud Junior didn't have the sand to deal a death's blow to anyone. Didn't occur to him until he reached down, took hold of Old Bowie's grip with both hands, pulled the knife out of his belly. Knew right away he'd made a mistake. The blood flowed faster, the pain grew worse instead of better.

"Emma, I can't see so good."

She hugged him to her. "There'll be an ambulance here soon. Just hold on."

Bud Junior came running in. "I called the police, there's an ambulance coming." He was crying. In the background, the girls sounded hysterical. "Dad, I didn't mean to hurt you so bad."

"Hey . . ." Wolf rejected the apology with a weak wave of his hand. "I'm proud of you, Junior." His vision was failing and he felt as if a strong hand had seized him by the throat. "This knife . . ." Wolf groped for Old Bowie, wanted to explain the history of the knife, its importance and value. He couldn't find Old Bowie, settled for pulling the de Baraga letter out of his shirt pocket and pressing it into his boy's hand.

Bud Junior threw the letter aside. "I'm sorry," the boy sobbed.

Wolf felt himself sliding along the wall. "Fuck it . . ." Then he was dead.

*        *        *

Scanner sneezed about five times over three minutes. "Excuse me, must be the damned cedars."

"We can find another place to park," Kay offered.

A sheriff's car came screaming past them and turned up the road leading to Wolf's house. It was followed by an ambulance and a second sheriff's car.

"What the hell's that all about?" Scanner reached for the ignition. "We'd better find out."

Kay grabbed the handhold on her door as Scanner sent the rental car flying up the road towards the house. "Wolf's in that house."

"How do you know?"

"Sheriff's cars? Ambulance? That's the kind of traffic Wolf generates."

They pulled up between the sheriff's cars and walked towards the house. A deputy posted at the door stopped them. Scanner showed his Treasury ID and told the deputy Kay was a witness to a crime committed by the owner of the house.

The deputy allowed them inside.

"Look . . ." Kay put a hand to her mouth. The police and ambulance attendants had gathered in the living room, where Bud Wolf lay slumped against a wall. He was dead, you could tell that from a distance. The amount of blood on Wolf, on the carpet, on the wall, on Emma and Bud Junior was lavish. The girls, Charlene and Mary, bawling in tandem, were being comforted by their mother.

"Stay here while I find out what happened." Scanner moved in and showed the deputies his ID, stretching a point as he told them Bud Wolf had been under federal investigation.

Kay, feeling out of place, edged into the living room.

". . . never was your solid citizen type," the senior deputy sheriff was saying. "We been lookin' at Bud for years, never nailed him 'cause he was smart enough to play his games outside the Amarillo area. Christ, lookit all the knives on the guy's body! Plus a Colt Python. Everyone knew he was an animal, nobody expected him to end up dead at the hands of his own boy."

Kay's foot touched something, sheets of paper folded in half. They looked familiar. She bent and picked them up. Oh God, yes indeed, this was the de Baraga boy's letter from the Alamo. That meant Old Bowie was close by.

No one noticed when she stuffed the letter into her purse.

Another carload of people arrived, including a crime technician who cleared everyone out of the living room and began taking pictures. The tech complained loudly that deputies had been tramping back and forth over a crime scene. Kay was moved back into the hallway rather rudely, though nobody seemed to care if she just stood watching all the activity from a reasonable distance. Bud Junior was taken into the kitchen for questioning, his sobs audible above all the other voices. She looked for Roy. He had gone into the kitchen to listen to the questioning.

The crime technician was collecting evidence, putting it all in separate plastic bags. One of the items bagged was the murder weapon, a great long Bowie knife. Kay saw it clearly and a chill ran through her. Wolf's son had killed his father with Old Bowie. The bag went into a cardboard box with other evidence.

Scanner came out of the kitchen and stopped to talk with the deputies before coming over to Kay. "I don't know where Wolf was hiding, but he came into the house through the back door not long after we left. Wolf was angry they were leaving. He hit the boy, terrified the girls, began beating his wife. Bud Junior stabbed him. I doubt the kid'll be put away for this. He's only fourteen."

"I should hope not," Kay said. "Everybody around here knows what kind of man Wolf was, I heard the deputies talking about him."

"Yeah, even so, the son'll have to go through the system." Scanner looked around. "I guess Wolf didn't have Old Bowie after all. He wasn't carrying any knives that size, I just looked at what they took off him. He carried plenty of blades, plus a pistol, but no Bowie knife."

"Too bad," Kay said meekly.

"You suppose he hid it somewhere? Or are you rethinking the whole thing, maybe Wolf didn't steal Old Bowie after all?"

"I don't know what to think, after all this." Not quite a lie, Kay decided.

Scanner looked around. "Let's get out of here, this is all pretty depressing."

Kay didn't object.

# CHAPTER 30

**F**ive months later, on an extremely bright and chilly November day about a week before Thanksgiving, Kay again boarded a plane from New York to Texas. She flew into the Dallas/Fort Worth airport, changed to a commuter flight that put her down in Amarillo, rented a car and drove fifty miles south to Bud Wolf's hometown of Quito, Texas.

A few days earlier she'd sent an E-mail note to Roy Scanner: *Dear Roy, too bad we haven't been able to touch base lately. I think the last time we talked was in September. (Do you get the feeling we're drifting apart?—you don't have to answer that!) Guess what—the saga of Old Bowie isn't over. If you're curious about what really happened to Jim Bowie's knife, meet me in Quito, Texas, at the municipal garage at two p.m. on November 17, that's three days from now. Thinking of you, Kay.*

She had no idea whether Scanner would come to Texas. After Bud Wolf was killed by his son, they had talked by phone several times a week for a couple of months. But they'd seen each other only twice. The first time, back in July, they spent a weekend together at the Plaza Hotel in New York City. Saw a couple of shows. Strolled through Greenwich Village. Had dinner in the Oak Room at the Algonquin. Made love at least three times a day. A wonderful weekend. In August Kay flew the shuttle down to Washington and they spent two more nights at a little inn on the Maryland shore. That was fun, too, though Kay wondered why Roy hadn't just taken her to his apartment. She had an uncomfortable feeling that he didn't want to let her that far into his life.

In September Kay flew off to London on a buying trip while Scanner was in California chasing down another counterfeiter. His California trip stretched to six weeks. Since then they'd exchanged E-mail notes a few times, talked on the phone twice, promised each other they'd stay in closer touch. The last couple of months they hadn't spoken to each other at all.

Kay put aside her questions about why another relationship apparently was going sour and tried to concentrate on something easier to deal with—like lunch. She was having a BLT at a coffee shop on Quito's main street when she saw Scanner walking the square, hands in his pockets, frowning as if he regretted coming here. He was dressed for late fall in denim pants, old boots, leather jacket with a sheepskin lining. His collar was turned up against the brisk Texas wind. As he passed the coffee shop, Kay rapped on the plateglass window.

He brightened, waved, and came into the coffee shop. "Kay, great to see you!" He kissed her and sat down, ordered only coffee from a waitress who came over promptly. "I'm not hungry, they served a sort of lunch on the flight from Denver."

"How long have you been in Denver?"

He looked pained. "More than a month. I've been transferred to Denver. It's taken me a month to find an apartment, move, get settled."

Kay felt wounded. "Why didn't you tell me? At least I'd have known why you were too busy to call. What made you move to Denver anyway?"

"Wasn't my idea." He got his shoulders squared up, knowing he had to tell her the whole story. "Fact is, I've been demoted. An assignment to Denver is the Treasury Department's equivalent of being put on a shelf. I'm still chasing counterfeiters, but now I report to the guy who took my job."

"Demoted! Why would they do that? You broke a big case when you confiscated Donin's counterfeit hundreds."

"Funny thing is, you'll appreciate this, they demoted me for burning down Mr. Marvin's house."

"What?"

Scanner offered up a grim smile. "Remember Deputy Bubba Pinchet? He wrote a long letter of complaint to the department about my actions on the day Wolf was trying to kill us. Said I'd deliberately burned down a man's house without any legal authorization to do so, which was true enough. Deputy Pinchet said that was just the sort of *wild excess* . . . Bubba's words . . . that's making U. S. citizens angry with the federal government. A review board took my testimony and did the politic thing. Demoted me two grades. Didn't help that Secretary Wright died in August. He was the one who pushed my career. Without Wallace Wright's backing, I'm just another T-man."

"Roy, I'm so sorry." Kay also regretted having made such a fuss herself about what Roy did to Mr. Marvin's house. "Are you going to stay with the Treasury Department?"

"Probably. Chasing counterfeiters is still an exciting job, even if I'm no longer in charge of the section."

"Denver's a long way from Connecticut." The statement popped out before Kay could censor herself.

"Yes, makes it harder for us to spend time together. I'm sorry I haven't been more communicative. My life has been crazy the past couple of months, the demotion and the move and all."

"Mine, too." She ventured a guess about the future. "I have a feeling our lives are always going to be hectic. And separate."

Scanner didn't really want to get into this discussion in a coffee shop, so he changed the subject. "Never expected to see this town again. Can you tell me what we're doing back in Quito, Texas?"

Kay looked at her watch. "I'd rather show you. Come on, let's walk over to the municipal garage. It's three blocks away, the waitress gave me directions."

They strolled arm in arm across the square, huddled together against the wind and looking to anyone who passed like a married couple grown very comfortable with each other. Kay rather wished that was what they were, but knew it would never happen. Roy had people to chase and he loved doing it. She had a life just as exciting. Neither was willing to give up or substantially change what they had.

"That auction was a disaster for most of those who took part," Scanner said as they walked. "Wolf. Melanie. Arthur. Goto's heart finally gave out when he got back to Tokyo, you must have seen his obituary in the *Times*. And a few weeks ago Donin was killed in Moscow."

That gave Kay a jolt, being the only bidder left alive. "How? By whom?"

"Nobody knows who did it. Donin and his wife were coming out of a theater, they'd been to the Bolshoi Ballet, when someone stepped up behind Donin and shot him once in the back of the head. Killer got away clean. I understand Donin's partners were sore because we not only confiscated his product, we busted their operation."

"Can't say I'll grieve over Leon Donin, or Nicolai Leontin, whatever name he was using when he died," Kay said.

"I'm not grieving over Bud Wolf, either. But here I am in his hometown. Beautiful Quito, Texas. Is this where Old Bowie is? Why are we going to a municipal garage?"

"Patience, my dear." Kay felt she deserved to have some fun with this, give Roy a genuine surprise.

They found the garage, a big old brick building that had once been a fire station and was now a center for servicing all county vehicles. One end of the garage was stacked with an assortment of county property, most of it old and dilapidated. In front of that mishmash was a riser and podium. Perhaps fifty people were milling around, mainly ranchers and their families, looking over the items on display.

Promptly at two o'clock an auctioneer stepped up to the podium. He had none of Stewart Ruddington's careful grooming or aristocratic air. This auctioneer wore bib overalls and boots, had on a mackinaw jacket against the draft from the open garage door and carried a Heinz soup can into which he occasionally spit his chewing tobacco. "Afternoon, folks. Hope it ain't too cold for you in here, we'll try to move this along right smart." He banged a gavel on the podium a couple of times, not to close a bid but just to work up the feeling of an auction. "Got a lot of good stuff on auction today, mostly old county property been replaced with new. Anything you buy has to be paid for with cash, right here in my hand, no checks. We used to take checks till Will Tuttle bought a county car with a real smelly piece of paper and left town."

A couple of people, apparently they knew Will Tuttle, laughed and chided the auctioneer for being dumb enough to take Will Tuttle's check, everyone knew he was a deadbeat.

"The Good Lord made me a trusting man," the auctioneer shot back. "Sometimes that's a curse, but I'm too old to ask Him to make any major adjustments in my character. Anyways, we don't take checks no more, I ain't totally stupid neither. So let's look at this fine old school bus, a real classic, ain't got but three hundred and fifty thousand miles on it, been maintained real good, y'all know what a fine mechanic Wally is, do I hear a bid of three hundred dollars?"

Only two people bid. A rancher bought the bus for three hundred and sixty dollars, said he planned to park it right next to his house during the winter, store firewood in it, keep the wood dry all the way through till spring. A few folks applauded the idea.

A dozen children's school desks and chairs sold quickly. So did an assortment of power tools, an ancient truck used by the sanitation department and still smelling of its former job, a complicated-looking machine for laying asphalt, several out-of-date personal computers and four Selectric typewriters, and some steel file cases dented and faded into ancient grays. Other pieces drew no bids at all. The auctioneer didn't mind, he just cast those items aside like the junk they were.

About half the items on auction had been bought when the auction-eer said, "Got here a Bowie knife, little bit old but still has an edge to it, ouch, see what I mean, cut my damned finger, excuse me, ladies." Sucked on the cut. "This item was held by the Sheriff's Department as evidence in a court case, owner didn't want it back. Do I hear a bid of ten dollars?"

Kay, never eager to put out the first bid, waited until a grizzled old rancher said, "Ten dollars."

"Twelve," Kay countered.

Next to her, Scanner stirred and whispered in her ear. "Are you kidding me? That's Old Bowie?"

She nodded tightly, focused on the rancher.

"Fourteen dollars," the rancher said.

"Seventeen-fifty." Kay didn't know why she tacked on fifty cents, except that she didn't want the rancher thinking in terms of whole dollars.

"Seventeen-fifty," the auctioneer repeated. "Do I hear twenty dollars? Twenty? Going once. Twice." He banged the gavel. "Sold to the lady for seventeen-fifty."

Kay worked her way through the crowd towards the podium, hearing the rancher say to his wife, "Hell, I can get a new Bowie knife at Sears for twenty dollars." She paid the seventeen-fifty to the auctioneer's assistant and insisted on receiving a handwritten receipt. The assistant put the knife into a brown paper bag and thanked Kay with a smile.

When they were on the street, walking back towards the square, Kay was jubilant. "I did it! I won Old Bowie at auction! Billy Boy Watkins is going to be so pleased! Pleased? He'll be *amazed*."

"Are you sure that's Old Bowie? Let me look at it." Scanner took the knife out of the bag and turned it over a few times. "Okay, I recognize the knife. Jesus, was that sale legal?"

"I've got a receipt from a government agency, that makes it legal." Kay felt on top of the world. "I've been following the case. Bud Junior stabbed his father with Old Bowie. How he got hold of it, I don't know. You didn't see the knife that afternoon because it was put into an evidence bag while you were in the kitchen listening to Bud Junior's statement."

"You did see that," Scanner said. "And you didn't tell me."

"I didn't tell anyone. I followed the case, found out that Bud Junior had to go through juvenile court. Wolf's history came out in court, the sheriff even found stolen goods and equipment for making fake license plates on Wolf's property. No one doubted Emma's word, or Bud Junior's, that Wolf had been beating Emma, his neighbors and Emma's sister testified he'd done it before. Bud Junior was released in Emma's custody, of course. As he should have been. After the proceedings the sheriff was willing to return the knife to Bud Junior or Emma, but they didn't want it. Why would they want it? The knife that killed the father? So the knife became public property and went into the quarterly county auction."

Scanner was bothered by the whole thing. "Doesn't Old Bowie really belong to the estates of Melanie and Arthur? They paid de Baraga a lot of money for it."

"A judge might put Old Bowie into their estates," she conceded. "But neither of them have heirs, so New York state and the state of California would probably get the knife, and what would they do with it? I'm not even sure such a case would go to court. Do you think Antonio de Baraga would testify that he sold this knife to Arthur and Melanie for more than three million dollars? And leave himself open to being taxed on that amount? I don't think so. I've talked to my lawyer about it, he agreed I'd have legal claim to Old Bowie if I could buy it at auction from a government agency."

"How can you prove this is Old Bowie?" Scanner wanted to know. "The letter from the de Baraga boy burned up in Melanie's hotel room."

"Not at all." Kay's eyes were actually twinkling. "I have the letter. Found it on the floor of Wolf's house the day he died. It's safely tucked away right here in my purse."

"You didn't tell me about that, either." Bitter thoughts from Scanner. "You weren't particularly honest with me the whole time we were in Austin. Or afterwards, for that matter."

Kay, stung not just by the words but by Roy's attitude, said, "Don't talk to me about honesty. You pretended to be a bidder for Old Bowie and used me to get at Leon Donin. I was almost killed, Roy, partly because you were in Donin's way and I was your ally. I thought you'd be happy Old Bowie hadn't been destroyed. Happy that I won out over everybody."

"That's all that's important to you." He was walking so fast now she could hardly keep up. "Winning out over everyone, even me. Otherwise you'd have told me earlier that you knew what had happened to Old Bowie."

Kay came to a dead stop, let Scanner walk on. He realized she wasn't at his side, turned and stared at her. From six feet away, Kay shouted, "You're worse than I am about winning! You break whatever rules you can get away with, I've seen you do that. You bully your own people like some tinpot dictator. Maybe demoting you wasn't a *politic* thing to do, maybe you deserved it."

"You were there!" Scanner shouted back. "If I hadn't burned down that house, covered our run, we'd have been killed!"

"You had no regrets at all, never gave Mr. Marvin's loss a second thought. Burn it and forget it, that was your attitude."

"The old man was dying in a nursing home."

"You didn't know that at the time."

They'd come to a standstill. Not just a standstill, Kay thought. A parting of the ways. "Good-bye, Roy. Good luck catching your counterfeiters."

Scanner acknowledged their parting with a curt duck of his chin. "So long, Kay. I hope you find lots more lovely antiques for your clients."

"Don't worry, I will."

Scanner turned and walked away, the tail of his leather jacket flapping in the breeze.

Kay waited until he was out of sight, then trudged in the direction of the street where she'd parked the rental car. She clutched the brown paper bag containing Old Bowie close to her, the only thing she'd gotten out of this trip. She'd expected, wanted, a reconciliation with Roy. At least an understanding of where their relationship stood. *I guess I did get that*, Kay thought with a flutter of sadness.

By the time she reached Quito's charming old downtown square, Kay's spirits had begun to lift. She found a pay phone and used a credit card to call Billy Boy Watkins's number in New Orleans. After getting the usual shuffle from a secretary to an administrative assistant to an executive secretary, she managed to reach Billy Boy himself.

"Honey, how y'doin'? Haven't heard from you in a dog's age, what's on your pretty mind?"

"Guess what," she told him, "I just bought Old Bowie for you at auction."

"You did what? I thought Old Bowie was gone, burned up. Shit-oh-dear, you ain't kiddin' this wasted old man, are you?"

"No, I'm not kidding you and you're hardly wasted. Somebody told me you just became engaged to a twenty-three-year-old girl."

"She's a sweet young thing, gives a great massage. Found her waitin' tables at an IHOP. Now what about that knife? How'd you get it?"

"It's a long story, in many ways a terrible story. I'll fly down to New Orleans today and tell you all about it when I deliver Old Bowie."

"You got provenance? You can prove it's Jim Bowie's own knife?"

"I've got that, too." There was silence. "Billy Boy, you there?"

"For once in my life, I don't have no words. Kay . . . honey . . . you didn't ask me for any money, didn't even tell me Old Bowie was up for sale again, how could you have bought it on your own?"

"I had enough funds to cover this particular auction."

"Lord, tell me how much this is gonna cost me. I've halfway recovered from my latest financial disaster, but my bank account's still dry. I hope you didn't commit me to a fortune I don't have."

"Billy Boy, you'll be glad to know Old Bowie is going to cost you only seventeen dollars and fifty cents. Plus my commission, of course."

"Honey, these old ears are goin' bad on me, got to see a doctor one of these days, except I hate doctors almost as much as I hate the IRS. I thought you said seventeen dollars and fifty cents."

"I did."

More silence. "Kay, where you callin' me from?" Billy Boy Watkins sounded out of breath.

"Quito, Texas. A small town in the Panhandle."

"Quito must have a little airport, every stinkpot of a town does these days. Kay, I want you to find the airport, wait a couple of hours, I'm sendin' my personal Learjet to bring you down to N'Orleans. I crave Old Bowie as much as I crave a new prostate, but I want to hear the story of how you got hold of it for seventeen dollars and fifty cents even more."

"The story will cost you extra. See you soon, Billy boy."

· A NOTE ON THE TYPE ·

The typeface used in this book, Transitional, is a digitized version of Fairfield, which was designed in 1937–40 by artist Rudolph Ruzicka (1883–1978), on a commission from Linotype. The assignment was the occasion for a well-known essay in the form of a letter from W. A. Dwiggins to Ruzicka, in response to the latter's request for advice. Dwiggins, who had recently designed Electra and Caledonia, relates that he would start by making very large scale drawings (10 and 64 times the size you are reading) and having test cuttings made, which were used to print on a variety of papers. "By looking at all these for two or three days I get an idea of how to go forward—or, if the result is a dud, how to start over again." At this stage he took *parts* of letters that satisfied him and made cardboard cutouts, which he then used to assemble other letters. This "template" method anticipated one that many contemporary computer type designers use.